Dear Reader,
A lot of you will [be taking your] summer vacation now. So whether you're planning to sit in the sun by a pool, have a sporting holiday or just laze around at home (*my* favourite form of relaxation!) I hope reading *Scarlet* will be part of your holiday fun.

This month we are proud to offer you: the first award-winning novel by Julia Wild; critically acclaimed author Jill Sheldon's third *Scarlet* romance; a peep into the glitz and glam world of international tennis from talented new author Kathryn Bellamy; and a skilfully woven second novel, with a delightful Scottish background, by Danielle Shaw. As ever, we hope there are stories to suit every mood and taste in this month's *Scarlet* selection.

I always seem to be asking you questions – and here is another! Are four *Scarlet* books a month enough? Would you like to buy more?

I am very grateful to all those readers who have taken the trouble to complete our questionnaires and/or write to me. We are very grateful for your comments and we *do* act upon them.

Till next month,

Sally Cooper

SALLY COOPER,
Editor-in-Chief – *Scarlet*

About the Author

Kathryn Bellamy was born in 1953 and educated at Queen Elizabeth's Grammar School in Horncastle, Lincolnshire.

After gaining excellent examination results, she worked in a bank until ill health forced her to resign. Since then, Kathryn has worked for her husband John, a chartered accountant, on a part-time basis, and has been able to spend more time writing fiction, which has always been a much-loved hobby.

Kathryn still lives in Lincoln, and her hobbies include reading, tennis and yoga.

We are delighted to offer you Kathryn's first *Scarlet* novel and to tell you that she is currently working on her second, which we hope will star the gorgeous Ace Delaney, who you will find featured in *Game, Set and Match*.

Other *Scarlet* titles available this month:

REVENGE IS SWEET – Jill Sheldon
DARK CANVAS – Julia Wild
MARRIED TO SINCLAIR – Danielle Shaw

KATHRYN BELLAMY

GAME, SET & MATCH

SCARLET

Enquiries to:
Robinson Publishing Ltd
7 Kensington Church Court
London W8 4SP

First published in the UK by Scarlet, 1997

Copyright © Kathryn Bellamy 1997

The right of Kathryn Bellamy to be identified as author
of this work has been asserted by her in accordance
with the Copyright, Designs and Patents Act 1988.

A copy of the British Library Cataloguing in
Publication data is available from the British Library

ISBN 1-85487-960-X

Printed and bound in the EC

10 9 8 7 6 5 4 3 2 1

CHAPTER 1

'I see the Press are calling it "The Battle of the Beauties", Captain Dale 'Coop' Coupland remarked to his close friend, Major Nick Lennox. Nick merely grunted, concentrating on his driving as he gunned the Jag above 90 mph to overtake a long line of slow-moving traffic.

'This Lucia Conti – she's the sultry Italian, isn't she?' Coop continued. 'Quite a glamour-puss. What's your Melissa Farrell like?'

'She's not my Melissa – yet. But I'm working on it,' Nick replied, with quiet determination. 'And she's adorable. Around five foot eight, most of it legs, long, dark hair and incredible navy-blue eyes, a kissable, rosebud mouth . . .'

'Okay, I get the picture,' Coop interrupted, wishing he hadn't asked. They were heading for the pre-Wimbledon tennis tournament at Beckenham, where eighteen-year-old Melissa Farrell was competing in her first professional match.

Media interest in Melissa was high, not only for her undoubted talent and good looks, but because she was following her older brother Jack onto the pro circuit.

1

Jack Farrell was a popular and successful player, the highest-ranked British male, and famous worldwide for his victories with Doubles partner, Ace Delaney, the volatile, amoral American bad boy of the sport.

They arrived shortly before the match was due to begin, and Nick frowned as he flicked through the programme.

'Damn! I hadn't realized the men were competing here, too,' he muttered.

'So?' Coop enquired.

'Ace Delaney's here,' Nick replied shortly, as if that were answer enough. Ace was reputed to be descended from an Apache warrior, and certainly looked the part with long, straight black hair, swarthy complexion and hawk-like features dominated by jet-black eyes. But what concerned Nick was the knowledge that Melissa had been besotted with Ace since she had first met him at the age of fourteen, and that she was determined to marry him one day, an intention which scared her parents witless and amused Ace enormously.

'From what I've read about Delaney, he's not a man with matrimony on his mind,' Coop said, when Nick apprised him of the situation. 'Pull rank,' he advised. 'Does she know about your title and estates in Scotland?'

'The only title that would impress Melissa is a Wimbledon one,' Nick said drily. 'As for ancestral homes, well, her family has lived at Bellwood, a magnificent sixteenth-century Tudor manor, for over three hundred years.'

'You'll just have to rely on your devastating charm, then!' Coop grinned. 'It usually works!'

2

'Melissa's different,' Nick said shortly, and turned his attention back to the programme. 'She's due on court two,' he added, and began walking towards the group of spectators.

Coop hung back; he'd already spied the refreshment tent and wasn't interested in watching two girls play tennis, anyway. He had only come along to have a look at Melissa. He and Nick had served in the same regiment for five years, and never before had Nick been this smitten with a girl.

'I'm going for a beer first – I'll catch up with you later,' Coop said.

'Okay,' Nick nodded and continued on his way. He was a tall man, powerfully built, with silvery-blond hair, cut short, and smoky-grey eyes above a straight nose, full mouth and a firm jaw which suggested he usually achieved his aims. Today, he was wearing Army fatigues, having dashed from his barracks in Aldershot to reach Beckenham in time for the start of the match. Men took one look at him and gave way as he shouldered a path to the side of the court. Women gave him a second look for a different reason, drawn by his ruggedly handsome looks and sensing correctly that he would use his obvious physical strength to protect the weak, not to exploit or attack.

Nick took a seat some yards away from the group of Melissa's supporters. He recognized Jack, a stocky fair-haired man with twinkling hazel eyes and a ready smile, a younger version of his father, Daniel. Rose Farrell, Melissa and Jack's mother, was still an extremely attractive woman with flawless skin and the glossy dark hair and huge navy-blue eyes she had bequeathed

3

to her daughter. Daniel and Rose had been divorced for several years, but the initial animosity had vanished, leaving in its wake a friendly truce.

'Excuse me!' A slim girl with bright red curls pushed past Nick to slip into the seat next to Jack, and began whispering to him.

'That's Katy Oliver,' someone sitting behind Nick said. 'Her knee injury has forced her to stop competing for a while, so she's agreed to coach and travel with Melissa for a year.'

'What the hell did Ace do to Lucia last night?' Katy asked Jack quietly. 'She's pea-green and swallowing painkillers by the bucketful!'

'He spiked her drinks with vodka and put laxative in her coffee,' Jack replied, and they both laughed despite their feelings of guilt. To take advantage of an opponent's injury or illness was perfectly acceptable, but to purposely cause it . . . Jack had asked Ace, as a favour, to take his ex-girlfriend out the night before the match for a little sabotage, but Ace had gone much further than Jack had expected, and he wasn't feeling too proud of himself.

A ripple of applause greeted the players and Nick turned his attention to them, instantly deciding that Melissa won the Battle of the Beauties. A year had passed since their first meeting, when Melissa had thrashed his niece, Jessica Stanton, in a junior competition, and he had fallen head over heels in love. His Army duties had taken him away from England for much of the intervening time, but he had been unable to put her from his mind. And each, rare, brief meeting since then had reinforced his conviction that this was the girl for him.

'She looks pale,' Rose said anxiously.

'She's okay,' Katy assured her. 'She's looking forward to it, just anxious to begin.'

They fell silent and watched tensely as Melissa hopped nervously from one foot to the other while waiting for the umpire to toss the coin, but once she was trading shots in the five-minute warm-up Jack and Katy relaxed a little. She was hitting the ball well, her movement around the court fluid and graceful; there was none of the awkwardness that denoted paralyzing nerves. She'll be okay, Jack thought, and turned his attention to Lucia – how well could she perform?

Lucia was feeling dreadful, cursing Ace and her own weakness for him with every stroke that intensified her pounding headache. She should never have accepted his invitation – 'just a quick drink,' he'd said, but, with Ace, that always meant bed. And not to sleep, either. Still, this British novice shouldn't pose any problems . . .

Lucia had won the toss and elected to receive, figuring that the loss of her first service game would demoralize the English kid, and Melissa certainly did feel a flutter of nerves as the crowd quietened and the umpire instructed her to 'play'. For an instant, she froze, then took a deep breath and tossed up the ball. She knew it was a good serve as soon as her racket connected and she rushed forward, perfectly placed to intercept Lucia's return, keeping the volley low and skidding out of Lucia's reach. Fifteen – love. She breathed a sigh of relief as she returned to the baseline.

'Good volley,' Jack approved, and Katy nodded her agreement. Rose and Daniel could hardly bear to watch.

Following Katy's advice, Melissa continued her net-rushing tactics, trying to avoid becoming embroiled in

5

any long rallies which would aid Lucia, the ground-stroke specialist. She won the game, losing only one point, and sat down, feeling pleased and relieved.

Lucia, not so pleased, threw down her racket, then winced as she bent to pick it up; there seemed to be a lead weight lodged in her skull! She was even less pleased twenty minutes later when she lost her own service game, to give Melissa the chance to serve for the set, which she did faultlessly, winning 6–3.

Lucia dropped into her chair and closed her eyes, dabbing her throbbing temples with cold water as she reviewed the situation. Her headache had worsened and she now had stomach cramps as well. There were no computer points at stake here, and she still had plenty of time to practise on grass before Wimbledon. So, did she want to slug out this match? Despite the ignominy of losing to a newcomer, the answer was a resounding 'no'. She eased up in the second set and, after only one hour's play –

'Game, set, and match, Farrell! She wins by two sets to love, 6–3, 6–2.' Melissa stood stock-still for a moment, and had to suppress an insane desire to ask him to repeat the score, it sounded so wonderful! Then she remembered Lucia and ran to the net.

'Well done,' Lucia said coolly, 'I guess we'll be seeing you around.' And I'll get you next time, she vowed silently. Melissa nodded and smiled before dashing off to her family, hugging and thanking everyone incoherently.

'Oh, my God, you're in the second round and I haven't a clue who you have to play next,' Katy realized suddenly. 'I'd better go and check.'

'Some people have no faith!' Melissa said indignantly, as if she had never harboured any doubts about the outcome of the match. Strangers began coming over to offer congratulations and Melissa revelled in the attention, and had to be dragged away by Jack.

'The Press want to talk to you,' he told her. 'Remember what I said – be nice, even when they ask silly questions, and never slag off your opponent,' he warned.

'I remember,' she nodded, and went warily into the Press Room. But they were mostly British and delighted with her win, asking her easy-to-answer questions about her future plans. After that, she took a quick shower before going in search of Katy, eager to discover the identity of her next opponent. She could hardly believe she was through to the second round! And had beaten a player in the top thirty to get there, even though Lucia was considered far more proficient on slow, clay courts than on fast grass.

'Melissa!' A familiar voice stopped her and she swung round to find Nick Lennox smiling down at her. 'Congratulations,' he said warmly.

'Thank you,' she responded, a little breathlessly. Jessica Stanton's uncle had always been kind to her, and was very good-looking too, but, suddenly, he seemed different . . . certainly not avuncular . . .

'I've never seen you in uniform before,' she blurted out, and instantly felt incredibly stupid. Nick hid a smile: khaki was a turn-on for a lot of girls, but he hadn't expected Melissa to fall into that catagory. 'Very macho!' she added mockingly, to cover her confusion. 'Is Jessica with you?'

'No, I drove here straight from Aldershot.'

'Oh,' Melissa knew he wasn't particularly interested in tennis. 'You came to . . . see me?' she ventured, tilting her head slightly and looking at him through long sooty lashes with more than a hint of coquetry. Good God, she's flirting with me, Nick thought, surprised and delighted.

'That's right. And to invite you out,' he added on impulse.

'Oh!' Melissa flushed with pleasure, then glanced away. You love Ace, she told herself sternly. Don't be so fickle!

'I'm spending this weekend in London – would you enjoy a day in town?' Nick continued, trying to sound casual.

'Well . . .' Melissa caught sight of Ace, fresh from victory on Centre Court, consoling Lucia, and she beamed at Nick. 'I'd love to,' she said brightly.

'Great.' Nick had noticed her reaction to the by-play between Delaney and Conti. He quickly made arrangements to meet, then took his leave of her before she could have second thoughts.

As he passed Ace, he subjected him to a long, hard stare. Everything he had read about the man – who appeared more often in gossip columns than in the sports pages – reinforced his dislike. Now that he had made his own move on Melissa, Nick resolved to drive the reprobate from her thoughts. Ace, usually impervious to the opinions of other men, couldn't fail to notice the malevolence emanating from the tough-looking blond guy and he glared back. There was a natural arrogance and self-assurance about Nick, born

8

of his aristocratic background, that instantly irritated Ace, a kid from the slums of LA.

Melissa quickly came down to earth with a bump. Losing her second-round match to another British player ranked around one hundred, made her realize just how hard it was going to be to climb to the top of her chosen sport. However, she was determined to succeed and knew she was lucky to have Katy to help her. At first, they had been wary of each other, Melissa a little afraid of the brash New Yorker with her sharp little features and even sharper tongue. She seriously thought Jack must be mad to want to take her to bed!

Katy, too, had had many doubts; Melissa in her sweet little tennis outfits with matching hair ribbons had seemed as if she wanted to bask in Jack's reflected glory, rather than do the necessary work to make her own mark on the game. She had agreed to coach Melissa, mainly because she was crazy about Jack, but also because of the recurrent knee injury which had forced her to drastically cut down her own playing schedule. However, Katy was slowly realizing that, behind the 'Little Miss Cute' exterior, was a determination and readiness to work hard that boded well for the future.

Melissa worked with both Jack and Katy for the rest of the week, but was looking forward to her meeting with Nick on Saturday. As the day approached, she began to feel unaccountably nervous. It was silly, irrational, she told herself, but the feeling persisted. Perhaps it was because she had only ever dated boys of her own age and Nick, she knew, was in his late twenties.

9

She tried on, and discarded, every item of clothing in her wardrobe and still hadn't decided what to wear when she awoke on Saturday morning. The day dawned bright and clear, the forecast promised hot and sunny weather, so she finally settled on a sleeveless, black lycra mini dress.

It was a little after ten o'clock when she arrived in London, and she scanned the crowd for a glimpse of Nick as she passed through the ticket barrier. Her heart gave a peculiar lurch of happiness when she spotted him, taller and broader than most men, making his way towards her. He looked tanned and fit, his fair hair bleached by the sun.

'Hi,' Nick smiled down at her, his grey eyes warm and friendly, but the nervous fluttering in her stomach didn't abate.

'Hello,' she responded, a little awkwardly.

'You look wonderful,' Nick said lightly. God, he had never wanted anything in his life as much as he wanted this girl. 'You also look . . . taller,' he added, perplexed, and Melissa giggled.

'It's my shoes – I'm wearing high heels.' She extended one foot for his inspection, but it was her bare, tanned, slender leg that drew his gaze.

'Mm,' was the best response he could manage. He cleared his throat and tried again. 'Is there anything special you would like to do today?' he asked, hailing a cab.

'No, it's just lovely to have some free time – Katy's running me ragged,' she said, but sounded remarkably cheerful about it.

Nick reasoned that all women, of whatever age, loved

shopping, so he asked Melissa to help him choose gifts for Jessica and her younger sister, Juliet, as they both had birthdays in the coming weeks. They strolled down Kensington High Street and, after purchasing the costume jewellery Melissa was sure his nieces would love, crossed over to Kensington Gardens, walking aimlessly, simply enjoying the sunshine and each other's company.

Melissa quickly relaxed and it seemed perfectly natural when Nick clasped her hand in his as they strolled along. She chattered away happily, answering his questions about Katy, her own future plans, and proudly telling him of her partnership with Jack in the Mixed Doubles at Wimbledon, just two weeks away.

'Jess is combining tennis with a degree course — didn't you consider doing the same?' he asked, for he knew that her father had tried to persuade her to attend university, instead of joining the tennis circuit.

'No,' Melissa said promptly, dashing his hopes. 'And, to be honest, I think Jess will regret it. I don't see how she can do justice to both. She'll probably fail her degree and the tournaments she'll compete in won't help her ranking much.'

'I see,' Nick couldn't fault her logic, unfortunately. 'Let's get some lunch,' he suggested.

They managed to find a pavement table at a restaurant and Melissa eased off her shoes after she sat down. Katy would kill her if she could see the height of the heels – a twisted ankle would ruin all their plans for the next few months.

Nick waited until they had been served their drinks, then raised his glass in a toast.

11

'To your future,' he said softly, adding silently, please let it include me!

'Thank you,' Melissa smiled and picked up her own glass of iced water. 'But what about your own future? Jess told me you might have to give up your Army career – something to do with your cousin dying recently?'

'Yes.' A shadow crossed Nick's face; it had been almost two years since the fatal accident, but it still hurt like hell. 'Rory was only my second cousin, but we were more like brothers,' he began slowly. 'We grew up together in a place called Glengarry, in Scotland. There's a title and an estate, which Rory would have inherited but, unfortunately for me, he and his wife didn't produce any heirs, which leaves me the next in line. The Old Man – that's what everyone calls my great-uncle, the present baronet – is over eighty now, and I know he'd like me to spend more time there. I owe him,' he finished simply.

'I see,' Melissa regarded him sympathetically. More and more she could understand why Jess adored her uncle. 'Couldn't you . . .' she began, but, at that moment, someone nearby screamed and Nick twisted around in his seat, scanning the crowd for the source of the disturbance. Twenty yards away, a man had snatched a girl's handbag and was running towards them, shoving people aside as he made his escape.

Nick had been resting his foot on the rung of a vacant chair and now pushed it into the path of the thief, then stood and grabbed him as he half-fell over the obstacle. Wrenching the man's arm behind his back and forcing him to his knees, Nick reached down and retrieved the bag, which he handed back to the girl. She was blonde and pretty, wearing a skirt up to her armpits and smiling adoringly at Nick in a way Melissa found she didn't like at all. Melissa was still in her chair, stunned by the speed of it all – she had barely begun to realize what was happening before Nick had reacted.

'Will someone please call the police?' Nick asked, then, 'I'd quite like to finish my lunch,' he drawled. This last was for Melissa's benefit; she looked pale and shaken and he gladly handed his captive over to the waiters who had rushed out of the restaurant to help. He brushed aside the victim's thanks and rejoined Melissa, reaching across to place his hand over hers.

'You okay, sweetheart?' he asked gently.

'Yes.' She gave a rather wan smile. 'You were very quick,' she said admiringly. 'I just froze – I don't know what I would do if I were attacked,' she shivered, despite the heat of the sun.

'If a guy just wants your cash, you let him take it,' Nick advised, to her surprise.

'You wouldn't,' she objected.

'No, because the odds will usually be stacked in my favour. But, believe me, if someone points a gun at me and demands my wallet, I'll swallow my pride and hand it over,' he said seriously. 'A dented ego mends quicker than a bullet wound. But you have more to lose than I do, Melissa – if you start struggling with a guy over your purse, he's soon going to have more than robbery on his mind.'

'Rape, you mean,' she said flatly.

'Yes, but let's drop the subject, I didn't mean to scare you,' he said quickly.

'Okay,' she nodded, but then, 'Could you teach me some self-defence?'

'Be glad to,' Nick said promptly. 'We can start this afternoon, if you don't mind coming to the flat,' he added. 'It's not far – just off the Kings Road in Chelsea. Would you like anything else to eat? Or coffee?' he asked.

'No, thank you,' she declined, and Nick beckoned to their waiter for the bill.

'Those shoes you're wearing are a pretty good weapon,' he told her, watching her ease her feet back into them. 'If someone grabs you from behind, scrape the heel down his shin and stamp hard on his instep. That should be enough to make him release you and then you run like hell,' he added. He hailed a passing cab and resumed the lesson as soon as they were inside.

'Always avoid trouble if you can and be alert, especially if you're walking alone at night, or in a deserted car-park. And have your keys ready in your hand – do you have them with you?'

'Yes.' Melissa delved into her bag and brought out the bunch of keys.

'Right.' Nick showed her how to hold them in her fist, jagged edges protruding. 'Aim for his eyes. Your lungs are another natural weapon – scream as loud as you can. These creeps don't like noise . . .' he stopped, seeing the troubled look in her eyes. 'This is frightening you, isn't it?'

'No. Well, yes, a bit, but I want to learn,' she said firmly. 'I'm going to be spending most of my time in strange cities and Katy won't be with me twenty-four hours a day.'

14

'Okay,' Nick managed not to plead with her to stay in England and let him protect her, and spent the afternoon doing all he could to ensure she would be as safe as possible on her travels.

It was a time of mingled pleasure and torture, holding her lovely body only to teach her how to escape him. Despite her slenderness, she was extremely strong, as Nick found to his cost, and he began defending himself with a cushion, encouraging her to hit out even more.

'Don't forget to shout – but just pretend, for now,' he added hastily, trying to imagine how he would explain the situation if one of his neighbours heard her and called the police! 'Now use your knee,' he instructed, quickly re-positioning the protective cushion. Her short dress rode higher up her thighs until he could no longer concentrate. Cold shower, think of being under an ice-cold shower, he told himself desperately.

'Let's take a break – I need a cool drink,' he said, and disappeared into the kitchen until he had regained control. 'Would you like a coke, or orange juice?' he called out.

'Just water, please,' Melissa replied.

When Nick re-entered the room, Melissa was gazing out of the window, with her back to him. He quietly set the drinks down and stole up behind her, snaking one arm around her throat and bracing himself for a sharp jab from her elbow, or a backwards kick to his knee. But she didn't react in the way he had expected; the way he had taught her.

Looking down at Nick's arm holding her captive, Melissa felt only safe and protected. He had strong, comforting arms, she thought, and absently stroked the fine covering of blond hairs, which were surprisingly soft in contrast to the hard-packed muscle beneath the skin.

'Melissa!' Nick sounded as if he were being strangled. 'When a man sneaks up behind you, you definitely do NOT stroke his arm!'

'I know.' She leaned her head back against his chest and smiled up at him. That smile, those eyes, Nick thought despairingly.

'Melissa,' he groaned, turning her in his arms and bending his head to kiss her. Her lips were the sweetest he'd ever tasted and her response, a little uncertain but welcoming, offered encouragement. He deepened the kiss, moulding her body to his.

For Melissa, the kiss was a revelation; his hands sure and confident as he sought out her curves. This was nothing like the inexpert fumblings of boys she had kissed, and desire for more leaped in her.

Nick lifted her until her face was level with his: one arm held her securely around the waist while his other hand raked through her long silky hair, holding her head captive while he plundered her mouth once more, this time dipping his tongue inside. He felt her body relax against his and moved his mouth to the pulse beating rapidly at her throat.

'We'd be more comfortable lying down,' he murmured. After a brief hesitation, Melissa nodded and he carried her through to the bedroom, laying her gently on top of the bed before sitting down beside her. She gazed up at him with a mixture of anticipation and apprehension evident in her huge, dark eyes.

'Nothing's going to happen if you don't want it to,' Nick assured her. 'I wouldn't have spent the past three

16

hours teaching you how to defend yourself if I intended hurting you, would I?' he asked drily.

'I guess not,' Melissa said softly.

'Promise me you won't gouge my eyes out? If I do something you don't like, a simple "no" will stop me in my tracks,' he went on, and she laughed, no longer uncertain. Just excited.

When he leaned down to kiss her, she reached up and wound her arms around his neck, pulling him closer. Take it easy, Nick was cautioning himself, trying to ignore his urgent need to possess her. He began to caress her, lightly at first, exulting in the sound of her rapid breathing; the way her nipples hardened at his touch. He broke the kiss to nuzzle her neck, working downwards until his mouth covered one taut peak. Melissa groaned in delight.

'Like that?' Nick asked huskily.

'Mm, yes,' Melissa sighed blissfully.

'It would feel even nicer if we removed your dress,' he suggested. Again, there was a slight hesitation, then Melissa sat up and helped him ease off the dress, leaving her clad only in black, skimpy briefs.

'You are exquisite,' Nick breathed, feasting his eyes on her beautiful body, so slender and firm, her breasts full and jutting proudly, her legs so long and shapely that he ached to have them wrapped around him.

He cupped her breasts in his hands and bent his head to suckle first one, then the other, urged on by her stifled moans of pleasure. He lay down beside her, kissing her with long, drugging kisses, while his hands gently explored her smooth skin, seeking out every curve and hollow.

Attuned to her every response, he felt her uncertainty when he ventured to remove her briefs and he stopped, leaving his hand resting lightly on her stomach, fingers splayed. As he had hoped, Melissa soon craved more and she squirmed against his hand. He waited until she moved again, more insistently, then slipped his fingers inside her briefs, almost losing control when he discovered how hot and wet she was. He slid the lacy garment down her legs and buried his face in her soft, damp hair.

'Oh!' Melissa cried out with delight at the wonderful sensations rippling through her body. When Nick tore at his shirt, needing to feel his naked skin against hers, she began to help him. Her hands were shaking a little as she began tentatively to stroke his shoulders and chest, curling her fingers into the matt of hair, her eyes widening in surprise when his nipples hardened at her touch. Nick noted her wonderment; he was sure now that Ace had never had his filthy hands on her and felt a primitive satisfaction.

Neither heard the slamming of the front door, but they both heard his name being called – by a woman, and one who obviously had a key to his flat, Melissa realized with horror.

'Nick? Are you here?' It was Sheena, Rory's widow, who had mistaken Nick's sympathy over the loss of her husband for something deeper. She had long ago decided that she still wished to become Lady Lennox and, since Rory had died, Nick, the next in line, could take his place.

I don't believe this, I do not believe this! Nick thought savagely, as Melissa shrank away from him.

'I phoned the Mess and they said you were in town

18

this weekend . . . Nick?' Oh, God, she'll come barging in here, Nick thought, scrambling quickly off the bed.

'Stay here, sweetheart,' he told Melissa, then left the bedroom, closing the door behind him.

'Oh, there you are,' Sheena turned, her expression changing as she took in his aroused, half-dressed state. 'My, you are pleased to see me,' she smiled.

'No, I'm not. What the hell are you doing here?' Nick raged and her smile faded.

'I have as much right to be here as you do,' she reminded him coolly. Nick raked his fingers through his hair.

'Yes, of course you do,' he agreed heavily. 'You couldn't go and do some shopping for a while, could you?' he suggested, without much hope.

'No, I could not. I've had a long journey and I'm tired. Either get rid of that scrubber you're hiding in the bedroom or take her to an hotel,' she snapped.

'Don't you dare insult her,' Nick said furiously, following her into the drawing room. 'If I have my way, she'll soon be part of the family, so you may as well start by being pleasant to her now.'

'Oh?' Sheena looked at him sharply. 'You intend marrying her?' she asked slowly.

'Yes, so watch what you say. I've been teaching her self-defence, so if you call her a scrubber to her face don't be surprised if she punches you in the kidneys,' he warned grimly.

'A charming girl, obviously,' Sheena sniffled, while Nick went to try and persuade Melissa to emerge from the bedroom. But the room was empty, as was the adjoining bathroom.

19

'Damn! She's gone!' Nick hastily checked the other rooms but the flat was empty. 'Look out of the window and see if you can spot her,' he called to Sheena, as he pulled on his shirt and headed for the front door. 'She's wearing a black dress.'

'Can't see a thing,' Sheena called back, without bothering to look. Really, what a fuss! 'Nick!' she yelled after him. 'She'll be back – she's gone without her shoes. And her bag,' she added, picking up Melissa's shoulder bag and peering interestedly inside until Nick snatched it from her.

'Oh, God,' he groaned. She was barefoot and penniless, he thought in horror. Her likely course of action was a reverse-charge call to her father . . . He felt himself break out into a cold sweat. 'I have to find her.'

'Oh, don't give her the satisfaction of chasing after her,' Sheena said impatiently. 'She'll come back once she realizes she has no money.'

'She might be too embarrassed; I'm going to look for her.' He paused on his way out. 'If she returns while I'm gone, you will be kind to her,' he said sternly.

'Else what?' Sheena muttered, but not until he was out of earshot.

Nick raced down the stairs and out of the building, guessed she would have headed for the Kings Road and took that direction himself. He spotted her after what seemed an eternity, sitting huddled on some steps, the very picture of misery, but he hardened his heart as he slowly walked towards her.

'It's only Sheena – why did you run away? It was a very stupid and childish thing to do,' he said coldly. Not to mention almost causing him to have a heart attack!

'You've been telling me all afternoon to run away from trouble!' Melissa yelled at him. Sheena? Jess had shown her family photographs which included the petite, exquisitely pretty widow, with her air of helplessness accentuated by huge brown eyes and a cloud of black hair. Jess had also confided that the family hoped Nick and Sheena would marry one day.

'From dangerous situations, not personal problems!' Nick yelled back, exasperated by her logic, then he sighed and hunkered down beside her.

'May I have my bag and shoes back, please?' Melissa asked politely.

'Not yet,' Nick hung onto them. 'We have to talk.'

'No! Just let me go,' Melissa pleaded, evidently near to tears and seeming even younger than her eighteen years. Nick felt ashamed; he'd behaved terribly trying to seduce her.

'I'm sorry, sweetheart, I shouldn't have let things get out of control,' he said quietly.

'Shouldn't you be apologizing to Sheena, not me?' she enquired coldly.

'Whatever for?' Nick asked blankly.

'Well, she does have a key to your flat, so presumably the two of you are . . . close,' she finished.

'Oh, Melissa,' Nick sighed, but with relief. She was jealous of an imagined relationship with Sheena? 'The flat belongs to the Old Man – all the family use it, not just me. Ask Jess if you doubt me; she probably has a set of keys, her mother certainly does.'

'Oh! I thought . . .'

'You were wrong,' he said firmly. 'Now, come and meet her . . .'

'No,' Melissa interrupted. She was still refusing to even look at him. She had never felt so embarrassed or ashamed in her entire life! 'I just want to go home,' she said. 'I should never have been with you – I love Ace,' she burst out. Her words seared Nick's soul and he lashed out in his pain.

'If you're still harbouring childish fantasies about that creep then I agree, you shouldn't have been with me,' he said savagely. 'I apologize for mistaking you for an adult!' Melissa bit her lip, then snatched up her bag and shoes, stumbling in her haste to get away. Nick let her go, watching only to ensure she found a cab before turning and retracing his steps. Well done, Lennox, he berated himself bitterly. You've pushed her right back to Ace Delaney! It hurt like hell, but he was afraid that she might have to learn from first hand experience what everyone else already knew – that Ace would break her heart and never even notice.

Melissa had loved Wimbledon fortnight ever since she was a little girl, pestering her parents to take her there, or, failing that, avidly watching the TV coverage. When Jack had played in the junior event, she had been so excited and proud of her big brother, watching all his matches while keeping an eye out for her heroes and heroines to pester for autographs. She had been in seventh heaven when Jack turned pro and passed her autograph book around the locker-room until it was overflowing with signatures.

This year, Jack and Ace had rented a house within walking distance of the All England Club. Katy and Melissa joined them after the tournament in Eastbourne and Rose went along, too, to act as housekeeper and to allay Daniel's fears over Melissa sharing a house with Ace. Katy was a little disgruntled by Rose's presence – she was somewhat in awe of Jack's classy mother and felt that Rose disapproved of her. In that, she was correct, but not because of her involvement with Jack. Rose considered that, at twenty-three, his romantic affairs were his own business and she sensed, with a mother's intuition, that Jack's emotions were not seriously involved, but what she did resent was Katy's bullying and constant criticism of Melissa. However, when Rose made no objection to Jack and Katy sharing a bedroom, the group settled down in an amicable fashion.

Melissa spent every day at the Club, living and breathing tennis. With Katy at her side, she watched the players she would soon be competing against, noting their strengths and weaknesses, the tactics they employed, soaking up the knowledge and experience Katy had gained in her five years on the circuit.

Melissa and Jack were scheduled to play their first round Mixed Doubles match late on Wednesday evening, their opponents being another brother and sister team from California, Hal and Lisa Renwick. Melissa had practised earlier and was waiting in the locker-room for the match currently on court fourteen to finish.

She wasn't nervous, just keyed-up and excited to be playing with Jack and hoping she wouldn't let him down. By partnering her, instead of a higher-ranked player, he had forfeited the advantage of being seeded, and she wanted desperately to justify his sacrifice.

'Melissa! Hurry up, you're on!' Katy rushed in. 'The

23

Singles on Centre finished earlier than expected, so you're going on there,' she told her.

'Centre Court?' Melissa said hollowly. That vast arena? Thousands of spectators and TV cameras? 'I can't go out there!' she panicked.

'Of course you can. Jack will be there to hold your hand,' Katy said caustically. 'Most players would give their eye-teeth to play on a show court.'

'I know,' Melissa took several deep breaths, then picked up her rackets and followed Katy outside. Her heart was hammering with fear, but she managed to summon up a rather wan smile for Jack. Her legs felt weak, as if she had flu, and she stumbled a little.

'I think I've got the wrong shoes on,' she whispered.

'No, you haven't,' Jack said calmly.

'I need to go to the loo!'

'You've just been.'

'I don't know how to curtsey!'

'You don't need to. The Royals have left, so have most of the spectators. And the TV coverage has switched to the match on number one,' he lied. 'Here are our opponents – don't let them see you're nervous,' he added quietly, and Melissa nodded. She already knew Hal and Lisa by sight; Hal was brown-haired, with soft-brown eyes and a ready smile, Lisa a tall, honey-blonde, who had already spent several years as a pro.

Fortunately for Melissa, they didn't have long to wait. The officials were already out on court and the four players were ushered out, passing beneath the famous engraving: 'If you can meet with triumph and disaster and treat those two imposters just the same . . .'

The applause which greeted their appearance seemed

24

deafening to Melissa, and she looked around her in awe. The huge arena seemed even larger from this viewpoint and the crowd was about a hundred times bigger than any other she had played in front of, despite the fact that many people had left their seats after the completion of the Singles contest.

'Wow,' she breathed, catching sight of the huge score-board. J.D. FARRELL & M.R. FARRELL v H.E. RENWICK & L.E. RENWICK. God, please don't let me make a fool of myself, she prayed, as she took out her rackets and selected one.

Jack won the toss and elected to receive, thereby giving Melissa three games to settle down before she had to serve. The five-minute warm-up helped her considerably and Jack smiled encouragingly as the umpire called 'time'. They had already discussed tactics, but he quickly reminded her of the signs he and Ace used to communicate unobtrusively during play.

'I remember,' Melissa nodded, and took the net position. Hal served first to Jack, a clean ace, which did nothing for Melissa's confidence as she backed down behind the baseline to return serve. Or try to, she amended silently, twirling her racket in her already perspiring hands.

The serve came, faster than she expected; she had no time to think, sheer instinct had her feet moving in the right direction and her racket connected with the ball. Lisa mis-hit the return and dumped it in the net. 15–15. She'd won a point! Hal won the game, though, then Jack evened up the score. Lisa struggled a little, but held to lead 2–1.

'Just concentrate on serving deep and I'll try and cut

off the returns,' Jack told her, as they walked out after the changeover. Melissa nodded, taking several deep, calming breaths as she prepared to serve. Her first serve went out, the second was so slow Jack was tempted to put out his racket and help it along, but at least it went in. Hal stepped in and swung hard, but Jack anticipated and volleyed sharply, placing the ball out of Lisa's reach.

Melissa heaved a huge sigh of relief as she returned to the baseline. She won the game, or, more accurately, she managed not to double-fault and Jack did the rest. 2–2. The match continued, with all players holding serve, with varying degrees of ease. 6–6. Tie-break.

The crowd was more involved now, cheering the home players, and the stadium had filled up again as people returned to their seats after leaving for refreshments at the end of the Singles match.

Hal opened with serve, Jack returned to Lisa, who hit at Melissa. She volleyed, hard, straight at Hal and the ball caught him in the groin. He yelped and clutched himself, and the crowd began to laugh as he hobbled, knock-kneed, around the court, using his racket as a walking stick.

'I'm awfully sorry,' Melissa said, trying to hide her own laughter.

'Are you trying to ruin my wedding night?' Hal squeaked, and she put her hand to her mouth.

'You okay, mate?' Jack asked, joining them at the net.

'Sure.' Hal minced away, to more laughter from the spectators. The incident not only relaxed Melissa, but gave her and Jack the one break of serve needed to clinch the tie-break, and the set.

Growing in confidence, she played a much greater part in the second set and was instrumental in breaking Lisa's serve and, more importantly, held her own. She and Jack won, 7–6, 6–3.

'I'm really sorry about hitting you,' she apologized again to Hal as they all shook hands. 'You didn't want children, did you?' she couldn't resist adding.

'Not until I met you,' Hal told her seriously, already smitten with the gorgeous brunette. Melissa smiled uncertainly, not sure how to respond. She turned to Jack, bubbling over with excitement.

'Isn't it terrific playing out here? I can't wait to play a Singles!' she said, a remark which, after her earlier paralyzing nerves, struck him temporarily speechless.

It took a long time for her to come down off cloud nine, but next day she reverted to her routine of practising and spectating. The fortnight passed quickly, as ever. The locker-rooms emptied as players were eliminated and flew home. She and Jack won their second round match, played on an outside court, to her disappointment, but lost in the third round to the top seeds. Jack also lost in the third round of the Singles, but he and Ace were still in contention for their main objective – the Men's Doubles title.

Melissa returned to Centre Court several times, but in the Players' Box, watching her brother and Ace. Ace had played quite brilliantly, reaching the quarter finals in Singles before losing a tense five-setter. His long black hair was held back from his face with a head-band, his tanned, hawk-like features giving credence to his claim to Apache ancestry.

'I'm surprised Ace doesn't stick feathers in that head-

27

band and put war-paint on his face!' Katy remarked caustically.

'You don't like him, do you?' Melissa asked curiously. Katy shook her head.

'Can't stand him. All that crap about being an Apache! It's all publicity hype. He's like me – a kid from the wrong side of the tracks.' She paused and shot Melissa a sidelong glance. 'You don't prattle on about him so much any more – have you come to your senses?' Melissa merely smiled and shrugged; she still found Ace utterly fascinating, yet more and more she found herself thinking of Nick. She had even phoned Jess to ask for his address and phone number, but had not summoned up the nerve to make use of the information.

With just three days left in England, Melissa began packing and saying her goodbyes, phoning friends and promising to write, although both Jack and Katy had warned her how difficult it was to sustain a long-distance relationship.

'They won't understand your life and you'll feel excluded from theirs,' Jack had told her. 'And it's hard to be close friends with a fellow pro; on court, they're the enemy and you can't afford to let them know if you're injured or depressed. You always have to keep a part of yourself hidden. It's different for Ace and me – we specialize in Doubles, but you intend concentrating on Singles. It's a tough path you've chosen.'

As the hour of departure drew near, Melissa knew she simply had to see Nick and, on Saturday evening, she dressed and made-up carefully and quietly left the house.

* * *

28

Nick was sitting in the Officers' Mess, idly watching the news on TV as he tried to unwind after a gruelling week's training on the Brecon Beacons. The phone rang and he reached out his hand.

'Lennox.' He listened for a moment, then, 'Say again,' he instructed, unable to believe his ears. 'Keep her there,' he said tersely. 'I'm on my way.'

He walked slowly towards the main gate of the barracks, not at all sure of the wisdom in seeing her again. By driving himself, and his men, to the point of exhaustion, he had partially succeeded in pushing her to the back of his mind. Now she was here, stirring up emotions and re-awakening his longing for her.

An ever-growing group of squaddies had gathered to admire both the BMW convertible and its driver when Nick arrived. His ferocious glare sent them scurrying away and he came to a standstill a yard from Melissa. He daren't go nearer; the desire to crush her in his arms warred with an almost equal desire to shake her. She looked stunning, wearing a bright pink sleeveless dress that accentuated her tanned skin and emphasized her glossy dark hair and huge, navy eyes. It also revealed too much leg and cleavage, he thought jealously.

'Are you crazy? Driving through a garrison town at night dressed like that! And with the top of your car down,' he noted furiously, then hated himself as her tentative smile faded and the sparkle in her lovely eyes dimmed. Then her chin jutted stubbornly.

'I got here safely, didn't I?' She didn't mention the drunken soldier who had tried to climb into her car when she had asked for directions, nor that she'd had to crash a red light to escape him.

29

'Yes. The question is: why?' Nick asked curtly.

'I'm leaving England tomorrow. I wanted to say goodbye,' Melissa faltered: she had never seen him look so stern, his grey eyes as cold as flint. She had to summon up all her courage to face him squarely. 'I just wanted to say I'm sorry I ran away that day in London, and that . . . I wish Sheena hadn't arrived,' she mumbled, blushing furiously. Nick's heart skipped a beat, yet he hardly dared allow himself to believe the implication behind those last words.

'Does anyone know you're here?' he asked carefully.

'No. My mother thinks I'm spending the night at Bellwood and I guess my father thinks I'm still in London,' she said, her cheeks now a brighter pink than her dress. Nick relaxed and smiled, then slowly, reverently, drew her into his arms and held her close, breathing in the heady scent of her skin, her hair.

A passing soldier, not immediately recognizing Nick, emitted a loud wolf-whistle, then a look of horror crossed his face when Nick jerked up his head and glowered at him.

'Oh, God! Sorry, sir,' he muttered, hurrying on his way.

'There's no privacy around here,' Nick grumbled. 'We're going to a hotel,' he decided, propelling a willing Melissa back into the car, then vaulting into the passenger seat. He gave her directions, then settled back to the pleasure of watching her as she drove, his gaze lingering on the smooth expanse of thigh. He'd never realized before how erotic watching a woman change gear could be!

'Damn!' he swore suddenly, remembering he needed condoms. 'We need to stop at a late-night chemist, or a

30

garage,' he explained, when Melissa glanced at him questioningly.

'Oh! Well, I'm on the Pill,' she informed him shyly, adding quickly, 'It was Katy's idea – to regulate . . . things,' she finished vaguely: her defeat at Beckenham had been due, in part, to the onset of her period.

'I see.' Nick guessed what she meant. 'There's more to safe sex than preventing pregnancy,' he told her. He had always used condoms, even pre-AIDS, never trusting a girl who claimed to be 'safe'. The Old Man had drummed that lesson into him and Rory when they were still in their early teens, afraid they might be trapped into paternity by girls attracted by the Lennox fortune and title. But now he knew he couldn't bear to have even that thin barrier between him and Melissa.

'You shouldn't be so trusting,' he told her.

'But I do trust you,' she said simply, with a lovely smile. Nick gently caressed her cheek, then snatched his hand away. He'd have to make love to her, now, in the car, if he continued touching her. He hoped to hell the Red Lion would have a vacant room!

Fortunately, they did. Nick hung out the 'do not disturb' sign, locked the door and unplugged the phone before turning to Melissa. He gazed at her for a moment, then they fell into each other's arms.

Immediately, his passion flared and ignited hers: it was as if they were back in his flat, re-living the moments before Sheena's interruption. Clothes were an unbearable barrier, hastily cast aside, and Nick lowered her to the bed and covered her nakedness with his own.

31

He kissed her hungrily, his hands caressing every inch of her body, before parting her thighs and dipping urgent fingers into her moist heat. Forcing himself to remember her innocence, he contained his desire until she was wet with longing, pushing against his hand and moaning softly. Only as he was poised to enter, did she remember a schoolfriend complaining about the pain of the first time, and she tensed.

'Relax, sweetheart, just relax,' Nick murmured against her mouth – he was stiff enough for both of them! Slowly, gently, he eased inside. God, she was so hot, so tight, so welcoming and he gritted his teeth against his need to thrust deeply, waiting until her own tentative movements urged him to continue. Slowly, carefully, he slid ever deeper inside her, increasing the speed and power of his thrusts, spurred on by the little cries of delight which grew in volume and intensity as he pushed them both near to climax.

Melissa had never expected sex to be this good: wave after wave of unimagined pleasure engulfed her entire body as she strove to become part of Nick. She wrapped her arms and legs around him, feeling herself being carried higher and higher to some pinnacle where the whole world exploded. She cried out, her body racked with shuddering spasms which slowly faded away, and she opened her eyes to find Nick smiling tenderly down at her.

'I never knew it would be like that,' she said shakily. 'Is it always so wonderful?'

'Only with me,' Nick said firmly. 'You'd hate it with any other man,' he added, kissing her mouth before easing his weight from her. He turned on his side, cradling her in his arms and Melissa snuggled closer, almost purring when he began stroking her shoulders and back.

'You're not sorry you're with me, instead of Ace?' Nick had to ask, and braced himself for the reply. Melissa twisted in his embrace and looked him straight in the eye, trying to find the words to describe her feelings regarding Ace Delaney.

'Most young female tennis players have a poster of Ace on their bedroom wall and day-dream about him,' she began slowly. 'And that's as far as it goes for most girls, but, for me, the man in the poster walked into my house when I was fourteen and said, "Hi, honey, you're going to be a beauty." I was sure he was the man for me.'

'Was? Past tense? What changed your mind?'

'You, I guess,' she smiled. 'You see, I was never jealous of Ace's girlfriends – I told myself they didn't matter to him, but really, they didn't matter to ME. But, when Sheena let herself into your flat as if she owned the place, as if she owned you . . .'

'I explained that,' Nick interrupted. He felt they had spent more than enough time talking about other people and was confident her crush on Ace had reached its end. He turned her onto her back, grasping her wrists to stretch her arms wide and nudged her legs apart with his knee.

This time, there was no need for haste, and he used all his skill to bring her to a fever-pitch of wanting before he took her. The intensity of their mutual orgasm surprised even him and shook Melissa to the core. Afterwards, Nick lay propped against a stack of pillows and held her as she slept. He refused to yield to his own tiredness, to waste a moment. Tomorrow, no today, he realized with a pang of impending loss, they had to say goodbye.

All too soon, the short summer night gave way to an early dawn and Melissa stirred, stretching languidly and smiling sleepily at Nick.

'Do you really have to leave this morning?' he asked, but didn't give her time to reply. 'Forget I said that; it was selfish of me. Of course you must go. This is your big chance to succeed.'

'If I don't go, I'll always wonder how good I could have been,' she said slowly. She had looked forward to this day for so long, yet now she wanted to cry!

'I'll come and see you, whenever I can,' Nick promised, although, with her constant travelling and his Army commitments, the chances of their being on the same continent at the same time were pretty remote. 'Let's make a definite date, here and now,' he said suddenly. 'Every year, on this weekend, we'll meet here, whatever else is happening in our lives.'

'Oh, yes, that's a wonderful idea,' Melissa readily agreed, then she sighed. 'Look, it's already light outside,' she said sadly. She clung to him and he held her close, wishing he could stop time, but the sun rose ever higher and soon there were sounds in the hotel indicating the start of another day. They breakfasted in bed, made love one more slow, delicious time, then had to prepare to leave.

They walked slowly outside, hands entwined, and stopped by Melissa's car. She was due to meet her parents at the airport and hand over the BMW for Rose to use during her absence.

34

'I'll say goodbye to you here, and phone a friend to come and collect me,' Nick said, trying to sound matter-of-fact when what he really wanted was to beg her to stay. He kissed her once more, hard and bruising, marking her as his, then released her and opened the car door. Melissa fumbled with the keys, her vision blurred by tears. She finally found the ignition and reached up to kiss him one last time before gunning the engine and driving away.

CHAPTER 2

The next few weeks flew by for Melissa. There was no time to feel homesick and she was so tired when she went to bed that thoughts of Nick quickly turned into dreams about him. Katy ran her ragged, training hard to hone her fitness and improve her game, trying out new rackets with varying tensions, even testing different shoes.

In between intensive training sessions, Melissa competed in small-money tournaments, in places she had never heard of, against equally unknown opponents and in front of meagre crowds.

She won some matches, mainly partnering Katy in Doubles, but in Singles never progressed beyond the second round. But she was gaining valuable experience and even more valuable computer ranking points. The little prize money she won was quickly spent and the amount she owed to Jack grew alarmingly.

'It's not as if we're flying by private jet or staying in luxury hotels,' she sighed one evening, as they were once again packing their bags. 'It's costing a fortune just to get to each tournament.'

'Welcome to the real world,' Katy said drily.

'How did you manage, when you first started out?' Melissa asked curiously, for she knew Katy's parents weren't wealthy enough to have subsidized her.

'I lived in a camper van and drove to tournaments. When I ran out of money, I took jobs as a waitress until I had enough to get back on the road,' Katy said, matter-of-factly. Melissa digested that in silence for a moment.

'I guess you think I'm having it easy?' she ventured at last. Katy shrugged.

'Sure I do, in some ways. Jack's money has put you on the first rung of the ladder, but you have to climb the rest of the way by yourself. And you're doing okay,' she added encouragingly, which was praise indeed from Katy.

'Am I?' Melissa beamed her delight, and the two exchanged a warm smile. The relationship, originally born out of mutual necessity and convenience, was blossoming into a strong friendship. Katy was pleased and surprised by Melissa's willingness to work hard and learn her craft.

They arrived in New York on a stifling hot day in August, and both were in high spirits as a cab took them to a rented house in Flushing Meadow, venue of the US Open. Katy was glad to be in her home city again and, for Melissa, there was the excitement of her first trip to the Big Apple. And they were both, for different reasons, looking forward to seeing Jack, although he and Ace wouldn't be arriving for several more days.

Melissa was facing the daunting prospect of needing to win through the pre-qualifying rounds, then three more qualifying matches before being included in the

Singles draw, but her places in the Women's Doubles, with Katy, and in the Mixed, with Jack, were assured.

'I want to play Mixed with Jack,' Katy had grumbled.

'You two can play a different sort of mixed,' Melissa had retorted, and suggested Katy team up with Ace; to their surprise, he had agreed to the partnership.

Now, Melissa craned her neck, trying to see as much of New York as possible, for she knew better than to ask if she might do some sight-seeing. She had asked, just once before, in Florida.

'Do you want to be a tourist or a tennis player?' Katy had snapped, and Melissa hadn't asked again. Maybe after the tournament, before they had to leave the city, Melissa decided silently. For now, it was too hot and humid to expend energy she would need on court.

As soon as they had unpacked, Katy took Melissa to Flushing Meadow.

'I always thought Wimbledon was huge but, compared to this, it's a vicarage garden party,' Melissa said, looking around her in awe.

'Stadium Court alone holds twenty thousand spectators,' Katy told her. 'Playing out here at night, under floodlights, is the craziest experience. You can't see much of the crowd; there's just this huge mass of noise and pandemonium, all bearing down on you. It's great if they're rooting for you, but pretty scary if they're not.'

Melissa nodded, trying to imagine the rows and rows of seating, seemingly rising to the sky, filled with cheering – or booing – fans.

'I don't suppose I'll be playing out here, not this year,' she said, both regretful and relieved.

'You might – if you win through the qualifying and draw Graf in the first round,' Katy said, then laughed at the expression of horror on Melissa's face. 'Come on, let's go and sort out a practice court and check the schedule,' she said, back to her usual, practical self.

Two days later, Melissa was practising hard when Jack appeared, earlier than expected. She dropped her racket and ran to him, just beating Katy.

'Hello, how's my investment coming along?' Jack asked, picking her off her feet and swinging her around.

'Don't call me that,' Melissa scolded.

'Okay – pension plan,' he amended, with a grin, before turning to Katy, hugging her briefly and dropping a light kiss on her cheek. 'How is she doing?' he asked.

'See for yourself,' Katy said, rather shortly, not exactly overwhelmed by the exuberance of his greeting! She had hoped coaching Melissa would bring her and Jack closer, but the reverse seemed to be happening. He still phoned regularly, at each stop of the tour, but more and more it seemed to her that Melissa's progress was his main reason for calling.

Jack took Katy's place on court and began to trade shots with Melissa, his experienced eye quickly noting the extra speed and power.

'Hit more to her backhand,' Katy told him. That was Melissa's weaker side and Jack raised a questioning eyebrow, but did as she suggested. The first cross-court pass took him by surprise; anticipating the second, he watched instead as Melissa drilled it down the sideline.

'And to think I told her to abandon that double-fisted

backhand,' he said ruefully. 'It's almost impossible to judge the direction.'

'I know,' Katy agreed, rather smugly. 'She's so much quicker to the ball now and has time to play an aggressive backhand instead of just pushing it back as she used to.'

'Doing it in practice is one thing – has she the confidence to do it in a match?' Jack asked.

'You'll find out in . . .' Katy consulted her watch, 'three hours. Okay, Melissa, that's enough,' she called. 'Have some lunch and a rest, and remember to drink plenty of water or you'll become dehydrated in this heat.'

'Okay,' Melissa towelled down and gathered up her rackets. 'Are you coming to watch me?' she asked her brother.

'Sure. I'm meeting Hal Renwick for a hit, but I'll be there,' he promised.

He was as good as his word and Hal, remembering the gorgeous brunette who had made such an impact on him at Wimbledon – in more ways than one! – joined Jack on the sidelines as Melissa's match got under way. She won in straight sets and beamed happily as she made her way over to them.

'Well done, you've definitely improved,' Jack said. Hal nodded his agreement, although he had never seen Melissa play a Singles match before. God, she was stunning! Even hot and sweaty . . . especially hot and sweaty, he thought, feeling decidedly hot himself.

'Why don't we all have dinner together this evening?' Hal suggested. Katy frowned, wanting Jack to herself, but Jack agreed readily. Melissa did, too, not relishing the prospect of playing 'gooseberry'.

'Melissa has another match tomorrow,' Katy reminded Jack sharply.

'So? She has to eat. She can still go to bed early,' he retorted. Oh, yes please! Hal thought longingly. Jack noted the look on his face and groaned inwardly. Hell! That was all he needed – a lovelorn Hal distracting Melissa from her tennis!

Jack would have been even more discomfited if he had known of her involvement with Nick. However, he was soon to find out, for Nick decided to fly to New York and visit Melissa. In the seven weeks, seven lifetimes, since her departure, he had covered for fellow officers on weekends and now called in the favours, taking a week's leave. The postcards and brief phone calls, although welcome, had merely made him want her more, and he flew over on the first Thursday of the tournament.

Melissa had won her qualifying matches and the first round in the main draw, before losing in the second to a player ranked in the top thirty. Although she hadn't really expected to win, she felt a little tired and dispirited and went early to bed. She was brushing her teeth when Katy entered the bedroom.

'You've a visitor waiting downstairs,' Katy said, sounding cross, Melissa thought.

'Mm? Who?' she asked, rinsing her mouth.

'Don't you know?' Katy queried.

'Haven't a clue,' Melissa replied.

'You must have given him the address,' she said accusingly.

'Who? I didn't . . . Nick?' Melissa asked incredulously, and, when Katy nodded, gave a scream of

41

delight. 'I was only expecting a letter!' she said, rushing out of the room, forgetting she was clad only in a skimpy nightie. She bounded down the stairs and threw herself into Nick's waiting arms.

'I can't believe you're here,' she said shakily, her voice muffled against his chest.

'And I can't believe this welcome,' Nick said huskily. The short satin nightie concealed none of her curves and he lifted her against him, moulding her to the contours of his body.

Ace sauntered past, his gaze lingering on Melissa's legs and bottom as the nightie rode up even higher.

'Nice arse, honey,' he drawled, looking challengingly at Nick. He didn't know the guy's name, but vaguely remembered seeing him in England. Apparently he'd succeeded in getting into Melissa's knickers! Nick gazed steadily back.

'Not even you can annoy me today,' he said evenly.

'No? Pity,' Ace said lightly, passing on into the kitchen.

'Why didn't you tell me you were coming?' Melissa asked, pulling back a little to look into his face. She was so happy to be back in his arms; everything else in her life had changed so drastically and so quickly, that she had sometimes been apprehensive about meeting him again, wondering if their feelings for each other would be the same. Now, all her doubts had vanished; she was where she belonged.

'I wanted to surprise you. There are too many people around here – I've got a cab waiting outside. Go and pack an overnight bag and put some clothes on.'

'Won't that be a waste of time?' Melissa murmured, and he grinned.

'Probably, but go and do it. You're too much of a temptation dressed like that.'

'Okay, I'll be five minutes,' she promised, racing towards the stairs. 'The kitchen's through there – help yourself to some coffee,' she called over her shoulder. In the kitchen with Ace? Not likely, Nick thought, and stayed where he was. He heard raised voices, recognized Jack's and assumed the other belonged to Katy Oliver. He guessed it was a lovers' tiff and closed his ears to it, but in fact, he – or rather his arrival – was the reason for their displeasure.

'He shouldn't be here,' Katy said crossly. 'In the middle of the US Open! Go and tell him she's not on holiday,' she ordered. Jack sighed, but went to talk to Nick.

'Where's Melissa?' he asked.

'Gone to get dressed, I'm taking her with me,' Nick told him.

'She was about to go to bed when you arrived, and she has to be up early tomorrow to practise,' Jack said. 'Look, I realize you've had a long journey to see her,' he went on uncomfortably, 'but it's not awfully convenient. I wish you'd let us know you were coming over . . .' he trailed off under Nick's quizzical gaze.

'I don't need your permission to spend a few days in New York,' he responded mildly.

'No, of course you don't,' Jack agreed hastily. 'But this is an important tournament for her.'

'I'm sure it is, and I don't intend disrupting her schedule, but presumably she does have some free time?' he asked, curbing his temper.

'Yes, but she's supposed to rest, not to . . . to . . .' Katy stammered.

'Get shagged out,' Ace supplied helpfully, as he re-entered the room.

'Shut up!' Three people yelled at him simultaneously, and he grinned, quite unabashed; he was enjoying the scene enormously.

'What's going on?' Melissa came slowly down the stairs, looking uncertainly from one angry face to another.

'Nothing, sweetheart,' Nick said firmly, taking her arm.

'Melissa – we have a court booked for ten o'clock tomorrow,' Katy reminded her.

'I know, I'll be there,' she said, before she was hauled bodily out of the house and Nick slammed the door behind them.

'What was all that about?' Melissa asked again, as she nestled in Nick's arms in the back of the cab.

'They're not too pleased to see me,' Nick said drily. 'They're afraid I'll distract you.'

'They got that right,' Melissa said happily. 'I'm so glad you came – how long are you staying?'

'Until next Wednesday. This is my first trip to New York and I'll be quite happy exploring alone. I realize you have to work,' he assured her. 'Jack's lecture was quite unnecessary. I'll get you a pass-key to my suite and you can come and go as you please,' he said easily.

'I'd rather just come,' Melissa said, then blushed. But Nick laughed out loud, delighted.

'I'll do my best,' he promised.

He was as good as his word, despite his long journey and lack of sleep; looking at her, touching her, was all the aphrodisiac he would ever need, even if he lived to be a hundred.

'Mm, that was lovely,' Melissa sighed blissfully, some time later, stretching like a contented cat basking in hot sunshine. 'I was a little afraid things might not be the same between us,' she confided. 'So much has happened since I left England, but it's as if we've never been apart.'

'Are you crazy? We've been separated for an eternity,' Nick grumbled good-naturedly, settling her into the crook of his arm. He reached out to switch off the light, then, tired but happy, they slept.

Melissa arrived at the practice courts only three minutes late the next morning, but still received a scowl from Katy, who was ready to begin. Melissa hastily changed and ran back out on court. They were preparing for a Women's Doubles match, so she and Katy hit against two other players, warming up and honing their skills as a team. Jack was there, too, loosening up before his third-round Singles.

'She seems happy,' he commented to Katy, as they took a breather.

'Too happy,' Katy said sourly. 'She doesn't care if we win or lose.'

'She'd care even less if she were miserable,' Jack snapped, sick of hearing her moan about Nick's arrival. 'I know we'd be better off without Nick Lennox but, now he's here, for God's sake make the best of it.'

Katy stomped off without answering: it wasn't just Nick who was making her bad-tempered. She was losing Jack, she just knew it, and her moods were only making him back off quicker. He sure as hell didn't look at her in the way Nick gazed at Melissa! She knew she

45

didn't have exclusive rights to Jack – nor he to her – but, for the past eighteen months, they had made the most of their times together.

It was another hot, sultry day, with the temperature soaring above a hundred degrees, and Melissa and Katy relaxed in the air-conditioned locker-room while waiting for their match to begin. The heat hit Melissa like a hammer blow as she walked onto court, but she was determined to prove to Katy that Nick's presence wasn't detrimental to her game, and it was her accurate volleying that won them the break of serve needed to clinch the first set.

The second went to a tie-break and Melissa, her energy sapped by the heat and humidity, put everything into the last, vital points. If they had to play a third set, she felt they would lose. On match-point, she served an ace and beamed with delight and relief as she moved to the net to shake hands with Katy and their beaten opponents.

'Well played,' Katy said, rather grudgingly, as they gathered up their belongings. 'Are you coming to watch Jack?'

'No, this heat's killing me,' Melissa said, which was true enough. She showered and dressed quickly, then made her way out to the car-park.

She let herself into Nick's suite and found him lounging on one of the kingsize beds, propped against a stack of pillows, and wearing only a towel around his hips. The TV was switched on, and he was idly watching Jack's match.

'Hello, sweetheart,' he moved to rise, but she motioned him to stay.

'Don't get up, you look comfortable,' she said, kicking off her shoes and stripping off her jeans and T-shirt before clambering up beside him and nestling into his arms. 'Is Jack winning?'

'He's two sets up,' Nick told her. 'They showed the end of your match. Katy will have to stop complaining about my being here – you played better than she did.'

'Oh? Since when have you become an expert?' Melissa teased.

'I haven't. The presenter said the pupil was outstripping the teacher,' he explained.

'Oh, God, I hope no one repeats that to Katy!' Melissa said feelingly. A loud burst of applause caused her to look at the TV and she saw the replay of Jack's shot to break serve. The camera panned to the spectators and focused briefly on Katy.

'There's Katy Oliver, Jack's girlfriend,' the commentator told the viewers. 'She's coaching Melissa Farrell, Jack's sister. I can't see Melissa, can you Bill? I wonder where she is?' Melissa laughed at that, twisting to look at Nick, then grimaced in pain.

'Ouch! I should have stayed for a massage . . . will you rub my back?' she asked.

'I didn't hurt you last night, did I?' Nick asked guiltily, as he gently tried to ease the soreness from her muscles.

'No, these cement courts are really hard on my body,' Melissa said, matter-of-factly. 'To the right a bit . . . lower . . . ooh, that's nice. Have you ever thought of becoming a masseur?'

'Only for you,' he dropped a kiss on her shoulder. 'Lie on your tummy and I'll massage your back,' he offered. Melissa obeyed gladly and gradually relaxed beneath his ministrations.

'I should have brought some oil,' she murmured. Nick thought for a moment then got off the bed and went into the bathroom.

'Bath oil?' He held up the bottle and Melissa nodded. He tipped some of the perfumed contents into his palms and gently kneaded her back, trying to ignore his mounting desire. But then he heard the quickened breathing that attested to her own arousal and dipped his oiled fingers into the cleft of her buttocks. Melissa moaned and wriggled seductively.

'You're the first physiotherapist to do that!' She giggled, and twisted around, her eyes widening as she noted his erection. 'My turn,' she said huskily, reaching for the bath oil. Her slippery fingers teased and stroked his engorged shaft until he could bear the torment no longer. Remembering her sore back, he lay down and gently eased her on top of him, closing his eyes in ecstasy as he buried himself in the hot depths of her body. However often he had her, he would always hunger for more, was his last coherent thought as they strove for, and reached together, a climax more earth-shattering than anything that had gone before. They lay, unspeaking and half asleep, bodies still joined.

'Bath,' Nick said finally. 'The tub's big enough for two – that oil is so strong, we smell like we've been in a Turkish brothel,' he said idly.

'How do you know?' Melissa opened one eye to regard him suspiciously. He merely winked in reply and, curiosity piqued, she raised herself on one elbow. 'I repeat; how do you know what a Turkish brothel

48

smells like?' He still didn't answer, so, 'You've never had to pay for it, have you?' she challenged mockingly.

'Don't be crude,' Nick said, trying not to laugh, then relented. 'I was very young,' he excused himself. 'We had been on NATO exercises with Turkey and then had a couple of days' leave. We went into what we thought was a nightclub, and . . .' he shrugged.

'But you didn't leave when you discovered it wasn't just a nightclub?' Melissa snorted.

'No,' he admitted. Melissa frowned slightly; she didn't like the thought of him making love to someone else, however casual the encounter and however long ago.

'I'll have to tell Ace that story,' she said, knowing the very mention of Ace would annoy him. 'You'll go up in his estimation no end.'

'I doubt it. He's probably been there, done that, and bought the T-shirt,' Nick said drily, well aware of her reason for mentioning the grease-ball. Melissa laughed and relaxed.

'I'm sorry, I shouldn't be jealous of women you knew when I was still in primary school,' she said innocently.

'Ouch, that was below the belt,' Nick complained. He pounced, scooping her up in his arms and carrying her through to the bathroom. 'Apologize . . . or have a cold shower,' he threatened.

'I'm sorry, I'm sorry,' she said quickly, and he set her on her feet, then began running hot water into the tub. It WAS big enough for two, although a great deal of water slopped over the side as they splashed like children. Then they soaped each other, definitely not

49

like children, and Melissa had her first experience of making love in the water.

They ordered dinner from Room Service, after which they abandoned the bed with its perfume-oiled sheets and settled down in the other, talking desultorily and watching TV. Melissa was pleased to hear Jack had won his Singles match and phoned the house to speak to him.

'Where the hell are you?' Jack demanded.

'With Nick.'

'I guessed that much! But where?'

'I'm not telling you,' she said firmly. 'What time do I have to practise tomorrow?'

'Hang on,' he conferred with Katy, then, 'Eleven o'clock,' he told her.

'I'll be there,' she promised.

'Don't forget we have a match tomorrow. Get a good night's sleep. Oh, God, what am I saying?' he sighed wearily. 'Try and get some rest, please. For me.'

'Of course I will; I'm in bed already,' Melissa said indignantly, Nick laughed and Jack, hearing him, sighed again.

'You would not believe the earache I'm getting,' he said, lowering his voice so Katy couldn't hear.

'Yes, I would. I've lived with it for weeks, remember? Goodnight, Jack, see you tomorrow.' She hung up and turned to Nick. 'I really must get some sleep.'

'I'm not arguing,' Nick said; the combination of jet-lag and lovemaking had worn him out.

'Will you come and watch our match tomorrow? It's Jack and me against Katy and Ace.'

'Sure,' he agreed, yawning. He switched off the TV

and the lights, holding her soft, warm body in the darkness as sleep overtook them both.

Quite a sizeable crowd had gathered to watch the Mixed Doubles match, despite Agassi's presence on nearby Stadium Court. Ace was a favourite with the New Yorkers, too, and there was always an added interest when he and Jack were on opposite sides of the net. And this was the first time Katy and Melissa had faced each other in competition.

Nick was enjoying himself, the noise and excitement of Flushing Meadow was impossible to resist and, even had Melissa not been playing, he would have been caught up in the electric atmosphere of the place. She had made sure he had a good vantage point, too, sitting with other players and their friends and families.

Neither Jack nor Ace was taking the event too seriously; both were still in the Singles and were working towards a second US Open Doubles title. Melissa wanted to win in front of Nick; Katy wanted to beat Melissa – she HAD heard the comment about the pupil outstripping the teacher and it rankled. Also Melissa was getting more sex than she was, and that rankled even more!

Both men played with less than their usual power. Jack was delighted with Melissa's prowess as she and Katy battled for supremacy at the net, Melissa more often then not winning the point. Katy grew more and more frustrated, especially with Ace.

'Not to her backhand!' she wailed, regretting the hours spent honing Melissa's new-found skill as she lunged at, and missed, yet another passing shot.

51

'Sorry, I thought that was her weaker side,' Ace lied, as he returned to the baseline. He served to Melissa, deliberately to her backhand. Katy intercepted and shot it back, Melissa, rushing the net, scooped up the ball and hit it back at Katy's feet. Jack found himself redundant and looked at Ace, jerking his head to the side of the court. Grinning, Ace joined him at the net, and they stood, arms crossed, and watched the girls fight it out. The crowd laughed and cheered as Melissa finally outfoxed Katy and put the ball away.

'It went thattaway!' she taunted, pointing to where Katy should have moved.

'Where the hell were you?' Katy screamed at Ace, swearing loudly at him.

'You girls want equal prize money – earn it,' he snapped.

'Warning, Miss Oliver, audible obscenity,' said the umpire.

'Tut tut,' Melissa wagged an admonishing finger at Katy, who glared murderously.

Jack and Melissa were now leading 5–4, and Jack served to clinch the first set. Ace, annoyed with Katy, and thinking of a potentially gruelling Singles the following day, eased up even more and Jack and Melissa quickly went into a 3–0 lead.

'Agassi's just won,' said a voice behind Nick as a newcomer entered the stand.

'Yeah? Ace is about to lose,' replied another. 'I'm playing him tomorrow – I hope he does this badly against me!'

'I shouldn't count on it.' Then, later, 'Ace isn't even trying, is he? What's he up to? Is he after Melissa Farrell?'

'Dunno. If he is, he'll have to fight Hal Renwick for her.' They'll both have to fight me, Nick thought grimly. And who in hell was Hal Renwick?

He asked Melissa about Hal later, when she joined him in the Players' lounge.

'Hal? I haven't seen him – he might be here somewhere,' she said vaguely, glancing around.

'Is he a fan?' Nick asked, watching closely for her reaction.

'No, he's a player,' she said absently, then looked directly at Nick, not understanding the intensity of his gaze. There was only innocence in her lovely dark eyes and Nick smiled and relaxed, his fingers stroking her cheek.

'You're my girl, aren't you?' he asked softly, and she felt weak with desire.

'Of course.' She reached up and kissed him and he held her close, oblivious to the people around them.

'Ready to go?' he murmured against her hair and she nodded, slipping her hand in his as they threaded their way outside.

Katy and Melissa lost their next Doubles match, and Katy threw her racket down in disgust at her own poor performance.

'I'm sorry, that was abysmal,' she mumbled.

'It's okay. Is anything wrong?' Melissa asked, relieved that Katy's errors, and not her own, had been their downfall.

'No. Yes. Has Jack said anything to you – about me, I mean?' Katy swallowed her pride to ask.

'No, but I haven't seen that much of him,' Melissa

said, for she had spent her spare time with Nick, and had only returned to the house for a change of clothes. 'Why?'

'I don't think he loves me any more,' Katy said miserably.

'Oh.' Melissa didn't think he ever had. 'Would you like me to speak to him?' she ventured, but Katy declined her offer.

The next day it was Melissa's turn to apologize for an error-strewn match.

'You've done really well to get this far,' Jack tried to comfort her, not too concerned about losing. 'When does Nick leave – Wednesday morning, isn't it? Go and enjoy yourself. You deserve a break from training – I'll square it with Katy.'

'Thank you,' Melissa cheered up immediately, and hurried away to shower and change. Thirty-six whole hours of parole! she thought happily.

Katy digested the news of Melissa's 'holiday' in silence. Then, 'Does this mean you and I can finally have some fun?' she asked. Jack shifted uncomfortably, wishing he could end relationships as easily as Ace. But, there was more at stake here than Katy's hurt feelings; Melissa really needed her. He just hoped Katy needed his financial backing too much to walk out on Melissa in a huff.

'I'm still competing,' he hedged.

'Yeah, just as you were last year, but that didn't stop us from having sex at every opportunity! Is there someone else, Jack?' she added, more quietly.

'No,' he said truthfully. 'But . . . you've changed, Katy,' he said, raking his fingers through his hair. 'Your coaching Melissa was a business proposition, beneficial to you as well as to her,' he hastened to add, 'but . . . you seemed to think it was some sort of marriage proposal! When I took you to Bellwood to meet her, you kept looking around the place as if you were planning to re-decorate!'

'That's not true!' Katy denied, but couldn't meet his gaze. She HAD enjoyed feeling part of the Farrell family, and had been overawed by Bellwood, wondering what it would be like to live in a house with such a history.

'I'm sorry,' she managed a tight smile. 'No hard feelings, huh?'

'Of course not,' Jack heaved a sigh of relief. 'And I am still . . .'

'If you say you're fond of me, I shall probably hit you!' she informed him. 'When will Melissa be back?'

'Er, Wednesday.'

'Right. I'll go and spend some time with my parents,' she said, and walked out with her head high before he could see her tears.

Melissa was happily unaware of Katy's distress, spending every precious minute with Nick. Unfortunately, the hours sped by; sight-seeing, shopping and, of course, making love.

'I'm going to need another holiday to recuperate from this one,' Nick said, on their last evening together, utterly spent.

'Are you complaining?' Melissa murmured drowsily.

'What do you think?' Nick retorted, but she had already fallen asleep. He smiled and settled her more comfortably in his arms, considering his – their – future.

I'm going to quit the Army, he thought suddenly. He had been toying with the idea for months, but now the reasons for resigning outnumbered those for staying.

The Old Man wasn't putting pressure on him, but Nick knew he wanted him at Glengarry, and felt he ought to comply. After all, his own childhood and teenage years would have been very different if his great-uncle hadn't stepped in and taken the confused and unhappy eight-year-old orphan to live in Scotland alongside Rory.

And Melissa . . . he glanced down at her and gently touched his lips to her brow. Glengarry was a beautiful place; he'd have a lovely home to offer her, instead of Army married quarters. He had enjoyed his ten years' soldiering, but it was time to go.

He had to leave for the airport at seven o'clock and quietly dressed and packed while Melissa continued sleeping the sleep of the exhausted, for he had already decided he didn't want her to accompany him to the airport – he preferred to remember her just as she was, sleeping in his bed. At the very last moment, he gently awakened her with a kiss.

'I have to go,' he said softly.

'Oh, Nick,' Melissa tightened her arms around his neck, trying not to cry. 'I do love you.' He went still.

'That's the first time you've said that.' He held her close, then reluctantly put her from him. 'I bought you a present,' he indicated a package on the bedside table. 'Don't open it until I've gone.'

'Okay,' Melissa agreed, puzzled. He bent and kissed her lips, then pulled away while he still could. Neither could say 'goodbye' and, after one last, lingering look,

Nick closed the door behind him and began his journey home. Melissa ran to the window and watched as he climbed into a cab and was driven away. Sadly, she returned to the bed and picked up her gift. She tore off the wrapping paper, gasped when she saw the contents and then began to laugh, which was exactly what Nick had intended.

'Look what Nick bought me!' Melissa said cheerfully, as she entered the sitting-room, later than morning. 'A vibrator!'

'A pity he didn't buy one for me, too,' Katy said sourly, glaring at Jack. Melissa grimaced sympathetically at her brother. 'I'm glad you're finally here,' Katy continued. 'I've entered you for a tournament in Virginia – we're leaving in a couple of hours. There's no reason to hang around here,' she added pointedly.

'Okay, I'll go and pack,' Melissa said peacably. She had wanted to stay to watch Jack and Ace in their pursuit of the Doubles title, but decided against mentioning it. She was just relieved that Katy evidently intended continuing to coach her, despite her quarrel with Jack, which her brother had briefly explained. She would be lost without her – she did everything; all the paperwork, travel arrangements and even ensured her laundry was done in time! And she knew all the players Melissa came up against, so her advice on how to beat them was invaluable.

The packing finished, she lay on her bed and watched TV until it was almost time to leave, then she picked up her luggage and left the room, pausing to knock on Ace's door.

'I've just come to say goodbye . . . oops!' She covered her eyes, for he had just emerged from the shower, stark naked.

'Come in and say it properly, then,' Ace dared her. She half-opened one eye, then removed her hand once she saw he had wrapped a towel around his hips. He was tanned mahogany brown, black hair plastered to his skull and covering his broad chest.

'You can't really be an Apache – they don't have body hair,' she informed him.

'Are you an expert on male bodies, now?' Ace teased.

'Only one man's body,' she said dreamily. Ace's eyes narrowed; he had enjoyed Melissa's adoration and he definitely didn't like the man she had chosen in his place.

'Is your soldier a good lover?' he asked.

'The best,' Melissa told him.

'How do you know? You've nothing to compare him with,' Ace scoffed, moving nearer. Melissa gazed up into his eyes and felt . . . nothing. A year ago, this close to an almost naked Ace, she would have swooned! But, just to be sure, she didn't back away when he leaned forward and kissed her. She even kissed him back, and enjoyed it, but there was none of the toe-curling, bones-melting desire she experienced with Nick. She was definitely Ace-proof! Ace broke the kiss and stepped back, watching her ruefully.

'I guess I've been around your brother too long,' he drawled. 'Kissing you feels almost incestuous!' Then, dark eyes glittering, he went on silkily, 'Mind you, incest is about the only thing I haven't tried!' Melissa backed off towards the door rather hastily.

' 'Bye, Ace. I hope you and Jack with the title,' she said.

'Thanks. 'Bye, honey,' he said. 'Hey!' he called. 'If you ever need help and Jack's not around – call me.' Melissa stared at him for a moment, then nodded, touched by his evident sincerity.

'I'll remember that. You're not as bad as everyone makes out, are you?'

'God, don't spread that around – I've my reputation to consider,' he said, truly appalled.

'I think your reputation is safe,' Melissa said drily.

'Melissa!' Katy called. 'The cab's here!'

'Coming.' She picked up her cases and ran downstairs.

' 'Bye, Jack; you'll be pleased to know I'm finally over Ace!'

'Don't be too complacent,' he warned. 'From what I've seen over the years, Ace is a bit like malaria – once infected, sufferers seem susceptible to recurrent bouts of fever!'

'Not me,' she said confidently, and hugged him, then clambered into the cab beside Katy. Jack waved them off, then, sighing his relief at Katy's departure, returned indoors.

'Now they've gone, can we party?' Ace asked.

'Later – I want this title,' Jack said firmly.

'Agreed. But, win or lose, we'll want to get plastered – and laid.'

'Agreed,' Jack said fervently, and they both laughed.

CHAPTER 3

Melissa and Katy quickly adjusted to being alone again, training and competing in tournaments throughout the States. The bond between them was strengthening daily; in the highly competitive atmosphere of the tour, they were united in their goal to see Melissa succeed. Katy said nothing about the argument with Jack, and concentrated all her efforts on Melissa's career.

Melissa steadily improved, increasing her prize money and, more importantly, her tally of computer points. She began beating girls ranked higher than herself and, when the seeded players checked their part of the draw, M.R. Farrell was one of the names they hoped not to see.

In early December, she broke into the top one hundred and Katy was as delighted as when she had passed through the same barrier herself. Melissa's Doubles ranking rose, too: she still occasionally partnered Katy, but had also experimented by teaming up with other girls, notably Lisa Renwick, with whom she enjoyed most success.

After another win, in her last tournament before Christmas, Melissa was curled up on her bed, chatting to Nick and finalizing plans for the holidays, which she was due to spend with him in Scotland. He was at Glengarry permanently now, his Army days over, sooner than he had expected, courtesy of the so-called 'peace dividend'.

'When will you be arriving?' Nick asked.

'That depends on whether I win tomorrow. And I'm going to see my parents first – I thought I ought to stop over at Bellwood for one night before flying up to Scotland.'

'Let me know which flight and I'll be there,' Nick said. 'I can't wait to see you.'

'I know, I miss you, too,' Melissa sighed.

'Isn't the vibrator an adequate substitute?' he teased, and she laughed.

'I don't know, I haven't tried it. I do share a room with Katy,' she reminded him.

'Is she there now?'

'No,' Melissa replied unthinkingly.

'What are you wearing?' Nick asked.

'My dressing-gown – I've just had a bath,' she stammered.

'Take it off and lie down on the bed.' Nick's voice was soft and seductive, and utterly compelling. Lying naked on the bed, her nipples hardened – in the chill air, she told herself.

'Close your eyes and pretend I'm there,' Nick said huskily. 'Where do you want me to touch you, Melissa?' Her ragged breathing was sweet torture to him and he closed his eyes as he imagined her stroking her lovely body. 'Is that good, sweetheart?'

'It's not as nice as when *you* do it – and I hope none of

the hotel staff are listening in!' she giggled breathlessly, amazed and delighted that the mere sound of his voice could bring her to a climax.

'I expect they've heard worse – get some rest now, sweetheart. I'll see you soon,' he said softly.

'Yes, soon,' she echoed longingly.

Melissa had guessed correctly about there being an eavesdropper, but it wasn't at her end of the line. Sheena, picking up the phone to make a call, had heard Nick's voice and continued listening, her anger and frustration rising as quickly as Nick's obvious desire. She had been delighted by Nick's decision to resign his Army commission, but her romantic hopes had been quickly dashed as he remained oblivious to her ever more blatant attempts at seduction. Too angry to think rationally, she stormed out of her room and marched into his.

'I heard you!' she spat, eyes blazing. 'It was disgusting! Perverted!'

'It seems to have turned you on,' Nick remarked dryly. 'It's about time you found yourself another man, Sheena.'

'Oh!' His brotherly advice was more than she could bear. 'How can you prefer that . . . that . . .'

'Careful,' Nick warned, his amusement vanishing abruptly. 'I know you think I'm here as a substitute for Rory, but I'm not. At least, not where you're concerned. I'm sorry; I agree it would be more convenient if I loved you instead of Melissa, but life isn't like that. She'll be here in a few days – you will make her welcome, won't you?' he asked, but it was an order not a question.

'Of course, I'm an excellent hostess,' she reminded him coolly, gathering the shreds of her dignity around her. 'I've put her in the turret room – it has such lovely views.'

'Don't be ridiculous; she'll sleep with me,' Nick said flatly. 'Now, would you mind leaving my room?' he asked pointedly, and sighed wearily when she flounced off, banging the door behind her.

'Well played! You face Lucia Conti in the next round,' Katy told her, then took a deep breath; it was confession time! 'Don't be too confident; I know you beat her at Beckenham, but . . .'

'I know, grass is her worst surface,' Melissa interrupted. 'She'll be tougher to beat here.'

'It wasn't just the surface,' Katy hesitated briefly. 'Ace took her out the night before and spiked her drink with vodka,' she told her.

'What?' Melissa stared at her. 'I was so thrilled to win that match!' She shook her head in disbelief, unsure whether to be angry or grateful, but it seemed so long ago it hardly mattered.

Lucia was determined to avenge her defeat at Beckenham – the 'Battle of the Beauties' write-up, favouring Melissa, had rankled more than losing the match. Lucia's Latin good looks had won her a host of lucrative sponsorship deals and, if the younger English girl rose much higher in the rankings, she might well be a rival for those, too.

She and her coach had watched Melissa's earlier match and worked out a strategy; Lucia's superior groundstrokes finally overcame Melissa's serve and volley tactics, but it took Lucia three sets and almost three hours to emerge the victor.

'Well played,' she said graciously. Melissa, feeling guilty about what had happened at Beckenham, returned the smile and wished her good luck for the remainder of the tournament, before going to gather up her things. She could go to England! It was almost Christmas and she didn't have to pick up a racket for two weeks!

Katy was spending the holidays in New York; Jack was in South Africa and Ace was away somewhere, being secretive, according to Jack. 'I think he's got a new bird – God knows why he can't even tell me her name – it's not you, is it?' he'd asked, in alarm, and she'd assured him that it definitely was not her. She was going to Nick!

Rose met Melissa at Gatwick and hugged her tightly.

'Darling, it's so good to see you! You're a little too thin, though,' she worried, holding her at arms' length. 'Have you been working too hard?'

'I'm certainly ready for a break,' Melissa admitted, as they retrieved her baggage and made their way outside. 'God, it's cold,' Melissa shivered, hurrying ahead to where Rose had parked the car. 'Nick tells me you're going away?'

'Er, yes,' Rose fidgetted nervously, but Melissa was too tired and cold to notice her agitation. 'It was very kind of him to invite me to Glengarry, but, once I knew neither you nor Jack would be here, I made other plans. Would you like to drive?' she asked, changing the subject.

'No, thanks, I'd feel I was on the wrong side of the road,' Melissa declined, settling into the passenger seat.

They spent the next few hours together, talking non-

64

stop. Rose wanted to know all about Melissa's new life and the cities she had visited, while Melissa was eager to hear all the local gossip. It was odd, but the trivia of village life that she had always scorned as being boring, now fascinated her. For six months, apart from the three weeks in New York, she had belonged nowhere, her only continuity being with Katy as they travelled from place to place, always the strangers.

Daniel joined them for dinner; he, too, commented worriedly on Melissa's appearance, but she privately thought he looked even more tired than she felt! Later, she asked her mother if there was anything wrong.

'He's not ill,' Rose assured her quickly. 'But he has had some financial troubles. His losses as a Lloyds "name" have been horrendous. But he's sold off a couple of the estate farms, which should be enough to sort everything out,' she added brightly.

'Does Jack know?' Melissa frowned.

'No, and you're not to tell him,' Rose said quickly. 'Your father would prefer to go bankrupt than accept money from his son!'

'But . . .'

'But nothing. Promise me, Melissa. I should never even have told you.'

'Oh, okay, I promise,' Melissa agreed reluctantly.

She had already booked a morning flight to Edinburgh, and phoned Glengarry to let Nick know her time of arrival. He was out, so she left a message with a woman she assumed was the housekeeper.

Melissa waited for Nick at the airport for over an hour, then went in search of a cab driver willing to take her to

Glengarry. The village was larger than she had expected, the castle ruins towering over the cottages below. There was a row of shops, two pubs and a hotel, all nestling between the mountains and the loch.

The driver had to stop and ask for directions to Glengarry House and the icy blast of air from his open window made Melissa huddle back miserably in her seat. It had been cold in England, but the temperature was several degrees lower north of the border. At last, the car drew up in front of a vast three-storey greybrick Victorian mansion, situated a short distance from the village on the side of the loch.

'Melissa!' Nick stared incredulously as he rounded a corner of the house and spotted her. 'What a wonderful surprise! Why didn't you phone me?' His obvious delight warmed her and she ran to him, and he scooped her up in his arms.

'I did, I phoned yesterday, but it doesn't matter,' she said, her voice muffled against his shoulder.

'It does matter! Come inside, you're frozen. I'll see to the taxi.' He opened the door and ushered her inside a huge, dark-panelled hall. 'Sheena! Maggie!' he yelled, and briefly introduced her to the two women who came at his bidding. Melissa recognized Sheena from Jessica's photographs, the other she knew was the housekeeper, a local woman who had mothered both Rory and Nick when they were young.

She was a little embarrassed to be meeting Sheena, after what had happened in the Chelsea flat. Presumably she was staying for Christmas, too – she should have guessed Rory's widow would be invited, but it hadn't occurred to her, and Nick hadn't mentioned it.

'Melissa phoned here yesterday,' Nick said accusingly, glancing from one to the other.

'Oh, yes!' Sheena clapped a hand to her mouth. 'I must have misunderstood – I thought you were arriving tomorrow!' she exclaimed. Like hell, Melissa thought wearily, but she let it go.

Nick went to collect her bags, and led the way up a long flight of wide, shallow steps. At the top, more stairs branched out on both sides.

'This is our room.' Nick kicked open the door, dropped the cases, and drew her into the circle of his arms. 'What's wrong, sweetheart?' he asked gently.

'Nothing, really. I'm just tired. Please hold me,' she begged. Nick picked her up and sat down with her curled on his lap in front of the open fire. He held her close, without speaking and, very gradually, she relaxed against him, soothed by the crackling log fire and his tender touch. After a while, she tilted her head back and smiled up at him.

'Hi,' she greeted him softly. Nick read the invitation in her eyes and bent to kiss her mouth.

'Hi,' he said huskily, tightening his hold. The first kiss sparked flames of desire and soon their clothes lay in a discarded heap as they made love on the rug in front of the fire.

'Mm, that was lovely,' Melissa sighed contentedly.

'You've lost weight.' Nick ran an expert hand over her curves. 'You need looking after – and I'm just the man for the job,' he decided.

'You've made a terrific start,' Melissa smiled lazily, then yawned hugely. 'I'm so sorry,' she apologized, 'but I'm really tired.'

'I know. Katy's obviously a slave-driver,' Nick gently touched the circles beneath her eyes. 'Get into bed and sleep,' he suggested. Melissa sat up and gazed longingly at the huge four-poster.

'I'd love to, but won't your uncle think I'm awfully rude?'

'Of course not. I'll explain you've been travelling for two days – he'll understand. Besides, he's at his best first thing in the morning and would prefer to meet you then,' Nick assured her.

'Great.' Melissa needed no further encouragement and snuggled down beneath the covers, pouting a little when Nick began to get dressed instead of joining her.

'You need some rest,' he said firmly, tucking her in as if she were a child. When he looked in twenty minutes later, she was fast asleep.

He brought her dinner on a tray and insisted she eat every scrap; not that she needed too much encouragement, happily spooning up the last of a delicious chocolate pavlova.

'Katy would have a fit – "there's no nutritional value in that",' she mimicked, and Nick laughed.

'Are you two still on good terms?'

'Yes, but I think we're both glad to be spending some time apart.' She paused and drank some coffee. 'I'm being a dreadful nuisance, having dinner in bed. What will your other guests think?'

'What other guests? You're the first to arrive,' he told her.

'What about Sheena?' Melissa frowned.

'She isn't a guest – she lives here,' Nick said, matter-of-factly.

68

'Lives here?' Melissa repeated incredulously. 'Why?'

'Why? Because it's her home, of course. She moved here when she married Rory.'

'But he died ages ago. This isn't her house – or is it?' she asked, confused.

'No, it's part of the entail, so it will come to me eventually,' Nick explained. 'I suppose she stays on because the Old Man likes having her around,' he shrugged.

'And do you?' Melissa asked sharply.

'Not particularly, but I can't insist she leave, can I?'

'Why not? Your uncle doesn't need her now you're living here. You wouldn't like it if I lived with another man . . .'

'Oh, shut up.' Nick stopped her words with his mouth, pushing aside the blankets and covering her body with his. The tray of dishes clattered loudly to the floor, but they didn't even notice.

Melissa was quite nervous about meeting Lord Douglas Lennox, and her teeth chattered with more than the cold as Nick escorted her to the Old Man's quarters.

'He won't mind my wearing jeans, will he?' she asked. She was also wearing tights, socks, boots and two sweaters, and still felt cold.

'No, you look fine,' Nick assured her. He knocked lightly on the door and opened it. 'Uncle? I've brought Melissa to meet you.'

'Bring her in,' Lord Lennox barked, and Melissa entered behind Nick. She recognized the small old man in the wheelchair from Jessica's photograph album. 'He can still walk,' Jess had told her, 'but he hates people to see him hobbling about on sticks, so usually uses his wheelchair. If he doesn't like someone, he deliberately rams into their legs!'

'How do you do?' Melissa walked towards him, extending her hand. Douglas Lennox leaned forward, his grip surprisingly firm. The grey eyes that scrutinized her were very like Nick's, and Melissa smiled.

'Well, you're a beauty, sure enough,' he growled, giving a small nod of approval. He had done some discreet checking on Melissa Farrell, and discovered that her family background was more than adequate; she seemed well-bred and bright, as well as being a picture to look at. She'd do.

'Hear you're a tennis player – wouldn't you prefer to be Lady Lennox?'

'Is that a proposal?' Melissa asked, and he gave a short laugh.

'If I were fifty years younger . . .' he mused.

'I'd challenge you to a duel,' Nick put in.

'Don't blame you, my boy.'

Sheena had been listening at the door, or trying to, and, although she couldn't hear the actual words, the tone of the conversation seemed decidedly cordial. She suddenly burst into the room.

'Grandfather, I . . . oh, sorry. I didn't realize you had company. Good morning, Melissa, did you sleep well?'

'Eventually,' Melissa replied smugly, and Nick hastily turned his laugh into a cough. Douglas Lennox' shrewd eyes noted Sheena's annoyance and he hid a smile of his own. By God, Nick had an explosive situation on his hands here! He envied the boy, indeed he did.

'Nick, why don't you show Melissa around Glengarry and introduce her to people? After all, she'll be mistress here one day,' he said, watching Sheena.

'You're an old rogue,' Nick told him, fully aware of what he was up to.

'Not many pleasures left at my time of life – setting the cat amongst the pigeons is the most fun I have these days. Now, Sheena, what do you want?' He turned towards her and Melissa noticed how he bumped his wheelchair into her legs. So, perhaps he wasn't as fond of her as Nick had implied? Maybe it was Nick who liked having her around? Nick guessed her thoughts as easily as if she had spoken out loud, but said nothing to reassure her. If jealousy of Sheena helped prompt her to quit tennis and marry him, he'd be an idiot to convince her she had nothing to worry about!

The days sped by, as always when they were together, every moment was precious and to be savoured. Melissa became a familiar figure in the village, chatting happily to people as she relaxed in her first break from tennis. She maintained her fitness level, though, jogging each day with Nick and was delighted to discover a fully-equipped gym and heated swimming pool at Glengarry House.

'Aren't you afraid of becoming muscular?' Sheena asked her.

'Aren't you afraid of becoming flabby?' Melissa retorted.

'The exercises she does are designed to make her muscles stronger, not bigger,' Nick explained hastily, trying not to laugh.

'What does she DO all day?' Melissa asked Nick later.

71

'I've been here for four days and I've not seen her do anything more strenuous than lift a teapot.'

'She's an excellent hostess,' Nick said, after a pause. 'And she does a lot of charity work, organizes the local meals-on-wheels and ferries the OAPs to hospital appointments – that sort of thing,' he added vaguely.

'Oh,' Melissa grimaced, and decided to change the subject. 'You ought to turn the castle into a hotel,' she said. 'Americans would pay a fortune to stay in a genuine Scottish castle.'

'They wouldn't appreciate the plumbing,' Nick said drily.

'I'm serious. You have so much to offer tourists – scenery, mountain climbing, fishing, and a golf course nearby. All you need are some tennis courts and a famous pro player as an attraction!'

'You're famous, are you?' he teased.

'Not yet, but I'm working on it,' she said confidently.

'It's not a bad idea,' Nick acknowledged. 'But I don't want to tread on The Old Man's toes – major changes will have to wait.'

'Yes, I guess so,' Melissa said slowly. He didn't really have a role here until he inherited the estate and title, she realized, and wondered if he regretted leaving the Army. She almost asked him if he were happy, but lacked the courage, a little afraid of what the answer might be – it was becoming clear to her that his great-uncle and the people of Glengarry assumed she would soon be his wife, and she wasn't ready for that.

On Christmas morning Nick awoke her by rattling her gift in her ear. She sat up groggily, then realized what day it was and smiled sleepily.

'Happy Christmas, sweetheart.' He handed her a small box which obviously contained a ring, and Melissa opened it slowly, beset by conflicting emotions when she saw the exquisite antique sapphire and diamond ring. She loved Nick, but had so much still to accomplish before settling down.

'It's beautiful,' she said, watching the gems sparkle as they caught the light. Nick guessed her dilemma and took the ring from its bed of velvet.

'Wear it on your right hand for now,' he said, slipping it on to her third finger. 'Any time you want to transfer it to your left is fine by me.'

'Oh, thank you! I love you,' she hugged him tightly, delighted as much by his understanding as by the gift. 'It fits perfectly, you are clever.'

'Not really. I know every inch of you, remember?'

'I remember.' She kissed him, then clambered out of bed to retrieve the present she had for him. It was a large, heavy parcel that had arrived by post three days previously and Nick was intrigued as to what she had bought.

'I hope you like it.' Melissa offered it to him, rather diffidently, and sat back to watch his reaction. He ripped away the wrapping and stared at the framed canvas, gazing at the portrait of Melissa smiling back at him. 'I didn't know what to buy you – it's rather narcissistic of me, but I don't want you to forget me when I'm not around,' she joked.

'It's wonderful,' Nick said slowly. 'When have you been in the same place long enough to sit for a portrait?'

'I haven't – one of the girls on the tour is married to an artist. Do you really like it?' she asked anxiously.

'I love it,' he said simply. He removed a painting already on the wall facing the bed and hung the portrait in its place. It was not only an excellent likeness, but the artist had captured the lively impishness that he loved so much. Her lovely dark eyes sparkled with gaiety and a mischievous smile curved her mouth.

'It's just what I wanted – you permanently in my bedroom,' he teased, climbing back into bed, and holding her close. 'But, for now, I have the original,' he murmured, pushing her back against the pillows.

'Do we have the time . . .?'

'Always, my love,' Nick said huskily. 'Always.'

They were, in fact, late for breakfast; the staff were already clearing the dishes when they appeared. Nick asked for fresh toast and coffee and they lingered over it, happy to be alone, for Melissa only had three days left before she headed out to Australia.

To please the Old Man, they both attended the church service, then returned to the house for a light lunch. After the meal, Nick went to check on the seating arrangements for the dinner party that evening. As he had suspected, Sheena had placed Melissa as far away from him as possible. He switched the cards just as Sheena entered, carrying a bowl of roses and carnations.

'Don't do that!' she shrieked. 'I spent ages working it out.'

'I know,' Nick said grimly. 'I'm not having Melissa sitting next to that boring old fart, Carmichael – he'll send her to sleep with his anecdotes and then grope her. She's sitting next to me.'

'Oh, for goodness' sake, are you two joined at the hip?' Sheena asked crossly.

'As often as possible, yes,' he retorted, and stalked out.

Melissa took great care over her appearance for dinner, wanting Nick to be proud of her. She wore her hair pinned up and looked older and very sophisticated in a cream lace dress, scooped low back and front, and with a pearl choker clasped around her neck.

'You look beautiful,' he told her, bestowing a kiss on her bare shoulder before taking her hand in his and walking downstairs to greet the guests.

Nick introduced her to everyone, and Melissa tried hard to memorize all the names. When they sat down for dinner, she found herself the centre of attention, and patiently answered endless questions about life on the tour, although none were original. Had she played against Graf or Sabatini . . . had she met Agassi . . . what were they like . . . was the travelling stimulating or merely tiring . . . And, predictably, from a Mrs Randall, a particularly silly woman:

'Aren't there an awful lot of, you know, lesbians?' she leaned across the table to whisper. 'I'd be afraid to take a shower in front of them!' she trilled.

'I'd be ashamed to, if I had a body like hers,' Melissa muttered to Nick. He pretended not to hear.

'What did you say? Why are there so many?' Mrs Randall persisted.

'I don't think there are that many,' Melissa said coolly. 'They just see no reason to hide their sexuality. The percentage of gays on the tour is probably no higher than it is around this table,' she added. Nick choked and there was a short, strained silence before someone began a discussion on the hunt due to take place the following day.

'I think I scored a direct hit!' Melissa whispered to Nick.

'And I think you're trying to give me heart failure. Behave yourself!' he snapped. Melissa subsided, toying miserably with her food. Sheena, sensing discord, glanced meaningfully at one of her cronies in a pre-arranged signal.

'I've just realized!' Isobel exclaimed theatrically. 'You must be Jack Farrell's sister?'

'That's right,' Melissa smiled.

'I saw him compete at Wembley a couple of years ago,' Isobel continued. 'He's rather cute, but I must say I preferred his partner . . . Ace Delaney, isn't it?'

'Oh yes,' Sheena took up the charade. 'You remember, Grandfather? Jessica used to talk about him constantly. He's the Apache; always in the gossip columns, and has a dreadful reputation with women. Jess had quite a crush on him . . .'

'So did I.' Melissa decided to jump before she was pushed.

'You must know him very well,' Isobel said meaningfully.

'He's a friend of the family,' Melissa said evenly.

'What? What?' the Old Man barked. 'Can't have you involved with some chap who claims to be an Apache!'

'That's just publicity hype,' Melissa told him, forcing a smile. 'As I said, he's a friend of the family.' She glanced at Nick for support, but the coldness of his answering gaze shrivelled her to the core. She wanted to yell at him that it wasn't her fault, but stayed silent.

'Do you ski, Melissa?' asked a kindly matron, coming to her rescue, and Melissa beamed a grateful smile.

'I have done, but I'm not awfully good and I daren't risk an injury,' she replied.

'How about coming over to the Club and playing tennis?' Mrs Randall asked. Melissa stared at the overweight, middle-aged woman in amazement; she must be joking!

'I'm only going to be here for a couple more days,' she prevaricated.

'So? Come tomorrow, while the men are out hunting.'

'I'm on holiday,' Melissa said lightly. 'I don't want to even look at a racket until I arrive in Australia.'

'Oh, do come – you can give us a few tips!' another woman tried to insist.

'No, really. I can't,' Melissa declined, again wishing Nick would come to her aid. Finally, he did, changing the topic of conversation, but later she was shocked by his anger.

'Would it really have hurt you to hit a few tennis balls?' he asked tightly. 'You don't hunt, won't ski – they were only trying to make you feel welcome!'

'Rubbish! They wanted free coaching from a pro,' Melissa said furiously. 'If I'd known I was expected to sing for my supper, I wouldn't have come! There was an accountant at dinner – I didn't notice him filling out tax returns!' she said wildly. 'And the doctor wasn't examining ingrowing toe-nails . . .'

'Grow up!' Nick turned on his heel and left the room, and that night they lay apart and sleepless in the huge bed.

Her imminent departure drove them back into each other's arms the next morning.

'I'm sorry,' Melissa mumbled, even though she wasn't sure that she had anything to apologize for. 'I love you.'

'I know, I love you, too.' Nick crushed her to him and they made love frantically, both trying not to wonder if she could ever fit in and be happy living with him at Glengarry.

'I've decided to travel back to London with you,' Nick said later. 'We can stay at the flat overnight and I'll take you to Heathrow before heading back here.'

'That would be lovely,' Melissa gratefully accepted what she took to be an olive branch.

They were both relieved to leave Glengarry behind: alone, everything was perfect again, and, this time, their sojourn at the flat was uninterrupted. Melissa was touched when, the next morning, Nick presented her with a set of keys to the flat.

'I thought you might prefer staying here instead of in an hotel if you ever have to stop over between flights,' he explained.

'Thank you.' She kissed him, and stowed the keys in her case. Nick watched sadly as she checked her travel documents, but resisted the urge to beg her to stay.

It was a rather quiet journey to Heathrow. Melissa was torn between the pain of leaving and the excitement of beginning her first full year on the tour. Nick was silently debating the wisdom of asking her to put a time limit on her quest for fame and fortune.

'I wish I had my passport with me,' he said suddenly, when she was checking in her luggage. Melissa smiled slightly.

'So do I,' she said, but could imagine the look of

horror on Katy's face if she arrived with Nick in tow. 'Don't wait with me – I'll end up in tears and you have a long drive ahead of you.'

'All right.' Nick held her close, unable to let go. 'Phone me when you arrive. And I'll fly out in seven weeks for your birthday,' he promised. After one last kiss he turned and walked away, wondering just how many more times they would have to say 'goodbye'; how many more times he could bear it.

CHAPTER 4

Three weeks later, Melissa and Katy arrived in Melbourne for the Australian Open at Flinders Park. Melissa had performed well in the warm-up tournaments, pushing her ranking higher, and had gained direct entry into the main draw at the Open. The climate and hard court surfaces suited her and she was eagerly anticipating the start of the Championships.

After they had settled in their hotel, she went, alone, to see Jack.

'How's everything at home?' he asked, and she hesitated, but reluctantly kept her promise to her mother and said everything was fine.

'How's Nick?' he asked next.

'Oh, he's lovely,' she beamed. 'Look what he bought me for Christmas.' She proudly displayed her ring and Jack admired it, noticing she wore it on her right hand but making no comment.

'You're playing Mixed with me,' he said. 'Are you partnering Katy in the Women's Doubles?'

'No, Lisa Renwick – we reached the final in Auckland.'

'That's good,' Jack said absently. Lisa Renwick –

Hal's sister? Interesting, he thought, and wasn't surprised when, later, the two Americans appeared on the practice courts while Katy was putting Melissa through her paces.

Hal was delighted his sister had teamed up with Melissa and greeted Jack as if he were a long-lost friend.

'It's great that the girls have got together, isn't it?' he asked.

'Is it?' Jack enquired blandly. 'One appearance in a final doesn't make them Navratilova and Shriver,' he said dismissively.

'They'll be terrific,' Hal said confidently. 'I call them the "Lissa and Lisa show" – the Press will love 'em!' He lowered his voice. 'That guy in England – is he still in the picture?'

'Afraid so. He's "lovely",' Jack mimicked Melissa. 'And look what he bought me for Christmas!' he flapped his hand and Hal laughed.

'I've already seen it – she's not wearing it on her engagement finger. Anyway, he's on the other side of the world. Can't you put in a good word for me?' he asked hopefully. 'I saw him a couple of times in New York – he obviously isn't interested in tennis. She needs a guy who'll help her career, not hinder it.'

'I can't argue with that,' Jack agreed, picking up his racket. 'Come on, let's get the "Lissa and Lisa" show on the road!'

Melissa stared moodily out of her hotel bedroom window, paying little attention to the discussion taking place about her future. She had done well in Melbourne, reaching the third round in Singles and quarter finals in both Doubles events. The prize money meant that, sooner than she had hoped or expected, her debt to Jack would begin to diminish. But the pleasure in her achievements had been spoiled by a phone call from Nick – the Old Man had suffered a stroke and Nick felt he had to cancel his plans to fly out for her birthday.

Now, Jack and Katy – thankfully friends again, due to Katy's invention of a new boyfriend in New York – were deciding her career-strategy for the coming months.

'Melissa? What do you think?' Jack asked. 'Melissa!' he repeated loudly, and she turned to face him.

'Katy's been right so far – I'll go along with whatever she thinks is best,' she said listlessly.

'Okay; that's settled. Katy? Would you mind if I had a private word with Melissa?' Jack asked, rather apologetically, for it was her room, too.

'Of course not,' Katy forced a smile, and sauntered out of the room.

'Is something wrong?' Melissa asked, finally sensing that she wasn't the only one with something on her mind.

'Mum phoned earlier – she thought we ought to know that Bellwood's up for sale,' he said. 'Dad's moving to one of the smaller farms.' Melissa gaped at him, shocked.

'Oh, no! I thought he'd worked everything out! It's your inheritance he's selling – are you thinking of buying it?'

'That's what I want to talk to you about,' Jack said heavily. 'It's your home, too. I can't see myself as the country squire, even when I quit tennis,' he continued, 'but Bellwood's been in our family for over three centuries.'

'Mm, I know.' Melissa stifled a pang of regret. 'How much is it likely to fetch?' she asked.

'Around two million,' Jack told her, and she grimaced.

'That's a lot to pay for sentiment and childhood memories,' she said, and he nodded.

'The auction is in three weeks. I'll let you know what I decide to do,' he said, glancing at his watch and getting to his feet. He had a flight to catch. 'I'm really proud of the way you played here,' he said, kissing her cheek.

'Thanks, but Katy deserves a lot of the credit,' she smiled, trying to hide her depression. She hated parting from him, hated not being with Nick, and wasn't as indifferent to losing Bellwood as she pretended. 'Give my love to Ace,' she said.

'I'll tell him you said "goodbye",' Jack amended drily, hugging her again before turning and walking out of the room.

Lord Douglas Lennox died three weeks later, peacefully in his sleep.

'I am sorry,' Melissa said, when Nick phoned to break the news. 'I'm glad I had the chance to meet him.'

'So was he, he liked you,' Nick told her. 'Look, you don't have to fly back for the funeral,' he continued. Melissa's jaw dropped: she was working, for heaven's sake, and had no intention of flying halfway around the world to attend the funeral of a man she barely knew.

83

'I'd prefer not to,' she said coolly. 'I do have a rather busy schedule.'

'I realize that,' Nick said absently. 'Things are pretty hectic here, too. I'll call you in a couple of days.'

'Fine.' She hung up and turned to Katy, fists clenched. 'I know he's got a lot on his mind, but he didn't even ask how I'm faring. I'm in my first Singles final and he doesn't give a damn!'

'Like you said, he has a lot on his mind,' Katy said peaceably. She was actually quite pleased about Nick's no-show, but didn't want Melissa getting into a state about it – her first final was far more important!

'Huh! He has Sheena to help him,' Melissa muttered. Would Sheena stay on at Glengarry now the Old Man was dead? Stupid question, of course she would, unless Nick asked her to leave, which she felt sure he wouldn't!

Despite her discontent over Nick and his attitude, or perhaps because of it, she concentrated hard on her tennis and won the final.

'I've won a tournament! I've actually won a tournament!' she kept saying excitedly, to everyone, even to her disgruntled opponent. She phoned Jack and her mother to tell them, but not Nick.

But, the following week, she returned to earth with a bump, losing in the first round to a girl ranked two hundred places below her.

'I knew you'd do that,' Katy sighed. 'You have to concentrate all the time. Last week's tournament is last week's news. You're potentially a better player than I ever was,' she continued, 'but you're not as tough mentally. I wish you could go on court with my mind.'

'I'm always going on court with a piece of your mind!'

84

Melissa retorted. 'But, I know you're right – I was still thinking of last week's final. I won't make that mistake again,' she vowed.

Nick travelled down to London the day before the auction, staying overnight at his flat in Chelsea and driving to Bellwood the following morning. The auction was taking place on the estate and he strolled around the grounds, glad of the opportunity to take another look at the place.

He spotted Daniel Farrell chatting to a group of men and made his way over.

'Hello, Nick, good to see you.' Daniel clasped him warmly by the hand, seemingly more cheerful than Nick had expected.

'I'm sorry it's under these circumstances,' he said.

'Not at all, best decision I've made in years,' Daniel replied, and went on to tell him of his imminent return to Brook Farm, the property he had farmed while his father still resided at Bellwood. 'There seemed no point in struggling to hang on to Bellwood any longer – Jack will never be a farmer, and Melissa will eventually marry and live elsewhere?' he finished on a questioning note. Nick smiled.

'I hope so,' he said lightly.

'Come on into the house and have a drink,' Daniel suggested next. 'I haven't packed the booze away yet!'

'Thanks, I will,' Nick accepted, and they walked indoors.

'Scotch?' Daniel offered, and Nick nodded. 'You're not here to buy, are you?' Daniel asked next, handing him his glass.

'No, I just wanted to see the place again. And Melissa asked me to collect her personal belongings,' he added.

'They're all safely boxed-up,' Daniel assured him. 'I was sorry to read about your uncle. I . . .' Daniel broke off as he heard voices in the hall. Both he and Nick recognized Melissa's clear tones and collided in their mutual haste to greet her. Nick won the race and lifted her in his arms, burying his face in her hair, savouring the scent and feel of her. He bent his head and kissed her hungrily, forgetting Daniel's presence and failing to notice that Rose had accompanied her daughter.

'God, I needed that,' he said, when they eventually came up for air. 'How long can you stay?'

'Just today. And tonight,' she smiled suggestively. 'Oops! I forgot to curtsey!' she suddenly remembered his new status. 'Sorry, sir!' She dipped her knee and tugged an imaginary forelock.

'Stop taking the mickey,' Nick scolded lightly. 'Do you want to go and watch the sale, or is it too upsetting?'

'No, but I'm glad . . .' she stopped speaking abruptly, for Jack had sworn her to secrecy. 'Come on, let's go,' she said briskly.

They wandered outside and she introduced him to various neighbours, most of whom were there out of curiosity, and then they sat down as the bidding for the house and land got under way.

Nick noticed that Melissa kept turning around to glance at someone; she also seemed excited by what was happening, not at all sad. Puzzled, he twisted around to try and see who had caught her attention.

'It's Greg Reynolds,' Melissa whispered, as if that were sufficient explanation, then she gripped his hand tightly as the auctioneer started the bidding.

'One million, five hundred thousand . . . six, thank you sir. One million seven at the back . . . one million eight. Come along, gentleman, one million nine? One million nine . . . thank you.'

'Damn,' Melissa muttered, as someone else entered the fray. 'Who's that?'

'One million nine . . . am I bid a round two million?' He looked around the group of bidders enquiringly. Nick suddenly remembered who Greg Reynolds was – Melissa's and Jack's business manager – and realized he must be representing Jack. That explained her attitude.

'Two million? Thank you, sir! Two million, one . . .?' He looked expectantly at Greg, who waited until the very last moment, before nodding his head. 'Two million one – am I bid two million two? No? At two million, one hundred thousand pounds . . .' Melissa held her breath until the gavel crashed down. 'Sold. Two million, one hundred thousand pounds!'

'That's great,' Nick said. 'It's a good price for your father and Bellwood remains in the family.'

'In the family?' Melissa repeated. 'I'd hardly call Ace family!' she laughed, and dashed off to talk to Greg. Nick stared after her in dismay. Ace Delaney! Why the hell did he want Bellwood? Or was it Melissa he wanted? One thing was sure – Melissa loved Bellwood a damn sight more than she would ever love Glengarry. Sick at heart, he followed her into the house. Daniel was initially just as incredulous when he learned the identity of the buyer, but then he nodded slowly.

'It makes sense, in an odd sort of way. He always plays the Lord of the Manor to the hilt whenever he stays here. I suppose he'll hire a manager to run things.'

'Yes, he will,' Melissa confirmed, 'But he also wants someone living in the house permanently. Someone who loves it and will care for it properly.' She paused for dramatic effect, then turned to Rose. 'He wants you to move back here, Mum,' she said softly. 'He thinks you're the best person to care for the house. Will you do it?'

'Me?' Rose looked around at the home she had thought was lost forever, and tears welled in her eyes. 'I'd love to,' she choked. 'Daniel?' she faltered, and he smiled at her.

'I'm glad you'll be living here. It's where you belong,' he said simply, which made her cry even more.

'Listen! There's a helicopter!' Melissa exclaimed, and ran to the window before running outside to greet the arrival. Nick watched Ace alight and went quickly in pursuit.

'Yes, you got it!' Melissa was saying. 'Greg was brilliant! Don't ever play poker with him,' she advised. 'And Mum's considering your offer, but she wants a huge salary,' she added wickedly.

'Melissa!' Rose scolded, laughing, then she looked rather shyly at Ace. 'I would love to return here,' she said quietly.

'Great,' Ace said casually. 'How much has it cost me?' he asked, even more casually, or so it seemed to Nick.

'2.1 million,' Melissa told him.

'Dollars?'

'Pounds!'

'Oh.' It obviously made little difference, and Nick

gritted his teeth, wishing it had occurred to him to buy the place himself. Not that he could raise two million quid as easily as Ace evidently had. He put his arm around Melissa to draw her closer to him. Ace noticed the gesture and grinned.

'Hi, your worship,' he said mockingly. 'Is that the correct title?'

'No, you can call me "sir",' Nick said tersely.

'Dream on,' Ace said scathingly. He glanced around at his newly acquired property. He was an incongruous figure, dressed in black leather, his long hair tied back in a pony-tail, but he nodded slowly in satisfaction. He had loved this place ever since Jack had first brought him here as a guest. The Farrells were his guests now . . .

'Congratulations – you've come a long way from . . . where was it? An Indian Reservation?' Nick asked cuttingly. Ace laughed.

'No, just a slum,' he said honestly, but retaliated swiftly by taking Melissa's hand in his. 'This is still your home, honey,' he drawled. 'It won't be necessary to pack your things off to Glen-whatever, after all.' Nick was well aware that the display of kindly hospitality was for his benefit and managed, just, not to rise to the bait. He only wished Melissa weren't so damned happy about it all! And he had the strange notion that Ace felt compelled to take over the entire Farrell family, but quickly dismissed it as folly – no doubt Daniel was right, and Ace simply fancied himself as Lord of the Manor.

He persuaded Melissa to leave shortly after the encounter with Ace and, later, felt reassured by her passionate response to his lovemaking. But, too soon, the night passed and she had to again pack and head for the airport.

'How long is this going to continue?' Nick asked, hurt, but he sounded angry to Melissa.

'What do you mean?' She looked up anxiously.

'Us! We meet up once every couple of months, make love like crazy and then part!' he said savagely.

'You can fly out to see me whenever you want to,' she said tentatively, knowing Katy would hate the disruption.

'I have responsibilities in Scotland, remember? I can't follow you around the world, twiddling my thumbs while you get on with your career!' he snapped.

'Why can't you? You told me that your steward can run Glengarry without you. And, if things had been different – if I'd not chosen tennis as a career and you'd stayed in the Army, you'd have expected me to sit at home and wait, or accompany you on postings abroad, wouldn't you?' she challenged. 'You're just being sexist and unreasonable!'

'I know,' Nick said quietly, after a long pause, deflating her anger. She went over to him and wrapped her arms around his waist.

'Please be patient,' she begged, and felt huge relief when he finally returned her embrace, holding her tightly.

'Come along, or you'll miss your flight,' he said briskly, releasing her and picking up her bags. Melissa smiled and nodded, and they talked easily of other things on the journey. But they were both aware that his question of 'how long?' remained unanswered.

* * *

Playing on the slow, clay courts of Europe was anathema to Melissa's natural serve and volley game – shots which would win her the point on a fast court came relentlessly back over the net, time after time.

'I hate this stuff,' she complained, trying in vain to brush the red clay dust from her legs, socks and shoes. 'Tennis should be played on grass, not powdered brick!'

'Oh, well let's just forget it then,' Katy said scathingly. 'Why don't you take a few months off every spring? We'll not bother with Hamburg, Barcelona or Rome. And, as for Paris, well, there are three other Grand Slams!' Her voice dripped sarcasm and Melissa sighed wearily as she straightened and prepared to resume. 'There's no reason why you can't do well on clay,' Katy continued. 'You just have to be more patient, concentrate, stay in the rallies longer, and wait for the opportunity to hit a winning shot.'

'I know the theory!' Melissa almost wailed.

'You just need more practice – so get to it.'

They were staying and working in Monaco when, in April, the Men's tour arrived for the Monte Carlo Open. Jack had never enjoyed much success on clay and, after a second-round loss in Singles, good-naturedly agreed to practise with Melissa. Being with her brother always lifted her spirits and she worked hard, never forgetting that, without his help, she wouldn't have achieved half so much as she had, or so quickly.

Jack was more than happy to accept the existence of Katy's 'new' boyfriend – even though Melissa, when asked, had blushingly been unable to remember his name – and the subterfuge enabled Katy to treat Jack with a casual friendliness. He and Ace took both girls out to enjoy the excellent night-life Monte Carlo had to offer. Hal was also competing in the event and eagerly took up his pursuit of Melissa, much to Ace's amusement.

'Do you think His Lordship knows about Hal and Melissa?' he asked Jack.

'There's nothing to know!' Jack said sharply, alerted by the gleam of malice in Ace's eyes.

'Okay, if you say so,' Ace shrugged, but, later, he tipped off one of his mates in the Press.

Melissa was unaware of the brief item appearing in the British paper until Rose telephoned to warn her. In a panic, Melissa phoned Nick.

'It's rubbish; there's no romance,' she assured him.

'I know,' Nick said, with a calmness he was far from feeling; the article had given him a nasty jolt.

'A whole group of us went out after the Awards dinner,' she went on. 'Jack and Ace won the Doubles Team of the Year,' she said proudly.

'Really?' Nick sounded bored, and she bit her lip. They finished the call rather coolly, something he regretted instantly and even more so two days later when another item appeared in a rival tabloid.

'Ace Delaney to marry?' was the by-line. 'Ace Delaney, long-time Doubles partner of British number one, Jack Farrell, looks set to enter into a different partnership with Jack's sister, Melissa, rising star on the women's tour. The two were spotted here in Monte Carlo, choosing an engagement ring in Cartier.'

Nick swore viciously and reached for the phone, stabbing out the number of Melissa's hotel. She'd better be in her own room . . .

'What the hell's going on?' he snarled, as soon as she answered.

'I don't know what you mean,' Melissa stammered. Nick icily read out the snippet and she sighed.

'It wasn't like that at all. It's Jack's birthday next week and I knew he'd been looking at watches in Cartier, so I asked Ace to point out which one Jack preferred, that's all. And don't swear at me,' she added indignantly.

'You always have an answer for everything, don't you?' Nick wasn't ready to be mollified.

'It's true! Anyhow, Katy and I are leaving today, so there won't be any more gossip about me.'

'I certainly hope not,' Nick said grimly. 'I think it's time we announced our engagement – that should put a stop to any rumours.'

'Huh! While you're living with another woman?' Melissa said scornfully. Sheena's continued presence at Glengarry was a constant source of irritation to her. 'You must be joking!'

'I can't throw her out; she has nowhere else to go,' Nick said tiredly.

'Oh, for heaven's sake! She's young, healthy and rich! She stays on at Glengarry because she wants to be Lady Lennox, and you know it! I have to go, I have a plane to catch. Goodbye!' She slammed down the phone and looked at Katy, who had heard all of Melissa's side of the conversation and guessed the rest. 'Men!' Melissa burst out and Katy nodded her agreement.

'Come on, cheer up,' she said briskly. 'You can't play good tennis if your mind is in Scotland.'

'I know,' Melissa agreed gloomily.

'Melissa, you may have to make a choice – Nick or your career,' Katy said bluntly.

'I want them both,' Melissa smiled sadly. 'Is that so impossible?'

'That depends on Nick,' Katy shrugged.

'I don't know why he's being so unreasonable!' Melissa said crossly. 'He's known from the beginning how important tennis is to me, and I thought he understood.'

'I bet he was understanding until he got you into bed? Or until you said you loved him? That's always a mistake – if you keep them guessing you retain the upper hand,' Katy said cynically. 'Let's go – the car's downstairs.'

Jack was in the lobby, waiting to say goodbye, and to warn Melissa, but saw at once that he was too late.

'Nick?' was all he said, and she nodded.

'I bet Ace did it on purpose!' she burst out.

'No, he didn't,' Jack said quickly. 'He's furious about it. When I left, he was on the phone to some bird, swearing it was all a pack of lies. I think he must be in love – usually, something like this would just make him laugh.'

'Is this the same woman he was so secretive about at Christmas?' Melissa asked, temporarily diverted from her own problem by the unlikelihood of Ace being in love. 'I wonder who she is? I suppose he told you why we were in Cartier?' she went on.

'Er, yes,' Jack admitted, and she sighed.

'Happy Birthday for next week,' she said. 'I left the watch with Ace.'

'I know, thanks.' Jack kissed her cheek. 'I'm sorry it caused you such trouble – it was a lovely thought.'

'Tell that to Nick,' Melissa said bitterly, as she

climbed into the car. Jack waved them off and returned thoughtfully to his own hotel. He knew Melissa hadn't meant him to take her final words literally, but he did phone Nick, and he didn't mince his words, either.

'Are you deliberately trying to upset Melissa?' he asked. 'She's under enough pressure as it is and doesn't need all the rubbish you're dishing out!'

'I beg your pardon?' Nick said icily.

'You heard. Why don't you give her some support instead of constantly undermining her? You should be proud of her success, not resentful! You take no interest in her career; in fact, you treat it as if it's some childish whim she ought to have outgrown by now.'

'I am proud of her,' Nick protested, ignoring Jack's final sentence, which was rather too near the truth to deny. 'But I think I'm entitled to be annoyed when her name is splashed all over the tabloids – especially when she's linked with Ace!'

'That wasn't her fault. And Ace isn't interested in her,' Jack said impatiently. 'But Hal Renwick is. So far, she hasn't given him a second glance, but he's willing to give her the support and encouragement you withhold. If you're not careful, you'll push her into his arms. Or I might do it for you,' he warned.

'Don't threaten me, Jack,' Nick said angrily.

'Then stop making my sister miserable!' His point made, Jack broke the connection.

In Glengarry, Nick slammed down the receiver before storming out of the house. He strode away from the village, skirting the loch and then began climbing until he reached a small plateau where he and Rory used to camp out on summer nights, many years before.

From his vantage point, he could see all of his property; the village, far below, seemingly made of toy houses; the mountains, tipped by mist; the loch glimmering darkly. Lord of all he surveyed, and he didn't want any of it.

'Damn you, Rory!' he shouted to the heavens. 'I don't want to live your life!' Maybe Rory hadn't, either, he realized suddenly. Perhaps the mountaineering, the motor racing, the recklessness in everything he did, had been a subconscious invitation to an early death. If so, he had got his wish – and left me to carry the burden, Nick thought grimly. Well, it's not wrecking my life, cousin!

He was tired of trying to bring new prosperity to Glengarry, his every suggestion met with resistance and suspicion by the community. The Old Man had reigned supreme for over fifty years – to the villagers, Nick was still 'the major'. Well, that suited him fine; he preferred a title he had earned to one he had inherited. He was the last of his line; he needed a wife and heirs . . . but what he wanted was Melissa.

Eventually, hunger drove him back down the mountain, and he asked Maggie for sandwiches and coffee in his study. Then he settled down to watch TV – tennis. The tournament at Monte Carlo was featured; a Doubles match between Ace and Jack against two men he'd never heard of was in progress.

He forced himself to watch and concentrate, until Ace began disputing a close line-call. The American yelled at the umpire, berated the unfortunate linesman, and then his two opponents. Finally, Jack defused the situation, laughing and grabbing the back of Ace's shirt to haul him bodily away from the umpire's chair, saying something to Ace which turned his scowl into a reluctant grin.

How could four grown men, no, five, including the umpire . . . the linesman . . . six, plus the two commentators who had replayed the point in question in slow motion at least three times while the argument raged – how could they attach so much importance to whether a ball had landed on a white line or an inch beyond it? He had seen enough, and switched over to the news channel.

CHAPTER 5

Melissa's first tournament on clay was in Hamburg, and she had the misfortune to be drawn against Lucia Conti, now ranked fifteenth in the world, and a renowned clay-court specialist.

Incensed by the rumours linking Melissa with Ace Delaney, Lucia was determined to beat the British girl. She outplayed and outgunned Melissa, still floundering on the alien surface, and won 6–2, 6–2.

Melissa cast an apologetic glance at Katy as she ran to the net to shake hands. Lucia had adopted the Latin custom of kissing her opponents and leaned towards Melissa.

'Ace Delaney's whore!' she hissed.

'Ace Delaney's cast-off!' Melissa retorted, air-kissing the other cheek, then she suppressed a yelp of pain as Lucia dug her fingernails savagely into her palm. Pretending it hadn't hurt, Melissa gathered up her belongings and walked off the court.

'Look what that bitch did!' She showed Katy the injury. 'She's drawn blood – I need a rabies shot!'

'You need more practice on clay,' Katy said, matter-of-factly. 'You'll have to do better than that in Rome.'

'Thanks for the sympathy,' Melissa said bitterly, walking back to the locker-room. There, she was joined by an equally disgruntled Lisa.

'We just get rid of one Martina beating us hands down and then another comes along!' Lisa groused, throwing her racket down in disgust. Melissa grinned, her own good humour restored. Later, she and Lisa did well in the Doubles, giving her valuable experience on clay.

Katy was quite optimistic about the draw for the Italian Open, deciding Melissa had a good chance of reaching the quarter finals before she would come up against an expert clay-court player – unfortunately, it would probably again be Lucia, a home favourite with the Italian crowd despite having lived in the United States for most of her life.

Melissa enjoyed playing at the Foro Italico; the noisy, romantic Italians loved her looks and grace around the court and cheered her to victory.

'I might even start to like playing on clay,' she told Katy happily, after her third-round win. 'Who's next?' she asked, for she never looked ahead in the draw, too superstitious to tempt fate by assuming she would win.

'Lucia,' Katy told her, and Melissa grimaced.

'Uh oh,' she said. They spent the evening studying the video of the match in Hamburg, going over each point until Melissa felt more confident.

'At least the crowd here likes me,' she said brightly.

'Not tomorrow, they won't,' Katy warned. 'They'll be behind Lucia, one hundred percent.'

Melissa shrugged off the warning, and was unprepared for the reaction from the spectators. Not only were they rooting for Lucia, they were actively hostile to Melissa, cheering her errors and booing her winning shots. It was a new and unwelcome experience for her, upsetting and humiliating.

Completely demoralized, she lost the first set, but a triumphant smirk from Lucia as they changed ends stiffened her resolve. Ignoring the crowd, concentrating hard, she began to play well. Suddenly, everything she tried, worked. The days and weeks spent practising on clay paid off; she slithered around the red clay, timing her shots to perfection, using her superior power to put Lucia on the defensive.

She knew Lucia was worried when she began disputing line-calls, something she only did when she felt herself in danger of losing. Melissa ignored the frequent interruptions as Lucia ranted at linesmen and forced the umpire to repeatedly climb down from his chair to check the mark left by the ball in the red clay.

He's getting more exercise than we are, Melissa thought, not bothering to hide her grin as he ran across the court yet again to investigate a complaint. Once more, he sided with Lucia, to the delight of the crowd, putting out his arm to indicate Melissa's shot had gone wide.

'It damn well didn't!' Melissa muttered, no longer amused, but she accepted the decision with as good a grace as she could muster, and became even more determined to win. The hostility of the crowd actually helped; she was damned if she was going to give them something to cheer about! She won the second set and towelled down tiredly before the start of the third, feeling as if Katy were the only friend she had in the world.

Lucia continued her tactics of disrupting the game on every close call that went against her. Melissa was tempted to do the same, but resisted. It was a long, exhausting set, with punishing rallies, and culminated in a tie-break.

At 4–5, Melissa served an ace. Lucia, pretending belief that it had been a fault, stayed where she was as if awaiting the second serve.

'5–5.'

'No!' Lucia threw up her hands in feigned amazement, encouraged by the boisterous crowd, but, this time, the umpire fixed her with a steely glare.

'5–5,' he repeated. Lucia pouted but moved across to the other side of the court.

Melissa served; Lucia hit a searing forehand down the line and Melissa could only turn and watch its path. She saw the linesman hesitate, then he put his palms down to indicate the ball was in. The hesitation was enough for Melissa.

'That was out,' she told the umpire, going over to the line and smearing the red clay with her racket. Perhaps he'd had enough of Lucia's tantrums, too, or maybe he genuinely felt the ball had just missed. He over-ruled the linesman.

'6–5, Farrell,' he said, and this time ignored Lucia's objections.

It's match point! Melissa realized, panicking. She had cheated to reach match point! She stood back to receive serve, holding her racket loosely, meaning to throw the point. Her panic increased as Lucia's first serve went into the net. To show she didn't intend making a return, she stepped back instead of moving forwards to attack. Either Lucia didn't notice, or she thought it a bluff. Her second serve also hit the net and fell back. A double fault.

'Game, set, match, Farrell.' Oh, my God, Melissa thought despairingly, but there was nothing she could do. Amidst the boos and cat-calls, she advanced warily to the net. Lucia didn't even look at her and spurned her outstretched hand, stalking angrily off court.

The next hour passed by in a haze; somehow, Melissa got through the Press interview, showered and tried to relax beneath the expert touch of a masseuse. But she felt sick, and developed a pounding headache.

'What's the matter with you?' Katy demanded angrily. 'You've beaten a player in the top twenty, and you're through to the semis of the Italian Open – don't you know how many computer points you've earned?'

'I don't care,' Melissa replied listlessly, rubbing her throbbing temples. 'I cheated, Katy,' she said miserably.

'Like hell you did!' Katy exploded, too loudly for Melissa's head to tolerate and she winced. 'The umpire was refereeing that match, not you. He wouldn't have over-ruled on such a vital point if he hadn't been sure the linesman had made an error. Snap out of it, Melissa, you're behaving like a silly schoolkid! Come on, let's get something to eat.'

'Ugh, no, I feel sick,' Melissa shuddered. 'And I have a splitting headache – I think I'll go back to the hotel and lie down,' she decided.

The pain worsened and she lay on her bed, craving sleep. But, when she closed her eyes, all she could see was the penultimate point of the match, the ball whizzing past, out of reach and just clipping the line. It hadn't been out . . . she groaned and clutched her head, feeling it might explode.

When Katy returned, she found Melissa hanging onto the wash basin, her eyes dark in a face drawn with pain.

'Still bad?' she asked.

'Yes, and I've been sick,' Melissa said wretchedly.

'It could be a migraine,' Katy said thoughtfully. 'Have you had one before?'

'No, and I don't ever want another,' Melissa tried to smile. 'I took some painkillers, but they're not working.'

'You'd better have a sleeping pill,' Katy decided, thinking of the match to be played the next day. Melissa didn't argue, but clambered into bed and swallowed the tablet.

She slept like a log and awoke feeling much better. The headache was still there, but with nothing like the same intensity as before, and she managed to eat breakfast without throwing up.

'Your match is on last, so you have a few hours to recover,' Katy told her. Melissa grimaced at the prospect of facing the Italian crowd again; besides, she didn't feel worthy of her place in the semis.

'Have the Press crucified me for yesterday's performance?' she asked apprehensively.

'Are you kidding? It was a great win,' Katy said stoutly. 'Any criticism is aimed at Lucia, not you,' she assured her, thinking privately that it was probably just as well they were unable to read the Italian papers!

It was another blisteringly hot day, and Melissa's

headache worsened as she warmed up for her match. The sun seemed to reflect off the red clay, hurting her eyes. Dark glasses helped a little, and she wore them for the match, hiding from the crowd as well as protecting her eyes from the dazzling sunlight.

Her heart wasn't in the task: she simply didn't feel she should be there; didn't want to be there; her head hurt and she felt lethargic and heavy-footed. Neither her brain nor her body worked properly and Katy watched in mounting despair as she lost the first set in only twenty minutes. She's not even trying! Katy thought angrily.

'Melissa! Stop being so unprofessional!' she yelled, as Melissa dropped serve at the beginning of the second set. The umpire looked around, recognized Melissa's coach and shot her a warning glance. Not that such abuse could be termed 'coaching', he thought. Besides, Farrell hadn't seemed to hear it.

'Time,' he called. Melissa got wearily to her feet; she just wanted it to be over. She went through the motions, but that was all, and felt only relief when yet another mistake handed the match to her opponent.

Katy was too annoyed to even speak to her and stormed off, but had calmed down somewhat when Melissa caught up with her at the hotel. She still looked ill, Katy thought, watching as Melissa downed a couple of painkillers.

'I think you need a break,' she said slowly. 'You're not entered in a tournament next week, so go home for a few days. See Nick, or your parents, and meet me in Paris next Friday.'

'Oh, thank you!' Melissa exclaimed, immediately

feeling better, and hurried to phone Nick. He joined her in London on Sunday and they spent the next three days in the flat, rarely venturing out. Melissa was heartily sick of hotel food and happily pottered around the kitchen – not a room she was normally familiar with! Nick ate everything she cooked, even the failures.

'Anyone who's served in the Army isn't too fussy about their food,' he explained, less than tactfully, and had to duck to avoid the saucepan lid she threw at him. Laughing, he pulled her on to his lap and nuzzled her neck. 'Mm, this tastes good . . . and this,' his lips moved lower to suckle her breast. Melissa squirmed in delight; no matter how often they made love, or how sated she believed herself to be, he could always arouse her in a moment.

Later, she fell asleep in his arms and he lay quietly beside her, watching her. It could be like this all the time, he thought, if only she would quit tennis. She had seemed so tired and depressed when she arrived, and she said she loved him, so what was driving her to pursue an arduous career which kept them apart?

On Thursday, they drove down to Bellwood. Rose was delighted to see them and looked younger and happier than Nick remembered ever seeing her.

'Ace has been so generous, giving me a free hand to redecorate and furnish,' she told them, as Melissa wandered through the familiar rooms, admiring her mother's taste.

'How is Dad?' she asked.

'He's well. And happy, I think,' Rose said. 'You'll be able to judge for yourself – I invited him over for lunch.'

When Daniel arrived, it was apparent he had benefited from selling Bellwood. Running the smaller farm with minimal help and no financial worries had given him back his health and vitality. He strode into the house with a light step and a beaming smile for his daughter.

'I've had satellite TV installed so I can watch your matches,' he told her. 'That Lucia Conti is a madam, isn't she? I'm surprised you didn't hit her over the head with your racket!'

'I was tempted, but I'm way behind in a long queue for that pleasure,' Melissa giggled, the horrors of the match having receded under Nick's loving care. He had no idea what Daniel was referring to and resolved to learn more about the sport and the people she spent her time with. Jack was right; he should be more involved and not ignore it, hoping she would tire of it. Hell, he would even learn how to play the game, he decided suddenly.

It was midnight before they left Bellwood, and Melissa fell asleep in the car, waking only briefly when Nick carried her into the flat and put her to bed. On Friday morning they made love slowly, savouring and prolonging every moment, until it was time for her to leave. Still determined to be supportive, Nick made no complaint about the seperation and took comfort from the knowledge that she would be back in England for the grass-court season in a couple of weeks.

Melissa had been to Roland Garros, home of the French Open, just once before, but then only as a spectator. Now, she was keyed-up and eager to play, fresh after her short break. Already the Grand Slams were special to her, and not only for the huge prize money and prestige at stake. She loved having Jack around, loved the huge crowds and high-profile Press and TV coverage; it was as if the entire city was involved in the event.

As usual, Melissa hadn't checked the draw, a habit which sometimes irked Katy, but, in Paris, she was relieved; Melissa had drawn Graf in the first round.

'Steffi?' Melissa repeated incredulously. 'Oh, hell!'

'What sort of attitude is that?' Katy scoffed. 'You have to play the best if you ever want to join them at the top. Unless you're content to play the tournaments they don't bother with, of course,' she added scathingly.

'You know I'm not,' Melissa said defensively, stiffening her spine.

She tried hard not to let nerves overcome her, tried to heed Katy's advice to forget just who was on the other side of the net and play the ball, not the player, but that was easier said than done.

'At least you kept her out there for more than an hour, which is better than most players can do,' Katy said afterwards. 'Cheer up, you played well and you're still in the Doubles,' she added encouragingly.

Hal had also lost his Singles match and Katy increasingly began to feel he was usurping her role as he acted as coach to both Lisa and Melissa.

'He's making it impossible for me to do my job,' she complained to Jack. 'Him and his "Lissa and Lisa show"!' she snorted disgustedly.

'If he bothers you that much, find Melissa another Doubles partner,' he suggested.

'It would be a pity to do that,' Katy said slowly. 'They're a good team.'

'You sound as if you have long-term plans,' Jack commented. 'The agreed year is almost over. Are you going to stay with Melissa?'

'Yeah, if she wants me to,' Katy had already decided on that. 'She can't afford to pay me much yet, but I'm willing to take a chance on her making it big.'

'I'm glad to hear that,' Jack said, relieved. Even after a year on the tour, he'd hate to think of Melissa travelling alone.

They all flew over to England in early June to prepare for Wimbledon. Nick journeyed down from Scotland to spend as much time as possible with Melissa, and she stayed at the flat with him whenever her schedule – or Katy – allowed.

'I'll be coming to Eastbourne next week, after all,' Nick told her one evening. 'Jess is competing in a junior event, and Juliet wants to go along and support her, so I told their mother I'd keep an eye on the two of them.'

'That's kind of you, Uncle Nick,' she teased. 'It'll be nice to see Jess again,' she added.

'She's very impressed with all you've achieved,' Nick said. 'She saw you playing in Paris . . . that reminds me – can't you wear longer skirts on court?' he growled. 'Those French cameramen kept focusing on your cute little backside!'

'So?' Melissa giggled. 'My knickers were clean!'

'My thoughts weren't,' Nick said ruefully.

'Oh? Can you remember what those thoughts were?' Melissa asked, rubbing her thigh suggestively against his, and they both forgot about Jessica.

It never occurred to Nick that his niece might have to

compete against Melissa, but Katy had decided to enter her in the Under Twenty-ones event, hoping for a succession of victories to boost her confidence going into Wimbledon the following week. Melissa wasn't too happy with the decision, not sure she liked being relegated to the more junior competition. She was even less happy when she asked Katy about her first opponent.

'I don't know much about her yet – she's a wild card entry – a British kid, name of J Stanton.'

'Jessica? Oh, God, she's Nick's niece,' Melissa frowned, 'I used to play her in the juniors.'

'Who won?' Katy asked, practical as ever.

'I did.'

'Good.'

Jessica was sick with nerves at the prospect of playing Melissa, and almost withdrew from the tournament.

'She's played against Graf!' she wailed to her mother.

'And lost,' Caroline Stanton replied tartly. 'Pull yourself together, Jessica – you've played her before.' Jess grimaced: sure she had, but she had never beaten her.

Nick watched the match with mixed emotions: he knew Melissa needed to do well here, but he also wanted Jess to experience some of the success Melissa had enjoyed over the past year.

It soon became clear who would win. Jessica performed terribly, at first from nerves and then from sheer panic at the speed of her annihilation. Melissa hated the match; it was difficult to play good tennis against such a dreadful opponent and she wrapped it up as quickly as possible, 6–0, 6–0, in just over thirty minutes. Jessica won only one point in the second set when Melissa, bored and losing her concentration, served a double fault.

It was only when she ran to the net to shake hands that she realized how badly Jessica was taking her defeat. Tears poured down her cheeks and she couldn't meet Melissa's eyes.

'God, Jess, I'm sorry,' Melissa said awkwardly. Jessica rushed off without speaking to anyone, and Melissa slowly packed her rackets away.

'You cow!' Melissa glanced up, startled, and found herself confronted by a kid who looked vaguely familiar . . . Oh, yes, Juliet, Jessica's sister. The girls were very alike, both with the same silvery-blonde hair and grey eyes as their mother and Nick. 'I'm going to be a professional player and, one day, I'm going to do to you what you've just done to Jess!' Juliet hissed.

'Oh, go and get your nappy changed!' Melissa snapped, pushing past her, only to find herself facing Nick.

'Was it necessary to humiliate Jess like that?' he asked coldly.

'Yes, it was!' Melissa said furiously. 'If Jess can't hack it, she should quit! You still think a tennis tournament is some sort of Sunday afternoon vicarage garden party, don't you? It's not – it's my career! Remember that word? You had one once,' she ground out. 'When you were fighting the Iraqis in the Gulf war, you didn't stop and say, "oh, hold on chaps, let's give them a sporting chance," did you?'

'Don't be so infantile – lives were at stake!' Nick snapped, incensed. 'That's hardly the case here.'

'Really? You do surprise me – the way you and Juliet are banging on, I thought Jess must have slit her wrists!' Melissa said scornfully.

'When did you become such a bitch?' He didn't wait for a reply, but turned on his heel and walked swiftly away to go and comfort Jessica. Melissa was almost in tears herself when Katy returned from watching the match which would provide Melissa's next opponent.

'What the hell's happened? You were coasting along when I left,' she frowned.

'That was the problem – Nick thinks I should have let her win a few games,' Melissa explained miserably.

'Oh, for God's sake! Come back Hal, all is forgiven,' Katy said dramatically. 'At least Hal lives in the real world.'

'The tennis world,' Melissa corrected.

'Yeah, right. But surely even Nick can understand that it's impossible to give away games? Not that you could have, today, even if you'd wanted to . . . well, only if you'd served four successive double faults,' she amended. 'Come on, cheer up – Nick's just playing the kind uncle – he'll cool down,' she said comfortingly.

Nick did cool down but, when he arrived at the Grand Hotel to meet Melissa for dinner, his anger resurfaced upon receiving a message informing him that Melissa had a headache. Thinking she was sulking, he stormed up to her room and banged on the door.

'Melissa! Open this door!' he thundered. It was Katy who opened it, and she gestured frantically for him to be quiet.

'What's this rubbish about a headache?' he demanded, before noticing the curtains were drawn against the light.

111

He crossed swiftly to the figure huddled on the bed, still not convinced she wasn't playing games.

'Melissa?' He bent over her and placed his hand gently on her forehead, It was very hot to his touch and, when she opened her eyes, he realized she found even the dim light hard to bear. 'How long has she been like this?' he asked Katy.

'Don't shout, please don't shout,' Melissa whispered.

'I'm not shouting,' he lowered his voice still further, then stood and indicated Katy should follow him from the room. 'Well?' he demanded.

'It's another migraine; I'm going to give her a sleeping pill . . .'

'Sleeping pill?' Nick interrupted. 'She's nineteen, she doesn't need sleeping pills!' he exploded. 'And what do you mean – "another" migraine? How often does she have them?'

'This is the second. The first was in Rome; I thought the heat triggered it, but I was wrong. They're obviously stress-related, and YOU caused this one,' she hissed.

Nick glared at her and walked back inside to tend to Melissa, soaking a flannel in cold water and placing it across her forehead. The cloth was hot within seconds and he repeated the action again and again until her skin felt a little cooler. But she was obviously still in great pain and, finally, he could bear it no longer.

'Okay, give her a sleeping pill,' he sighed. He sat by the bedside until it took effect and the lines of pain gradually eased as she fell asleep.

'She'll sleep for hours now,' Katy told him, and he got to his feet.

112

'She must consult a doctor about this,' he said, and Katy nodded, for once agreeing with him. 'I'll take her back to London tomorrow, or Bellwood if she prefers,' he continued. Katy stared at him.

'She has another match tomorrow,' she reminded him.

'She can't possibly play,' Nick objected.

'Do you want to bet?' Katy had heard enough, and pointedly opened the door wide for him to leave. With a last glance and tender touch for the sleeping Melissa, Nick returned to his own hotel.

Melissa still felt ill when she awoke but, as before, the migraine had subsided to a dull ache. She felt as if she were recovering from flu, a little nauseous and very weak. Practising made her feel worse and they retreated to the locker-room, glancing constantly at the lowering sky and praying for rain to postpone her match.

Shortly before four o'clock, she was called on to court. It was cold and windy; dark clouds scudded overhead but no rain fell. Melissa's opponent was Karina Svenson, a girl Melissa should have beaten easily, ranked outside the top one hundred and none too proficient on grass. But Melissa's mind and body were too slow; each serve made her feel dizzy and hitting the ball hard sent shock waves of pain up her arm and into her head.

'I wish she'd played this badly yesterday,' Jessica muttered.

'Shut up,' Nick advised her tersely. He had made his peace with Melissa earlier, but now wished she would quit – why the hell was she putting herself through this? Melissa lost the first set, 6–1, and felt the first drop of rain fall as she took a much-needed breather.

113

'It's raining – can we go off?' she asked the umpire, but he refused. She lost her opening service game and appealed to him again at the changeover.

'It's too dark to see the ball properly,' she objected, but he again refused to suspend play. Knowing a downpour was her only hope, she dallied as much as she dared, taking the maximum time allowed between points, until Karina complained about the delay.

Melissa was trailing 1–5 when the heavens opened and they dashed for cover. Melissa exchanged a relieved grin with Katy, but they both wondered if the reprieve had come too late to help.

There was no further play that day, and the match resumed at two the following afternoon. Melissa, happy to be feeling healthy again, went out determined to win. Karina, lulled into a false sense of security, never recovered from the shock of Melissa's opening display of power and aggression.

Katy watched worriedly until Melissa evened the second set score at 5–5, and relaxed even more when she won it 7–5. Melissa then reeled off the next six games for a whitewash third set.

'Was that your twin sister out here yesterday?' Karina asked ruefully, as they shook hands. Melissa grinned at her, then turned to Nick and Katy, beaming with relief.

'That was great, I enjoyed it,' she said happily. Katy laughed. Nick wanted to throttle her for putting everyone, especially herself, through such torment, but hugged her instead.

Still on a high, she breezed through her remaining matches and won the event, looking forward to Wimbledon and hoping she wouldn't have the bad luck to be drawn against one of the top seeds in the first round. Jack and Ace had again rented a house near the All England Club, only this year Melissa insisted on paying a third of the rent. Nick was displeased by her decision to join them, but couldn't argue against the logic of staying within walking distance of the courts, instead of in central London.

'Mum will be there, if you're worried about Ace,' Melissa assured him. 'And I'll make it up to you, I promise.'

'I'll make sure that you do!' He kissed her hard, possessively, wanting so much more than she could, or would, give.

CHAPTER 6

'I think you'll enjoy your first match,' Katy told Melissa. 'It's against Dianne Bannister – she beat you at Beckenham last year.'

'Yes,' Melissa nodded thoughtfully. They hadn't played since but, in the intervening months, Melissa's ranking had risen sharply, overtaking the older girl as the highest-ranked British player. 'As it's an all-British match, we might be on Centre Court,' she realized happily.

'Is this the same girl who was terrified of going out there last year, even with her big brother to hold her hand?' Katy asked mockingly. Melissa just smiled, thinking she had come a long way since then.

Many of the top seeds were in action on the opening day of the Championships and Melissa's match began at noon on an outside court, attracting only a few spectators. However, she did have the distinction of being the first player to reach the second round, beating Dianne easily, 6–2, 6–2.

She faced a much sterner test on Wednesday, meeting Carlotta Mendoza, the number eight seed, for the first time. Carlotta – nicknamed Carthorse by Ace – was tall and strong, an experienced player on all surfaces. When they walked onto number one court, the stands were already packed and Melissa glanced briefly to her left, where the players' supporters had gathered.

Her parents were there, Jack and Katy, and, of course, Nick. He seemed far more interested in the sport, now, and she had been delighted to learn that he had been taking lessons at a club in Edinburgh. His coach, Gavin Bruce, had tried life on the circuit, but had given up after eighteen months, readily admitting that it had been too tough and he had returned home, exhausted, lonely and broke after having only ever won two matches. Gavin's admiration for those who succeeded had coloured Nick's opinion, as had his own attempts to play. It wasn't as easy as it looked! He had reasoned that, being fit and strong, he would soon become proficient. After all, one only needed to serve, to know how to hit a forehand and a backhand, keep the ball over the net and inside the lines – right? Wrong: he had quickly discovered he had a lot to learn.

Melissa smiled slightly then continued on her way, lifting her head to gaze at the tiers of applauding spectators. If she lived to be a hundred, the smell of freshly-mown grass would always recall this moment, she thought; this, her first Singles match on one of Wimbledon's show courts. She had a few butterflies in her tummy, but knew they would disappear as soon as they began to play.

Greg Reynolds was also present, unusually for him. He rarely watched the matches, being too busy behind the scenes making deals for the players he represented to actually see them at work. But he was becoming increasingly interested in Melissa. She was climbing the rankings quicker than anyone had expected, the Press loved her and the snippets of gossip concerning possible romances with Hal and Ace were doing her no harm at all. Already she had a high profile and a few more matches on world-famous stages would put her in line for some lucrative sponsorship deals.

From the very first point, Melissa knew she had the crowd behind her, willing her to play well, as they did every British player. It was a long, hard-fought first set, but Melissa had the advantage of serving first. At 5–4, urged on by the thousands of yelling spectators, she hit out boldly, knowing this was her best chance to break serve and take the opening set. '30–40.' Set point. Melissa put the thought from her mind and watched the ball closely. It was a rather tentative serve and Melissa stepped in, timing her shot perfectly, blasting a double-fisted backhand into the corner of the court.

'Game and first set, Farrell, 6–4.'

Again, Melissa served to open the set, and won easily, then immediately broke Carlotta, who was evidently brooding over the loss of the first set. Melissa held grimly onto her lead, countering Carlotta's differing tactics and maintaining her own aggressive strategy. The score slowly crept up, each game a battle until, eventually, Melissa was leading 5–3.

Her heart thumping, she turned to a ball-boy and nodded calmly. She was serving for the match! At Wimbledon, against the number eight seed! Forget that, she chided herself, just play one point at a time. 15–0, 30–0, 40–0. Three match points! She tossed the ball and swung her racket. It was a good first serve, but

Carlotta's return was excellent and Melissa had to scramble to reach it, scorching the two-fisted backhand past Carlotta, clipping the line. She'd done it! She'd . . .

'40–15.'

'What?' Melissa stared at the umpire, then at the linesman. She had not heard his call of 'out', but his arm remained outstretched, indicating her shot had gone wide.

'40–15,' the umpire repeated.

'Shit, Bugger, Bollocks,' Melissa swore under her breath. She was sure she had won the match, but, after the controversial win over Lucia in Rome, she had resolved never again to be drawn into a dispute over a line call, not even if the officials came onto court with white sticks and guide dogs!

'She still has two match points,' Jack said, sounding a lot calmer than he felt. To lose a match point in such a way was enough to put even an experienced player off their stride, and Melissa only had the one break of serve. If Carlotta broke back now . . . He leaned forward, willing Melissa to remain calm, hardly aware of Katy's nails digging into his arm.

Melissa bounced the ball several times to compose herself, hit a good serve and rushed to the net, intercepting Carlotta's return and smashing it, with rather more force than was necessary, way out of reach.

'Game, set, match, Farrell!' Melissa turned at once to Nick and her family, grinning broadly as she waited at the net for Carlotta to approach.

'Well played,' Carlotta said, rather stiffly, and quickly left the court. Melissa took her time, enjoying the applause and the good will that enveloped her from all around the stadium. She never wanted to leave!

She ran over to be congratulated by her family, and Nick hugged her tightly. Rose was dabbing at her eyes and Daniel looked as proud as if he had won the match himself. But only Jack and Katy truly knew how she felt; how great a triumph it was. She and Katy exchanged a long look, each silently acknowledging the other's part in the victory.

After that, everything became a blur; so many people talking to her at once, their voices merging and becoming incomprehensible.

'Go and have a shower – it's the only place you'll get any peace,' Katy advised, sensing Melissa was becoming overwhelmed by it all. Melissa did as she suggested, but couldn't relax. She was still on a 'high', her mind a confused jumble, part of her still on the court, her ears ringing with the sound of the applause.

She beamed happily as she entered the Interview Room and took her seat facing the assembled Press corps. Their questions were friendly and easy to answer; trained by Katy, Melissa was always careful not to say anything controversial.

'You thought you had won on the first match point – how do you feel about that decision?'

'The linesman was in a better position to judge – I guess it was just wishful thinking on my part,' Melissa smiled sweetly, easing past the awkward question.

'You've beaten the number eight seed – the way is clear to the quarter finals now, isn't it?' Melissa stared at the man who had spoken, her euphoria evaporating, and she felt a slight twinge of pain in her right temple.

'No!' she denied, rather too forcefully: they couldn't expect this of her, they couldn't! 'I don't even know who my next opponent is – I never look at the draw,' she explained. 'Please, don't tell me,' she quickly put up hand to forestall them. 'That's Katy's job,' she added, forcing a smile, and the line of questioning changed as they asked about Katy's role as her coach. Melissa gradually relaxed but was glad to escape and she rushed back to the locker-room, where she swallowed two of the tablets prescribed to prevent another attack of migraine.

'Oh, God, not a headache?' Katy hovered anxiously.

'No, not yet, anyway.' Melissa rubbed her forehead. 'I just felt a niggle during the interview, but I seem to be okay,' she said cautiously, crossing her fingers.

'You're supposed to take those as soon as you feel any indication of pain,' Katy fussed.

'I know, but I can hardly start popping pills in front of a bunch of journalists, can I?' Melissa retorted.

'I guess not – what did they say to upset you?' Katy asked shrewdly.

'They seem to expect me to get through to the quarter finals now,' Melissa sighed. 'Don't they know how difficult that is?'

'Sure they do; they're just desperate for a Brit to do well,' Katy said soothingly. 'Wait here a minute,' she said, and disappeared, going in search of Nick. Perhaps the guy had his uses, after all.

'Can you take Melissa back to your flat?' she asked.

'Sure.' Nick wasn't certain he'd heard correctly.

'The Press won't bother her there,' Katy explained. 'Can you feed her, calm her down and see that she gets a

121

good night's sleep?' Well, two out of three, Nick thought.

'Of course. But I thought she wanted to stay and support Jack?'

'She's had enough,' Katy decided for her. 'She needs to rest and unwind. Jack will understand.'

They avoided the main entrance and slipped away unnoticed. Nick quickly realized why Katy was so concerned; Melissa's mood changed from one minute to the next, from over-excited, non-stop chatter to introspective, frowning silence, before reverting to the fast monologue. She was the same once they were at the flat, restlessly pacing, switching on the TV and then turning it off, picking things up and putting them down somewhere else. Silently, Nick made tea and she drank half a cup, forgetting the rest.

'Come here.' Nick held out his hand, deciding there was only one way to deal with her – horizontally – and led her into the bedroom. He closed the drapes to cut out most of the light and gathered her into his arms, nuzzling her neck, feeling the pulse there leaping too quickly. Not from desire, he guessed, not yet, anyway.

Several hours later, he awoke and moved cautiously away from Melissa, so as not to disturb her. He watched her closely as she slept, her body relaxed, her breathing deep and even, a small smile curving her lips – dreaming of him, or her match? He daren't pursue the thought and, after picking up his clothes, quietly left the room.

Two victories in the Doubles events on Thursday boosted Melissa's confidence even more, and the news that her third round Singles match would take place on

Centre Court added to her delight. Katy had spent some time scouting for information on her opponent, a little-known Australian named Susan Carlton.

'She's just nineteen and is ranked 188 so she had to qualify for this tournament. Like you, she's a serve-volleyer, so you'll have to get to the net before she does, which shouldn't be difficult as she's too slow around the court,' Katy told Melissa. 'And this is her first Grand Slam, so she'll be as nervous as hell at going out on Centre,' she added. Melissa nodded her agreement, remembering her own apprehension the year before.

Melissa was out on the practice court early on Friday morning, too intent on what she was doing to notice the tall, stocky girl who paused to watch for a while before continuing on her way. Katy spotted her, though, and pointed her out to Melissa. Melissa looked, blinked, and looked again.

'She ought to be in the men's draw. She's not an Australian – she's an Amazon!' she said, horrified.

'Don't be defeatist,' Katy scolded. 'She's overweight; lumbers around the court like an elephant.'

'That hardly matters – she's got arms like a gorilla; all she has to do is stand in the middle of the court and reach out. She doesn't need to move!'

'Rubbish. If you keep your returns low to her feet and take the net position, you'll be okay,' Katy said. Her gaze slid past Melissa and, from the look of yearning on her face, Melissa knew Jack was near. She turned and watched him approach with Ace; they had a Doubles match scheduled for later that day.

'Have you seen that giant I have to play?' Melissa asked, nodding to where the Australian was warming up on a nearby court. Jack grimaced in sympathy. Ace laughed.

'If she beats you, demand a drug test,' he said. 'She's got more testosterone in her body than I have!'

'I bet she hasn't got as much alcohol,' Jack said sourly. Ace's drinking was really annoying him; his continual late nights meant he wasn't performing at his best, and Jack badly wanted to win the Wimbledon title. Ace tried, and failed, to look contrite.

'I'm in trouble,' he confided to Melissa, in a stage whisper. 'I forgot to ask for a late-night pass!'

'I know the feeling,' Melissa giggled, with a sideways glance at Katy.

'Come on, let's get to work,' Jack and Katy said in unison. Ace grinned.

'Why you two ever broke up is a mystery to me,' he drawled. 'You're obviously made for each other.'

'Shut up!' Jack ground out, cast an apologetic smile at Katy and began walking away, turning around to wish Melissa luck.

Melissa's match was the first on court, which pleased her; a definite starting time was preferable to hanging around the locker-room waiting for an earlier match to finish.

The minutes ticked slowly by as they waited in silence for the occupants of the Royal Box to take their seats. The delay irked her – who had the crowd come to see, for God's sake? They're here to see you win, said a small voice in her head. You've beaten the player ranked eighth in the world, so someone they've never heard of, ranked 188, should be a piece of cake . . . That's what they were thinking, but they were wrong, Melissa thought. She didn't underestimate a girl who had won through the qualifying rounds and had already beaten two players ranked higher than herself in the main draw.

Finally, they were ushered onto court. Melissa let Susan walk ahead of her; the muted applause increased tenfold when Melissa came into view. She felt, and looked, tiny compared to her opponent. The faces she saw were smiling and friendly, and the weight of expectation lifted a little from her shoulders. Perhaps they would understand and sympathize if she lost, and not heap recriminations upon her head, she thought hopefully.

They reached the service line and turned to face the Royal Box. Melissa executed a dainty, if rather perfunctory, curtsey. Susan made a hash of hers, feet together, bending both knees awkwardly. Either she was a Paul Keating supporter or she was stiff with nerves. Melissa hoped it was the latter.

Melissa won the toss and chose to receive – if she was right about the giant's jitters, she might win an immediate break of serve. She soon realized that Susan hit the ball as hard as any man, but fortunately she wasn't as accurate, at least not today. None of her first serves were in, and Melissa pounced on the second. Susan was slow to react and Melissa hurried the match along, eager to have a strong lead before her opponent could calm down and begin to play well.

She romped to a 4–0 lead, dropping only one point before Susan found any rhythm and started to serve with confidence. She was still slow to move and Melissa swung her from side to side, then wrong-footed her and went in for the kill. That fifth game was tough, with three deuces, but Melissa won it and flashed a grin at Katy was she went to sit down.

Melissa served out a 6–0 first set, accompanied by loud cheers from the partisan crowd. The games were becoming harder to win, though, and Susan won her first game, her serves too fast and powerful for Melissa to control the returns as well as she would have liked. She had to win her own serve to maintain her grip on the match and Susan was more confident now, up from her chair before Melissa and moving more easily.

Melissa held serve, but couldn't break Susan. The score was 3–3, then 4–4, but Susan had the advantage of serving first. The crowd, although still on her side, had wanted a repeat of the easy first set and there were impatient cries of 'Come ON, Melissa!' as if she were dragging her feet instead of running and hitting as hard as she could. Couldn't they see that the Australian's standard of play had risen dramatically?

Melissa badly wanted to finish the match in two sets, and took advantage of some weaker second serves, firing returns to each corner of the court. She broke to lead 5–4, and the noise was deafening as she walked back out to serve for the match, the crowd oblivious to the umpire's repeated calls for silence. Melissa didn't mind the hubbub, the cheers were for her and she didn't let them down, serving well and volleying crisply to a downhearted opponent.

'Game, set, match, Farrell!' The crowd went wild and Melissa punched the air in delight. In some ways, this victory was even sweeter than the one over Carlotta – she had proved to the home crowd that the earlier win hadn't been a fluke; that she was a winner! She ran over to shake hands and turned to Nick, Katy and her family. Jack grinned broadly and put up his thumb in a gesture of approval before dashing off to prepare for his own Men's Doubles match with Ace.

He made his way to the locker-room, where Ace was already waiting, chatting to other players and flicking idly through a magazine featuring the top female tennis stars.

'Which of the girls has the best tits?' Ace asked, of no one in particular.

'Melissa Farrell,' said a besotted Hal promptly.

'Oh, what a surprise!' Ace said sarcastically. 'Who has the best legs?'

'Farrell,' Hal said again.

'Ooh, thanks very much!' Jack squealed, mincing up and down the room, hand on hip.

'Not you, asshole!' Ace laughed, and threw the magazine at him. 'You can forget her, Renwick. You don't stand a chance,' he told Hal.

'We'll see. I'm going to ask her to come away on holiday with me, somewhere really romantic,' Hal said.

'Yeah? Thousand bucks says she turns you down,' Ace challenged.

'A thousand bucks? Okay, you're on,' Hal agreed.

'Do you mind? That's my sister you're betting on,' Jack protested.

'No offence,' Hal apologized quickly. 'I'd marry her tomorrow if she'd have me.'

'She wouldn't,' Ace interrupted.

'Not even for a honeymoon in the Seychelles?' Hal asked hopefully.

'Not even if you bought the Seychelles!' Ace retorted. 'It is nice there . . . mind you, it's nice anywhere!'

'When were you in the Seychelles?' Jack asked.

'Last Christmas . . . oh, look at the score – we'd better shift,' Ace pointed to the monitor as he got to his feet and collected up his rackets and towels. Jack followed suit; there was something niggling at the back of his mind, something about a holiday in the Seychelles, but he couldn't quite pinpoint the source of his unease. Mentally he shrugged it aside and turned his thoughts to the coming match.

The fans were eager for another Farrell victory, and they weren't disappointed. Ace's awesome serve lived up to its reputation and Jack was his usual efficient self at the net. They won in three straight sets in under two hours, an easier win than they had anticiapted. They exchanged a meaningful glance as they approached the net to shake hands with their opponents.

'I think this could be our year,' Jack murmured. '*If* you stay off the booze!'

'I will, I really want this title,' Ace said, and Jack nodded, satisfied. When Ace really concentrated on a goal, he generally achieved it.

Nick knew the middle Sunday of the Championships was a 'rest' day, and had anticipated spending it alone with Melissa, preferably in bed, and was dismayed to find she was already dressed to leave when he awoke.

'You're not going to practise?' he protested.

'Of course I am. I have a big match tomorrow,' she replied, in the absent tone of voice he hated, the tone which meant her mind was on her tennis.

'I know, but . . . oh, go ahead,' he sighed.

'I won't be late,' she promised, leaning over to kiss him and dancing back out of reach when he tried to grab her. 'No, you don't! You'll have to wait until tonight,' she grinned, blew another kiss from the safety of the doorway and disappeared.

Katy and Lisa were waiting for her at the practice courts and Melissa apologized profusely for her tardiness. She knew Katy disapproved of her staying overnight with Nick in central London, and didn't want it to become a bone of contention.

'Who am I playing tomorrow?' she asked. 'A seed, I suppose?'

'Afraid so,' Katy nodded. 'Lucia Conti.'

'Oh, hell!' Melissa muttered.

'You beat her on clay, so you can beat her on grass,' Katy said swiftly. 'And don't give me any rubbish about winning the match in Rome unfairly,' she added softly, so that Lisa couldn't hear. Melissa nodded, but they both knew it would be a 'grudge' match. 'You realize she's bound to complain over any close line calls?'

'Is the Pope a Catholic? I'll be prepared for that – she won't get to me this time,' Melissa said confidently. 'And this is my home crowd, not hers.'

'True,' Katy relaxed slightly.

The three girls practised for a couple of hours, broke off for a light lunch and then Lisa and Melissa resumed, with Katy watching closely from the sidelines. Her injured knee caused problems if she played too much, but she found it less and less irksome as coaching Melissa and guiding her to the top became more important than her own career.

129

When Katy decided they had done enough for the day, the three of them walked back to the house and relaxed in the garden, drinking the fresh lemonade Rose had prepared. Jack and Ace returned from their own practice session soon after; Jack joined them in the garden while Ace disappeared indoors to shower and change.

'Hello, Lisa, where's Hal?' Jack asked.

'Hal? I'm not sure – why? Oh!' She looked at Melissa and grinned. 'I think he's playing hard to get!'

'Oh, stop it. Hal's just a friend; he knows about Nick,' Melissa said, flushing.

'Yeah?' Jack raised an eyebrow. 'He obviously hasn't got around to inviting you to the Seychelles yet?'

'He'd be wasting his time,' Melissa said quickly, with a meaningful glance at Lisa, who nodded; she would pass on the message to save her brother the embarrassment of being rejected.

'The Seychelles? Oh, it's lovely there!' Rose exclaimed.

'I didn't know you had ever been,' Melissa said, surprised.

'Mm, last Christmas,' Rose told her. Jack stared at his mother in horror. Of course. It all added up – why hadn't he guessed before? Ace's unusual secrecy, his occasional disappearing acts, buying Bellwood. Jack had wondered why Ace hadn't taken any of his tarts home; but of course he didn't need to, he had one permanently installed! Ace and my mother? Dear God, Ace and my mother! He went cold as he heard Melissa's bright laughter – had Ace ensnared her, too? He'd love that scenario; to have both the mother and the daughter, with neither knowing about the other.

He stood up and strode indoors, furious now, and barged into Ace's room, then pounded his fist on the wall in frustration when he realized he had already left the house. He watched the group on the lawn from the window, saw Melissa and Lisa leave, followed later by Katy. Rose gathered up the empty glasses and he heard her bustling about in the kitchen, then her footsteps on the stairs and the soft closing of her bedroom door. He crossed the landing swiftly and entered her room.

'Oh, Jack, it's you,' Rose turned and smiled.

'You sound surprised. Who were you expecting – Ace?' he asked coldly, and watched the colour drain from her face.

'Ace?' Rose repeated faintly, sinking on to the dressing table stool. 'Why . . .?'

'Don't deny it,' Jack advised tersely.

'Jack! I'm your mother, and . . .'

'And one of Ace's broads. That's what he calls them, broads,' Jack informed her cruelly. 'Brainless bimbos with morals as loose as their knicker elastic! Are you completely off your head?' he asked incredulously. 'He treats women like dirt, you know that. How long has it been going on?'

'I don't have to answer . . .'

'How long!' Jack shouted.

'About eighteen months,' Rose said finally. 'I was still feeling so depressed and lonely after the divorce, and Ace just . . .' she bit her lip and looked away.

'Oh, I know how he operates,' Jack told her. 'I've witnessed it, a thousand times. Eighteen months? Melissa was crazy about him then – did you stop and think how much this would hurt her?'

'Melissa loves Nick,' Rose said, but rather uncomfortably.

'Now she does, but eighteen months ago she was infatuated with Ace, and you knew it.'

'I'd never hurt Melissa,' Rose protested. 'She was the main reason I insisted on secrecy. I was afraid she would think I'd betrayed her . . . you're not going to tell her, are you?' she pleaded. Jack stared at her broodingly, mulling over his options; if Melissa were told, she'd be safe from Ace, but she would also be very hurt. He sighed heavily.

'I haven't decided yet. You're a fool,' he said contemptuously. 'Do you know how many other women he's had over the past eighteen months? He's not even faithful to you when you're in the same city . . . or the same house!' he realized suddenly, for Ace had been absent most nights since they had arrived in London.

'I know.' Rose bit her lip. 'He's sulking, punishing me because I won't . . . won't sleep with him when you or Melissa are here,' she explained.

'Oh, my God,' Jack said heavily, his anger replaced by pity. He shook his head slightly and turned and walked away. He threw some things in a bag and left the house to find a room in an hotel.

He caught up with Ace the following morning, in the men's locker-room, and knew from the guarded look on his face that Rose had warned him they had been found out.

'You already know what a bastard you are,' Jack gritted, quietly, for other players were within earshot, 'so I won't bother telling you what I think of you. We finish this tournament and then it's goodbye.

132

Win or lose, we tell the world we've accomplished as much as we can as a team and we're both moving on; an amicable split – right?'

'That's stupid – you're over-reacting,' Ace protested; he'd expected a row, but not this.

'I said; we're through!' Jack glared at him with loathing before stalking off.

Ace sat down and lit a cigarette, with shaking hands, oblivious to the howls of protest that rose up around him. He couldn't believe Jack was taking it this badly – anyone would think he had been the cause of Daniel and Rose's divorce, instead of merely giving Rose the comfort she had needed! He hadn't planned it – Rose Farrell was one of the few women he had ever genuinely liked or respected. He would always remember his first visit to Bellwood, five years earlier; how impressed he had been by the ancient beauty of the place, the traditions – walking into the village when the local hunt gathered was like walking onto a film set!

He had envied Jack coming from such a background; had even envied Daniel having such a gracious wife, but he had never had designs on Rose. Or Melissa, for that matter; virgins were too much like hard work! Jack's warning to leave his kid sister alone hadn't been necessary; besides, even then Ace had known he drank too much, took too many drugs, and needed Jack's calming influence, both on and off court. He still needed Jack . . . no, damn it, he didn't. He had Rose, he owned Bellwood, he was a millionaire . . . he didn't need Jack Farrell, he decided. But his hands still shook.

* * *

Rose, unable to face Melissa, had phoned her at Nick's flat earlier to say she was feeling unwell, just a touch of flu, but had returned to Bellwood so as not to infect anyone else, and would watch her match on TV.

It was almost six o'clock when a marathon Men's Singles on court one ended, and Lucia and Melissa walked onto court. The long delay had shredded Melissa's nerves and, from the very first point, she knew she was in trouble. Lucia was hitting out in confident form, finding the lines with unerring accuracy, and earned herself an early break of serve which was enough to win her the first set, 6–4.

The second was a real battle; Melissa broke serve, but then lost her own, and Lucia's smirk had her fuming. Lucia kept up a running commentary, too, but in her native Italian. Melissa couldn't understand the words spat at her, but the tone was unmistakably hostile and it began to wear her down. She wasn't enjoying the match, not one bit, but dug in her heels and won the second set tie-break, which wiped the smile from Lucia's face.

Early in the third set, Melissa fell heavily, wrenching her ankle; only a slight injury, but painful enough to hamper her movement. Lucia took heart from Melissa's misfortune, openly gloating as she raced to what proved to be an unassailable lead.

'Game, set, match, Conti!' Melissa and Lucia exchanged terse nods as they shook hands, then Lucia grinned maliciously.

'Thanks for getting Carlotta Mendoza out of my path,' she said. 'I've never beaten her, but now I should get through to the semis, at least!'

134

'Bitch!' Melissa muttered, as she gathered up her rackets. Bitterly disappointed, she limped off court, brushing aside Katy's anxious enquiry about her ankle. She didn't even want to talk to Nick, and hid away, wallowing in a hot bath – and self-pity – before giving herself a stern talking-to and prepared to meet the Press.

She was able to shrug off her defeat, relieved that her ankle was as good as new after a night's rest, and finding consolation in reaching the semis in both Doubles events before bowing out of the tournament. There was satisfaction, too, in being able to present Jack with a cheque that repaid him every penny, plus interest.

'You mean I can't write you off against tax any more?' He feigned annoyance, then grinned. 'Well done, it took me two years to repay Dad, and I only had my own expenses to cover. I assume you're staying with Katy?'

'Yes, she and Greg have worked out a deal,' Melissa told him. 'I think I still have a lot to learn from her.'

'I agree,' he said, and later sought Katy out. 'No-one else knows this yet,' he began, 'But Ace and I are splitting up. I'm sick of the way he carries on, but you know what a vindictive sod he can be. I'm afraid he might try to get back at me through Melissa – maybe lead her on and then publicly humiliate her, just for the sheer hell of it. Does she still fancy him?'

'I don't think so,' Katy shook her head. 'She hardly mentions him these days.

'Good,' Jack relaxed slightly, feeling he needn't tell Melissa about their mother's affair. 'Watch out for Ace pulling a stunt, though,' he cautioned.

'I will,' Katy promised. 'I'll call you if I think he's trying anything.'

'Thanks.' Jack touched her cheek briefly, then went on his way, unaware of the half-longing, half-resentful look from Katy. *He only ever bothers to talk to me about Melissa,* she thought, sighing.

Jack and Ace continued their progress in the Men's Doubles; they had been partners for so long that they didn't need to communicate much on court.

Their mutual anger actually helped their cause, both determined to be the better player. Ace was at his brilliant best, living up to his name as he fired a record number of aces at a succession of hapless opponents. They achieved their goal of taking the title, but the victory was one they would both remember for all the wrong reasons. They hoisted the trophy aloft and smiled at the cheering crowd.

'Enjoy it,' Ace hissed. 'You'll never win another Grand Slam without me!'

'Rubbish! You're over the hill,' Jack snarled back.

Melissa had watched their final on TV; she and Nick were spending her last few days in England at the Red Lion hotel in the New Forest, the hotel where they had spent their first night together, just one year before. It was a wonderful break, alone, with Melissa not having to watch the clock and dash off to practise or compete, but the precious time passed all too swiftly.

On the morning of her departure, Nick awoke first and lay still for a while, content to watch her sleep, her body curled against his. Then he began gently caressing her soft, warm skin; her nipples hardened to his touch

136

and her thighs parted easily when his hand brushed against her curls. When Melissa awoke, she was fully aroused.

'Good morning,' Nick smiled down at her.

'Mm, good morning; I'm going to miss waking up with you,' she murmured, reaching up to pull him closer. But Nick refused to be hurried; he teased and tormented her with his hands and his mouth, driving her to a frenzy of need. Even when he entered her, he knew her body so well that he was able to take her time and time again to the brink of fulfilment, then drew back, prolonging their climax until he could bear to wait no longer. One final deep thrust toppled them both over the edge and he felt her convulse wildly as he spilled his seed into her.

Afterwards came the sadness of parting as they showered and dressed. Melissa grew despondent; she didn't want to leave, but nor could she stay. When it was time to go she paused and looked around the room.

'We will come back here next year?' she asked urgently, seized by a sudden premonition that they wouldn't.

'Of course we will. Every year, even when we're old and grey,' he assured her. Melissa nodded and slowly followed him out to the car-park.

'I love you.' She clung to him desperately, still gripped by the unknown fear.

'I love you, too.' Nick kissed her one last time. 'Go on, you'll miss your flight.' He watched her drive away, his heart heavy, then he turned and clambered into his Jag to begin the long journey back to Scotland.

CHAPTER 7

The summer passed quickly and exhaustingly for Melissa, as she competed each week on the hard cement courts of America and Canada in preparation for the US Open in September. After her successes at Wimbledon, her ranking had risen to thirty-five and continued to edge up even higher.

Katy had checked the draw for the Open and was fairly optimistic about Melissa's chances of reaching the last sixteen and, with a bit of luck, even further. So far, there had been no more attacks of migraine and Katy was hoping the heat and noise of New York would not trigger one. She soon had something more serious to worry about.

'Katy?' Melissa ventured, rather nervously, on the first Monday of the Championships.

'Mm? What's up?'

'I think . . .' Melissa took a deep breath. 'I think I might be pregnant,' she said miserably.

'Oh, no!' Katy stared at her in horror. 'You can't be!'

'I think I am. That last night in England . . . I forgot to take my pill,' she confessed. 'I decided to take a break from them last week, before the Open, and I should have had my period by now . . .'

'Damn!' Katy said, and had to bite back further recriminations. After all my hard work! Our hard work, she amended fairly. But, hell, do I have to do everything for her? she wondered savagely. 'You're probably worrying needlessly,' she tried to calm Melissa – and herself – while thinking what to do. 'You haven't said anything to anyone else? Not even Nick?'

'No.' Melissa shook her head.

'Good. We'll have to make sure no one knows about this,' Katy said, thinking aloud. 'It would be awful if it became known that you even suspected you might be pregnant – I'll buy a home-pregnancy test; they're very reliable, these days. You go and meet Lisa at the courts, as arranged and don't say anything about this. Leave a urine sample here and I'll do the test, and then come and tell you the result. Okay?'

'Okay,' Melissa agreed, relieved to have spoken her fears out loud. Katy stood up and pushed her red curls under a baseball cap, then picked up her sunglasses.

'I'll be as quick as I can,' she assured her.

Despite her disguise, Katy took the subway to a shopping mall far from Flushing Meadow and bought the kit from a busy drug-store. Back at the hotel, she scanned the instructions, being careful to place all packaging in her bag to dispose of later, fearful that a maid might see the paraphernalia and alert the media. The test took only minutes and her heart sank as she watched the indicator change colour.

'You stupid little bitch,' she swore softly. Nick Lennox was going to win, after all. Maybe not . . . she began thinking furiously as she methodically erased all traces of the test from the room. Maybe not . . .

She hurried to the practice courts and Melissa ran over as soon as she spotted her. Katy forced a cheerful grin.

'Panic over; there's nothing to worry about,' she said brightly.

'You're sure?' Melissa asked eagerly.

'Positive,' Katy said unthinkingly, and inwardly cringed at the word. Fortunately, Melissa didn't notice.

'Thank you, God! Oh, Katy, what a relief! I've been feeling a bit off-colour, I really thought I . . .'

'Just the heat,' Katy interrupted quickly. 'And the worry. Lisa will be wondering what's going on; you'd better get back to work.'

'Sure.' Melissa smiled happily, and dashed back on to the court.

Katy's guilt grew over the days that followed, as did her frustration over what had happened. Melissa, free of her burden, or so she believed, had never played better. In temperatures soaring above one hundred degrees, many players had to be stretchered off court, some requiring hospital treatment for dehydration, but not Melissa. She romped through the early rounds in all three events, gaining confidence daily and hoping she and Jack might take the Mixed Doubles title.

Jack wasn't enjoying the Open. He had avoided Ace since Wimbledon, competing in different tournaments, but knew a clash here was almost inevitable. He was partnering Hal in the Doubles and they were seeded five, one place lower than Ace and his partner, Alfredo Montoya, and both teams progressed to their scheduled meeting in the quarter finals.

The match took place on Stadium Court, late at night, under floodlights. The crowd, mostly exuberant New Yorkers, were rooting for Ace. Ace wanted to win the match so badly that it hurt, and he began the match in superb form, not losing a single point on his own serve and playing excellently at net on his partner's. Jack and Hal held theirs with more difficulty but stayed level to end the first set on a tie-break. Ace and Alfredo won that 10–8, but Jack wasn't too discouraged.

'Ace can't concentrate like this for much longer,' he told Hal, as they towelled down at the change-over. 'He'll hit a slump sooner or later.' Jack knew just how to provoke the loss of form, too. For five years he'd had to hold Ace together after a row over bad calls, so he began hitting for the lines, knowing Ace would inevitably disagree with some of the decisions.

The argument, when it came, surpassed even Jack's expectations. He had forgotten that Montoya was as excitable as Ace; the Mexican joined in the haranguing of the umpire and the linesman concerned, earning them a warning for an audible obscenity. An insulting comment regarding the umpire's mother earned them a point deducted and still they continued yelling.

Jack just stood and grinned at Ace, inflaming him further. The next penalty would be a whole game awarded to Hal and Jack; after that, disqualification.

'You're losing it, buddy boy,' Jack goaded Ace, but that was one taunt too many. Ace pulled himself together, spoke urgently to Montoya, and they continued the match. Instead, it was Hal who went to pieces; unnerved by the hostility of his home crowd, he served a double fault to lose the game, and hand their opponents the advantage. Ace laughed, gesturing obscenely at Jack.

'I can't believe I did that,' Hal groaned, throwing his racket to the ground as they sat down. Jack couldn't believe it, either, but he used the ninety seconds to reassure and encourage his partner.

'Ace is knackered; he'll run out of steam,' he said confidently. He was right, Ace was exhausted but adrenalin and sheer determination forced him on, plus the vociferous support of the crowd.

'Hey! I'm American too!' Hal yelled angrily at a group of particularly vocal Delaney fans. Thoroughly dispirited, he again lost his serve and the match.

Jack approached the net warily, bracing himself for Ace's gloating.

'You lost it . . . buddy boy,' Ace threw back Jack's earlier words, and laughed. 'I told you you'd never win another Grand Slam without me!'

'I'd prefer to never win another match than partner you again!' Jack gritted out.

Katy pondered long and hard over how best to deal with Melissa's pregnancy. To continue with it was out of the question, so far as Katy was concerned, but she sensed Melissa would balk at the obvious solution. Katy needed help and, after casting around in her mind for someone to advise her, she discarded everyone but Ace. She didn't like him, or trust him, but eventually sought him out at his hotel.

'I need your help. Or, rather, Melissa does,' she amended. Ace hid his surprise.

'Why come to me and not Jack?' he asked casually.

'I can't go to Jack with this; he might come over all noble,' she said disgustedly. She might have confided in him, once, but not now – he'd made it perfectly clear that she was only on the scene to help Melissa's career! 'Melissa's pregnant,' she blurted out. Ace whistled soundlessly, then he arched one brow when she added, 'Melissa doesn't know.'

'Excuse me?' He wasn't sure he'd heard correctly.

'I lied to her about the result of a pregnancy test,' Katy admitted.

'Why? Don't you think she'll notice, sooner or later?' he asked sarcastically.

'Of course she will! But I couldn't tell her the truth, not at the start of the Open, could I?'

'I guess not. She is the goose that lays your golden eggs these days, isn't she?' Ace said mockingly. Katy flushed.

'That isn't the reason I lied. It isn't,' she insisted, at his sceptical glance.

'You were hoping she'd miscarry, playing three events in this punishing heat,' he said suddenly. Katy's deepening flush confirmed his guess, and he grinned. 'Why do you think I care whether she has a kid or not?'

'Nick Lennox will be in heaven if she quits tennis, marries him and starts a family,' Katy replied obliquely. Ace's grin vanished.

'What do you want me to do?' he asked curtly.

'Help me convince her to get rid of it. And you must know of a clinic, a really discreet place,' she stressed. 'Melissa is one of the sport's blue-eyed girls right now – if this got out, the Press would crucify her and she could

143

kiss goodbye to all those sponsorship deals Greg Reynolds has lined up for her.'

'Okay, I'll help you,' Ace decided. 'First, you mustn't tell her you lied, or she'll lose confidence in you. Persuade her to take another test . . . after Jack's left New York,' he added. 'I'll make the arrangements and, when it's over, we'll send her home to Rose to recuperate.'

'She'll have to pull out of at least one tournament,' Katy frowned. 'How do I explain that?'

'Say she's exhausted,' Ace shrugged. 'But don't let a doctor near her, for God's sake. If necessary, she'll just have to pay the fine for a late withdrawal; that's the least of your worries. I'll phone you when it's all organized,' he said. Katy nodded, and took her leave, feeling distinctly uncomfortable about what she was doing. But it wasn't as if she was forcing Melissa to have an abortion, she reasoned; it would be her choice . . .

'Melissa? Have you had your period yet?' Katy asked casually, several days later; the Open had drawn to a close and Jack had called in to say goodbye on his way to the airport.

'No,' Melissa frowned. 'Do you think something's wrong?'

'It might be a good idea to do another pregnancy test,' Katy said, getting to her feet. 'I'll go and buy another kit, just to be sure.

'Okay,' Melissa agreed, her anxiety returning as Katy left on her errand. Katy had, in fact, already made the purchase and phoned Ace from the hotel lobby to arrange a time for him to call, supposedly by chance.

He could hear Melissa sobbing when he knocked on the door, but pretended not to notice her distress when Katy first ushered him inside.

'Hi, I just popped in to . . . hey, what's wrong?' he asked, going over to Melissa and putting one arm around her shoulder.

'Nothing,' she sniffled and he raised his eyebrows in a 'now what?' grimace at Katy. He could hardly offer a solution to the problem if she wouldn't confide in him!

'Tell him,' Katy urged quickly. 'He's probably used to this situation,' she added waspishly.

'I have to talk to Nick . . .' Melissa began.

'No! Not until you've decided what to do,' Katy stood guard over the phone.

'Will one of you please tell me what's going on?' Ace asked. 'Come on, honey, I might be able to help,' he hugged Melissa, genuinely sorry for her predicament.

'I don't know what to do!' she wailed. 'Oh, Ace, I'm pregnant!' She buried her face in his shoulder and he wrapped his arms around her.

'It's okay; it can be sorted out,' he soothed her.

'How?'

'You don't have to go ahead with it,' he said, choosing his words carefully.

'You mean, have an abortion? I can't do that!' Melissa pulled away from him.

'Why not?' Katy put in. 'You don't want a baby, do you?'

'No, of course I don't, but . . . I just wish I weren't pregnant,' she said, her lip trembling.

'Well, you are,' Katy said bluntly. 'But you don't have to be – it can all be over in a day or so, and you can

145

get on with your life.' She softened her tone. 'Melissa, you've worked too hard to throw away your career for a kid you don't even want!'

'But Nick will want me to have it, and it's his baby, too,' Melissa said.

'He's not pregnant. And he won't have to give up everything he's worked for, but you will.'

'Maybe not; maybe I can have both,' Melissa said slowly. The first, numbing shock had eased, enabling her to think. 'I'm only nineteen; I could regain my ranking . . .'

'No, you couldn't,' Katy said flatly. 'Even if you had the healthiest pregnancy on record and the easiest birth, you'd never make up the lost ground; it's been tried before. But, just supposing you could,' she hurried on, sensing Melissa was about to interrupt. 'What about the baby? Who's going to look after it on a daily basis? You won't be able to, not if you're serious about returning to tennis – are you going to leave it in Scotland for Nick and Sheena to raise?' Oh, nice touch, Ace thought admiringly; Katy didn't really need his help at all!

'No, I . . .' Melissa frowned and shook her head slightly.

'You don't seriously believe Nick will let you traipse all over the world with his baby in tow, do you? Not when he can give it a settled home?' Katy asked incredulously. Knowing she was taking a huge risk, she picked up the phone and held it out to Melissa. 'If you tell him you're pregnant, he'll lock you up in that castle of his and never let you out,' she warned. Melissa hesitated, then turned away. Katy flashed a look of triumph at Ace.

146

'Leave it to me, honey,' he said softly to Melissa. 'Don't worry; it will be over soon.' He walked towards the door and jerked his head at Katy, indicating she should follow. 'Here,' he handed her a card, bearing the name and address of the clinic. 'She's booked in for ten tomorrow morning, name of Smith. For God's sake, pay the bill with cash. And here's a couple of sleeping pills to keep her quiet until then.' Katy nodded, pocketing the card and pills.

'How long will she be in?'

'I'm not sure – I've never hung around long enough to collect anyone afterwards,' he admitted cheerfully. 'Overnight, I expect. Book her a flight for Tuesday and ring Rose – just tell her Melissa's exhausted and needs a rest. What are you going to do about His Lordship?'

'Nick? Nothing,' Katy shrugged. 'He's already phoned her today, so he won't ring again until it's too late to stop her. He need never know,' she added airily.

Nick grew increasingly worried when he was unable to speak to Melissa. At first, he accepted Katy's explanations that she was attending a Press interview, or shopping, but began to feel something was wrong when Melissa failed to return his calls. Then he discovered she had checked out of her hotel in New York, but had not arrived at the next stop on the tour.

Striving to keep calm, he phoned Bellwood.

'She's here,' Rose told him, to his relief.

'Can I speak to her?'

'She's sleeping,' Rose said, reluctant to wake her. 'She's absolutely exhausted, Nick. She's hardly spoken two words since I picked her up at the airport.'

'Is she ill?' he asked, concerned.

'She says not; just tired after the Open. She played a great many matches and it was extremely hot for the whole two weeks. I kept telling her she was working too hard but you know how ambitious she is. Katy phoned to tell me she was sending her home for a break – apparently, she suffered a migraine and Katy decided to pull her out of this week's tournament.'

'I see,' Nick said slowly; it sounded plausible, but why hadn't Katy told him the truth? If it was the truth . . .

'Why don't you come down?' Rose suggested. 'I'm sure she'd love to see you and she should be feeling better after another good night's sleep.'

'Yes, I'll drive down tomorrow,' Nick decided, although he wasn't as sure as Rose seemed to be that Melissa would be pleased to see him. He hoped his fears were groundless, but he couldn't quite rid himself of the suspicion that Melissa had been unfaithful to him.

He'd always known it might happen; she was only nineteen, and they spent more time apart than together. She had been in New York for a couple of weeks with Ace and Hal in pursuit, and Nick didn't trust either of them as far as he could throw them! He thought back to the last conversation he'd had with Melissa; she'd been her usual bright self. He shook his head and, with some difficulty, stopped torturing himself. He'd discover the truth, soon enough.

Melissa was still asleep when Rose checked on her at tea-time and again in the evening. She still looked . . . haggard, Rose thought worriedly. Despite her healthy tan, her features were drawn and dark rings of fatigue circled her eyes. Rose left sandwiches and milk on the bedside table and quietly left the room, hoping news of Nick's impending arrival would lift Melissa's spirits.

'Nick's coming here? Today?' Melissa stared at her mother in horror, then she pushed back the bed-clothes. 'I have to leave, I can't face him yet,' she said desperately. 'Will you take me to the airport?'

'No, I will not,' Rose said firmly, pushing her back against the pillows. 'You're staying right there,' she said, sitting down on the bed to prevent Melissa's escape. 'Now. Why don't you want to see Nick?'

'I can't.' Melissa's face crumpled. 'He'll hate me,' she whispered.

'Of course he won't,' Rose said gently, smoothing her hair back from her face, then she sighed. 'What is it? Or should I say who is it?' she asked, jumping to the same conclusion as Nick. Melissa shook her head.

'I can't tell you; you'll hate me, too,' she said miserably.

'Never,' she declared stoutly. 'No matter what you've done, I could never hate you, darling. You'll under-stand that when you have children of your own . . .' she broke off when Melissa began to cry, dreadful huge sobs torn from her body. Rose pulled her into her arms and began to rock her, trying to soothe her. 'Tell me, please,' she urged.

'I didn't want to do it! But . . . I didn't want to be pregnant, either,' Melissa wept. Rose closed her eyes; oh God, no, not that. She hid her shock and dismay, and gently coaxed the details from Melissa; frowning as she realized the speed with which it had all been done.

149

Surely, even in New York, it couldn't have been arranged so quickly?

'Didn't you have counselling before . . . the operation?' she asked.

'No. I just wanted the nightmare to be over. I thought that once I'd done it, that would be it. But it isn't.

'No, I don't suppose it is,' Rose sighed.

'Will you tell Nick I can't see him? Or that I've already left?' Melissa asked desperately.

'No,' Rose said regretfully. 'He's already worried about you. You'll have to see him.'

'What do I say to him?' Melissa looked at her mother as if she possessed the answer, and Rose couldn't meet her gaze.

'I've no idea,' she said helplessly. 'He'll be hurt, and angry. But you have to tell him the truth . . . oh, God!' she gasped, seeing a flash of sunlight on metal as the silver-grey Jag eased up the drive. 'He's here already, he must have driven half the night.'

'Oh, no!' Melissa buried her head beneath the bed covers. Rose hesitated, then went slowly downstairs to meet Nick.

'Hello, how is she this morning?' Nick greeted her.

'Not good, I'm afraid,' Rose faltered. Nick sensed her distress and felt sick; his gut reaction had been right. 'Try and understand,' Rose pleaded, and he drew a deep breath, then nodded.

'Where is she?'

'Still in bed,' Rose told him, and watched sadly as he slowly climbed the stairs.

Nick paused before entering her bedroom; he'd

thought himself prepared for this, but he wasn't. He was never tempted to stray; he knew what he had with Melissa was special, but she had nothing to compare their lovemaking with. At least, she hadn't . . . He drew another deep, steadying breath, then stepped inside the room. She was lying in bed, her face averted, with unmistakable signs of recent tears on her cheek.

'Please look at me,' Nick said quietly.

'I can't,' Melissa whispered.

'Do you still love me?'

'Yes,' she nodded, and he felt a slight lessening of the pain.

'If you love me, we can work it out,' he said calmly, walking forward to sit on the edge of the bed, but making no attempt to touch her. Melissa looked up, hope flaring.

'Did Mum tell you . . .?'

'No. Tell me – what, Melissa?' His voice was strained and she bit her lip; she had to tell him. How could she ever have been so stupid as to believe she could some-how keep this from him and continue as before?

She sat up straighter, her fingers nervously pleating the sheet. She peeked at him once again, briefly, then had to look away, unable to bear the pain and concern evident on his face. Even more unbearable would be the icy contempt and hatred he would feel once he knew what she had done.

'Melissa! You're driving me crazy!' Nick raked his fingers through his hair. 'Tell me what's happened!'

'It was . . . that last night we spent together at the Red Lion,' she began haltingly. 'I forgot to take my contra-ceptive pill . . .' she stopped; God, this was so hard!

'You're pregnant? But that's wonderful . . .'

'I was; I'm not now,' Melissa interrupted quickly.

'You've had a miscarriage.' Nick offered her an easy way out, making a statement, not asking a question. Melissa wanted desperately to lie, and sensed he also wanted her to; he'd accept it, or pretend to, for now, at least. But their relationship couldn't survive it.

'No.' The whispered denial hovered in the air, shattering Nick's hopes and dreams. He stood and moved to the window, staring unseeingly outside while he fought for control.

Melissa made a tentative move towards him, but his tightly clenched fists and the rigid set to his jaw robbed her of the courage to try and explain; to plead for understanding and forgiveness. The silence lengthened and the tension in the room became unbearable.

'Nick?' she ventured timidly. He gave vent to a huge sigh, then turned his head slowly and looked directly at her, his grey eyes cold and assessing, as if he were wondering why he had ever loved her, Melissa thought wretchedly, trying not to flinch beneath his icy gaze.

But, when he finally spoke, his voice was surprisingly calm and controlled, betraying nothing of his emotions.

'It's strange,' he said, almost musingly. 'The one word reverberating in my brain is "why?", which is stupid, because I know why. Your career.' The last was spat at her and she cringed. 'Didn't I even deserve to be consulted?' he ground out.

'I'm sorry.' Tears spilled over and she gazed at him imploringly. 'I do love you . . .' she began, but the harsh sound of his bitter laughter stopped her. She stared as he turned and walked towards the door, and was galvanized

152

into action when she realized he was going to leave, scrambling out of bed and hurrying after him.

'Don't . . . please, Nick. What are you going to do?'

'I'm going back to Glengarry.' He paused and looked down at her, and a small smile touched his lips. 'I'm going to do what I should have done a long time ago – marry Sheena.'

'No!' Melissa reached for his arm but he shrugged her off and headed for the stairs. She ran after him, sobbing, but Rose restrained her.

'Not now, darling, he needs time,' she said. 'You must give him time.' Melissa sank to her knees, crying as if her heart were breaking.

The staff at Glengarry House had already retired to bed and Sheena was about to follow suit when she heard Nick return. She went to greet him, but her welcoming smile faded when she caught sight of him.

'Whatever's wrong?' she asked fearfully. 'Why are you back so soon?' Nick didn't bother to answer and she trailed after him as he walked past her and into the dining-room. Her eyes widened when he took two full bottles of scotch from the cabinet. 'Nick?' She stood determinedly in his path as he tried to pass her, and he focused on her, briefly, his eyes chips of ice.

'I intend getting extremely drunk, and it won't be a pretty sight, so I suggest you go to bed and forget you saw me,' he growled. Sheena stepped aside and watched him wearily climb the stairs, then she went into the kitchen and microwaved some leftover casserole, adding bread and cheese to the tray before carrying it to his room.

She knocked and entered, then almost dropped the tray in alarm. The window was wide open and Nick was leaning dangerously far out.

'Nick!' Sheena screamed. To her relief, he turned and closed the window. 'Oh, God,' she sighed, placing the food carefully on the bedside table. 'I thought . . .'

'What? That I was going to jump?' Nick laughed mirthlessly. 'No. There's already been too much death in our family,' he added savagely.

'What's happened? Is it Caroline, or one of the girls?'

'No.' He wrenched the top off the bottle of scotch and took a long swallow. Sheena glanced away, hating to watch him, and noticed the empty space on the wall where Melissa's portrait usually hung.

'Melissa's picture!' she exclaimed. Nick jerked his head towards the window.

'I chucked it out.' He took another pull at the whisky. 'It's over. And don't pretend you're sorry,' he warned.

'I am truly sorry to see you hurting like this,' she said softly. Nick looked at her, hard.

'Maybe you are,' he said indifferently.

'Has she found someone else?' Sheena asked.

'No.' Nick slumped into an armchair, swigging more scotch. It wasn't working; instead of numbing his senses, it was melting the ice around his heart and only adding to the pain. He closed his eyes against it, but then all he could see was Melissa – the face of an angel and a heart of stone. How could she have done it? He wasn't aware he had spoken aloud until Sheena asked,

'How could she have done what?'

'Abort my child,' he said flatly.

154

'Oh, God, that's awful. Nick, I'm so sorry,' she said. He shrugged and drank some more. Sheena inched nearer the second bottle and hid it behind her back.

'She didn't even tell me; she knew I'd have welcomed it. How can hitting a tennis ball be more important to her than the life of a child?' He took another large slug of the scotch, then regarded Sheena thoughtfully. He hadn't meant his parting shot to Melissa, but what the hell? He needed an heir. 'How about we both settle for second best and get married?' he asked casually. Sheena hesitated, sorely tempted. To live at Glengarry House forever? To have a husband and children, the settled life she'd craved? She glanced at Nick: he was leaning back in his chair, eyes closed, obviously not caring what her answer would be.

'Ask me again, when you're over Melissa,' she said quietly. She moved to the door, taking the second bottle with her. Hopefully, by the time he had emptied the first, he would have forgotten about the spare, or be in no condition to go in search of it.

After replacing the scotch in the dining-room, she took a flashlight and ventured out into the courtyard, searching for the portrait she felt sure Nick would regret discarding. She found it directly beneath his window and carried it indoors to inspect it for damage. The frame had splintered along one side but the canvas itself remained intact. Sheena stared at Melissa's happy, smiling face and shook her head slightly.

'You silly girl,' she said softly. Strangely, she felt pity for Melissa, as well as for Nick. She'd wanted her out of his life, but not in this way.

* * *

The pain of Nick's hangover almost equalled the ferocity of the migraine which afflicted Melissa after his departure. But, while he strode around the Glengarry estate, barking orders and finding fault, Melissa huddled miserably in bed with the curtains closed. She didn't take any medication; she felt she deserved to suffer the blinding agony of the worst-ever attack, and at least it stopped her thinking about the horrors of the abortion or of losing Nick.

It was Rose's threat to summon both the family doctor and Daniel that finally roused her. Pale and nauseous, she showered and washed her hair, then forced down some soup while her mother hovered over her.

'Don't tell Dad, please.' Melissa begged. 'Or Jack.'

'I won't. Your father thinks exhaustion triggered a migraine, that's all,' Rose assured her. And Jack's not speaking to me at all, she thought sadly.

Katy phoned that evening to check on Melissa's progress. She had already called twice and knew about Nick's visit and the resulting migraine – something else for her to feel guilty about.

'How are you feeling?'

'Physically, I'm okay now,' Melissa replied listlessly.

'I'm not trying to push you,' Katy hesitated, 'but you're entered in the tournament in Zurich next week. Questions will be asked if you don't show up.' Melissa closed her eyes: what did it matter? she thought wearily.

'Melissa? Getting back to work and making a success of your career is the only thing that makes sense,' Katy said earnestly.

'I guess you're right,' Melissa agreed. 'I can't feel

worse than I do right now. I'll fly out tomorrow,' she decided.

Rose, tight-lipped with disapproval, drove her to Heathrow.

'It's too soon,' she said repeatedly. 'Stay with me until you feel strong again,' she urged.

'No, I'll go crazy if I just mope around,' Melissa told her, but, all the same, she clung tightly to Rose at the moment of departure.

'Will I ever be happy again?' she whispered, and Rose struggled to contain her tears. 'Sorry, unfair question. Don't try to answer it.' Melissa made a brave attempt at a smile and kissed her mother's cheek. ''Bye, Mum.'

'Goodbye, darling. Take care,' Rose said sadly.

When Ace learned of Melissa's departure, he made his own travel plans, deliberately arriving in England in the early hours of the morning. He hadn't even phoned Rose since the abortion, so had no idea how much she knew of his part in it, but figured any necessary fence-mending could be accomplished more easily if Rose were only half-awake.

He paid off the cab on the road-side and walked slowly up the drive, feasting his eyes on the ancient manor house bathed silver in the moonlight. Owning Bellwood thrilled him to the core; he had come a long way from the slums of LA to this piece of English history, a house mentioned in guide books and where royalty had stayed.

He let himself into the house and stealthily climbed the stairs, dumping his holdall in the guest room which was supposedly 'his', so far as other people were concerned, and shed his clothes before entering the master bedroom which Rose had once shared with Daniel.

'What!' Rose gasped, waking abruptly when he slipped into bed beside her. She tried to sit up, but Ace pulled her back down.

'Sh, it's me,' he murmured, nibbling her ear and sliding his hands beneath her nightdress.

'Ace!' Rose hastily pulled her stomach in, wishing she had not indulged in so much comfort eating since Melissa had left.

'What the hell are you wearing?' he demanded, tugging at yards and yards of material.

'It's chilly here at night,' Rose said defensively, as she discarded the offending garment.

'Not now I'm here,' Ace declared. He pushed her back on to the mattress and began running his hands over her lush curves, cupping her full breasts and suckling greedily. He heard her breathing quicken and slipped one hand between her legs.

'Is Melissa okay?' he asked, nuzzling her neck.

'No, she's . . . ooh, that's nice,' Rose sighed, then put her hand firmly over his to stop the delicious stroking; she couldn't think straight while he was doing that! 'Why didn't you tell me?' she asked reproachfully. 'How could you make the arrangements without talking to me about it?'

'There wasn't time for a family conference,' Ace said patiently. 'Katy contacted me when she couldn't find Jack,' he lied. 'She and Melissa were panicking like crazy; the whole world would have known about it if I'd not sorted it out. Sure, she's feeling bad right now, but she didn't want the kid. She's going to be a great player.'

'She can't cuddle a tennis trophy,' Rose said sadly. 'She could have resumed her career after the birth; I'd have travelled with her and looked after the baby.'

'I'm sorry,' Ace tried to sound penitent. 'I thought I was doing the right thing. She'll have children one day, when she's ready.' He caught her fingers in his mouth and then planted a kiss on the palm of her hand. 'His Lordship ought to be shot for getting her into such a mess,' he added self-righteously, although the sentiment rather lacked credibility when, a short time later, he had to be reminded to put on a condom. But, by then, Rose had temporarily forgotten her daughter's plight.

CHAPTER 8

After a shaky start, losing two first round matches and enduring several attacks of migraine, Melissa buckled down to some hard work. She pushed herself mercilessly, making herself stronger and fitter, practising endlessly to hone her skills and continue her rise up the rankings. Also she hoped that, by going to bed exhausted every night, she might fall asleep before futile regrets crowded her brain to keep her awake and brooding.

The pain didn't lessen; she missed Nick terribly, for, despite their long separations, they had phoned each other almost every day. At least a hundred times, she picked up the phone and began dialling, so strong was her need to talk to him, but always she resisted the urge. After all, what could she possibly say? As for the baby . . . she shied away from even thinking about it; the shock of discovering she was pregnant, the horror of the clinic, the confrontation with Nick – all had taken on a nightmarish quality, as if it had happened to someone else. But the loneliness and emptiness were real enough.

Her relationship with Katy had undergone a subtle change; the knowledge of the abortion hovered, unspoken, between them. And, now that hotel costs were no longer an issue, they stopped sharing rooms, and Melissa began spending most of her free time with Lisa Renwick.

'Are you going to England for Christmas?' Lisa asked one day, while they waited to be called onto court for a Doubles match.

'No,' Melissa shook her head: she didn't want any reminders of the last year spent at Glengarry with Nick. 'I've already told my parents I'm going to go and soak up the sun somewhere.'

'Come to California with me,' Lisa suggested.

'Thanks, I'd like that,' Melissa accepted gratefully.

Hal was already in San Francisco when Lisa and Melissa arrived and he was delighted to have Melissa in his parents' home, especially when he learned of her break-up with Nick. But Lisa knew Melissa was deeply unhappy about it and warned him to keep his distance, so he was careful to treat her with the same casual friendliness he accorded all Lisa's guests.

Joshua and Hannah Renwick, both busy successful lawyers, also welcomed her warmly. Melissa quickly discovered that Lisa's and Hal's parents held 'open house', and there was a constant stream of visitors. Many of Hal's and Lisa's friends from school and college dropped in to lounge around the pool and exchange gossip, or to play tennis. The three professional players avoided the court, however, needing to relax and unwind after a gruelling year. It didn't seem at all like Christmas to Melissa, which was a bonus, and the holiday sped by.

On her last evening there, Melissa finished packing

161

and wandered outside to lie on a sun-lounger, enjoying the mild night air and watching the star-filled sky.

'May I join you? Or did you come out here to be alone?' She looked up to see Hal standing over her, and smiled a welcome.

'No, it was just a little too hot and noisy indoors,' she said, for, as usual, the house was full of guests. Hal pulled up another sun-bed and sat, facing her. Despite Lisa's warning, he hadn't been able to let Melissa leave without talking seriously with her.

'You've been putting on a brave show, but you're not happy, are you?' he asked quietly. Melissa sighed.

'No,' she admitted.

'I'm sorry. Is it that guy you broke up with – Nick?'

'Yes. He doesn't want me any more,' she said sadly.

'Is he blind or senile?' Hal asked interestedly, and she smiled slightly.

'Neither. I hurt him and he won't ever forgive me,' she whispered, blinking back tears. Hal longed to take her in his arms but instead merely reached out to touch her hand.

'I can't believe you did anything so terrible you can't be forgiven,' he said gently. 'Do you want to talk about it? My shoulders are broad enough for problems and soft enough to mop up tears,' he said, reminding her of Jack.

'Oh, Hal.' Suddenly she felt the need to unburden herself. 'Promise you won't tell anyone? Not even Lisa?'

'I promise.'

'Nick hates me because,' she paused to take a deep breath, 'because I had an abortion,' she muttered, averting her gaze lest she see contempt in his eyes.

'Oh, you poor darling!' he exclaimed. 'What an appalling thing to go through! And he hates you? He should hate himself for being so damned irresponsible!'

'You don't think I'm awful?' Melissa asked, hardly daring to believe his reaction, yet it was obviously sincere.

'Of course not. What else could you have done?'

'I could have had the baby . . .'

'At nineteen? It would have ended your career just when you're beginning to make your mark. Didn't he consider that?'

'My career was never very high on Nick's list of priorities,' Melissa said bitterly.

'No, I think we all received that particular message, loud and clear,' Hal agreed slowly. 'The arrogant pig!'

'But I didn't even tell him I was pregnant,' Melissa said, wondering why on earth she was playing devil's advocate. 'I knew he would never agree to a termination.'

'It wasn't his decision to make,' Hal said hotly. 'You're not married to the guy; it's your body and your career at stake. You did the right thing, Melissa,' he said earnestly, 'so stop beating yourself up about it.'

'Do you really mean that?' Melissa asked, beginning to feel some of the weight of guilt lifting from her shoulders. If a nice guy like Hal felt she'd done nothing wrong, then perhaps she wasn't so dreadful after all, she reasoned. It didn't occur to her, or Hal, that he might not be quite so philosophical had it been his baby she had conceived.

'You bet I do,' he said firmly. 'And, I admit to being biased here,' he grinned at her. 'But I think you're better off without him. Arrogant pig,' he repeated scornfully.

The 'arrogant pig' under discussion was at Glengarry, trying, unsuccessfully, not to think about Melissa. The portrait, repaired and handed silently back to him by Sheena, was stashed away in his wardrobe, facing the wall. He had invited his sister Caroline, her husband Gerald, and his two nieces to spend Christmas and New Year in Scotland, hoping their presence would help ease his loneliness and despair. It didn't, and he spent most of his time outdoors, leaving Sheena with the task of entertaining his family.

One afternoon, Sheena and Caroline took tea in the smaller, cosy sitting-room, neither woman noticing that Juliet was curled up on the window-seat, with the curtains drawn to afford her a better view of the snow falling steadily outside.

'Whatever's wrong with Nick?' Caroline asked, settling herself comfortably by the fire and accepting a cup of tea.

'Melissa Farrell,' Sheena said succinctly. Juliet overheard and decided to remain in hiding. 'He doesn't see her any more.'

'I gathered that much,' Caroline sniffed. 'He bit my head off when I asked if she would be coming here for part of the holidays. I'm not really surprised – she's so much younger and constantly travelling. Another man, I suppose?' she arched one brow questioningly.

'No, it was something worse than that,' Sheena confided. 'He hasn't mentioned it since, so don't say anything . . .' she hesitated.

'I won't breathe a word,' Caroline promised hastily.

'Well,' Sheena paused again, not sure of the wisdom of her actions. Caroline leaned forward eagerly.

'Yes?' she prompted.

'Melissa had an abortion,' Sheena said quietly. Juliet's gasp was fortunately drowned out by a similar exclamation from her mother.

'No! How awful! Poor Nick,' she sighed, and shook her head sorrowfully, then looked across at Sheena. 'At least this leaves the field open for you, dear.'

'He did suggest marriage, but I don't want him, not in the state he is now,' Sheena said firmly. 'I think he sees a woman in Edinburgh, maybe more than one. All I know is that he often stays out all night – not that it seems to do him much good, he always comes home in a foul temper,' she added feelingly.

'How long has he been like this?'

'More than three months,' Sheena sighed. 'I thought Rory was a moody devil, but it never lasted very long with him. But Nick . . .' she shook her head despairingly. 'He's lost interest in everything. He was so full of ideas and plans for the estate and the village, but he's abandoned them all. He just doesn't seem to care about his heritage – the only thing he bothers with are his tennis lessons, as if they're some link to Melissa.'

'Oh, nonsense.' That was far too whimsical an idea for Caroline to consider. 'He's always been keen on sports.'

'I know, but he only began tennis lessons to please her,' Sheena insisted. 'I think he still loves her.'

'How could he, after what she did? No, he'll soon be back to his old self and, this time next year, you'll be

Lady Lennox,' Caroline said confidently. Sheena shrugged; she wasn't so sure.

Juliet had to wait, shivering with cold, until the two women had left the room before she could emerge from her hiding place. She stretched her cramped limbs in front of the fire and pinched the remaining sandwiches and cake before scampering off to tell Jessica what she had learned.

When Nick came down to breakfast the next morning wearing a track suit and carrying a tennis racket, Juliet piped up.

'May I come with you, Uncle Nick?'

'Yes, I suppose so,' he said grudgingly, since he was unable to think of a good reason to refuse. And he was uncomfortably aware that, so far, he had been a lousy host.

'I'm going to be a professional player,' Juliet told him, once they were in the car.

'I seem to recall your sister saying the same thing,' Nick remarked.

'I know, but I'm better than Jess. I can beat her easily and, one day,' she cast a sideways glance at Nick, 'I'm going to beat Melissa Farrell. I hate her.'

'You do? Why?' Nick kept his face and voice impassive.

'Don't you remember how she humiliated poor Jess at Eastbourne?' Juliet demanded. 'Jess could have been good, but she never played enough. I want to go to a tennis camp in the States and play every day,' she confided. 'Mummy would let me go, but Daddy says it's too expensive,' she added glumly. Nick made no comment but, when they arrived at the club, he gave up his court time and asked Gavin Bruce to put Juliet through her paces.

Nick watched from the sidelines and it seemed to him that Juliet was indeed better than her older sister, and later discussed with Gavin the pros and cons of the intensive training provided by the various tennis academies.

'If she thinks it will be an extended holiday in the sun, she's in for a rude awakening,' Gavin said. 'She'd have to work extremely hard. We hear a lot about the success stories – Agassi, Seles etc., but we never hear of the thousands who fail.'

'So it would either make her or break her?' Nick said thoughtfully, and turned to Juliet. 'If your parents agree, I'll help with the expenses,' he told her.

'Thank you, Uncle Nick!' Juliet squealed with delight. 'I'll work hard. And I meant what I said earlier – one day, I'll thrash Melissa Farrell!'

'That's not the reason I'm helping you,' Nick said sharply, but silently wondered about his motive. Had he stooped that low? Did he really want to witness Melissa's humiliation at the hands of his niece and know that he had helped bring it about?

From San Francisco Melissa flew to Perth, where she and Jack represented Great Britain in a Mixed Doubles event. From there, they travelled together to Sydney for a warm-up tournament prior to the Australian Open in Melbourne the following week. Katy was already in Sydney awaiting Melissa's arrival, and they were due to meet up with the Renwicks again in Melbourne.

'Are you and Hal an item now?' Jack asked.

'No.' Melissa involuntarily glanced down at the sapphire and diamond ring she still wore.

'No chance of a reconciliation?' Jack asked gently, noticing the gesture. Melissa simply shook her head and fell silent, debating whether or not to take her brother into her confidence.

'Jack? If Katy had become pregnant while you were together, what would you have done about it?' she asked, rather too casually. Oh God, was that the cause of the break-up? Jack thought wretchedly. Poor little kid.

'We were always careful that wouldn't happen,' he began sternly, although she had no doubt learned her lesson. 'I guess I would have gone along with whatever Katy wanted,' he said slowly. 'I wouldn't have married her, but I'd have supported her if she'd wanted to keep the child.'

'And if she didn't?' Melissa persisted, and Jack shrugged.

'Like I said, I'd have gone along with what she decided – she would have had a lot more to lose.'

'Mm,' Melissa smiled and relaxed a little. Jack agreed with Hal; perhaps she wasn't so dreadful, after all. If only Nick could understand what a dilemma she had faced; would consider how much of an ordeal she had suffered, and was still suffering.

Jack dropped the subject, but realized that, if his guess were correct and Melissa had undergone an abortion, Katy must have known about it. As soon as he could, he sought her out.

'I want to talk to you,' he said brusquely, with an unusually stern expression on his face.

'Melissa's abortion,' he said.

'She told you?' Katy gaped in surprise: Melissa had been adamant that it remain a secret.

'No, you just did,' Jack said grimly. 'You're supposed to be looking after her, Katy.'

'What do you expect me to do – supervise her sex sessions to make sure she takes precautions?' Katy demanded crossly. Jack sighed, raking his fingers through his hair.

'No, of course not. I'm sorry, that was unfair,' he acknowledged readily, and Katy's anger melted as quickly as it had flared. 'You obviously handled it well; there's never been so much as a hint of gossip about it. Just who does know?' he asked.

'Only your mother and Nick, unless Melissa's confided in Lisa. Oh, and Ace of course.'

'Ace knows?' Jack asked, appalled. 'Oh, hell!' he groaned.

'I couldn't think of anyone better to advise us,' Katy said defensively. 'You had already left New York and I could hardly walk into the locker-room and ask if anyone knew of a discreet abortion clinic!'

'No, but . . . oh, hell!' Jack ground out. 'Don't trust Ace with any more secrets!' He turned and strode off, thinking furiously. Damn, I'll have to be nice to the bastard, he thought. If Ace decided to go public about his affair with Rose, and Melissa's abortion, the Press would have a field day!

Unlike Melissa, Jack always looked at the draw, checking out potential opponents and already knew that, if he and Ace both won their first round matches, they would have to compete against each

169

other. He thought, hoped, that Ace would lose his encounter with the number four seed but, instead, he pulled off one of the best Singles victories of his career and, on Wednesday afternoon, the two former friends and Doubles partners faced each other.

For the first time in his career, Jack 'tanked', that is, he deliberately lost a match. He was afraid of what Ace, disgruntled and vindictive in defeat, might say at the Press interview. Jack knew Ace's game better than anyone and could read and return the lightning Delaney serves which left most players floundering.

But not this time: he was consistently a split-second late, too consistently, perhaps, and a narrow-eyed, speculative glance from Ace at the conclusion of the second set caused him to raise his game. Jack won the third and fourth sets before allowing Ace to regain supremacy in the fifth to take the match. He knew he could have won and the defeat was a bitter one; the first Grand Slam of the year and the number four seed out of his path . . .

'You're sharp today – you must be off the booze,' Jack said pleasantly, as they shook hands.

'Yeah, I am,' Ace nodded, looking rather wary. 'Not tomorrow, though – I'm throwing a birthday party for Al Montoya. Do you want to come along?' he added casually.

'Sure,' Jack agreed amiably: anything to keep the so-and-so happy, he thought savagely, as he gathered up his rackets and towels and headed back towards the locker-room. Scores of fans clamoured for autographs and Ace scribbled a few before losing patience and walking off, but Jack dallied longer than usual, signing programmes and chatting to people in the crowd in a bid to avoid further conversation with Ace.

He felt he couldn't avoid the party, though, but purposely arrived late. As he had hoped, a large crowd had already gathered in Ace's hotel suite, but his heart sank when he saw Melissa was one of the guests. At least Hal was also there, hovering over her, his arm possessively around her waist.

'Glad you could make it.' Ace pushed his way through the throng to greet Jack. 'Grab a drink, or a girl.'

'Can't I have both?' Jack forced a smile, and Ace grinned.

'Help yourself.' He hesitated, then asked quietly, 'Stopped sulking, have you?' Jack shrugged.

'You're both single, I guess it's none of my business. But don't expect me to like it – I know how badly you treat women and, besides, no one wants to think their mother has a sex life, do they?' he asked lightly.

'Maybe not where you come from,' Ace said flatly. 'Where I grew up, everyone's mother was a whore.' *Which isn't a reason to turn my mother into one*, Jack thought furiously, but he kept silent and gazed casually around the room as if he were more interested in the other people present. He smiled warmly as Melissa, looking stunning in a minuscule black lace dress, approached, with Hal in close attendance. *The things I do for you*, Jack thought ruefully. But he had loved her and taken care of her since the day of her birth, and knew he'd do a lot more than lose a tennis match to save her pain.

'Hello and goodbye,' Melissa said cheerfully. 'I'm leaving.'

171

'Oh yeah?' Ace glanced suggestively at Hal. 'Early night, honey?'

'Yes, but not for what you're thinking,' she said sternly. 'I have two matches scheduled for tomorrow.'

'Bad luck, Hal,' Ace said, laughing at his discomfiture. He thought Hal was too soft with her – it had been months since the split with Lennox and still Hal hadn't got her into bed, he thought contemptuously. All he'd get in return for offering a shoulder to cry on was rheumatism!

Ace eyed Melissa speculatively; she definitely needed a new lover, he decided, but regretfully dismissed the idea – for now. At the moment, he needed Jack more than he wanted Melissa, or Rose, for that matter.

'You are awful,' Melissa scolded, then looked from Ace to Jack, and back again: she had never believed the official reason given for the dissolution of their successful partnership. 'Are you two friends again? What did you quarrel about?' she wanted to know.

'Oh, Jack decided everyone else has been right about me all along – I'm just a sonofabitch – a real mother——' Ace drawled, speaking to Melissa but watching for Jack's reaction. Jack almost made the mistake of pretending to be amused, then realized that the remark was some sort of test of his true feelings. Ace was well aware he wouldn't consider the comment to be at all humorous. He narrowed his eyes.

'Don't push your luck,' he warned softly, turning slightly so Melissa couldn't hear.

'Sorry, couldn't resist it,' Ace said, trying to look repentant.

'Resist what?' Melissa asked, exasperated.

'Nothing,' Jack and Ace spoke in unison, and she sighed heavily.

'Oh, keep your stupid secrets,' she said loftily. 'Come on, Hal, let's go.' She walked off, with Hal trailing after her.

'Hal the sheepdog,' Ace said scornfully.

'Better a sheepdog than a wolf,' Jack retorted. 'Say, who's that blonde over there?' he asked, pointing to one of the guests, anxious for an excuse to be rid of Ace.

'Don't know her name,' Ace eyed her assessingly. 'She came with Alfredo.'

'Well, she's leaving with me,' Jack decided. 'And I don't care if it is his birthday!' Ace laughed.

'Great to have you back, buddy,' he said sincerely.

Hal and Melissa strolled the short distance to her hotel, their hands loosely clasped. He had made no mention of their conversation that last evening in San Francisco, but it was obvious his feelings for her remained the same, despite knowing her dreadful secret. His brown eyes were still full of warmth and admiration, and he had been great, practising with her and helping her prepare for her matches while poor Katy was suffering with flu and had stayed in her room lest she infect Melissa.

Melissa had begun the tournament a little nervously. Now world ranked nineteen, she had squeezed in as the sixteenth seed due to a couple of no-shows by higher-ranked players. This was a new experience for her, and new pressure, to be expected to reach the fourth round of a Grand Slam.

She had always disliked the way TV presenters showed viewers a list of seeded players and blacked

173

out the names of those who had lost – as if they were dead! A 'roll of dishonour', Katy called it, but now Melissa was safely through to the third round and gaining in confidence, while several higher seeds had fallen by the wayside.

Melissa collected her pass-key, then turned back to Hal, reaching up to kiss his cheek. She stepped back, then hesitated, knowing he wanted far more from her. She had resisted, so far, but she was so lonely, so tired of waiting for a word from Nick, a word that would never come. Here was a man who wanted her, who understood her, her ambitions and her way of life better than Nick ever had.

'Would you like to stay?' she whispered. Hal's mouth went dry and he could only nod dumbly, and silently thank God he had a pack of condoms in his pocket.

Alone with him in her room, Melissa felt shy and awkward, as nervous as a virgin, and she fiddled with the contents of her bag, avoiding eye-contact with Hal.

'If you've changed your mind, just say so and I'll go and kill myself,' he offered lightly. Melissa laughed and moved over to him, gazing up into the warm brown eyes that regarded her so lovingly.

'Don't do that. I haven't changed my mind; it's just that there's never been anyone but Nick.'

'I guessed that much,' Hal said, gently drawing her closer. He forced himself to proceed slowly, which was agony when what he really craved was to rip off her clothes and ravish her until she forgot the bastard's name. But, despite his experience, he was unbearably excited by bedding the girl he had fantasized about for so long, and climaxed far too quickly.

'God, I'm sorry,' he groaned, mortified. 'I'm like a schoolkid on a first date when I'm near you.'

'Don't apologize; it was lovely,' Melissa lied politely, as if she were at a boring English vicarage tea party, Hal thought wretchedly. He slid down the bed, pausing to kiss her breasts before moving lower and burrowing his face between her thighs.

'Hal, it doesn't matter,' Melissa said quickly, pulling away. He might expect her to reciprocate . . . 'I'm tired, and we both have matches tomorrow. Let's just go to sleep,' she suggested.

'Okay,' Hal agreed, after a pause. 'It'll be better next time,' he promised, drawing her into his arms. Melissa smiled and nodded, and lay in his embrace until he drifted off to sleep. Then she edged cautiously away from him; she couldn't sleep so close to him, she didn't fit into his body the way she had with Nick. Frustrated and miserable, and feeling absurdly guilty, as if she had cheated on Nick, she turned on her side and closed her eyes.

She awoke some time later, warm and comfortable, to discover Hal's hands gently caressing her back and buttocks. She half turned towards him and one hand moved to cup her breast, teasing the nipple until it hardened. Melissa sighed with relief; this was better . . .

She caught her breath when his hands moved lower to spread her legs apart, and she moaned, pushing back against him and feeling his huge erection pressing into her spine. She twisted around and his mouth fastened greedily on hers, his tongue probing deeply. Melissa closed her eyes and let herself be swept up in his passion; her healthy young body responded to his

175

powerful thrusts and finally she shuddered and arched against him, then laughed out loud.

'I had an orgasm!' she gasped, sounding so amazed that Hal assumed it was her first experience of one. Delighted, he smiled and showered her with kisses. Damn cold Englishmen – they were notoriously bad in bed, he thought smugly; she certainly wouldn't want to return to him now.

'I love you,' he said softly.

'Oh, Hal!' Melissa hugged him tightly, wishing she felt the same, but he was too happy to notice the wistful note in her voice and soon drifted back to sleep, utterly content.

Katy was more than a little surprised when, phoning Melissa early next morning to discuss the tactics of her forthcoming match, she found herself talking to Hal. 'She's in the shower,' he said cheerfully. 'You don't have to worry about Nick Lennox any more – he's history.' In your dreams! Katy thought scornfully.

Anxious to see for herself how this new development might affect Melissa's attitude towards her tennis, Katy forced herself out of her sick bed and stood on the sidelines, coughing and sneezing, and watched closely while Melissa practised with Hal and Lisa. She thought Melissa seemed relaxed, yet eager to work and there was no sign of the dreamy where-am-I, what-am-I-supposed-to-be-doing mood that had usually been the aftermath of a night spent with Nick, and which had so infuriated Katy.

Later, Katy accompanied Melissa back to the locker-room.

'I don't want to nag,' she began.

'Since when?' Melissa asked, good-naturedly. 'Sorry, go on.'

'You were careful, weren't you? Last night, I mean?'

'Of course. Belt and braces,' Melissa assured her.

'Good. So, how was he?' Katy asked interestedly. Melissa laughed, but refused to answer.

After the Australian Open, Melissa competed in the Far East before returning to the States to play on the American green clay courts. The surface was faster than the European red clay she disliked, and more suited to her natural game.

The affair with Hal continued, but on a rather casual on-off basis, which suited Melissa a lot more than it did Hal. Their schedules meant they were usually in different States, but Hal would often fly out to wherever Melissa was playing to snatch a couple of days in her company before he had to leave for his next stop on the tour.

Their sex life improved, and she was always happy to see him, but refused to let him distract her from her tennis. She worked harder than ever, pushing herself until Hal, and even Katy, protested that she was overdoing it. Melissa refused to discuss it, but Katy knew what was driving her to mind-numbing exhaustion – it was getting very close to the time when the baby would have been born, and Melissa couldn't forget it, couldn't bear to look at pregnant women or young babies. She continued on her not so merry-go-round of travel, practise, play, eat and sleep, while Katy watched and waited for an inevitable explosion.

It came one hot, humid afternoon in Florida. Melissa

was competing against Lisa, which she disliked doing, and, as the seeded player, she was expected to win. The crowd was solidly behind the American, especially a very vocal group of schoolkids who cheered Melissa's mistakes and went wild with delight when Lisa broke Melissa's serve to take the second set.

Melissa glanced at them as she passed on the way to her chair, then swivelled her head around for a second look, for she thought she recognized one of them. Juliet Stanton! It couldn't be . . . unless . . . maybe Nick had brought his nieces to Florida on holiday?

She forced herself to stop thinking about it, and settled down to concentrate on the third set, but Lisa won the opening game with ease. Angry with herself, Melissa walked out to serve, determined to silence the jeering by winning.

She tossed the ball high and prepared to swing her racket through: a baby's shrill cry rent the air and she faltered, then let the ball drop, bounced it several times to steady herself, then restarted the point. She battled on, but so did the baby; the crying continued until Melissa could bear it no longer – what sort of moron brought a baby to watch a tennis match?

'Will you get that damned baby out of here!' she screamed and added a few choice swear words. Katy groaned and dropped her head in her hands. Lisa gaped, open-mouthed, unable to believe her ears. One of the schoolkids laughed, but most of the crowd tutted disapprovingly, and the woman nursing the baby flushed beet-red as she hurried out of the stands.

'Warning, Miss Farrell, audible obscenity.' The umpire fixed her with a stern eye. Melissa bit her lip, and tried to put the incident from her mind. But the crowd wasn't willing to let her do that, and Lisa raced to a 4–1 lead. Again, when they changed ends, Melissa was sure she saw Juliet Stanton and it was the smug malevolence on the girl's face that finally forced her to regroup. She was NOT going to lose this match!

She blocked out everything but the task in hand; forgot the heat, the hostile crowd, her tiredness and depression, forgot she was playing against a friend. Katy watched the transformation with pride and approval, and relaxed when Melissa evened the score at 4–4. She then broke Lisa to lead 5–4 and successfully served for the match, finishing with an ace.

'Game, set, match, Farrell!'

'I nearly had you this time,' Lisa said ruefully, as they clasped hands. Melissa smiled and turned to look at Katy.

'That took guts; well played,' she said quietly. 'But, next time you yell at a spectator, try and make sure she's not the tournament director's wife,' she added resignedly.

'Oh, hell, was she really?' Melissa exclaimed. She knew she would face censure for her outburst, but couldn't help but laugh. 'I guess I won't be offered appearance money to return next year,' she said ruefully. Her amusement died when she saw Juliet, and she nudged Katy.

'See that tall, blonde kid over there? I'm sure she's Nick's niece.'

'It can't be – what would she be doing here . . . you mean the girl who slagged you off at Eastbourne when you thrashed her sister?' Katy asked thoughtfully, remembering how that encounter had resulted in a migraine.

'That's the one,' Melissa nodded.

'It certainly looks like her,' Katy agreed slowly. 'Oh, forget it, let's go,' she decided. Lisa was busy signing autographs but, for once, no one asked Melissa, and she began following the security guard off court.

'Melissa!' She turned towards the voice – it WAS Juliet.

'Hello, Juliet,' she said coolly. 'Are you here on holiday?'

'No, I'm attending a tennis academy. Uncle Nick is paying for my tuition,' Juliet told her, and her grey eyes that were so like Nick's gleamed with malice. 'He wants me to be the British number one.'

'Really? I doubt he has enough money to accomplish that!' Melissa retorted. 'Besides, if you were that good, the academy would offer you free coaching,' she added.

'Well said,' Katy muttered from behind her, taking her arm and ushering her away before Juliet had a chance to upset her further.

'Uncle Nick has asked Sheena to marry him!' Juliet yelled at Melissa's retreating back. Katy felt her stiffen and resolutely propelled her forward.

'I bet that's a lie – she's just being bitchy,' Katy said quickly.

'God, he really hates me,' Melissa groaned, as she slumped down on a bench in the locker-room. 'He never took any interest in my career, but he's willing to pay a fortune so that brat can beat me. And do you know what's really stupid?' she asked, her voice shaking, and went on before Katy could reply. 'When I first

180

saw Juliet in the crowd, I hoped Nick was here, that he had come to see me and make up.' She blinked back tears. 'Isn't that the most pathetic thing you've ever heard?'

'No,' Katy said gently. 'Come on, you'll feel better after a shower and a massage,' she said, and shook out a couple of the tablets prescribed to block a migraine attack.

'I don't need those, I'm okay,' Melissa shook her head.

'Take them, just as a precaution. You have to play a Doubles later,' Katy reminded her. Melissa shrugged and obediently swallowed them.

While a physiotherapist eased the tension and stiffness from Melissa's muscles, Katy wandered off in search of refreshment and was, for once, delighted to bump into Hal.

'I'm glad you're here,' she greeted him enthusiastically. 'Melissa could use a shoulder to cry on.'

'Did Lisa beat her?' Hal asked, surprised.

'No, but Nick Lennox is trying to,' Katy said grimly, and quickly briefed him about what had happened earlier.

Unlike Katy, Lisa was not pleased to see her brother – again.

'Not another first round loss?' she sighed.

'Yeah – so what?' Hal said cheerfully. Lisa shrugged, but said nothing further. If he thought seeing Melissa was more important than his career, well, it was his decision.

Melissa, too, was not exactly thrilled to see him. Her thoughts were too full of Nick, of Juliet's spite, and the

181

incident on court, of which she was now deeply ashamed. She maintained her composure and performed well enough to win her Doubles match in the evening, but simply had nothing left to offer Hal. She certainly couldn't summon up any enthusiasm for sex, but didn't like to refuse him when he had flown such a long way to be with her.

'You can join in, you know,' Hal said tightly, hurt by her lack of response.

'I'm sorry, I'm tired,' Melissa excused herself, relieved when he withdrew and lay down beside her.

'You're not supposed to say that until after we're married,' he said, forcing a laugh.

'I'm sorry,' she repeated lamely. Sorry I can't love you; sorry I still love Nick . . .

CHAPTER 9

After two more tournaments in the States, Melissa flew to Europe where she was due to compete on the slow red clay courts in Spain, Italy and Germany before the second Grand Slam of the year, the French Open in Paris at the end of May.

The furore over her on-court outburst had soon died down; she made her apologies and paid her fine, but unfortunately details of the incident appeared in the British Press. Despite her continued success, the 'English Rose' was no longer held in such high regard, mainly because of her refusal to represent her country in the Fed Cup, the women's equivalent to the Davis Cup.

The decision not to take part had actually been Katy's, not Melissa's, but this was either not generally known or was ignored. Katy's caustic comment that Melissa would have to carry the rest of the team and would bear the blame for their inevitable defeat, had been attributed to 'Malicious Farrell'.

Melissa wondered unhappily if Nick read the Press reports, guessing that he would disapprove of her for not representing her country. Thoughts of him intruded more and more as the summer progressed and she began to count the weeks to the beginning of the grass-court season in England.

Always, lurking at the back of her mind, was the prospect of the 'date' she had with Nick: 'whatever happens,' he had said, they would meet up on the last weekend of Wimbledon fortnight at the Red Lion hotel. She had to believe that he would be there.

But, first, she had to concentrate all her energies on maintaining her ranking whilst playing on her least favourite surface. She adjusted to the slow red clay more easily than she had the previous year and was seeded in all three events for the French Open. Hal had suggested she partner him in the Mixed, but Melissa had declined, saying, untruthfully, that she had already promised to team up with Jack as usual. She then had to phone Jack to ensure he corroborated her story.

'I only wish he was as keen to partner me!' Jack grumbled. 'He's always letting me down, I'm sick of being left to find a substitute at the last minute. And it's your fault,' he added, most unfairly, Melissa thought.

'How do you work that out?' she demanded.

'Do you know how far his Singles ranking has dropped this year?' he asked.

'Er, no,' she admitted.

'From twenty-five down to eighty-five,' Jack informed her. 'He's a joke in the locker-room – all the guys know he's an easy target. He doesn't really care if he loses, because then he can leave town and go to visit you.'

'Oh, no, that's awful.' Melissa was truly appalled, and decided she had to stop Hal from ruining his career. But how to do it without hurting his feelings?

'I'll play the heavy, if you like,' Katy offered. 'I'll tell him he's disrupting your schedule.'

'I don't think that would work,' Melissa said doubtfully. 'He'd probably start believing we're star-crossed lovers, kept apart by cruel fate! Or a cruel coach, in this case. No, I'll have to do it myself,' she sighed, not relishing the task.

'What do you mean – you want to cool it?' Hal demanded, when she tried to dissuade him from flying to meet her in Rome.

'Just what I said. We both need to concentrate and work hard at the French Open and then Wimbledon,' she said placatingly.

'But we'll be in Paris and London together . . .'

'Katy's already booked hotels for us,' Melissa interrupted quickly. 'I intend to work, not play.'

'But I can help you prepare for your matches,' Hal protested.

'That's Katy's job. Besides, you should be preparing for your own matches, not mine,' she pointed out. Perfectly reasonably, she thought.

'Are you going to see Lennox when you're back in England?' Hal asked suspiciously, and she hesitated.

'Maybe,' she prevaricated.

'Will you sleep with him?' he asked jealously.

'I don't think he wants me,' Melissa replied, and her voice sounded wistful to Hal.

'But you want him,' he stated bitterly.

'Oh, Hal, you're twisting my words,' she said, rather uncomfortably.

'Right now, I'd like to twist your neck!' Hal slammed down the phone and stalked off to the hotel bar. 'Your

185

damned sister!' he said wrathfully to Jack, who was sitting quietly, reading and minding his own business. He looked up, startled, opened his mouth to ask what was wrong, then closed it again. He figured he was better off not knowing.

Melissa met up with Hal again in Paris, which was inevitable, as he was partnering Jack and she Lisa. They circled each other warily at first, but Melissa relaxed a little when she realized he was resigned to their relationship being a purely platonic one. In fact, Hal was merely biding his time, hoping she would turn to him again when she finally had Nick out of her system.

Although Melissa progressed further at Roland Garros than she had previously, she was glad to exchange the Parisian red clay for the green grass courts of England. While other players struggled to adjust, complaining about bad bounces and even worse weather, Melissa swept through the warm-up tournaments and rose to her highest ever ranking of twelve. Her confidence was high as they entered Wimbledon fortnight, as were her spirits, for a phone call to the Red Lion hotel confirmed a reservation for the second Saturday.

She hugged the knowledge to herself, trying not to feel too optimistic about the outcome. He might not turn up; might have simply forgotten to cancel the booking. But she decided she would definitely go. If Nick didn't arrive, then she would spend the time quietly by herself, remembering their times together and then say a silent and determined farewell to that part of her life.

It was late on Monday afternoon when Melissa faced

her first-round opponent, a lowly-ranked Danish qualifier, Kristen Haardraad, on court three. During the long delay, she had been allowing herself to day-dream about Nick; unfortunately, she carried the day-dream onto court, and dropped the first set before giving herself a stern talking-to. Luckily for her, Katy wasn't there to witness her lacklustre performance – she had been confident of Melissa's victory and decided her time would be better spent in watching the match which would produce her second-round opponent.

Luckily, Melissa realized that it was her preoccupation with the possibilty of seeing Nick that was hampering her game. She WOULD see him, but at the Red Lion hotel in twelve days' time. Before that, she had a lot of matches to play and win! She must, if only to justify choosing a career over a family.

From that moment, her standard of play rose dramatically, and Kristen was soon floundering, finding herself blitzed off the court as Melissa hit winning shots from both wings, and blasted down aces. Melissa took the second set 6–1, and grinned at Katy, who had been told she was in trouble and had come hurrying courtside.

After losing her opening service game, Kristen was thoroughly demoralized and Melissa romped through a 6–0 final set, cheered on by relieved fans and her family.

'What the hell happened?' Katy demanded. 'I can't leave you alone for a minute!'

'It just took me a while to find my timing,' Melissa shrugged, not daring to tell her the truth.

After that scare, she concentrated fully on her tennis. Her other matches were on the show courts and the support of the crowds helped. A group of teenagers sported 'I LOVE MELISSA' T-shirts and were particularly vocal in their encouragement. She improved on the previous year's performance, reaching the quarter finals in the Singles and the semi-finals in both Doubles events. She and Lisa lost on Friday evening, but her match with Jack was scheduled for Saturday afternoon.

She hadn't looked that far ahead, and pleasure at still being part of the Championships on the final weekend warred with apprehension over being late for her meeting with Nick. But, she reasoned, unless he had not switched on a TV or read the newspapers, he must know exactly where she was and what she was doing. She just prayed he was proud of her achievements and now had some understanding of why she had reacted to her pregnancy as she had.

She had told no one of her planned trip to the New Forest, but had secretly arranged for a hire car to take her straight to the hotel from the All England Club. Fortunately, their match was the first semi-final to take place, and they began playing on court one shortly after the Ladies' Singles final got under way on Centre.

Melissa desperately wanted to win in two sets and, after they broke serve, tried to rush the match along, becoming over-eager and trying over-ambitious, outright winners.

'Steady on,' Jack cautioned, after one rather wild shot. 'Have you got a train to catch?'

'No,' she smiled angelically.

'Well, slow down then. You're making me look bad,' he complained.

'Sorry.' She forced herself to think about what she

188

was doing, and they did win in straight sets. Melissa didn't even stay long enough to shower and change and, after telling Katy she was going to watch the end of the final on Centre, paused only to collect her bag containing a change of clothing before slipping away to the waiting limo.

Her relief at the ease of her getaway was soon tempered by the anxiety of wondering if Nick would actually show up, or what his frame of mind might be if he did. She was a bundle of nerves when she checked in. Nick hadn't arrived . . . yet, she assured herself. She was early; he wouldn't expect her to be here for at least an hour.

She ordered tea and sandwiches from Room Service and began running a hot bath while laying out fresh clothes and make-up. She sat down to remove her shoes, then yelped in pain and hastily lifted her bare foot from the carpet: tiny shards of glass caught her eye, hundreds of sharp particles covered the floor and she hopped on one foot to the phone, asking for a maid to come and clean the mess. By the time one arrived, the bath was full and Melissa was impatient to get on, to be dressed and made-up before Nick arrived.

'I'm going to take a bath – you will lock the door when you leave, won't you?' she asked anxiously. Reassured, she entered the bathroom and closed the door, quickly finished undressing and sank into the hot, soothing water, closing her eyes as she tried to relax.

'I've finished!' the maid called out. 'I'm sorry I missed it earlier.'

'That's okay, thank you,' Melissa called back.

* * *

189

Nick walked slowly along the corridor. Even after enduring the most miserable nine months of his entire life, he still had no idea how he would react to seeing Melissa again: he had missed her dreadfully, yet sometimes the anger still burned as hotly as it had that day at Bellwood.

He was startled when the door opened and the maid emerged, then stood aside for her to leave before stepping inside. The sound of splashing water told him where Melissa was and, after taking a deep breath, he pushed open the bathroom door.

Melissa had just stood up to rinse her hair and, for long moments, they stared at each other, both stunned into immobility.

'Nick,' Melissa breathed: he looked tanned and fit, but was unsmiling, his expressionless grey eyes unfathomable.

Nick gazed at her, drinking in the beauty of her glistening nude body. She was still so slender and shapely, and he ached with wanting her, ached to touch and taste her firm breasts, to span her tiny waist with his hands and have those long legs wrapped around him. But she shouldn't look the same, he thought suddenly; her breasts should be fuller and larger, her body rounded and more womanly from bearing and nurturing his child. The child she had callously flushed down the pan!

A potent, awesome mixture of lust and rage engulfed him and he stepped forward, grabbing her wrists to haul her out of the bath.

'Nick!' Melissa, with both hands imprisoned in his, fell forwards awkwardly and was unable to prevent the right side of her face slamming against the wash basin.

She cried out in pain, but Nick didn't even notice, and tossed her onto the bed as if she were a rag doll.

Dazed with pain, Melissa didn't realize his intent until she felt rough hands forcing her legs apart.

'Nick! No! Not like this!' She tried to wriggle away but he was too strong for her, easily holding both her wrists with one hand. 'Please don't,' she begged. 'Let's talk . . .'

'There's nothing to talk about. There never was. All we ever had was good sex,' he said harshly. 'That's all I'm here for,' he lied. 'And so are you – it's a little late to worry about cheating on Hal Renwick!' He squeezed her breasts painfully before unzipping his fly, and Melissa increased her struggle to be free, a sob of humiliation catching in her throat. Nick made the mistake of looking into her eyes; they were luminous dark pools, brimming with tears as she silently pleaded with him.

'Hell! What have you turned me into?' he growled, his voice filled with loathing as he pushed himself away from her. The disgust was for himself, not for her, but Melissa didn't realize that, and tried not to cry as she cautiously sat up, rubbing at her wrists and then the side of her face which had begun to throb.

'Did . . . did you marry Sheena?' she whispered. Nick blinked in surprise at the question and frowned slightly.

'No,' he said shortly, but refused to give her the satisfaction of believing herself irreplaceable. 'I did ask her, but she turned me down. Still, there are plenty of available women in Edinburgh,' he added. Melissa flinched.

'You're so cruel,' she said sadly.

'At least I don't kill babies!' Nick snarled. Again,

Melissa attempted to stem the tears but they flowed freely. Nick watched her for a moment, torn by the conflicting emotions of love, hate, sorrow and anger. He had to forgive her, or forget her, but, God help him, he couldn't seem to do either. A persistent knocking at the door finally gained his attention.

'What?' he bellowed.

'Room Service,' was the rather timid reply.

'Cover yourself!' he ordered sharply, then belatedly remembered his own dishevelled state and hastily adjusted his clothing, while Melissa stumbled into the bathroom to put on a robe. She stayed to compose herself and placed a cold flannel over her face, which was already showing signs of swelling, and to cool her eyes, red and sore from weeping.

When she stepped back into the bedroom, it was deserted. A tray of tea and sandwiches lay on the table – how many years ago had she ordered that? Then she gasped as she saw the message Nick had left on the mirror. Using her lipstick, he had scrawled 'NEXT YEAR' across the glass. He intended to return next year? For what? To finish the rape he had so nearly inflicted on her? Not likely, she thought savagely, rubbing away the words. He must be crazy if he thinks I'll come back here next year!

Shaking like a leaf, she huddled on the bed, too distraught to think coherently. She drank some tea and searched for her painkillers; it wasn't a migraine, but her head hurt almost as much and, besides, the little red tablet would send her to sleep and that was what she craved now – oblivion.

* * *

She slept for almost twelve hours, waking at six o'clock. She groaned at the memory of what had happened and winced at the pain in her head. Dragging herself into the bathroom, she stared in horror at her reflection – the whole right side of her face was discoloured and swollen.

'Oh, God!' All she wanted was to crawl back into bed, but she wouldn't let herself do that. She had a match to play; she couldn't let Jack down and certainly wouldn't give Nick the satisfaction of ruining her first appearance in a Grand Slam final.

She ordered breakfast and a car to drive her back to London, then phoned Katy, hoping her overnight absence hadn't been noticed. No such luck.

'Where the hell have you been?' Katy demanded. 'I was about to call the cops!' Melissa grimaced.

'Who knows I went missing?' she asked.

'Only me. I covered for you,' Katy said grudgingly. 'Where did you disappear to?'

'I'd arranged to meet Nick,' Melissa admitted.

'Oh, Melissa,' Katy groaned. 'Are you okay? You sound awful.'

'I look even worse, but I'll live. Can you take my kit to the courts, please? I should be there around ten.'

'Sure. I'll tell Jack to meet us there. What . . .?'

'See you later,' Melissa interrupted her, and ended the call.

She tried to disguise the bruising with make-up, but it wasn't very successful, and Katy's eyes widened in disbelief at the sight of her.

'Nick did that?' she gasped.

'No,' Melissa denied quickly, already regretting ever

193

mentioning Nick. 'I'll go and get changed – who won the other semi?' she asked, as an afterthought.

'Lucia Conti and Steve Barton,' Katy replied, frowning as she watched her go.

Jack arrived shortly after and did a double-take when he saw Melissa.

'How did that happen?'

'I slipped getting out of the bath and fell against the wash basin,' Melissa said glibly.

'A wash basin named Nick Lennox,' Katy put in. Melissa glared at her.

'Nick? Where is he now? He can't get away with this!' Jack exploded.

'It wasn't Nick! I was supposed to meet him, but he didn't show up. I was crying and I missed my footing when I climbed out of the bath,' Melissa insisted. 'Are we going to practise for this match, or not?' she asked impatiently, moving out onto the court to indicate the discussion was over, at least so far as she was concerned. Jack looked helplessly at Katy, who shrugged.

'Better do what she wants – the routine will calm her down,' she said shrewdly.

'She might be concussed,' Jack said doubtfully. 'Maybe she ought to have an x-ray on that cheek?' he suggested. Katy hadn't considered that.

'You could be right – I'll go and organize it,' she said briskly, glad to have something practical to do.

Hal and Lisa had offered to help them prepare for the match, and Melissa stoically endured more shocked looks and questions when the pair arrived. The other three seemed to think she might drop dead at any moment and kept the ball away from her, much to her exasperation.

'You don't think Lucia is going to do me any favours just because I've bruised my face, do you?' she demanded. 'I'm fine! Hit the ball to me, or I'm not playing!' she added petulantly, sticking out her tongue at Jack. 'If you treat me like a child, I'll act like one,' she informed him.

'Tell me something I don't know,' he retorted. She did seem in fairly good form, he thought, watching her carefully as they continued practising, but he still cut short the session and insisted she receive medical treatment for her injury.

'Oh, very well,' Melissa capitulated. 'On condition you keep Mum and Dad away from me?'

'Deal,' Jack agreed.

The match would take place on Centre Court after the completion of the Men's Singles final, and Melissa spent the afternoon in the locker-room, lying down with a cold compress over her throbbing cheek. When Lucia entered to change, she stopped dead at the sight of her rival.

'Well, well,' she surveyed Melissa, hands on hips. 'Battle of the Beauties, huh?' she said, referring to the phrase used by the tabloids whenever the two competed. 'More like Beauty and the Beast, today!'

'Shut up, Lucia!' Katy said crossly; she had been hovering over Melissa like a mother hen. 'You'd better get ready to play,' she added to Melissa. 'The presentation is about to take place.'

Melissa nodded and stood up, grimacing a little.

'Do you want some more painkillers?' Katy asked, noticing the gesture.

'No, I'll be too dopey to play,' Melissa declined. She drew her hair back to confine it in her usual pony-tail, but that showed too clearly the bruises and swelling, so she decided to wear it loose.

'I feel like I have mumps,' she complained, surveying her appearance with dismay.

'You look okay,' Katy lied. 'I don't know what we're going to do about that photo shoot you're supposed to be doing tomorrow, though. The sponsors are going to go nuts!'

'Sod 'em,' Melissa said succinctly. She picked up her bag and rackets and walked outside to meet Jack. The trek to the waiting-room behind Centre Court was now a familiar one, but still nerve-racking, especially today when she felt so self-conscious.

'I hope all the TV cameras blow a fuse,' she muttered to Jack, then groaned as she saw Ace walking towards them. He was the last person in the world she wanted to see! He raised one eyebrow at the sight of her.

'Hi, honey. Had a run-in with Mike Tyson?' he enquired, grinning.

'Leave her alone!' Jack snapped, taking her arm and hustling her along.

For Melissa, walking onto Centre Court that day was almost as bad as the first time, two years earlier, for her first ever pro match at Wimbledon. Then, it had been her ability she had doubted; now she just felt like an accident victim on show to ghoulish spectators.

At first, no one seemed to notice anything amiss, but then she had to turn and curtsey to the occupants of the Royal Box, thereby exposing the injury to a section of the crowd. She heard gasps of shock and dismay, followed by the excited buzzing of a hundred speculative conversations.

'Hold your head up,' Jack told her. 'You've done nothing to be ashamed of.'

The umpire glanced at her, then quickly away, and directed his remarks to Jack. As Melissa walked out on to the court to begin the warm-up, she looked across to the Players' Box for support. Katy gave her a thumbs-up; Hal and Lisa were there, too, and Daniel and Rose. Jack had indeed kept them from seeing Melissa, and told them only that she had slipped and given herself a black eye, making light of the incident. Suddenly, Ace appeared in the box; he winked and held up one of the 'I LOVE MELISSA' T-shirts which had been on sale, then draped it over the side of the box. Melissa nodded her appreciation, then turned away, mentally going through the routine of shutting her mind to everything but the task in hand.

After his second long drive in two days, Nick left the car at Glengarry House and strode off in the direction of the mountains, needing the physical exercise and the fresh air to clear his tortured brain. He had done what he had once accused Melissa of – run away from an emotional problem. But he hadn't dared stay; he simply couldn't trust himself. His loss of control had shaken him to the core – all his life he had hated bullies, yet had become one; had so very nearly inflicted the most despicable of crimes on a girl he had once loved. Still loved, he finally admitted. Not that the admission helped, for the gulf between them was now even wider.

Sighing heavily, he stopped to gaze at the beauty surrounding him, the mountainside green and lush, the loch water smooth and sparkling in the sunlight. So often over the past months he had tried to find peace of mind up here, but, since he had lost Melissa, for him solitude only equalled loneliness.

Finally, he retraced his steps and returned home. As he entered the house, he heard the noise of the TV in the small sitting-room Sheena used. She was evidently watching Wimbledon – again. He was sure she had only watched so much of the coverage to wind him up! Sheena had noticed his car earlier and had been listening out for him, and now rushed out to intercept him.

'I thought you were going to an Army reunion last night,' she said, almost accusingly, he thought. 'But you were with Melissa Farrell, weren't you?'

'So?' Nick sighed.

'So?' she repeated. 'What did you do, Nick? She looks dreadful!'

'She's here?' he stepped forward eagerly, and Sheena shook her head pityingly.

'No, on TV. She and her brother are in the Mixed Doubles final,' she explained, and watched the light die from his eyes and the shutters come down once more.

'Of course. How stupid of me,' he said bitterly, but he followed her into the sitting-room and watched the match for a few moments. Melissa had her back to the camera and seemed perfectly fit as she chased down a lob from Conti.

'She looks okay to me . . . oh, hell!' He moved closer to the screen when her bruised face was momentarily shown in close-up. 'You think I did that?' he asked incredulously.

'The commentator said she slipped while getting out of the bath and fell against the wash basin,' Sheena told him, her tone of voice betraying her doubts. Nick closed his eyes and groaned, dropping down into a chair and holding his head in his hands. Oh, God, he had done it, he realized wretchedly, as the ugly scene unfolded in his mind. He had been so out of control, it was as if someone else had manhandled her out of the bath, but he was responsible, for that and for what had followed.

'Nick?' Sheena ventured. He raised his head and looked at her.

'You were right,' he said bleakly. 'I did it. Not intentionally, but I did.'

'So why are you here? Go back and talk to her . . .' Sheena began.

'Talk? That's what I intended doing yesterday, and look what happened!' he gestured to the screen. 'I honestly thought enough time had passed for us to be able to talk calmly about the abortion, but, as soon as I saw her . . .' he shrugged helplessly. 'I don't trust myself to go within a mile of her.'

'I don't understand. You said you hurt her accidentally,' Sheena said, bewildered.

'I almost raped her, Sheena!' Nick ground out. 'Do you still think I should go back?' he demanded, but he was talking to an empty room. Sheena had fled in horror at his words.

Nick turned his attention to the match. Melissa and Jack had won the first set and, as he watched, they broke Steve Barton to take a 2–0 lead in the second, and Melissa took up position on the baseline to begin her service game.

Outwardly calm, Melissa turned to the ball-boy and

waited for him to toss a ball to her. The physical exertion was taking its toll; her head was throbbing painfully now and she desperately wanted to avoid a third set, which meant she couldn't afford to drop her serve.

She took several deep breaths, then tossed up the ball and served hard into the corner, then rushed to the net as Lucia mis-hit the return.

'Leave it!' Jack called, knowing the shot would go wide. Melissa quickly side-stepped, pulling her racket away from the ball.

Afterwards, she couldn't remember exactly how it happened, but somehow she managed to hit herself in the face with the end of the racket handle, splitting the already bruised skin. The pain was intense and, involuntarily, she dropped to her knees, clutching at her cheek. The spectators murmured in sympathy and Jack rushed over to her, gently pulling her hand away so he could inspect the damage.

'God, you're bleeding,' he said, appalled at what he saw. 'Get the trainer out here!' he yelled at the umpire, as he helped Melissa stand up and guided her to her chair.

'Are you okay, Melissa?' Lucia enquired sweetly, when she was near enough for the courtside microphone to convey her concern to the viewers.

'Oh, dear, this is most unfortunate,' remarked the commentator. 'And she touched the ball, too, and so lost the point. What a pity.'

'You prat,' Nick muttered, watching helplessly as Jack and the trainer fussed around Melissa, trying to stem the bleeding.

'We can quit, you know; it doesn't matter,' Jack said quietly.

'Are you kidding? This is my first Grand Slam final,' she protested. 'I'll be okay,' she assured him.

She received a rousing cheer when she walked back onto court and she managed a rather lop-sided smile of thanks. With Jack's considerable help and the support from the spectators, she was able to continue, but wasn't sure how much longer she could do so. Her head ached badly and she felt dizzy and nauseous. But they already had the necessary break of serve, and she held grimly onto her own, fighting back from 15–40 to win, for a 3–0 lead.

The changeover gained her a breathing space and then they managed to break Lucia for a 4–0 lead. Jack held serve easily, as did Steve Barton, which left Melissa to serve for the match, and the title, at 5–1.

She stood at the baseline and took a moment to steady herself. Serving for a match was always a little nerve-racking, but for a title, her first Wimbledon title, it was awesome. She wished Jack was serving to finish the match instead . . . if I bottle out now, he'll probably have to, she thought drily, but by then their opponents would have regained some confidence and be harder to beat.

Jack, poised at the net, glanced back questioningly at the delay, and she nodded. Sheer will-power and endless practice enabled her to serve proficiently and Jack did the rest, seemingly everywhere as he pounced on every ball and volleyed them out of reach.

'Game, set, match! . . .' Melissa practically fell into Jack's arms and he continued to support her as they shook hands with their opponents and the umpire. She had a few minutes' respite before the presentation ceremony, but the climb up to the Royal Box seemed endless and she forgot to curtsey to the Duke and Duchess of Kent. They didn't seem to mind, though, delighted at being able to present the trophy to British players.

The noise from the crowd was already deafening, but the volume increased as they stepped forward and held the trophy aloft. Melissa glanced around the vast arena, at the thousands of people clapping and cheering, and elation temporarily blocked out the pain and nausea. She just wished there weren't so many cameras pointing at her!

'These pictures are definitely not for the family album,' she muttered to Jack, pulling her hair over her cheek in an effort to hide the disfigurement.

'You're so vain,' he said, giving her an affectionate hug. 'I'm really proud of you,' he added quietly, and she smiled.

'I wouldn't be here without your help,' she said, remembering his endless patience with her when she was a child, trading shots for hours with a little girl who so wanted to emulate her adored older brother.

'I think you would. It might have taken you longer, but you'd have succeeded,' he told her. His words meant more to her than the silver trophy they were holding, and she reached up to kiss his cheek.

'Oh, isn't that lovely,' the commentator remarked to the millions of TV viewers, Nick included. 'How wonderful to have a British win on this, the last day of the Championships. The first Grand Slam title for

Melissa Farrell, but surely not the last. She is still only twenty, and has already achieved so much, but we all feel there are greater triumphs ahead for this talented player. A Singles quarter-finalist this year, a result which will place her in the top ten, she has the potential to be the Ladies' Singles Champion here. And wouldn't that be a terrific day for Great Britain? For British tennis? Maybe next year . . .'

Nick switched off the set as Melissa left the Royal Box. Pride and pleasure at her achievement warred with self-disgust that he had almost ruined it for her. That's where she belongs, he thought, with Jack and Katy, with . . . his gut twisted with jealousy, with Hal, Even Ace had never hurt her or tried to stand in her way as he, Nick, had.

He went upstairs to shower and change, and took the portrait of Melissa from its hiding-place. He gazed at the lovely, unblemished face for a long time, then lightly caressed the painted cheek.

'I'm sorry, sweetheart,' he murmured, before walking over to the wall to hang the picture in its original place. 'Maybe next year,' he repeated the commentator's words. She must have seen his message on the mirror – next year. Would she meet him again? Would she hell, he answered himself bitterly, but the portrait remained on the wall, both a pleasure and a torment in the months ahead.

CHAPTER 10

Melissa stuck resolutely to her story about how she had sustained her injury, flatly denying that she had seen Nick and insisting Katy must have misunderstood.

'What about the bruises on your wrists?' Katy asked caustically. 'I suppose your toothbrush attacked you?'

'Leave it, Katy, please,' Melissa begged. 'I don't want Jack charging up to Scotland or, worse, my father finding out exactly why Nick is so angry with me.'

'Okay,' Katy agreed reluctantly.

For a few days, speculation was rife in the media, her picture splashed across the tabloids, much to her annoyance, but then, with Wimbledon over, the incident was forgotten.

But not by Nick. Nor by Melissa. The shock and horror of Nick's violence gradually receded, and she even allowed herself to feel cautiously optimistic about their future. Maybe she was clutching at straws, but she didn't believe that he had gone to the Red Lion merely for sex, or that he had found solace with another woman – if that were true, surely he wouldn't have bothered making the trip?

Often, before she drifted off to sleep at night, or

dozed during a flight, she would see in her mind's eye that message on the mirror – next year – and felt sure they would both be there for that rendezvous, a meeting that would surely end more happily than the last?

Meanwhile, she had to work hard, consolidating her position in the top ten, defending the computer points she had amassed the year before and always trying to go one step further up the ladder.

Money was rolling in, now; not just higher prize money, but lucrative sponsorship deals. Greg had been working busily on her behalf and she had signed contracts with companies to wear their clothes and shoes, and use their rackets. She was offered a huge amount to endorse a new high-energy health drink on court.

'But I only drink water during matches,' she said, ingenuously.

'You can drink straight vodka, for all they care, just so long as you use their bottles,' Greg explained, so Melissa shrugged and signed on the dotted line. There was also a range of swimwear, but she declined to model lingerie.

The most recent offer was for her to promote wrist-watches, by wearing a selection of styles on court.

'As accurate and elegant as Melissa Farrell!' Katy snorted derisively at the proposed slogan but, as her own percentage of Melissa's earnings was now considerable, she made no objection to Melissa's acceptance of the offer. However, her main objective was still to push Melissa as far up the rankings as possible.

They arrived in New York at the end of August; they were both finding it difficult to forget what had hap-

205

pened the previous year, although neither ever mentioned the abortion. However, Melissa cheered up when Jack arrived, two days before the Open began. They were staying at the same hotel and he phoned her from his room to suggest they meet for dinner.

'I've just got in and I'm knackered, so do you mind if we eat here?' he asked.

'No, of course not. I'll book a table – what time?'

'Give me half an hour to shower and change and I'll meet you in the bar,' Jack said.

'Great.' Melissa made the reservation, then, her spirits already higher just knowing her brother was around, she quickly changed into tight white jeans and a scarlet top, before making her way downstairs. Although they had spoken often on the phone, she hadn't seen him since leaving England in early July, and she chattered non-stop while he relaxed with a cold beer.

As they entered the dining-room, Melissa spotted Ace sitting with a stunning redhead, and darted over before Jack could restrain her.

'Hi, honey, you're looking great,' Ace stood up and kissed her cheek, and nodded a greeting to Jack. 'Join us for dinner?' he suggested, and beckoned for a waiter to lay extra places without waiting for a reply.

'Are you staying here, too?' Melissa asked Ace. 'What a coincidence,' she remarked. Coincidence, my foot, Jack thought irritably, as he reluctantly sat down. He tried to avoid Ace away from the tournaments and had purposely booked himself and Melissa into a new hotel.

Jack realized that the redhead looked about as pleased as he felt, and he smiled at her.

'Hi, I'm Jack Farrell and this is my sister, Melissa,' he reached over to shake her hand.

'Oh, yeah,' Ace belatedly remembered his manners. 'This is . . .' he paused to think. 'Sally-Lou. Where's your watchdog?' he asked Melissa.

'Katy? She's gone to visit her parents,' she told him.

'I meant Hal. I can't usually get near you without tripping over him.'

'He does have some uses, then,' Jack put in acidly. 'I knew there must be a reason why I put up with him.'

'Oh, stop it, he's sweet,' Melissa protested.

'Sweet?' Ace grimaced. 'All "sweet" will do for you is make you fat and rot your teeth,' he drawled. Melissa giggled.

'You've been in England recently, haven't you?' she asked. 'How's everything at home? Are Mum and Dad okay?'

'Fine. They send their love.' Ace shot a look at Jack, who was carefully studying the menu and avoiding his gaze. 'I tried to persuade your mother to come over for the Open, but she wouldn't,' he said, rather edgily. In fact, he had decided that he had proffered his last invitation to Rose; if she wanted to stay at Bellwood, well, that was fine by him.

He didn't realize, as did Rose, that the secrecy of the affair had added to its longevity. Also, Rose was shrewd enough to know that she couldn't hope to compete with the young lovelies who followed the tour – she didn't even want to try. The very thought was exhausting. And even less did she relish the public ridicule which would follow the inevitable break-up.

Melissa didn't notice Ace's tone – she was busy

checking out Sally-Lou, who was breathtakingly beautiful, but looked bored as she played with the gold bangles on her slender wrist.

'Do you live in New York?' Melissa asked her politely.

'Yeah.'

'You're a model?' she guessed.

'Yeah. And you're another tennis player, aren't you?' Sally-Lou added, making it sound as if a plague of locusts had descended upon the city.

'Yeah,' Melissa imitated the other girl's petulant drawl, but Sally-Lou was too thick to notice the sarcasm.

'Melissa models, too,' Ace put in quickly. 'And I bet she earns more than you,' he added maliciously. 'A million bucks for those swimwear ads, wasn't it, honey?'

'No, not that much,' Melissa denied hastily. 'You should know better than to believe what you read in the tabloids,' she added.

'I saw that spread,' Sally-Lou said, eyeing Melissa with professional interest. 'Did they use a body double?'

'No, they didn't!' Melissa said furiously. Ace and Jack laughed and exchanged glances of amusement, briefly recapturing the old rapport, then Jack looked away. Sally-Lou pouted sulkily and Melissa tried to make amends.

'I suppose you must get as tired of travelling as we do?' she asked.

'Yeah,' Sally-Lou nodded. Melissa sighed as she received the standard reply. Where did Ace pick them up? Still, he never had chosen girls for their conversational skills!

'Excuse me for a minute,' she stood up. 'Order the

chicken and salad for me, will you?' she asked Jack, then made her way to the powder room. After a moment, Sally-Lou followed her and a silence fell between the two men.

'I see you've got a tough first-round draw,' Jack said finally.

'Yeah, but I've beaten him before,' Ace replied, and they both relaxed a little as they talked 'shop'.

Meanwhile Sally-Lou had joined Melissa in front of the mirror in the powder room and was fiddling with her hair, shooting sideways glances at her.

'You're the one the Press call the English Rose, aren't you?' she asked abruptly.

'Amongst other things,' Melissa agreed drily.

'I thought so – you're the girl Ace told me about. Well, you needn't worry – I'm catching the red-eye to LA tonight, so he's all yours,' she sniffed. Melissa stared at her, open-mouthed, then she grinned.

'He must have been winding you up – there's nothing going on between us,' she said.

'Oh, come off it!' Sally-Lou snorted. 'The English Rose. He bought your house in England, didn't he?'

'Well, yes, but not for me . . .'

'That's what he told me,' Sally-Lou said flatly. She snapped her bag shut and walked out of the room. Melissa frowned in puzzlement; Ace must have been joking, or perhaps trying to make Sally-Lou jealous? He had often said that fear of a rival kept a girl on her toes or, more importantly, on her back, She leaned nearer the mirror to re-apply her lip-gloss. Next year! It was as if the words were actually written on the glass, so clearly did she see them.

'Damn you, Nick,' she muttered resentfully. A stack of mail had caught up with her in New York; hundreds of people, strangers, had written, congratulating her on her Wimbledon title and commiserating over her injury. But had Nick contacted her? Had he hell! Just those two words, commanding her to meet him for one night the following July!

What if Ace hadn't merely been teasing Sally-Lou? She had been besotted with him for years, before she ever met Nick. Ace was reputed to be the best lover on the tour . . . who better to make her forget Nick, if only for a short while?

She returned to the table and toyed with her food while covertly watching Ace from beneath her lashes. She remembered how excited she used to be by his proximity and tried to recapture the old emotions. He was still drop-dead gorgeous, dark and dangerous, his body hard and lean. She watched his hands, the long, tanned fingers tapping restlessly as he spoke . . . magical hands, according to Lucia, and she should know, since she had enjoyed at least three different affairs with him over the past few years . . . 'enjoyed' being the operative word!

'Oh, excuse me.' Jack put his hand to his mouth as he yawned. 'I'm bushed, I'm off to bed.' He stood up; it never occurred to him that Sally-Lou wouldn't be staying with Ace overnight, or he would have waited until Melissa had finished her meal and escorted her back to her room.

'Goodnight, Jack,' Melissa smiled sweetly, helping herself to more coffee. Later, she hovered in the hotel lobby while Ace put Sally-Lou in a cab, and approached him when he returned.

'Buy me a night-cap?' she asked, feeling in need of some Dutch Courage.

'Sure,' Ace turned towards the bar, but Melissa put a restraining hand on his arm.

'In your suite?' she suggested. Ace hesitated.

'You're not in trouble, are you, honey?' he asked. Again. He didn't say the word out loud, but for a brief moment, they both recalled the tearful scene in her hotel room almost one year earlier. Melissa took a deep breath and smiled.

'No,' she said softly, gazing up at him. Ace looked at her sharply – and a little warily.

'Are you coming on to me?' he asked incredulously. Melissa didn't reply, but sauntered over to the elevator, trying to seem calm and in control.

'Which floor?'

'Er, seven,' Ace stepped in beside her and punched out the number. He leaned against the wall and regarded her with some suspicion. This was a trap, designed by Jack, he thought, but quickly discarded the notion. Jack would never use Melissa as bait. However, he still checked his suite for signs of her brother.

'What would you like to drink?' he asked.

'Brandy?' Melissa suggested. He nodded and poured her a small glass, watching her as she walked around and inspected his rooms. God, she was lovely, he thought. So like Rose, but younger, prettier, slimmer, more confident of her sexuality . . . although she was nervous now, he realized. He wondered why she was handing herself to him on a plate, but only briefly – who cared about her reasons?

211

'Come here,' he ordered softly. Melissa, her heart thumping, obeyed. He took the glass from her and cast it aside without taking his eyes from her face.

'Why tonight?' he asked.

'Why not?' she countered softly, closing her eyes as he pulled her towards him and kissed her hungrily. Oh, he's good, she thought blissfully, sliding her arms around his neck and leaning into him.

Ace ran his fingers lightly down her spine, slipping beneath her top and caressing her skin with a feather-light touch that made her want more. His thumbs circled her navel and then, oh so slowly, his hands moved upwards to cup her breasts, teasing the nipples until they were rock-hard. Melissa moaned as waves of desire swept over her. It had never been like this with Hal, and she had begun to fear that no man but Nick could fully arouse her, but she had been wrong.

Ace began moving her into the bedroom, his body moulded to hers as he backed her towards the bed, then lowered her to the counterpane and stretched out beside her. His hand, fingers splayed and seemingly every-where, caressed her tummy while he expertly unfas-tened her jeans.

'I used to fantasize about this moment when I was fourteen,' Melissa said dreamily. Ace smiled and looked down at her; at the large blue eyes, even darker than usual with passion, so like Rose . . . Both of them will hate me for this.

His hand stilled as a battle raged within him; if only Melissa didn't look so trusting, even innocent! Which she certainly wasn't; there had been the uptight English bastard who had got her pregnant, Hal, maybe dozens more for all he knew, or cared. But he did care, unfortunately.

'Aw, hell!' Ace cursed as he turned abruptly away.

'What's wrong?' Melissa asked anxiously.

'I've just discovered that I have scruples. And it's damned inconvenient!' he added fervently.

'I don't understand; I'm not fourteen now . . .' Melissa began.

'It's not that,' Ace denied.

'Then what?' she persisted, before pride came to her rescue and she sat up, straightening her clothes. He was rejecting her! 'Let's just forget it,' she said quickly, so humiliated she didn't think she would ever be able to face him again. She slid off the bed, intent on escape, but Ace caught at her hand.

'Let me explain,' he said, but she shrugged him off.

'What's to explain? You don't want to sleep with me,' she said flatly, heading for the door.

'Oh, I do, honey. Believe me, I do,' Ace sighed heavily, so obviously sincere that Melissa paused and looked back at him.

'So why are you turning me down?'

'Do you remember, a couple of years ago, I said making love to you would seem incestuous?' he asked slowly.

'Yes. So?'

'I wasn't referring to my partnership with your brother. I was thinking of Rose,' he said.

'Mum? What does she have to do with . . .' Melissa's eyes widened as comprehension dawned.

'You were having an affair with my mother? You still are,' she stated, suddenly understanding which English Rose Sally-Lou had been talking about.

'Mm,' Ace admitted, rather guardedly.

'You and Mum?' she said incredulously, needing confirmation.

'Yes.'

'You and Mum,' she repeated, half to herself, struggling to assimilate the information. She felt shocked, confused, concerned for her mother's happiness and . . . jealous, decidedly jealous. So many emotions warred for supremacy, and she shook her head in an effort to clear her thoughts.

'Does Jack know? Of course he does,' she immediately answered her own question. 'That's what you quarrelled about, isn't it? The real reason you broke up your partnership?'

'Yes,' Ace confirmed. 'You're taking this a lot better than he did,' he commented, still a little wary, half-expecting tears and recriminations.

'Am I? He's very protective; I guess he's worried you'll hurt her – he knows more about your debauchery than I do! Besides, I . . .' she stopped abruptly. I can understand perfectly why Mum succumbed, she thought. Jack could only see the possible problems and pain, not the undoubted pleasures.

'Why is it such a big secret?' she asked, and he shrugged.

'Rose was afraid that Jack would be upset, but mostly she didn't want to hurt you – you had quite a crush on me at the time it started,' he added, with a grin.

'I grew out of that,' Melissa retorted loftily. Ace merely glanced towards the bed where they had lain so recently – at her instigation – and she flushed.

'Bastard!'

'Probably,' he agreed. 'You're not mad at me, are you, honey? I'm good for her,' he added arrogantly. I bet you are, Melissa thought wistfully.

'No, I'm not' she said truthfully. 'But I would have been, if you had waited and . . .'

'Told you tomorrow morning?' Ace guessed. 'I figured that. But, now you know the score, I don't suppose . . .?' he arched one dark brow suggestively.

'No,' Melissa said, although she was sorely tempted.

'Sure?'

'No,' she admitted, and he grinned. Lounging back against the headboard, he was devilishly handsome and made no effort to hide his obvious arousal. He held out his hand and Melissa took a step forward, but then backed off. 'How could I ever look Mum in the eye again?' she exclaimed in horror. Ace sighed. He'd lost her, for now.

'Kiss me goodnight, then you can go off to your cold, lonely bed,' he said mockingly. Melissa wasn't that stupid! She blew him a kiss from a safe distance and then turned and walked resolutely away.

As the Open entered its second week, Melissa and Jack were again the sole British survivors, although Jack had lost in the Singles. Melissa was still in contention in all three events, seeded ninth in Singles and even higher in Doubles.

This was to be Hal's last tournament. After another first-round Singles defeat, he had surprised everyone by announcing that he was retiring from competition and would in future be coaching his sister, Lisa.

Melissa wasn't sure how she felt about that – he had

made no overt attempt to rekindle their affair, and was always friendly when he helped her and Lisa prepare for their Doubles matches, but she was uneasily aware that he was still in love with her, and often gazed at her with the look of a rejected puppy.

'What are we going to do about Hal?' She turned, as always, to Katy.

'Use him,' Katy said promptly. 'Make it official, put him on the payroll. You'll benefit from having a man as a hitting partner and, if it doesn't work out, we'll just have to find someone to replace Lisa in Doubles.'

On Monday evening Melissa went to watch Hal and Jack compete in a Men's Doubles match. She had only been there for a few moments when Ace joined her in the Players' Box, pushing past other players to squeeze in beside her. Melissa pretended not to notice him, staring straight ahead at the action on court.

'Hi, lovely,' he ran his hand over her bare thigh and she bit her lip. 'You're looking tired – aren't you sleeping well?' he asked, his eyes glinting with mischief.

'No, I'm not,' Melissa retorted, through gritted teeth. She was sure he knew damned well she had been in a state of frustration since the encounter in his suite. Despite her gruelling physical schedule, she had been sleeping fitfully, tormented by vivid dreams filled with erotic images of Nick or Ace and, shockingly, both! And Ace wasn't even gentlemanly enough to pretend she had never propositioned him – his sly looks and knowing grins seemed to follow her everywhere. She felt as if she had prodded a sleeping panther.

She ignored him, or tried to, and concentrated on the match. Ace sat back and watched her. He had been cursing himself for letting her go; he certainly wouldn't make that mistake again! He reached out and idly brushed a lock of hair back from her face, letting his fingers linger on her neck as he did so.

'Have you told Jack?' Ace murmured.

'That I was in your bedroom? I'm still alive, aren't I?' Melissa asked sardonically, and he grinned.

'Not that part. I meant, have you told him that you know about me and Rose, and that you're okay about it,' he clarified.

'No,' she shook her head, and jerked away from his caressing fingers. 'Stop that! Jack's noticed,' she hissed.

'I know. So has Hal. If they don't start concentrating, they'll lose this match,' Ace said reprovingly, as if he had nothing to do with distracting them. Melissa rolled her eyes, then visibly jumped and slapped at his hand as he stroked her inner thigh.

'If you don't stop, I'll get up and walk out,' she threatened.

'If you do, I'll follow,' Ace countered. 'Then they'll definitely lose the match,' he said, draping an arm around her shoulders. 'They'll probably default, and . . .'

'What do you want?' Melissa asked resignedly.

'Just one small favour. Persuade Jack to resume our partnership. He and I are both losing money, and he'll be looking for another partner now Hal's quitting,' he said.

'Okay, I'll do it – IF you stop touching me!' she ground out. Katy joined them at that moment and immediately noticed Melissa's discomfiture.

'What's going on?' she asked suspiciously.

217

'Nothing – he's got scruples,' Melissa said tartly.

'Got what?' Katy hadn't heard properly. 'What's that – a new strain of AIDS?' she asked, horrified. Melissa laughed, hoping the cameras weren't on them – Jack had warned her years earlier to be careful about what she said when spectating; according to him, there was always someone watching on TV who could lip-read!

'It might as well be – it's just as inhibiting,' Ace grumbled, then, having accomplished what he had set out to, he stood up and left. Melissa was both relieved and sorry to see him go, but at least his departure helped Jack and Hal pull the match around, and they easily clinched the final set, 6–1.

Later, Melissa had a drink with Jack at their hotel and asked his advice about hiring Hal. He agreed with Katy but suggested a six-month trial period.

'I'd feel happier – and I know Dad would – if you had a guy travelling with you. You girls attract too much of the wrong sort of attention.'

'We can look after ourselves,' Melissa declared. 'Have you seen Katy's kick-boxing?'

'Seen it? I've felt it!' Jack grimaced and she laughed.

'What are you going to do without Hal?' she asked next. 'Found a replacement?'

'Not yet,' Jack replied.

'What about Ace? You were a great team, and neither of you has accomplished as much since you split,' she pointed out.

'No, not Ace,' Jack said flatly.

'Why not? Because he sleeps with Mum?' she asked calmly. Jack choked on his drink, then stared at her.

'How do you know about that?'

218

'I made Ace tell me,' she said, which was true enough, in a way.

'And you're not upset?'

'Not really. A little jealous,' she grinned, then sobered. 'I think it's great for Mum, a terrific ego-boost. She was so down after the divorce, and she needed someone to make her feel young and sexy again.'

'Maybe, but not Ace. He treats women like dirt,' Jack objected.

'I know that. So does Mum. I've talked to her about it, and she's not expecting fidelity, or a long-term relationship. Don't be stubborn, Jack,' she pleaded. 'You and Ace were the best.'

'Well, okay,' he capitulated finally. 'But I'm just in it for the money – off court, we go our separate ways. And he has to cut out the drugs; if he gets caught, I'd be disqualified, too.'

'I'm sure he'll agree,' Melissa said quickly.

'Right; I'll have a word with him. Now, have you finished nagging?' Jack growled. 'I'd quite like to be the top Mixed Doubles team, too, so go and get some sleep.'

'Okay,' Melissa kissed his cheek and scampered off.

The following day a small package was delivered to her at the hotel. She opened the Cartier box and lifted out a pair of exquisite diamond ear-rings. The accompanying card read simply 'Thanks, honey'.

'Nick?' Sheena tapped lightly on his study door. 'May I talk to you?'

'Of course.' He threw down his pen and looked at her. 'What's on your mind?'

'There's someone I'd like you to meet,' she began,

twisting her hands together nervously. 'I've been seeing someone, a man . . .'

'You don't need my permission,' Nick said lightly.

'I know. It's all rather sudden, and a little strange . . .' she broke off. 'You'll understand when you see him. He's here now – will you come?'

'Sure,' Nick got to his feet and followed her out of the room, wondering idly why she was in such a tizz.

He quickly discovered the reason; the man waiting in the drawing room bore a remarkable resemblance to Rory, same features, same eyes, even the deep cleft in the chin was the same. But this man was older, in his early forties, Nick guessed, as he moved towards him.

'Nick, I'd like to introduce you to Richard. Richard Lennox,' Sheena added softly. Nick stretched out his hand and forced a smile.

'Lennox? You must be a distant cousin,' he said lightly. Or a con-artist. Perhaps both.

'So Sheena tells me.' Richard shook his hand firmly; the voice was different, deeper and faintly accented, as if he had spent a lot of time in Australia, or maybe South Africa, Nick thought. 'She almost fainted when we first met,' he cast a warm smile in her direction and she blushed. 'I thought my devastating charm was at work until she showed me a photograph of her husband!'

'When did you meet?' Nick enquired.

'I was over here earlier in the summer – I knew my ancestors originated from this part of the country and came to have a look around,' Richard said easily. And found a rich widow whose dead husband could have been your kid brother, Nick thought.

'It was just after Wimbledon,' Sheena put in quietly. 'You were . . . busy, Nick.' He nodded; not busy, just preoccupied, moody and unapproachable. He wished, too late, that he had been aware of what was going on. However, he hid his misgivings and invited Richard to dinner and then, upon learning he was staying locally at the Glengarry Arms, suggested he be their guest instead. Keep your friends close, and your enemies closer still . . .

Over the weeks that followed, he got to know his new 'cousin' and grew to like him enormously. It also eased his mind to discover that Richard possessed a fortune that made Sheena's inheritance look paltry. Richard had liquidated most of his assets abroad and was searching for a property in Scotland.

'Do you think Balmoral might be for sale?' he asked Nick, only half joking.

'I don't think things are that bad for the Royals,' Nick said drily. He stopped listening to Richard, remembering a time when Melissa was devouring the latest scandal to afflict the Windsors.

'I bet it's all those family holidays that cause the trouble – imagine having the only mother-in-law in the country who can answer the question: you and whose army?' He smiled slightly at the recollection. She had spent so little time at Glengarry, yet memories of her were everywhere.

'Sorry, what were you saying?' Reluctantly, he forced his thoughts back to the present.

'About asking Sheena to marry me – I want to be sure she doesn't look at me and see Rory,' Richard explained. Nick understood his doubts, but knew they were groundless from conversations he'd had with Sheena. She was positive about her feelings, more secure with the mature and easy-going Richard than she ever had been with the mercurial Rory.

Nick did a little match-making to speed matters along and was genuinely delighted when Sheena proudly showed off a diamond engagement ring. It was difficult not to feel excluded from their happiness, and he was pleased when his friend from Army days, Dale Coupland, newly-retired from the Forces, came for an extended visit before setting up in business.

'Crime is about the only growth industry there is,' Coop told Nick. 'People are frightened; they want protection for themselves and their property and they're prepared to pay for it.'

'Don't tell me you're going to install burglar alarms?' Nick queried.

'No, of course not. I'm talking about personal body-guards, minders. And I know just where to look for a suitable work-force – do you know how many ex-soldiers are looking for employment?'

'It's a problem, I know,' Nick nodded. 'Most of them joined up when they left school; the Army fed them, housed them, clothed them and told them what to do for up to twenty years. They're finding it hard to adjust.'

'Right. But they were good soldiers, and ideal for what I have in mind.' Coop leaned forward eagerly. 'They can look after themslves and the people who hire them! This could be one helluva successful business, Nick. Why don't you join me?'

'You need money? Sure,' Nick said easily.

'I didn't mean that!' Coop said impatiently. 'Come in with me, as an equal partner – what do you say?'

'I can't. I have too many responsibilities here,' Nick shook his head.

'That's rubbish. Sell out to Richard. And give him the title while you're at it! You don't want it – come on, Nick, what's keeping you here? Family loyalty? Well, Richard's family, isn't he?'

'Oh, sure. I had him checked out when he first arrived,' Nick admitted. He was a little ashamed of that now, but it had seemed necessary at the time. 'We share an ancestor, five generations back.'

'And the way things are now, he's probably your heir,' Coop pointed out.

'Well, the jury's still out on that,' Nick demurred.

'But he IS family. And he wants to settle in Scotland. Sell him what isn't entailed and get your lawyer working on ridding you of the rest,' Coop urged.

'The Old Man would start spinning in his grave,' Nick said slowly, sorely tempted to do as Coop suggested. It just seemed so disloyal; he owed his great-uncle so much.

'Oh, well, I can't argue with a ghost,' Coop sighed and dropped the subject.

But Nick mulled the conversation over and consulted his lawyer, his accountant and also spoke at length to Alan Duncan, the man who had been Glengarry's steward for almost forty years. A few days later, after listening to Richard and Sheena discuss and reject the property they had viewed that day, he made his decision.

'How would you feel about buying this place?' he

asked suddenly. Sheena gasped and put a hand to her mouth, gazing beseechingly at Richard.

'Name your price,' Richard said simply.

Sheena married Richard in late October, in Glengarry church where she had married Rory seven years before. Nick had acted as best man on that earlier occasion; this time, he gave away the bride. No ghosts were present, neither Rory nor the Old Man, and Nick tried to forget that he had once hoped the next Lennox bride would be Melissa. Sheena, alight with her own happiness, nevertheless guessed how he was feeling and took Coop to one side.

'Don't let him brood, will you? As soon as he's settled in London, introduce him to some girls. There must be one who can take his mind off Melissa Farrell!'

'Still her, is it? I told him years ago that he needed good booze and bad women to get her out of his system!'

'He's tried both,' Sheena told him. 'Nothing seems to work.'

'So why doesn't he patch things up with Melissa?' Coop asked, rather impatiently.

'He tried that, too,' Sheena said, after a pause. 'You probably saw the result – her picture was splashed all over the papers.'

'No,' Coop shook his head, then his eyes widened. 'You mean . . . when she fell . . .?'

'Yes, Nick told me he was responsible for that. And worse . . .'

'My God!' Coop was shocked. 'I'd have bet my life Nick could never do such a thing. What . . .?' he broke off, remembering it was her wedding day and forced a smile. 'Don't worry, I'll find somebody for him. Coupland and Lennox are an irresistible team!'

'Lennox and Coupland,' Nick corrected, overhearing the last few words as he came to join them. Luckily, he assumed Coop was referring to their business partnership. 'I outrank you, remember?' He turned to Sheena and kissed her cheek. 'Your husband's waiting for you. Good luck, love.'

'Thank you, Nick. For everything.' Sheena hugged him tightly, then hurried off to join Richard.

Nick had agreed to remain at Glengarry while Richard and Sheena spent their honeymoon in Kenya, and his spirits rose as he shipped his personal belongings to the Chelsea flat that was to be his permanent home. Coop had returned to London immediately after the wedding and had already obtained an office and someone to run it. The initial advertising had brought in floods of enquiries from ex-soldiers seeking work and from scared and angry members of the public eager for their services.

It was early December when Nick finally handed over the running of Glengarry to Richard and, feeling like a prisoner out on parole, climbed into his car and headed south. He had his life back, the chance to build something of his own. And Melissa would never have settled happily in Glengarry . . . the thought came from nowhere and he groaned, then shook his head impatiently. Damn it, he wasn't doing this for Melissa! Or was he?

CHAPTER 11

Hal couldn't believe his luck – he was actually being paid to watch Melissa play! He knew he was on probation, though, and was careful not to tread on Katy's toes. He coached Lisa, trying to improve her game to lift her above the mid-thirties spot where she had languished for several years, but acted only as a hitting partner for Melissa until Katy asked for his suggestions on how to push her ranking ever higher.

Practising constantly with a man was beneficial to Melissa's game; she began to hit the ball even harder and became even faster around the court. She added two more Singles titles to her growing tally and hoped the next year would bring her first Grand Slam title. Next year . . . those damned words on the mirror haunted her; however hard she pushed them aside during waking hours, they returned in her dreams, mocking and tantalizing her.

They were all in New York for the WTA Championships in early December, after which Hal and Lisa headed home to California, where Melissa was to join them for Christmas. Katy had declined an invitation to do likewise and remained in New York with her family, while Melissa flew to France for a lucrative exhibition event. Hal suggested Jack might also like to spend the holidays in San Francisco, so Melissa telephoned him at a tournament in Germany to ask him.

'Yeah, why not?' he said. 'But we ought to go and see Mum and Dad first. Why don't you meet me in London next week and we'll visit them both before going to the States?'

'Okay,' Melissa agreed. 'I haven't been home in ages – the British Press are giving me a bad time again, just because I didn't bother competing in the British National Championships in October,' she sighed.

'I know,' Jack said sympathetically: he had competed and most of the questions at his Press interviews had been about his sister chasing computer points and bigger prize money elsewhere. 'Don't worry about it, you were the blue-eyed girl once before and will be again,' he said comfortingly. 'They seem to enjoy putting someone on a pedestal just for the sheer pleasure of knocking them off.'

'I'm not worried,' Melissa denied, not altogether truthfully. She used to love reading her Press clippings, but not any longer.

They stayed in London for two days, to exchange news and Christmas gifts with their parents, and also for a meeting with Greg, their agent. Greg took them both out to lunch: unfortunately, the restaurant he chose was one where Melissa and Nick had often eaten, within easy walking distance of his flat. She found it increasingly difficult to concentrate on the conversation. She still carried a set of keys with her and the temptation to pay a visit grew irresistible.

It was bitterly cold and already growing dark when they emerged from the restaurant.

'God, look at this traffic,' Jack grumbled. 'It would be quicker to walk back to the hotel.'

'You go ahead,' Melissa said quickly. 'I still have some shopping to do – I haven't bought anything for Mr and Mrs Renwick yet,' she lied.

'Don't be too long – we ought to leave for the airport no later than five-thirty,' Jack called after her. Melissa waved in acknowledgement as she was swallowed up in the crowd of Christmas shoppers.

She pulled her coat collar up around her ears, and hurried along the Kings Road, pausing outside a phone-box and stamping her feet impatiently until she could take her turn. She punched out the well-remembered number and let it ring until she was certain no one was in the flat.

She left the booth and ran the remaining distance, pausing outside the block of flats to look up at the darkened windows. Despite shaking with trepidation, she couldn't fight the impulse to go inside and let herself into the building. Slowly, she climbed the stairs, belatedly wondering if Nick had changed the lock.

But her key fit easily and she pushed open the door, stepping inside and reaching unerringly to switch on the light. She blinked in the sudden glare and memories flooded over her as she walked slowly around the flat, lightly touching pieces of furniture and other familiar objects.

The master bedroom was the last room she entered, and she hesitated on the threshold. Eighteen months had passed since she had been here, happy and in love. It was as if she were a different person, that younger Melissa.

She opened the wardrobe door and burrowed her face in a tweed jacket hanging there; it smelled of Nick, a clean, male scent that was uniquely his. Suddenly angry with herself, she slammed the door shut and whirled around. Then she gasped, noticing her portrait hanging on the wall beside the bed. Probably Sheena had banished it from Glengarry, she thought, with a stab of pain. She had been stupid to come – what had she achieved?

About to leave, she paused; something in her demanded Nick know she had been here. She rummaged in her bag and her hand closed over her lipstick. A small smile curved her mouth as she walked over to the mirror and scrawled NEXT YEAR across it. She stepped back to study her handiwork; it would be of no significance to anyone else, but Nick would know she had been here. Satisfied, she left the flat and hurried back to the Kings Road to hail a taxi.

It was sunny and warm in California, and Melissa quickly began to relax and enjoy a much-needed break from competition. After a few days spent lounging around, she felt full of renewed energy and ready to explore San Francisco and the surrounding area. The previous year she had felt too tired and dispirited to do much sight-seeing, so now Hal and Lisa were happy to escort Jack and Melissa around their city. They indulged Melissa's passion for travelling by cable-car and pointed out all the historic places of interest.

'Historic?' Jack teased. 'You don't know the meaning of the word – you describe any building left standing after the 1906 earthquake as 'historic'! You should see Bellwood.'

'Which Ace now owns,' Hal couldn't resist saying.

'Oh, shush, you two. I love this place,' Melissa enthused, her eyes shining with delight. 'I might buy a house and retire here,' she added lightly. The offhand comment struck a chord; after all, she DID need a place of her very own, somewhere to escape to when she needed a respite from the constant travelling and competing. It made sense for her to invest some of her money in property, but not in England, there was too much Press attention whenever she set foot in the country.

A few days later, she saw the perfect house. The four of them were driving through the wine-growing area of the Napa valley, and she had been idly enjoying the scenery when she spotted it.

'Stop!' she said urgently. Hal slammed on the brakes.

'What's up?'

'That house – look!' She pointed to the white-washed hacienda nestling amongst the sloping hillsides covered in acres of vines. 'It's for sale!'

'Oh, Melissa, what would you do with a vineyard?' Jack sighed.

'I'd sell most of the land,' she said airily. 'Drive up to the house,' she instructed Hal.

'It's private property,' he objected, but reversed and swung up the long driveway.

'They want to sell it, don't they?' she retorted, scrambling out of the car almost before he had braked to a halt.

The house was surrounded by a deep verandah, and she stepped into its shade to knock on the carved oak door. When no one answered she began walking around, peering in windows.

'Melissa, stop that!' Jack protested.

'It's empty,' she told him and continued her inspection, walking slowly around the outside of the house, visualizing the rooms filled with her choice of furnishings. It was perfectly situated, she thought, wonderfully peaceful yet only about an hour's drive from the city, and they had passed through a small town a couple of miles back which would supply groceries and other everyday items. Best of all, she would be left alone here – the American Press had enough home players to write about without bothering overmuch with the English.

'Okay, I've seen enough,' she said brightly, returning to the car. She made a mental note of the realtor's name, then settled back in her seat and changed the subject; if she were to have a secret hideaway, she wouldn't tell anyone, maybe not even Jack.

'Melissa! Ace phoned while you were out shopping,' Jack said, meeting her in the doorway and quickly hustling her out of Lisa's hearing. 'He wasn't at Bellwood; he was in LA, waiting for his flight to be called. He didn't have time to talk for long, but he's flying here and wants us to meet him at The Pacific at seven-thirty.'

'Both of us?' Melissa frowned. 'Why does he want to see me?'

'I guess it has something to do with Mum,' Jack sighed. 'You don't suppose he's proposed to her, do you?'

'God, I hope not!' Melissa said feelingly, just as appalled

by the prospect as Jack, but for an entirely different reason. Ace as her stepfather? The mind boggled!

They were at the hotel early, sitting in silence, each busy with their own thoughts, and sipping their drinks when Ace entered the bar and sauntered over.

'Hi, children,' he said benignly, placing a hand on the top of their heads. Jack groaned, fearing the worst.

'We don't have to call you Daddy, do we?' Melissa giggled nervously.

'No.' Ace beckoned to a barman and sat down. He was unusually nervous, but hid it well. Ever since Melissa had come on to him in New York, he'd been searching for a way out of his relationship with Rose. Ending an affair had never been a problem in the past, but this was different; there was so much dependent on a friendly parting. He'd had to do it in a way that wouldn't alienate Jack or Melissa. And he'd realized that meant letting Rose think the split had been her idea, so he had sulked all over Christmas because she had, as she always did, refused to accompany him to Australia in the New Year.

'Thanks for coming; I'll get straight to it. Rose and I had a long discussion and decided we're going nowhere. She wanted to end it, and I agreed. There are no hard feelings, and I've told her she can stay on at Bellwood for as long as she wants – I'm hardly ever there, anyway, so that won't be a problem until I quit playing tennis,' he said calmly. Jack sighed with relief.

'Oh,' was all Melissa could say. Mum must be off her head, she thought.

'You're keeping Bellwood, though?' Jack asked. 'You don't want to sell?'

'I haven't thought about it,' Ace said slowly. Actually, the novelty of owning such a property was wearing thin; he was sure the manager he had installed was ripping him off. The countryside was a nice place to visit, but he didn't think he would want to live there permamently; at heart, he was a city person. 'Why? Would you be interested in buying it?' he asked.

'I might,' Jack said, to Melissa's surprise.

'You weren't interested when Dad had to sell,' she reminded him.

'I know, but I'm not going to be on the tour forever, am I? Eventually I'll want to settle down, and I'd just as soon do it at Bellwood as anywhere.'

'Is there something, or someone, I should know about?' Melissa asked suspiciously, but Jack just grinned and refused to answer. Ace drained his scotch and put down the glass.

'I'll give you first refusal if I decide to sell,' he said. 'Have you two eaten yet?'

'No, Mrs Renwick's expecting us back – you're invited too,' Melissa told him.

'No, thanks, I'm bushed. I'll order something from Room Service and crash out for a few hours.' He stood up, then added, ultra-casual, 'I'll see you both tomorrow?'

'Sure,' Jack agreed: after I've spoken to Mum, he thought.

'Okay. Goodnight.'

'Goodnight, Ace,' they echoed.

'Let's get back to the Renwicks,' Jack said. 'They'll be waiting for us.'

'Okay.' Melissa glanced at her watch to work out the

UK time – she couldn't wait to talk to her mother about this!

Rose felt very uncomfortable about discussing her sex life with her daughter, even over a long-distance phone call, and parried Melissa's questions for quite a while before capitulating.

'I know I can't hold him,' she said finally. 'I've always known that. And I couldn't bear the humiliation when he publicly replaced me with someone younger.'

'That's a defeatist attitude,' Melissa objected.

'No, just realistic,' Rose sighed. 'You don't understand; how could you, you're too young to worry about wrinkles and gaining weight, losing your figure, counting grey hairs . . . need I go on?'

'You look terrific,' Melissa told her.

'For my age,' Rose amended. 'I simply couldn't cope with Ace on a full-time basis,' she said, rather regretfully. 'It's such a strain, having to get up early and put on my face before he's awake! I even considered going to a health farm!'

'There's nothing wrong with that,' Melissa said.

'No, not if I wanted to do it for myself. But I didn't. I just don't want to make the effort any more. No, it was lovely while it lasted, but I'm not sorry it's over. I'm going to act my age and look forward to becoming a doting grandmother . . . oh, God, darling! I'm sorry . . .'

'It doesn't matter,' Melissa interrupted. 'Have a word with Jack,' she added, and quickly passed the phone to her brother.

'Is she all right?' Rose asked urgently. 'I can't believe I mentioned grandchildren!' she groaned.

'She's dashed off somewhere – what DID you say? Are you okay?' he demanded.

'Oh, I'm fine,' she said impatiently. 'Just give Melissa a hug for me, will you?'

'Sure, but what about you?' Jack said, exasperated.

'I told you; I'm fine, never better. You're not to be angry with Ace; he's being very generous, as always. I'm more worried about Melissa – I wasn't sure whether to tell her this, or not,' Rose went on. 'Nick Lennox called here, the day after you two came to visit.'

'What did he want?' Jack asked.

'To know where she was. I think he must have read in the Press that she was in the country. He made some excuse about her leaving something in his flat, but that couldn't be true, could it?'

'No. What did you tell him?'

'That she had been here, but had left and was on her way to spend Christmas with Hal,' Rose said, a little guiltily. 'I deliberately gave him the wrong impression – I know he had good reason to be angry with her, but I can't forgive him for hitting her.'

'Nor me,' Jack said grimly. 'And I'm sure he did, despite her denials. You did the right thing; he was always bad news. Don't mention it to Melissa, it might unsettle her again, and I'd like her to make a go of it with Hal – he's a good bloke and a great help to her career, which is more than Lennox ever tried to be.'

'I know, and I'm glad you approve of what I did,' Rose sighed with relief. Nick had sounded so eager to contact Melissa and then so hurt, but trying desperately to hide it, when she told him Melissa had already left the country.

After Rose finished talking to Jack, she went and cut herself a huge slice of Christmas cake, and kicked off her shoes to curl up on the sofa in front of the TV. She missed Ace, but it was so wonderful to let oneself go! she thought happily, reaching for a box of chocolates.

The first week of the Australian Open passed quickly; Melissa's schedule too hectic for her to spend more than a few minutes in conversation with Ace. But, on Sunday evening, she was waiting for Lisa in the Players' Bar, and found him sitting alone, sipping unenthusiastically from a glass of orange juice, for he was sticking to his promise to Jack not to drink alcohol during tournaments. She watched him for a few moments; he had a new image – for the first time anyone could remember, he had rid himself of his trademark Apache-style long hair, and was now wearing it cropped to his skull.

'Great match yesterday,' she said. 'I like your hair short,' she approved. He still looked devilishly handsome, hard and dangerous. 'Katy thinks you look almost normal now!'

'Good God, I'd better start growing it again,' Ace said, truly appalled at being described as 'normal'. 'Do you want a drink, honey?'

'No, thanks,' she shook her head. 'Lisa should be here any minute – we've got to go and talk to the Press.'

'And after that?' Ace asked idly.

'Bed,' she replied absently.

'With anyone interesting?' he drawled, dark eyes glinting. Melissa looked at him quickly, and a thrill of excitement coursed through her body.

'I've been kicking myself for letting you go last

September,' Ace continued huskily. 'How about you? Has anyone replaced Hal in your bed yet?'

'No,' Melissa shook her head; but her thoughts flew to Nick, not Hal. She had wondered constantly if he had been to London yet and seen her message and, if so, what his reaction had been. She felt she had burned her bridges by writing those words. Nick had thrown down the gauntlet in the Red Lion and, by leaving her message, she had accepted the challenge.

Ace was watching her closely. He knew nothing of the past or possible future meetings with Nick, but he guessed the uptight English bastard was the reason she had found no one else.

'You're still hung up on His Lordship, aren't you?'

'Yes,' she admitted.

'I could make you forget him,' he said confidently.

'Satisfaction guaranteed, huh?' Melissa mocked.

'Definitely,' he affirmed, and a slow seductive smile curved his mouth. 'You know where I'm staying – suite 612,' he said, then stood up and walked away, leaving her to make her own decision.

Melissa gazed after him, rather wistfully. She was sorely tempted, but . . . what about Mum? she thought. But she need never know, she decided, which was exactly the same conclusion Rose had reached several years earlier when worrying about hurting her daughter.

Next morning, Katy was frowning as she watched Melissa practising with Hal in preparation for her quarter final. Melissa was listless, moving sluggishly and timing her shots badly; suddenly, she yawned hugely and stretched. Katy's eyes narrowed; Melissa

237

had the same demeanour Katy associated with a night spent with Nick. She shot a suspicious look at Hal, then dismissed the idea – he looked as irritated as she felt! Not Hal, then, but someone . . . Melissa ran over to exchange her racket for another.

'It's not your racket that's at fault!' Katy hissed at her. 'What – or should I say who – has got into you?'

'I don't know what you mean,' Melissa lied cheerfully. 'Don't worry, Katykins, I'm fine.' Katykins?! Katy's expression of disgust spoke volumes and Melissa laughed as she moved back onto the court.

She felt wonderful, if rather tired! Ace certainly deserved his reputation of being the best lover on the tour – it had been a night of hot, blistering passion, a terrific release from the sexual frustration she had only been vaguely aware of, but which had been building for months. Best of all, her heart had remained untouched and she supposed she ought to feel like a slut, but she didn't.

'Wipe that smirk off your face!' Katy snapped.

'Sorry,' Melissa said perfunctorily, and tried to focus her mind on her tennis. She was meeting Ace again later; he had already booked another hotel room, using an assumed name, since they both felt the possibility of discovery was high if they stayed in their allotted suites. And neither relished that, being especially apprehensive about Jack's reaction.

Melissa had never played her opponent before; a relative newcomer to the tour who, ranked around one hundred, had played superbly to reach the quarter finals in her first ever Grand Slam. The Press, always alert for a rising star, had been praising Renata all week, and the attitude in the senior locker-room was one of,

'Come on, Melissa, teach the kid a lesson!' Although there was too much rivalry for great friendships to flourish amongst the top players, they did tend to close ranks against those they considered upstarts.

So Melissa, tired, unfocused and with the expectations of her peers on her shoulders, went out to face the unknown. Renata naturally knew far more about Melissa's game than Hal and Katy had been able to glean about the Russian. Melissa's mind was still in Ace's bed and she found herself up against a player in top form and high in confidence. Renata won the first set, 6–1.

'Time to switch to Plan B,' Hal muttered to Katy.

'Any damn plan would be an improvement!' Katy snapped back, thoroughly irate.

Melissa's poor form continued and soon she was facing defeat, trailing 2–5. At the changeover she glanced over to where her supporters were sitting. Jack and Lisa were looking concerned, Hal was frowning in puzzlement, while Katy merely looked cross. I'm letting them all down, Melissa thought, and she recalled Hal talking to her after she had narrowly lost to Steffi, a match she felt she should have won. 'Champions don't ever quit, not even on an off day. They summon up pride, guts and determination. They're not invincible; they can be beaten, but they never lose – the opponent has to win,' he'd stressed the difference.

Okay, lady, let's see if you can win, Melissa thought grimly, and went through the trick she had learned of mentally closing each door in her mind until only the match remained. It was a totally different Melissa who marched back onto court needing to serve to stay in the match and Katy recognized it at once.

'Thank God, she's woken up!' she said fervently. They were still on the edges of their seats, though, relaxing slightly when Melissa served four crisp, fast first serves to narrow the gap, 3–5. They relaxed even more when Melissa broke Renata for the first time in the match; 4–5. When Melissa served again to level at 5–5, Renata was losing confidence as fast as Melissa was gaining it, and began to make errors which Melissa happily capitalized on to take the second set, 7–5.

The third set was over in twenty minutes and Melissa triumphed, 1–6, 7–5, 6–1. She was through to her first Grand Slam Singles semi-final! She beamed her delight as she walked tiredly off court, but couldn't quite meet Katy's gaze. She knew she had almost blown it and would have had only herself – and Ace – to blame. She also knew it was madness to conduct an affair during a Grand Slam, but still she went to meet Ace as arranged.

Melissa stretched languidlly, lying naked beside Ace on the bed, utterly sated after five glorious, sex-filled days and nights.

'I'm going to miss this,' she sighed. The tournament was over and they were all leaving Melbourne to go their separate ways. 'It's been great – you don't want me to change my life, as Nick did, or to love you, which is what Hal wanted. Just pure sex.'

'Pure? I must be slipping,' Ace drawled, and she giggled.

'Wrong word,' she agreed, rolling over onto her stomach and propping her head in her hands. 'It's probably just as well it's over, though; I'm sure Katy suspects and I'm surprised Jack hasn't realized there's something going on.'

'He's too busy with his own affair to notice what you're doing,' Ace told her.

'Affair? Who is she? Not Katy, she's too miserable.'

'No, not Katy.' That was all Ace would say; he was peeved about her easy assumption that the affair was over. The it's-been-great-but-now-it's-time-to-say-goodbye speech was his prerogative. But he wasn't too worried; he felt he could get her back again easily enough and was confident she wouldn't find anyone to replace him while they were apart. Hal was obviously out of the picture and she would be in a different city each week, with no opportunity to strike up a relationship, and she wasn't the type to sleep around. She was only complacent about their separation now because she was sexually replete, but a couple of months of celibacy would have her scuttling back to his bed!

It was stiflingly hot in the room and Melissa reached across him to take some cubes from the ice-bucket, which she used to cool her temples and wrists.

'That looks fun.' Ace grabbed a handful of the cubes and began toying with her, circling her nipples with the ice until they puckered, then bending and tugging the buds into his warm mouth. He slid more ice down her ribs until it melted and puddled in her navel, then he bent and licked that, too. Melissa groaned and grabbed his hair.

'We don't have time . . .' she began half-heartedly. 'We have to meet the others for a farewell drink,' she reminded him. 'Besides, I'm sore!' she complained.

'Shut up,' Ace advised, reaching for more cubes. Melissa gasped in shock as he slipped one deep inside her, and followed it with another.

'Ooh, that's nice,' she decided she rather liked the contrast between heat and cold and began to squirm against his hand.

'You're so hot, they're melting too fast,' Ace told her, replacing the cubes with fresh ones, then parted her legs wide to retrieve them with his tongue. Melissa bit her lip to stop herself screaming.

'Ace?' she pleaded.

'We don't have time, remember?' he teased, pulling away so that she moaned with deprivation. He studied her for a moment; the lovely face, flushed with passion, her dark eyes smouldering, rosy mouth pouting, the gorgeous body wantonly sprawled.

He would miss her, too, he suddenly realized; not just the great sex, but she was one of the few women he enjoyed being with. She interested him, could make him laugh, and she was independent – she didn't demand more of his time than he was prepared to give and didn't want his money. Hell, he might even marry her! He said as much and Melissa hooted with derisive laughter. Ace's black eyes narrowed – perhaps she was too independent!

He said nothing, but re-started his slow tormenting of her body, arousing her until she was near to orgasm and then he deliberately stopped and moved away from the bed.

'Ace!' Melissa got to her knees and stared at him beseechingly, aching with frustration. 'What's wrong?'

'You want me to finish you off?' he asked, grinning.

'Yes!'

'Then say you love me, and want to marry me,' he instructed. 'Go on, say it,' he insisted. Melissa hesi-

242

tated, then crossed her fingers behind her back, out of sight.

'Yes, I love you, and I want to marry you!' she declared. 'Now, come here and make love to me . . .' Ace laughed, delighted with her capitulation, and returned to the bed.

He tipped her onto her back and, grasping her bent legs, pushed them until her knees rested flat against her shoulders. Even Melissa's supple limbs protested at such treatment, but his huge, deep thrusts, seemingly filling her entire body, drove every thought from her mind. She cried out as she came, and then again and again, feeling as if she would never stop convulsing, trying to draw him even deeper inside her. Finally, Ace collapsed on top of her, his breathing as ragged as her own. He released his grip on her and she carefully stretched out her legs.

'You're a sadist,' she complained.

'You loved it,' he said confidently, withdrawing and ridding himself of the used condom. Melissa didn't bother to deny it. She felt too exhausted to move, but a glance at her watch made her scramble off the bed and pick up her discarded clothing.

'Do you think it's a good idea for us both to show up at this "do" tonight?' she asked, as she quickly dressed. They had studiously avoided each other in public since beginning the affair.

'No, but it's an even worse idea for us not to,' Ace replied. 'Jack organized it and he'll expect us both to be there. We don't want him wondering why we don't show up, do we?'

'God, no,' Melissa agreed fervently. 'Just don't say or

do anything provocative,' she pleaded, kissing him one last time before she slipped out of the room.

When he was sure she had gone, Ace went over to the shelf, on which he had hidden a video camera behind a potted plant. The film would have been better with Melissa's co-operation, of course, but he hadn't dared risk asking her.

He showered and allowed himself just one cigarette now the tournament was over, then returned to his hotel. When he joined the others in the bar later, he saw Melissa sitting between Katy and Hal, looking demure in a midnight-blue shift dress. She avoided eye-contact with him as he sauntered over.

'My round – what's everyone drinking?' he asked amiably, passing the orders back to the barman. 'Melissa?'

'Just orange juice, please,' she requested.

'Do you want ice in that, honey?' he enquired blandly. Melissa suppressed a laugh and began to choke, which at least explained the sudden rush of colour to her cheeks. Ace obligingly reached over and thumped her between her shoulder blades.

'What's up – ice cube gone the wrong way?' he asked innocently, which only made matters worse for her. She shot him a beseeching look and he took pity on her, turning to talk to Jack instead.

Melissa tried to pretend he wasn't present, and began thinking about the house in California. She had received word that the owners were prepared to split the property, selling most of the land to a neighbour and the house plus a few acres to Melissa. It was called 'Rose Arbor', which had clinched her decision to buy, and she was eager to spend some time there, making it her very own private place. Not even Jack knew about it and she intended hugging the secret to herself until the house was perfect and ready for visitors.

'You're quiet,' Katy observed. 'Are you feeling okay?'

'Yes, just tired,' Melissa smiled.

'Let's go then.' Katy glanced over to Jack, who had barely spoken to her. 'We have an early flight to catch.'

'Fine.' Melissa gladly followed her lead, pausing only to kiss her brother. ' 'Bye, Jack, I'll talk to you soon. Oh, I almost forgot – what's this I hear about you having a new girlfriend?' she asked. 'Why didn't you tell me?'

'There's nothing to tell – yet,' he replied, frowning a little. 'Who told you, anyhow?'

'Oh, just something I heard in the locker-room,' Melissa said quickly.

'You don't listen to locker-room gossip, do you?'

'Listen to it? I start most of it!' she retorted, and he laughed.

'I believe you,' he said drily. 'Which is why I'm not telling you any of my secrets! Go on, get out of here!' he added, with mock ferocity, then hugged her.

'Leaving so soon, honey?' Ace towered over her. 'You've put on some terrific performances here this year,' he paused for what seemed an eternity to Melissa before continuing. 'Semi-finalist in Singles and finalist in both Doubles events; that's really great. And you'll do even better next time,' he added, with a wicked grin, and knew from her deep blush that she realized he wasn't referring to her tennis! He hadn't been able to resist teasing her, but they both hoped no one else sensed there was a double meaning to his words.

245

CHAPTER 12

Following her semi-final appearance in Melbourne, Melissa's ranking rose to a new career high of six. Unfortunately, a bout of flu prevented her defending the points she had earned the previous year and, when she did re-commence competing, she struggled to produce anything near her best tennis, and had slipped out of the top ten at the start of the European clay-court season.

'I can't play on this stuff!' she raged in frustration, hitting a ball so hard that a player practising on the adjacent court had to duck sharply to avoid possible decapitation. 'Sorry,' Melissa called guiltily, then turned back to Hal and Katy. 'I'm only twenty-one and already past it,' she said glumly.

'Stop being so melodramatic,' Katy sighed. 'Everyone goes through a bad patch occasionally. You're too impatient on clay.'

'She's still not fully fit,' Hal excused her poor performances. 'Perhaps she should stop playing Doubles for a while and put all her energy into her Singles matches,' he suggested.

'Okay, we'll try that,' Katy agreed, but it was to no

avail. Melissa's confidence ebbed as she lost time and again to lower ranked players in Rome, Hamburg and Berlin. The French Open was fast approaching and she still hadn't found her form on the slow red clay, and only just squeezed in the seedings at number sixteen.

'I think she needs a break from training,' Hal said, when they arrived in Paris. 'She's too tense – she'll benefit more from a few days' shopping and sight-seeing than practising.'

'I think I should pull out of the Open and announce my retirement,' Melissa said dolefully.

'Fine,' Katy called her bluff. 'I hate to see a has-been clinging on and gradually slipping down the ranking,' she said briskly. Melissa stared at her.

'I was joking,' she protested.

'Good. Then do what Hal suggests, relax for a few days and then come back prepared to concentrate and win. You'll feel better when Jack gets here,' she added encouragingly. Melissa nodded. That was true, the only problem was that Ace would accompany him!

Her illness and their differing schedules had prevented their meeting since Melbourne, but they had spoken on the phone and, during the last call a few days earlier, he had made it clear he expected her to resume their affair. Her body craved for that to happen, but her heart said 'no'. She was too near Nick, both geographically and in the number of days until she would see him, for her to succumb to Ace. Facing Nick was going to be difficult enough without the guilty knowledge that she had only recently left another man's bed. But, if Nick still hates me, I'll go back to Ace, she thought recklessly.

She was relieved, albeit a relief tinged with disappointment, when Jack arrived in Paris alone.

'Ace pulled a back muscle in Rome,' he told Melissa, and she daren't ask how, or with whom. 'It's not too serious, but he's decided to pull out of the Open to avoid any long five-setters. He wants to make sure he's fully fit for Wimbledon,' he explained.

Melissa's first-round match was very nearly a disaster. She was playing a wild-card entry, a young low-ranked French girl whom she should have beaten easily.

But, yet again, there was the now-familiar feeling of having someone else's racket; her timing was awry, her hand-eye co-ordination almost non-existent. Melissa committed error after error and struggled to win the first set tie-break, then hung on grimly to take the second set, after having served a humiliating total of twelve double faults.

'That was abysmal,' she said afterwards to Katy, almost in tears. 'I think the spectators ought to ask for a refund! Thank God I wasn't on a show court!'

'You toughed it out and you won,' Hal put in firmly. 'That's what matters.' Katy nodded her agreement, but she was worried. Melissa wouldn't get away with such an atrocious performance again.

Fortunately, that first match proved to be a turning point. Melissa had hit rock bottom and still won, which gave her back some confidence. The second match on Wednesday – 'enfants' day, when thousands of shrieking kids packed Roland Garros – was another struggle with herself as well as her opponent, but she emerged triumphant in three sets.

A couple of Mixed Doubles matches with Jack helped

her to relax and enjoy playing again, and on Friday she won her third-round match to take her allotted place in the last sixteen, where she faced Fleur Pascale, another French girl, and a favourite with the crowd. Melissa anticipated that the spectators would be rooting for their home player and ignored them, succeeding in closing her ears and mind to the noise from the partisan crowd.

Fleur was a player who put great pace on her strokes, which suited Melissa perfectly – it was the slow, high balls that frustrated her and lured her into rushing and making errors. However fast Fleur hit the ball, Melissa hit it back faster and harder and, for today at least, more accurately. In a little over an hour, Melissa had notched up one of her easiest wins over the French girl and advanced to the net to submit to the ritual kissing of both cheeks that she disliked.

Her quarter final was more of a tussle, but, this time, she had the crowd on her side and, at long last, felt fit and healthy, and full of renewed confidence. She hung on grimly in a tight third set, eventually winning 8–6.

She tossed her racket in the air and allowed her delight to show as she glanced across to Katy and Hal. A semi-finalist in Australia and now in Paris! Katy held up her hands, fingers splayed, to indicate that this victory placed her back in the top ten.

Melissa narrowly lost her semi-final, but felt she had acquitted herself well against a clay-court specialist and had silenced the critics who had suggested over recent months that she had reached her peak and could progress no further. She'd shown them! And, back in England, on grass, she could accomplish anything, she thought happily, with no premonition of the nightmare about to unfold.

'Uncle Nick! Come quickly!' Juliet pounded on the bathroom door, startling him, and he cursed softly as his razor nicked his chin. Grabbing a towel, he wiped lather from his face as he strode out.

'What is it?' he growled irritably. His nieces had only been staying with him for two days and already he was regretting his invitation!

'Melissa Farrell's on TV,' Juliet told him, disappearing back into the drawing room.

'So what? It is the first day of Wimbledon,' Nick said casually, but he followed her into the room. Jess looked up at him, her face pale.

'It's Jack Farrell – he and Lisa Renwick were in a bad car smash yesterday,' she said breathlessly. 'He swerved to avoid a cyclist and crashed into a wall. They,' she nodded towards the TV, 'showed a picture of Melissa's car – it's a write-off,' she shuddered. Nick winced, glad he had missed seeing it.

'Is he going to be okay?' he asked, glancing at the screen, but the item had finished, for now.

'It doesn't sound very good – they said he's critical, but stable,' Jess repeated the hospital spokesman's words. 'He's in Intensive Care, in a coma.'

'Oh, God,' Nick muttered. 'Try the other channel,' he suggested, sitting down to wait for further news. 'Juliet – get me some coffee and toast, will you?' he requested. She obeyed with an alacrity which would have amazed her parents, but she had an ulterior motive for being helpful; having left the tennis academy in

250

Florida, she was now hoping to persuade Nick to fund her launch onto the pro circuit.

'Melissa will be devastated if he dies,' Jess said, and Nick nodded his agreement. He glanced up as Juliet returned with his breakfast, and sipped coffee while he waited for the latest news bulletin.

'Melissa's supposed to be playing today – do you think she'll show up?' Juliet asked.

'Of course she won't,' Nick said dismissively, then shushed her and leaned forward as the newscaster began talking about Jack. The picture they showed was of Jack and Melissa winning the Mixed Doubles title the year before, and Nick flinched at the sight of Melissa's bruised and swollen face. It seemed incredible to him, now, that he had lost control so completely and inflicted that injury on her. But he had, and there was no excuse.

Jess turned up the volume and they listened in silence, but learned nothing new until the coverage switched to a pre-recorded outside broadcast. The reporter struggled to make herself heard above the noise and confusion created by the dozens of journalists and photographers surging towards Melissa as she emerged from the hospital. She was wearing dark glasses and kept her head lowered, refusing to talk as she tried to make her way to a waiting car.

'Vultures! Leave her alone!' Nick muttered, wishing he had been there to shield her. But she was better off without his protection, he thought, grimacing anew at the violence he had subjected her to. Yet, she had been here in the flat, leaving a message and promising to meet him. That had fuelled his optimism until Rose had told him she had left to spend Christmas with Hal, which had dashed his hopes. He'd know her true feelings in thirteen, no, twelve days' time . . . at least, he would have, but now, with Jack badly injured, maybe dying . . .

'You selfish sod!' he said out loud, disgusted with himself for considering how Jack's misfortune might affect his own plans. Meanwhile, the reporters were pestering Melissa mercilessly.

'How is Jack?'

'Is it true he's suffered brain damage?'

'Will he be paralyzed?'

'Are you competing at Wimbledon this afternoon?'

Melissa ignored all the questions fired at her and ducked her head away from the cameras. Nick saw Katy's bright curls and spotted Hal, then noticed a tall, dark-haired man begin to efficiently clear a path for Melissa.

'Well done, mate. Want a job?' Nick said, then, with a deep sense of shock, realized the man was Ace Delaney. With his hair cropped short, he looks almost human, Nick thought, then promptly revised his opinion when Ace turned, black eyes glittering, a ferocious scowl distorting his features as he snarled a bleeped-out obscenity at a photographer. But at least the cameraman stepped back. Ace was at his rib-breaking, eye-gouging, camera-smashing best, or worst, depending on one's point of view. But he did hustle Melissa and Katy safely into a car, which immediately sped off, destination unknown.

Nick sat back in his chair and watched Hal, not as ruthless as Ace, become enmeshed in the crowd of reporters.

'How is your sister?' someone called.

'Thanks for asking,' Hal said, rather sarcastically, for, until that moment, all the attention had been focused on Jack and Melissa. 'She has concussion and superficial cuts and bruises, but she'll probably be leaving hospital later today.'

'Where's Melissa gone? Will she be playing today?'

'Give her a break!' Hal snapped. 'She hasn't had any sleep – none of us has. Excuse me, I have to contact my parents . . .' Losing patience, he refused to answer any more questions and pushed his way through the crowd.

Melissa and Katy were sitting silently in the back of the car, both too exhausted and occupied with their own dark thoughts to talk. Melissa closed her eyes, but then all she could see was Jack lying so still and pale, kept alive only by a machine. She breathed deeply to fight off a sudden nausea and opened the car window for a gulp of fresh air, trying to rid her nostrils of the stuffy, overheated antiseptic smell of the hospital.

'We're going the wrong way,' she realized suddenly, and leaned forward to re-direct the driver.

'No, we're not,' Katy forestalled her. 'We're going back to Wimbledon, so you can get some rest,' she said firmly. Melissa shook her head tiredly.

'We're going to Bellwood, to collect some things for Mum.'

'Ace is doing that – the cleaning lady is packing a case for him to pick up.' She paused and took a deep breath. 'I spoke to your parents about this, and they agree with me – you're going to play this afternoon.'

'Are you crazy?' Melissa stared at her; she knew Katy was deeply upset about what had happened, yet tennis was still uppermost in her mind? 'I'm not playing. And don't tell me Jack would want me to,' she added.

'He would, actually, but that's not why I want you to play.' Katy frowned as she struggled for words. 'Maybe I am crazy, or just light-headed, but I have this strange feeling that, if you quit, Jack will, too. But, if you win your battle, he'll win his,' she said earnestly, and with obvious sincerity. Melissa shook her head doubtfully; was this practical Katy talking, the girl who mocked Melissa's superstitions?

'Please, Melissa?' Katy begged. 'I've got the mobile phone with me and your father's promised to call if there's any news. And I'll have a car and driver standing by – if necessary, you can default and leave the court, but will you at least try? Please?'

'Oh, God, I don't know. I'm so tired,' Melissa sighed wearily.

'I know, but you can rest for a few hours before you have to prepare for the match.'

'Okay, I'll try,' Melissa agreed reluctantly. She didn't share Katy's premonition, but didn't dare dismiss it, either. What if Katy were right?

The Press hadn't yet discovered the address of their temporary home in Wimbledon, and she was able to lie down quietly for a while, but didn't manage to sleep. At noon, she wandered downstairs and drank some milk, but couldn't face the food Katy tried to press on her.

Katy had switched on the TV; Melissa's match on court one was scheduled to begin at two o'clock, but play had already commenced on the outside courts. However, all the talk was of Jack and Lisa, and of Melissa's decision to take part.

254

Watching in his office in Belgravia, Nick couldn't believe his ears when he heard Melissa would be playing. God, does nothing stop her? he wondered, shaking his head in bewilderment. Not a baby, not Jack lying in a coma. And yet, she loved her brother, hero-worshipped him, even.

'Ambitious little thing, isn't she?' Coop remarked, a trifle disapprovingly.

'Tell me about it,' Nick responded dourly. He'd never understand what drove her, never.

Melissa walked onto court one in a trance-like state, her opponent, a young British wild-card entry, Mandy Lane, a few paces behind her. The applause which greeted them was rather subdued; the spectators hadn't been sure Melissa would appear, even after her name had flashed up on the score-board.

'Heartless!' sniffed one woman, rooting in her bag for a punnet of strawberries. 'Do you want one of these?' she offered them to her neighbour. 'I bought them on the market this morning – I'm not paying the prices they charge here!'

'Thanks.' They chewed for a moment in silence, watching as the players began the five-minute warm-up. Melissa was as elegant as usual, dressed in pristine white, the only colour the Wimbledon green and purple braiding on her shirt. Those watching courtside could detect no difference in her; only the more perceptive of those seeing her in close-up on TV noticed how her eyes showed her desolation; how lost and frightened she looked.

Melissa had gone through her regular exercise routine in the locker-room, but her body was stiff and tense, and she moved awkwardly around the court, mechanically going through the motions, her mind elsewhere.

The match began with Mandy Lane, playing in her first ever Wimbledon, serving. She was extremely nervous and served slowly and cautiously, something for which Melissa would normally have punished her severely, but today she completely mis-hit her returns, dumping two in the net and two way outside the lines. A love game to the inexperienced Mandy.

Melissa walked back to her chair and slumped down, glancing across at the Players' stand. Only Katy was there to support her, trying not to betray her anxiety. Melissa's thoughts flashed back to her triumph over Carlotta Mendoza, two years earlier on this same court. Then, Jack had been here, with her parents, and Nick. Would Jack ever come and watch her again? Would he ever tease her, scold her, be here to advise her? Tears welled in her eyes and she grabbed a towel to cover her face. But her distress became obvious and a murmur of sympathy rose from the crowd.

'Ah, poor love,' muttered one woman, who had earlier denounced her as being callous.

The seconds ticked by; Katy willed Melissa to get a grip of herself, convinced that her and Jack's differing battles were linked. Please, Melissa, she entreated silently.

'Time,' the umpire called. Melissa didn't even hear him. Mandy moved back onto court, glancing uncertainly at Melissa as she passed her.

'Time,' he repeated, then switched off the microphone and leaned down to speak to her. 'Can you continue?' he asked quietly, but received no reply. He looked at his watch, then stifled a sigh, knowing he was about to become the most reviled man in Britain. Reluctantly, he switched the microphone back on.

'Warning, Miss Farrell. Code violation. Time delay,' he announced. The crowd booed and hissed, and he closed his ears to the clamour.

'Bastard!' someone yelled. The hubbub roused Melissa and she stood up, gazing around rather bemusedly.

'It's okay,' she said, to no one in particular. 'He had to do that; it's the rules.'

'Can you continue?' he asked her again, and, this time, she nodded, squaring her shoulders and walking back onto court. Katy sat back with a sigh of relief.

The tears had begun a release of the tension which gripped her and, once she began to play, the physical exertion continued the process. The frustration of being unable to help her brother added venom to her shots and she hit the ball as if it were responsible for what had happened. In a little under an hour she completed what the TV commentator admiringly called 'a remarkable display of courage and professionalism', winning, 6–1, 6–1.

'Is the car waiting?' she asked Katy urgently, who nodded. 'I'll be ten minutes,' she said, and quickly showered and changed, foregoing a much needed massage and ignoring a request to attend a Press interview. She also ignored the crowd outside as, flanked by security guards, she emerged from the Club and dashed to the car.

'I phoned the hospital – there's no change,' Katy

informed her dully. Melissa bit her lip, but stayed silent. She had been stupid to believe Katy's nonsense, but she had and now felt cheated.

There were no guards at the hospital and they had to fight their way through a horde of reporters to reach the entrance.

'How's Jack?' they called out to her.

'If you'd all get out of my way, I'd be able to find out!' she snapped, averting her face from a cameraflash. They hurried up to the ICU; the doctor was in Jack's room, talking to Rose and Daniel, and Melissa paced restlessly as she waited. Ace was lounging in a chair, long legs stretched out before him, and he watched Melissa for a few moments.

'Stop that, you're making me feel dizzy,' he complained.

'Sorry.' She sat down beside him, twisting her fingers nervously as she watched her parents through the glass partition. God, she's ready to explode, Ace thought. He leaned towards her and lowered his voice.

'Are you sure this place is kosher? Some guy in the canteen told me the treatment here is free – shouldn't we hire a real doctor, not leave Jack to an amateur?' he asked solemnly.

'Oh, Ace,' Melissa sighed heavily, and was about to try and explain the NHS when she suddenly realized he was winding her up. 'Don't tease; I'm not in the mood!'

'You're as bad as your brother, no sense of humour. I've spent hours this afternoon, telling him the filthiest jokes I know and he hasn't cracked a smile once!'

'Oh, Ace!' Melissa said again, but this time with a smile.

'That's better,' Ace said softly. 'He'll be okay, honey. He's a tough old sod.'

'I know . . .' she stopped and jumped up as her father emerged from Jack's room. 'Daddy!' She threw herself at him and Daniel forced a smile as he hugged her. 'What did the doctor say?' she demanded.

'They've been running some tests and Jack's going to need an operation if he . . . when he's stronger,' Daniel amended. 'They'll have to do extensive work on his right leg as it's badly shattered, I'm afraid, and there is some damage to his spine, but that's not as bad as they first feared.'

'I'm sorry, but I'm going to be sick.' Melissa pulled away from him and dashed to the loo, bitterly ashamed of her weakness as she clung, retching, to the bowl.

'Take these.' Katy was bending over her, migraine-prevention pills in one hand and a glass of water in the other.

'Thanks. God, I'm so pathetic,' Melissa said miserably. 'Mum and Dad need me to be strong and I'm useless!'

'No, you're not; you can't help feeling ill,' Katy said soothingly. 'Hal's here to take Lisa home. Do you want to go with them?'

'No, I'm staying here; I'm okay. How is Lisa?' she asked, rather guiltily, for she had hardly spared her a thought.

'She's fine,' Katy said, rather shortly, but Melissa didn't notice her tone. She merely nodded, and splashed cold water on her face before returning to the waiting-room.

'May I sit with Jack for a while?' she asked Daniel.

'Of course. Take your mother some tea and try to persuade her to rest,' he urged.

Rose glanced up briefly when Melissa entered and managed a wan smile as she took the cup of tea. She looks awful, Melissa thought, as pale as Jack, her face drawn with worry and sleeplessness.

'I think he has a better colour,' Rose said, almost defiantly, as if daring Melissa to contradict. 'And I'm sure he brightened up when we told him you'd won your match.'

'That's good,' Melissa tried to sound as if she believed it. She sat down and tentatively touched Jack's hand, trying to ignore the array of machinery that was keeping him alive.

'Hi,' she whispered. 'We had a deal – didn't anyone tell you? If I won my match, you were supposed to wake up!' She paused; it felt strange, talking to him while he was so unresponsive, but they had been told that he might be able to hear what was being said, so she battled on gamely while Rose dozed off in the chair on the opposite side of the bed.

It was hot in the room and that, plus the sleepless night and tension-filled match, caused Melissa's eyelids to droop, and she had actually nodded off when Katy tiptoed in some hours later. She gazed at Jack for a moment, then placed a gentle hand on Melissa's shoulder.

'There are some security guys downstairs to take us back to Wimbledon when you're ready,' she told her. Melissa nodded sleepily as she massaged a crick in her neck, taking it for granted that Katy had arranged the escort.

Rose awoke, with a start, and rubbed her eyes, glancing hopefully at Jack, then biting her lip and trying to hide her disappointment when she realized there was no improvement.

'Yes, you must go,' she said to Melissa. 'It doesn't matter if the rest of us mope around here, tiring ourselves out, but you must look after yourself so you can compete.'

'It doesn't seem important now,' Melissa said listlessly.

'It's important to us,' Rose insisted. 'We need some good news, too.'

'I'll go back to the house if you'll come, too,' Melissa offered. Rose demurred, but Daniel added his voice to Melissa's and they finally persuaded her to leave.

When Melissa, with Rose and Katy, emerged from the lift, a stocky dark-haired man of around thirty stepped forward.

'Melissa? We met briefly at Beckenham several years ago – I'm Dale Coupland, Nick's friend and business partner,' he introduced himself quickly, handing over a small card, which bore the legend: Lennox and Coupland. Security Consultants. 'Nick asked me to look after you.'

'Nick did? You're a bodyguard?' she asked slowly. He was in business with Nick?

'That's right. I have a couple of cars outside – where do you want to go?' he asked briskly.

'Back to Wimbledon,' Melissa told him. Coop spoke briefly into a walkie-talkie and, within seconds, two other men appeared to usher them out to the waiting cars.

'Rawlins. Mallory.' Coop nodded to each in turn and Melissa smiled, a little confused. She vaguely remembered Coop, Nick's friend from Army days, and guessed he had invested some money in Coop's business. It never occurred to her that he was living in London and taking an active part in the venture.

The three men quickly and efficiently guided the women out to the cars and they sped off, Melissa with Coop and Rawlins, while Katy and Rose were in the car behind driven by Mallory. Unbeknownst to Melissa, a third car, with Nick at the wheel, pulled out to follow at a distance.

'Nick saw you on TV, being mobbed by reporters and guessed you might need some help,' Coop explained to Melissa.

'I did. Thanks,' she said briefly, feeling somewhat comforted that Nick had bothered to call Coop. She was too tired to carry on a polite conversation, even one concerning Nick, and she sat back and closed her eyes, trying to relax.

A small knot of Press had gathered outside the house, but they kept to the pavement and fell back to let them pass. Coop checked the house was secure, then took his leave.

'Rawlins and Mallory will stay until the night shift arrives, and they'll be back to take over tomorrow morning. Call if you need anything,' he told Melissa. I need Nick, she thought longingly, but only smiled and nodded.

Coop spoke briefly to the two men on watch, then strode over to where Nick had parked his Jag.

'How is she?' Nick asked tersely.

'Exhausted. Unhappy.' Coop shrugged. 'Why don't you go and find out for yourself?' he suggested, curious as to why Nick had delegated the task of protecting Melissa to others.

'No,' Nick shook his head regretfully. 'I haven't seen her for a year, and we parted on bad terms. Very bad. She must be almost at breaking point and seeing me might do her more harm than good.'

'Suit yourself. Here's her phone number,' Coop passed over the piece of paper on which he had jotted it down. 'I'm heading back to town. How long do you intend staying?'

'Not long,' Nick prevaricated. He wasn't even sure why he was there at all. He considered her problem with the Press to be largely self-inflicted, due to her decision to compete but, as the day wore on, he had been unable to sit idly by and ignore her plight.

He sighed and settled more comfortably in his seat. Briefly, he saw Melissa at an upstairs window. She glanced down at the reporters huddled outside, then closed the curtains. The bedroom light stayed on for a few minutes longer and was then extinguished. Still, Nick remained; at midnight, the light showed once more and he reached for his phone, fearing she might have received bad news from the hospital. He dialled the number she had given Coop and the receiver was picked up immediately.

'Hello?' There was unmistakable fear in her voice.

'It's Nick,' he said quickly. 'Sorry, I didn't mean to alarm you.'

'That's okay; I had just got up to fetch a drink, anyway. I can't sleep,' she said, gripping the phone tightly. The late call had frightened her dreadfully and, now, her heart was still pounding heavily, but for a different reason. 'Thank you for sending Coop,' she said politely. 'There are two of his men outside now.' Three, Nick amended silently.

'I know,' he said aloud. 'They'll drive you wherever you want to go and make sure you're not pestered.' He paused; there was so much to say, but now wasn't the time. Melissa was also silent, for much the same reason. 'How's your mother coping?' Nick asked finally.

'Not too good, but at least she's asleep. She asked for some aspirins for a headache and Katy gave her sleeping pills instead – that girl's a walking drug-store.' I remember, Nick thought, rather grimly; he had always considered Katy a little too eager to hand out pills. His silence spoke volumes to Melissa and she went on, rather defensively, 'Mum needed to sleep – Jack could be in a coma for days, or,' she swallowed, 'even weeks.' Or even longer, Nick thought, but he realized she knew that; she just couldn't bear to contemplate the prospect.

'I know,' he said. 'You did the right thing – is there anything you need?' he asked, rather hoping she would say, 'Yes, you.' Yes, you, Melissa thought, longing for the protective strength of his arms around her, and, had she known he was only a hundred yards from the house and not almost five hundred miles away in Glengarry, she might have said so. But she didn't.

'No, I'm okay,' she said, obviously lying, but Nick let it go. His reason for sending Coop in his place was still valid; there was too much unresolved bitterness between them, and Melissa already had more trauma than she could handle.

'I'll be in touch,' he contented himself with saying, and Melissa felt somewhat comforted by that. After checking Rose was still asleep, she returned to her own bed and fell into an exhausted slumber.

There was no change in Jack's condition on Tuesday morning, but he did improve slightly as the day wore on and, although still comatose, he began breathing unaided, and they all felt a surge of optimism and hope.

By the time Geoff Rawlins and Steve Mallory dropped her off at the house that evening, Melissa felt as if they had been a part of her life forever. She had been bundled in and out of cars, hospital and practice courts with a speed that made her head spin. It was as if they each had eight pairs of arms, fending off reporters even more efficiently than Ace and considerably more politely!

She managed to eat some dinner and then hovered by the phone, hoping Nick might call, and she snatched up the receiver the moment it rang, relaxing as soon as she heard his voice.

'Are Rawlins and Mallory looking after you well?' he asked.

'Yes, they've been wonderful,' Melissa said gratefully.

'Good. They'll be with you again tomorrow.' he paused. 'The newspapers are singing your praises today.'

'Only because of Jack. It won't last,' Melissa sighed. 'They're usually banging on about how I've earned millions from the sport and don't put anything back. They should see my tax returns,' she added bitterly, and Nick smiled slightly. She sounded more like her usual self; he'd barely recognized her voice the night before, she'd sounded so strained.

However, he was careful to keep the conversation away from personal, controversial subjects, but he was beginning to feel hopeful that they could find a way through the problems that had beset them for almost two years. How soon they could begin to do that depended on Jack.

CHAPTER 13

On Wednesday afternoon, Melissa played her second-round match, again on court one, and, this time, Hal joined Katy in the supporters' stand. Ace had just lost his match on an outside court and dropped by to see how Melissa was coping.

Nick, watching on TV in his office, grimaced at the sight of Ace and turned away from the screen, concentrating on re-working the roster, for Melissa's round-the-clock protection was wreaking havoc with their schedules.

'Oh, I say, what's happening now?' Nick looked up sharply at the concerned tone. The camera was trained on Melissa; she had stopped playing and was staring intently across at Katy, who had her mobile phone glued to her ear. 'We think there's news of Jack . . . we'll let you know as soon as we hear . . .' The camera stayed with Melissa, invading her privacy, Nick thought angrily, yet, no one had forced her to appear in public. Her face betrayed her fear, then a tremulous smile appeared and the nation smiled with her.

'He's awake?' she mouthed and, receiving vigorous nods of affirmation from Katy and Hal, turned away to hide her tears of relief.

Ace moved quickly to check with Katy, then disappeared from the stand. The umpire, who had pretended not to see the by-play, reminded Melissa of the score.

Her concentration faltered for a couple of games and she almost defaulted, so eager was she to see Jack, but she knew he would hate it if she quit. He would also feel guilty and it was that thought that forced her to buckle down and re-take control of the match.

'I'm sure you'll all be delighted to know that Jack Farrell has regained consciousness,' the commentator informed those watching at home. 'He's suffering serious leg and spinal injuries, but we all hope he will make a full recovery.' Amen, Nick thought, genuinely pleased for Jack and hopeful that his meeting with Melissa could now take place. He watched, with a mixture of pride and bemusement, as she won her match before quickly leaving the court.

'Come on, let's get out of here,' Melissa said to Katy, but the other girl hung back.

'You go, I'll see him tomorrow. This is a family time – besides, one of us ought to stay and talk to the Press,' she added prosaically, and Melissa didn't bother to argue. The news had spread like wild-fire and it was evidence of Jack's popularity that everyone wore beaming smiles and stopped to tell her how pleased they were.

When she finally arrived at the hospital, she was delighted to learn that Jack was out of Intensive Care and had been settled in a comfortable private room. Ace was the only visitor; he'd persuaded Rose and Daniel to go and catch up on lost sleep.

'Hi,' Melissa choked, and was unable to say anything else. She sat down and squeezed his hand. Jack forced a strained smile; he had asked the doctors for the truth and knew his career was probably over.

'I'm sorry I wrecked your car,' he managed, then, over Melissa's head, looked beseechingly at Ace. It was too much, pretending, when what he wanted to do was to vent his frustration and anger. Ace understood and stepped forward.

'Come on, honey, he's tired. You can talk to him tomorrow,' he said firmly.

'But I've only just arrived,' Melissa protested.

'Tough.' Ace hauled her to her feet.

'Jack?' Melissa appealed to him, then belatedly noticed the tension on her brother's face. 'Oh, okay, but how can you possibly be tired when you've been asleep for three days?' she asked lightly, as she stooped to kiss his cheek. 'I love you,' she whispered, then slipped out of the room. Jack angrily dashed tears from his eyes.

'Sod it!'

'Yeah,' Ace regarded him sympathetically. 'Beats me why you chose to hit a brick wall instead of a cyclist. I'd have run the idiot down!'

'And then sued him for scratching the paintwork!' Jack retorted, and Ace didn't bother to deny it. 'I don't remember any of it,' Jack added.

'That's what Lisa told the cops – the cretin shot out of a footpath, right in front of you. It was his fault, not yours, even he admits that, which hasn't stopped him selling his story to the tabloids,' he added disgustedly. Jack just shrugged, then something occurred to him, and he looked at Ace in alarm.

'The Press – has there been any speculation about Lisa and me?' he asked.

'No, surprisingly, but I think Katy's twigged you're more than friends,' Ace told him, with a grin. 'You wouldn't believe the weeping and wailing that's been going on these past few days! Lisa rather gave the game away, I'm afraid.'

'Damn!' Jack swore softly. 'I didn't want Katy to know until after Wimbledon – Melissa relies on her so much, and she's the only one earning any decent money now. Hal and Katy have stopped competing, Lisa had to pull out of the tournament, you lost in Singles and were too bone idle to find yourself another Doubles partner,' he grumbled.

'It's no fun without you, buddy,' Ace said lightly.

'Get used to it!' Jack replied bitterly.

'Sod that for an attitude! I'll get you back on your feet,' he vowed. 'And this orthopaedic guy who's flying in from the States – he's the best.'

'Sure,' Jack said tiredly, obviously unconvinced.

During the following days, it was Ace who kept Jack sane. He sat and listened when Jack needed to let off steam, but jollied him along at other times. Jack knew he was lucky not to have been killed; extremely lucky not to have suffered permanent paralysis, but he didn't feel at all lucky, and fell into a deep depression which he tried to hide from everyone but Ace.

He had a TV set in his room, but couldn't bring himself to watch any of the Wimbledon coverage until Melissa's match on Friday afternoon. He was proud of her, but, for a moment, he wallowed in self-pity, wondering if he would ever again set foot on the almost sacred turf of the Centre Court.

He forced the negative thoughts away and concentrated on Melissa. She had 'presence' on court now, he thought fondly, watching as she waited for the crowd to settle before she began playing. She glanced around imperiously, not because the noise distracted her, but because she expected their attention to be focused on her, not on chatting, reading programmes or eating ice-cream.

She won easily and he switched off the set and began half-heartedly sifting through the bags of mail that had arrived at the hospital. That soon palled and he leaned back, sighing heavily. Drugs kept the pain at bay; it was the inactivity which was driving him mad.

'The last time I spent this much time in bed, I had an air-stewardess with me,' he grumbled later to Ace.

'Want me to fetch you one?' Ace enquired seriously, and Jack smiled slightly.

'No, thanks,' he declined. 'Say, what's this I hear about Nick Lennox?' he asked. Ace's eyes narrowed.

'His Lordship? He's not back on the scene, is he?'

'Apparently Melissa's minders work for him; they used to be in his regiment before the Army cutbacks.'

'Really? I hadn't realized that,' Ace said slowly; since Jack's accident he had been feeling both protective and possessive over Melissa and definitely didn't want Nick usurping his role.

'I don't want him around her again,' Jack continued. 'He's screwed her life up enough already. He tried to stop her career, got her pregnant, beat her up . . .'

'Beat her up?' Ace repeated incredulously. 'When was that?'

'A year ago – don't you remember the state she was in for the Mixed Doubles Final? She admitted to Katy that she'd been with him before she came out with that fairytale about slipping in the bathroom. Katy's afraid they might have arranged to meet up after Wimbledon.'

'Really?' Ace said thoughtfully. 'I'll have to put a stop to that, won't I?'

'Yes. No,' Jack said, in some alarm. Woolly-headed from the drugs, he was belatedly aware that he ought to be having this conversation with his father, or perhaps Hal. Asking Ace to look after Melissa was rather like asking a fox to guard the hen house. 'You're not to upset her!'

'Of course not – what do you take me for? Don't answer that,' he said hastily. 'I'll make His Lordship back off,' he said confidently. 'That's what you want, isn't it?'

'Well, yes,' Jack said, rather doubtfully.

'I can do that. Trust me.' Ace smiled broadly.

'Oh, God,' Jack muttered.

On Saturday, while Jack was undergoing surgery, Ace drove to Bellwood to retrieve the film he had secretly taken of himself and Melissa in bed. It was stacked with others on a shelf – he'd figured a locked cupboard would arouse Rose's curiosity – but he had taken the precaution of placing it in a box depicting a gory war movie, something Rose would never be tempted to watch.

He slotted the cassette into the VCR and sat back to watch, searching for a particularly erotic scene. Before long, he was fully aroused and wished Melissa were with him. Or Rose. Or anyone . . . Hell, he was Lord of the Manor – wasn't one of the perks supposed to be hordes of nubile village girls at his beck and call? Only

Mrs Charles, the cleaning lady, was in the house and she must be pushing sixty, he thought regretfully. Suddenly, he sat forward and stopped the tape before slowly re-winding.

'I'd forgotten about that; that's perfect!' he crowed, a small smile of satisfaction curving the cruel lines of his mouth. If that didn't stop Lennox, nothing would. Of course, there was a risk that Nick would come gunning for him, with half the British Army in tow, but Ace doubted it. He guessed Nick would distance himself from Melissa, maintain a dignified silence and stiff upper lip. And, if he watched much of the tape, his lip won't be the only part of his anatomy that's stiff! he thought, grinning. He was well-pleased with himself as he headed back to London in search of an outlet for his frustration.

Melissa was on court again on Monday, more relaxed now that Jack had successfully come through the operation to repair the damage to his spine and shattered leg. It was going to be a long haul back to full fitness, but she was sure he would make it and looked forward to the day when they could resume their Mixed Doubles partnership in the major tournaments around the world.

She won easily, to take her seeded place in the quarter finals and, this time, stayed to talk to the Press as requested, and then took tea in the Players' lounge before meeting up with her two minders. She didn't really need them, now, but pretended she did as they were her link with Nick. He phoned her every evening to check her security arrangements for the following day; he was always friendly, but casual, and hadn't yet mentioned their 'date' for the weekend.

She was sitting in the back of the car on her way to visit Jack, idly listening to Geoff and Steve chatting in the front and pricked up her ears when Geoff said something about Nick at the office.

'Excuse me,' she leaned forward eagerly. 'Did you just say Major Lennox is in London?' she asked, her heart racing with excitement.

'That's right.' Geoff exchanged a puzzled glance with Steve.

'When did he arrive?' she asked, and again the two men glanced at each other.

'He hasn't been out of London,' Geoff told her. Melissa stared at him, frowning slightly.

'You mean, he's been here for the past week? Since you've been guarding me?' she said slowly.

'That's right,' Geoff confirmed, and she sank back against the upholstery, her brow furrowed. Evidently he didn't care enough to help her personally, but why had he sent Coop? she wondered. Because he hates to see anyone being bullied, even you, she decided miserably, and was quite cool when he phoned that evening.

The Ladies' quarter finals were held on Tuesday, and Melissa was up against her old foe, Lucia. Their rivalry had grown over the years, but they now treated each other with wary respect as they battled for titles on court and lucrative sponsorship deals off it. Lucia, courtesy of an excellent clay-court season, was the higher ranked of the two, but the Italian was aware that Melissa had the more superior grasscourt game and, moreover, was the crowd favourite.

Nick was watching the match on TV in his office when Coop walked in and handed over a bulky envelope.

'From Melissa, marked "private and personal" – Mallory's just dropped it in,' he said, glancing at the screen. 'Ah, the golden girl herself – how's she doing?' he asked casually.

'She lost the first set, got mad with herself and romped through the second and she's leading in the decider,' Nick said promptly.

'You're not watching too closely, then,' Coop commented drily, and Nick grinned. He opened the envelope, took out the unmarked video cassette and regarded it curiously.

'Was there any message?' he asked Coop.

'Don't think so – I'll go and check, though,' Coop offered, and walked towards the door, just as Melissa broke serve to lead 5–2. He glanced back as Nick switched the set to the VCR channel and slotted in the cassette, then both men did a double take as the picture changed dramatically. Seconds before, Melissa had been on the screen, neat and elegant as she sipped water. Now, she was naked, kneeling spread-legged on a bed, breasts thrust forwards, her hair tumbling about her shoulders as she spoke to someone out of view.

'Yes, I love you, and I want to marry you!' she declared joyously. 'Now, come here and make love to me . . .'

'Hell!' Coop exclaimed, then he turned away when Ace Delaney moved towards the bed, just as naked and very obviously ready and willing to comply. Coop dared not look at Nick and hastily escaped from the room, uncomfortably aware of his own arousal. God, she was a sexy piece!

275

The first shock waves of disbelief had stunned Nick into immobility, then, with a snarl of rage, he ripped out the cassette, smashed it violently against the edge of the desk and pulled out the reel of tape. Anger, hatred and jealousy washed over him in sickening waves and he fought desperately for control.

He moved clumsily and sat down, holding his head in his hands. For a brief second, he had thought her message was for him . . . that was funny, that was really funny, he thought savagely; he'd have to be sure and tell her, give her and Delaney a good laugh at his expense. Ace Delaney! Hell! he groaned. How could she let that depraved, immoral bastard touch her, let alone agree to marry him! Her schoolgirl crush on Ace had been understandable, if intensely irritating, but this! And to torture him, Nick, with it? Bitch! His fingers curved into claws, as if already anticipating the pleasure of slowly throttling her. And as for Delaney . . .

'Here, drink this.' Coop interrupted his murderous thoughts by shoving a glass of scotch into his hands, aware it was an inadequate gesture, but the best he could think of. The TV set was still on and Melissa was grinning broadly in triumph as she advanced, the victor, to the net. Coop hastily switched it off before it received the same treatment as the cassette.

'Melissa didn't send it – Delaney gave it to Mallory and told him it was from her, but I'd guess she doesn't know anything about it,' Coop said, trying to find some words of comfort.

'It hardly matters which one of them sent it!' Nick ground out.

'You . . . you're not thinking of doing anything . . .

rash, are you?' Coop asked quietly. Nick looked at him, his expression bleak and uncompromising, and Coop shifted restlessly. 'I mean, you're not going to kill him, or kidnap her, or pull some other stunt?'

'Why would I kidnap her? She didn't look to be under duress, did she?' Nick asked bitterly.

'Precisely,' Coop nodded.

'What the hell does that mean?' Nick snapped.

'It means, you have no valid reason for going after Delaney. Sure, sending that video was a rotten thing to do, but he hasn't stolen your girl – she hasn't been yours for a couple of years . . .'

'Is there a point to this conversation?' Nick interrupted.

'Yes. I know you want to go and rip his guts out, but you can't. He'll wind up in hospital and you'll be in jail! At the very least, the Press will get hold of the story. We're rapidly making a success of this business and it means helluva lot to me – I haven't got a private income to fall back on,' he reminded Nick. 'If you go and beat up Delaney, our current and potential clients will think we're nothing but a bunch of hired thugs! And they'd be right,' he added.

'Do you have to be so rational?' Nick growled.

'One of us has to be,' Coop pointed out. 'Leave it alone, Nick,' he pleaded. 'She's made her choice – don't go near either of them.'

'All right,' Nick agreed, after a pause.

'You mean that?' Coop eyed him worriedly; he'd expected to have a really tough time arguing his case.

'You have my word on it.' Nick looked him squarely in the eye and Coop nodded, satisfied.

'That's good enough for me,' he said. Although Coop's reasoning had been perfectly logical, it wasn't that which had swayed Nick from his first impulse to seek out and destroy Ace. It was the memory of the last time he'd had Melissa naked on a bed. Then, she had been crying and struggling to be free, pleading with him to release her.

The contrast between that and the scene he had just witnessed was unbearable, her words etched like acid on his brain. Even during the most intensely loving times of their relationship, she had side-stepped talk of marriage; he could only ever have dreamed of such an impassioned acceptance of a proposal.

Nick sighed heavily and drained the last of his scotch. Then, with Coop still hovering anxiously, he checked his address book and reached for the phone.

'You don't have to stand over me,' he said irritably, as he waited to be connected. 'I had a date with Melissa on Saturday – I'm cancelling the reservation – okay?'

'Fine,' Coop nodded, vastly relieved, but he remained within earshot until Nick had completed the call. 'Why don't you go up to Glengarry for a few days?' he suggested.

'Run away, you mean?' Nick arched one eyebrow. 'I think not,' he said dismissively.

'I just thought it might be easier for you,' Coop said. 'They might go public now her brother's on the mend.'

'I'd guess they'll make an announcement at the Savoy Ball next weekend,' Nick had already considered their next step. 'But I think London's big enough for the three of us.'

'Mm,' Coop wasn't so sure. 'One other thing – are we

sending Melissa a bill? It's adding up to quite a tidy sum.'

'Yes, she can afford it,' Nick said, and instantly changed his mind. 'No, I'm standing the cost personally; it was my idea to help her – she didn't ask us to,' he said, his innate sense of fair-play winning over his impulse to strike back.

'Fair enough,' Coop nodded. 'Do you want some company this evening? We could go out, get drunk and pull a couple of birds,' he suggested.

'No, thanks, I've got the girls staying with me,' Nick grimaced. 'You can do me a favour, though – take over Melissa's case? I don't want to talk to her.'

'Sure,' Coop agreed readily, and, when Melissa asked, he told her Nick was out of town on business for a couple of days.

Melissa's semi-final opponent was Carlotta Mendoza, the girl dubbed The Carthorse by Ace. She was undoubtedly one of the strongest players on the tour, tall and powerfully built, and Melissa knew it would be a tough match to win, even with the crowd rooting for her. But she had beaten Carlotta before at Wimbledon and at the US Open, so wasn't deterred by the challenge.

Melissa began in top form, easily holding her own service games and constantly threatening Carlotta's with deadly accurate passing shots on both wings. She finally managed to break in the tenth game to take the set, 6–4.

The second set mirrored the first, with Melissa that one, comforting service game ahead. Just one more break and I can take the match, Melissa dared to think, when she led 5–4. But Carlotta wasn't world ranked number three for no good reason and she hung on grimly, forcing a second set tie-break.

The points mounted, neither player yielding an inch, and Carlotta stoically ignored the tumultuous yelling of the partisan crowd. Melissa also closed her ears to the clamour, concentrating with every fibre of her being. She was so close to a Wimbledon Singles final!

They changed ends at 3–3, again at 6–6. Melissa paused and took several deep, steadying breaths before serving. She tossed the ball high and hit it cleanly down the centre line; Carlotta just managed to reach it but couldn't control her return, and Melissa raced in to intercept, volleying it crisply out of reach.

'7–6, Farrell.' Match point! Melissa wiped her palms on her skirt and gripped the racket tightly, bouncing lightly on the balls of her feet, watching intently as Carlotta prepared to serve. She was told later that it was the fastest woman's serve recorded during the Championships – over 120 mph – but, at the time, all she knew was that she read its direction wrongly and never had a hope of reaching it.

'7–7.' Damn! Melissa thought, but her face was impassive as she moved to receive the second of Carlotta's service points. Her mind was still on the previous, lost match point and she mis-timed her return, hitting it marginally long over the baseline.

'8–7, Mendoza.' Set point for Carlotta. Melissa turned to accept a ball and took her time over her preparation. It was a good, fast serve and Carlotta hit the return high; Melissa ran in to take what was arguably the easiest volley of the match and . . . dumped it in the net.

'Game, second set, Mendoza.' The crowd, as one, groaned its disappointment and disbelief. Melissa struggled for composure as she walked back to her chair, careful not to let her body language betray her to her opponent. She sat, outwardly calm, as she thirstily drank cold water and mopped her face and hands with her towel. She didn't dare look over at Katy, knowing she would be rightly furious and making no attempt to hide it.

'Final set, Miss Mendoza to serve.' Both players stood up and walked back onto court. Carlotta won her service game with ease, which meant she was leading, for the first time since the match began, a fact which obviously increased her confidence and on which Melissa preferred not to dwell.

The set became an endurance test, a battle of wills as well as skill. Melissa was already exhausted and now it was she who needed to hold serve to even the score. Her body was protesting at the battering it was taking; her legs were cramping, the recurrent tendinitis in her right shoulder began to gnaw ever more painfully, and a blister at the base of her thumb throbbed and finally burst, causing a stab of pain with every shot.

She held on grimly; 4–4, after a tussle, 5–5. Carlotta, with an apparent burst of renewed energy, served four brilliant first serves to edge ahead 6–5.

Melissa could feel her physical and mental strength failing rapidly, and she served poorly to trail, 0–40. An hour after Melissa had held one match point, Carlotta now held three.

Summoning up all of her pride and resources, Melissa ignored her body's plea for rest and put everything she had into her serving. An ace brought cheers and some hope; 15–40. An error from Carlotta edged the score to 30–40. The crowd roared as if Melissa had taken the match, but she was still match point down.

She took her time, controlling her breathing and wiping the perspiration from her hands and out of her eyes. Her first serve missed the line by a centimetre and she took her time before the second, bouncing it several times as she tried to relax.

Melissa tossed up the ball, her racket handle digging agonizingly into the raw flesh of her blistered hand, and she knew, even as she swung through, that she had missed. A double fault; the most ignominious end to any match, let alone a semi-final of a Grand Slam. She bit her lip as she took the seemingly endless walk to the net to shake hands.

'Game, set, match Mendoza' By two sets to one, 4–6, 7–6. 7–5.

All Melissa wanted was to get off the court and be alone. She felt she had let everyone down. A double fault! Bitterly disappointed, tired and depressed, she endured the post-match interview, then slipped quietly out of Wimbledon: the Championships were over, for her, for another year. And, this year, there would be no consolation in either Doubles events, for she had not replaced Lisa, and certainly not Jack, with other partners.

She shut herself away in her room, refusing to talk to anyone and alternately re-living the one match point she had held and cringing at the memory of the double fault that had ended it.

On Friday morning, she emerged, still aching in body and spirit, relieved to find the house empty. Steve Mallory was waiting outside and she asked him to drive her to the hospital. Before entering Jack's room she paused to straighten her shoulders and plaster a broad smile on her face.

'Hi,' she greeted him cheerfully. He wasn't deceived for a second and regarded her sympathetically.

'You don't have to pretend with me; I can guess how rotten you're feeling.'

'I'll get over it,' Melissa shrugged, sitting down beside him but avoiding eye contact. 'It doesn't matter; I'll have other chances. It was just a tennis match,' she said airily, and promptly burst into tears. Jack smiled sadly and pulled her head down to rest on his shoulder.

'Of course it matters,' he said gently. 'You were one point away from a crack at the title – it's what you've dreamed of since you were a little kid; what you've worked so hard for all these years.' he paused, then added intuitively, 'Just because you're gutted about the match doesn't mean you don't care about me.'

'I know,' she sniffed, searching for a tissue. 'But I shouldn't be feeling so sorry for myself . . .'

'Of course you should – I would be, in your position,' Jack assured her.

'But I'm supposed to be cheering you up, not the other way around,' she said guiltily.

'What are big brothers for? I've been feeling useless, lying here. Besides, I'm sick of everyone being cheerful,' he said truthfully.

'I'm your ideal visitor today, then,' she said glumly, then forced a watery grin.

They dropped the subject of the match and began reading some of the thousands of 'Get Well' cards that were still streaming into the hospital. Melissa left at lunchtime, when Rose arrived, and was driven back to Wimbledon.

As she let herself into the house, she heard voices raised in anger and, sighing, headed towards the source. Katy and Hal were both yelling, neither listening to the other, and they didn't notice Melissa enter. After a moment, she put two fingers in her mouth and let rip with an ear-piercing whistle. The sudden silence was deafening.

'What the hell's going on?' Melissa demanded.

'I quit!' Katy snapped, her face as red as her hair.

'You what? Why?' Melissa gaped at her in shock and disbelief. 'Do you want to stay in England, to be near Jack?' she guessed, innocently adding fuel to the fire. Hal groaned.

'No, it's Lisa who's staying with Jack,' he explained quickly.

'Lisa? Lisa and Jack?' Melissa said slowly. 'Oh, God, Katy, I'm sorry.'

'Spare me your hypocritical sympathy!' Katy spat. She had never felt so humiliated in her entire life. All this time, Jack had merely pretended to believe she no longer loved him; pretending to believe that story about a new boyfriend; he'd been humouring her simply because he wanted her to continue looking after his kid sister! In her fury, she forgot the satisfaction – and cash – she had derived from Melissa's success. She felt she'd been ridiculed and used; right now, she hated the lot of them!

'You knew, all of you. You've been lying to me, laughing behind my back . . .' she broke off and turned away, but not before Melissa saw the tears in her eyes.

'Katy, I swear I had no idea. And no one's been trying to make a fool of you. I'm sure they kept quiet to spare your feelings, not out of malice,' she said earnestly.

'How could you not know? It began in San Francisco last Christmas – you and Hal were in the same house!'

'I never guessed they were more than friends,' Melissa said truthfully.

'Oh, okay, I believe you. You're so self-obsessed you probably didn't notice,' Katy said snidely. 'But it makes no difference – I'm still quitting. Hal can take over – it'll be interesting to see how long he can put up with you!' She glared at Melissa, then turned to Hal. 'I hope you realize what you're letting yourself in for. She doesn't just need a coach; you'll have to be her travel agent, her secretary, her doctor, act as go-between with her sponsors – even chase up her laundry, although you'll probably enjoy that part,' she added nastily.

'Hold on a minute!' Melissa was becoming incensed. 'You've done very well out of my success – you've earned more from my tennis than you ever did from your own,' she pointed out, truthfully but tactlessly. Katy's lips tightened and her eyes shot sparks of fury.

'Thanks for the reminder,' she said icily. 'We'll soon see which one of us needs the other the most, won't we?'

'You're not really serious about quitting?' Melissa couldn't imagine life on the tour without Katy.

'Damn right I am! I can get another job coaching just like that!' Katy snapped her fingers.

'Then I guess I'll see you around,' Melissa shrugged, feigning an indifference she didn't feel.

'I guess so.' They stared at each other for a long moment, then Katy stalked out, her head held high.

'Just you and me now, babe,' Hal said lightly, giving her a comforting hug. 'I've always wanted Jack for a brother-in-law but this wasn't exactly what I had in mind!' he added ruefully.

Katy quickly packed and ordered a taxi. Her departure, with her luggage, was noted by the Press and she admitted she and Melissa were parting company, but declined to say why. Melissa, when asked, refused to say anything at all. Rumours spread through the All England Club and the split was announced to the TV viewers at the end of the evening's highlights programme.

Juliet Stanton was quick to see the possible advantage to her own career – everyone knew it was Katy who had pushed Melissa from obscurity to the top. Unfortunately for her, Nick was out that evening and she had to wait until Saturday morning when, even more unfortunately, he was hungover and in a thoroughly bad temper.

'Melissa Farrell's coach has resigned,' she informed him, dutifully preparing him a breakfast he couldn't face.

'I'm not surprised,' Nick grunted. He even felt a fleeting stab of sympathy for Hal – the poor sod must be feeling as sick as I am, he thought.

'I need a full-time coach . . .' Juliet began.

'Don't bother me now!' Nick snapped, retreating to the privacy of his bedroom. In the doorway, he bumped into Jess. 'Isn't it time you two were going home?' he demanded irritably; he felt as if they had been staying for at least a year!

He quickly dressed and left the flat, heading for the gym where he vented his frustration and rage on the equipment, in particular beating the hell out of the punch-bag, imagining his fist was smashing into Ace Delaney's evil face.

Meanwhile, Melissa was visiting Jack, making light of Katy's defection.

'I'm really sorry I've screwed things up for you,' Jack said contritely. 'I hoped Katy wouldn't react like this if you knew nothing about it.'

'I know, Lisa explained.' Melissa shrugged. 'You're as bad as Mum, being secretive about your love life,' she teased. It must be a family trait, she reflected silently, remembering Ace, and, more importantly, her date with Nick. She shivered in anticipation; maybe, this time tomorrow, she would have some romantic news of her own to impart.

'There didn't seem any point in telling you until we were sure it was leading somewhere,' Jack was saying. 'You know how difficult it is to maintain a relationship on the tour.'

'Yeah,' Melissa agreed dreamily, her thoughts still with Nick. 'Er, sorry, what did you say?'

'I asked if you were going to watch the Women's final this afternoon,' he repeated his question.

'Not likely – I hope it rains,' Melissa said moodily, and was instantly ashamed of herself. But Jack merely laughed.

She tried to forget about the match in which she should have been playing a major role, and went shopping, choosing a new dress for her meeting with Nick, settling on the same fuschia shade of pink she had worn so successfully three years before when she had plucked up the courage to go to Nick's barracks. She also had a relaxing massage and went to a beauty salon for the first time in her life, where she had her hair and nails done and her make-up professionally applied.

Feeling very glamorous, she returned to Wimbledon and dithered over whether she should ask Steve to drive her to the hotel – would Nick want his employees knowing about his personal life? She hedged around the subject with Steve until he, rather confused, phoned the office to talk to Nick. He reached Coop instead.

'Miss Farrell wants to go down to the New Forest, but she seems to think Major Lennox might be driving her there,' he explained.

'Damn!' Coop swore softly: surely the little bitch didn't imagine Nick wanted to see her? 'I'll drive over,' he decided. 'Stay there until I arrive – if she wants to leave before I get there, tell her you've got a flat tyre or something.'

'Yes, sir,' Steve said, more confused than ever.

Coop drove as fast as the traffic allowed, and reached the house to find Melissa, looking utterly ravishing but rather impatient, while Steve fiddled with the car's engine. Melissa spun round as Coop approached, then her face fell as she realized he wasn't Nick.

'Mallory says you're going to the New Forest – I hope you're not expecting Nick to join you,' Coop said coldly. Melissa swallowed and looked so stricken that Coop frowned and had an insane urge to bundle her into his car and take her to Nick. Then he remembered the video and the impulse fled. 'He doesn't want to see you, Melissa.'

'Wh . . . why not?' she whispered finally, her eyes glistening with tears.

'Because of you and Ace Delaney of course!'

'Ace?' Her face blanched. 'Nick knows about Ace?' she asked, horrified.

'Yes,' Coop said curtly. He wondered if she even knew of the film's existence; she certainly didn't know a copy had been sent to Nick. 'Do you still need Mallory to drive you this evening?' he asked, after a long pause.

'No,' Melissa shook her head, then changed her mind. The others would be returning to the house soon and she couldn't face them, or their questions; she had told them she was spending the night with an old schoolfriend. 'Yes. I want to go to Bellwood,' she said in a small voice. 'I want to go home.'

She sat, numb with misery and trying not to cry, while Steve drove, rousing occasionally when he asked for directions, and unaware that he constantly glanced at her in his rear-view mirror. Steve liked her; she treated him and the other minders as if they were equals, not servants, as some of the other clients did, and she had guts. If he had understood correctly, the Major was dumping her, in which case he needed his head examined, Steve decided. Officers!

'Are you okay?' he asked, when she scrambled out of the car.

'Yes, I'm fine,' Melissa lied. 'Can you come and pick me up tomorrow, around ten?'

'Sure. Goodnight.' He sketched a casual salute and drove off.

Melissa retrieved the key to the back door from its hiding place and let herself into the kitchen, dropped her overnight bag on the floor and began filling the kettle.

'Melissa!' Ace stood in the doorway, staring at her. Come into my parlour, he thought. This was an unexpected bonus.

'Oh, Ace, I'm sorry. I forgot I don't live here any more,' she said, and burst into tears.

'Honey, what's wrong?' Ace swiftly crossed the floor and gathered her into his arms. 'Is it Jack?' he asked, knowing damn well it wasn't since he had been talking to him on the phone when he had heard the car pull up outside.

'No, he's fine. It's . . . Nick! I was going to see him tonight and he stood me up!' she wailed.

'The bastard!' Ace said indignantly, as if he had never been guilty of such a thing.

'I bought a new dress! And went to a beauty salon!'

'Was it shut?' Ace enquired blandly, and she choked on a sob.

'Don't you dare make fun of me! He knows about us,' she said, and, for the first time wondered just how he knew. She wiped her eyes and glared at Ace.

'I haven't spoken to him,' he said quickly, and truthfully.

'Oh, well I suppose it doesn't matter how he found out,' Melissa sniffed. Phew, Ace thought with relief. 'I bet he hasn't been living like a monk,' she said resentfully. 'I didn't cheat on him.'

'Course you didn't – I always thought he was an uptight bastard. Typical Englishman, one set of rules for himself and another for you. You didn't do anything wrong, honey,' he said firmly. All the time they had been speaking he had been gently stroking her back and shoulders, gradually drawing her closer to him. He felt her begin to relax and let her cry for a few more minutes then kissed away her tears before lightly brushing his mouth against hers.

'I'm glad you came to me for comfort,' he murmured.

'So am I,' Melissa whispered, forgetting she had come to Bellwood to be alone. She determinedly pushed thoughts of Nick away and gave herself up to Ace's expert touch.

He restrained the urge to take her right there and then on the kitchen table, sensing she would reject such an aggressive approach. Instead he offered the solace he knew she needed, lulling her with soft words and tender caresses. Gradually, he inched her out of the kitchen and up the stairs, discarding his clothing and hers as they went.

Tenderly he made love to her, soothing the hurt and humiliation Nick had inflicted on her. Much later, he gave rein to the streak of savagery from which no female was exempt, unleashing the full force of his passion which left his bed partners bruised and sore, but sated. Very definitely sated, Melissa thought tiredly, when he finally allowed her to sleep.

She woke briefly, when Ace's alarm call disturbed her at six. 'Gotta go – I'm flying to Rhode Island,' Ace told her, leaning down to kiss her briefly. 'Bye, honey, see you around.' Melissa smiled sleepily then turned over and buried her head in the pillows, instantly asleep.

* * *

Rose, knowing of Ace's dawn departure, arrived soon after eight to check the house was tidy, to pick up her mail and to collect more clothes, for she intended staying in London until Jack was out of hospital.

She tripped over a high-heeled shoe in the hall, then noticed the splashes of colour on the stairs which, upon inspection, turned out to be assorted items of clothing. Her lips tightened in annoyance – Ace had promised not to bring his sluts to Bellwood! And, unless the scrubber had left without her dress, she was still here!

Muttering angrily, Rose stomped up the stairs and marched into Ace's bedroom, stopping dead at the sight of her daughter's nude body tangled in the sheets. A confusing mixture of emotions swept over her as she absorbed the fact that Ace's 'slut' was in fact her own child. Memories of her own intimacy with Ace flooded over her and she felt racked with jealousy that Melissa had taken her place in his bed.

Her first instinct was to flee, to pretend she had never witnessed the scene, but something kept her rooted to the spot. My body used to be as slender and firm as hers, she thought enviously. When I was her age, I . . . she frowned; no, that wasn't true. At her age, I was happily married and Jack was toddling around the house at my heels, such a joy and delight. She thought of all Melissa had lost, and the last vestiges of envy vanished as she realized that, not even for all Melissa's fame and fortune would she want to trade places.

She quietly backed out of the room, packed the things she needed and wrote out a list of instructions for the cleaning lady before making breakfast. She was pouring herself a second cup of coffee when Melissa, hair-tousled, yawning hugely, and clad only in a dressing-gown belonging to Ace, wandered into the room.

'Oh, God!' Melissa paused in mid-yawn, and hastily tied the belt of the gown more securely around her nudity. 'You know, don't you?' she guessed, and Rose nodded slightly. 'Are you angry?' she ventured.

'No,' Rose said truthfully. 'Just rather worried. Don't fall in love with him, darling. Monogamy is a dirty word to Ace.'

'I know, and he can't hurt me – I don't love him,' Melissa said positively. 'Last night wasn't planned. The "friend" I was supposed to meet was Nick, but he dumped me and I came here to lick my wounds,' she explained. 'I didn't even know Ace was here.'

'Let me guess – you were in tears and he offered a shoulder to cry on,' Rose said drily.

'Mm. Is that how it started with you?' Melissa asked.

'Yes. I was still upset about the divorce, and Ace . . .' Rose stopped, flushing slightly. Really, what an impossible conversation to be having with one's daughter! 'You'd better have some breakfast,' she said briskly.

'Okay,' Melissa complied, then took a long hot shower before getting dressed. Tactfully, she stripped Ace's bed and bundled the linen in the washing machine before sitting down with Rose over another pot of coffee.

'I really thought Nick and I might get back together,' Melissa confided. 'I thought he'd sent his minders to look after me because he still loved me, but evidently he was just being kind. I suppose he would have come personally if he really cared.'

'Are you going to try and contact him?' Rose asked.

293

'No,' Melissa shook her head firmly. 'He obviously still hasn't forgiven me for having the abortion. I guess I don't blame him for that, but I just wish he hadn't built up my hopes . . . no, it's better if I just continue with my career,' she decided.

'How soon will you be leaving?' Rose asked sadly: she hated the end of Wimbledon fortnight, watching Jack and Melissa fly off to the next stop on the tour. But, this year, she would give anything to see Jack climb into an airplane . . .

'As soon as possible,' Melissa said vehemently. She had two free weeks before her next tournament and, now that Jack was recovering well, decided to stick with her original plan and spend the time in California, turning Rose Arbor into a home. 'I'm going to . . .' she broke off when a knock sounded on the front door. 'Oh, that's Steve come to collect me – I'd forgotten about him!' she exclaimed.

'Drive back with me,' Rose urged. 'I borrowed your father's car.'

'Okay.' While Rose went to speak to Steve, Melissa rummaged for an envelope and took the keys to Nick's flat from her bag and dropped them in. After a slight hesitation, she slowly eased off the sapphire and diamond ring and placed that in the envelope, too.

She went outside and apologized for wasting Steve's time, then handed over the envelope.

'Will you give this to Major Lennox?' she asked painfully. 'And tell him to send his bill to my manager – he knows the address. Oh, one other thing,' she scrabbled in her bag and pressed her spare cash into his hands. 'You and Geoff have been great. Buy yourselves a drink. Please,' she insisted, when he tried to refuse. Steve shrugged and took the money, wished her luck, and then drove off.

He didn't see Nick until Monday morning, by which time Melissa had left for California.

'Not another package from Melissa,' Nick muttered, holding it as if it were an unexploded bomb. 'What is it this time – a wedding invitation?' He felt the outline of a key and ripped open the envelope. He hadn't foreseen the return of the ring, though, and winced when the jewel dropped into his palm. He sat down heavily and watched the light catch the sparkle of the gem stones as he slowly twisted the ring in his fingers. After the video, he'd thought she couldn't inflict any more pain on him. He had been wrong.

CHAPTER 14

When Melissa arrived in California, she was delighted with the progress that had been made with Rose Arbor. The tennis court had been laid and a sophisticated security system installed – if so much as a stray dog wandered onto her property the local cops would be on the scene within minutes!

While decorators were busy inside, she indulged in an orgy of shopping – furniture, carpets, pictures – every day, delivery vans arrived from San Francisco and disgorged their contents. Nor did she neglect her wardrobe; despite her vast earnings, constant travel and living out of a suitcase had deterred her from splurging on clothes, an omission she now compensated for.

She didn't even pick up a racket for the entire fortnight, and her body recovered from the minor injuries, aches and pains which were an accepted part of her working life. Her emotional state improved, too. Jack was at Bellwood, slowly recuperating and undergoing daily treatment from a physiotherapist he dubbed 'The Torturer'. She spoke to him often and he seemed in good spirits, and happy to have Lisa constantly by his side.

The hurt of Katy's defection faded, leaving in its

wake a steely determination to achieve even more without her. The top five beckoned, as did the US Open, where she resolved to do better than reach the semi-final, to eradicate the memory of her defeat at Wimbledon. Nick, she tried not to think about at all, and mostly succeeded, at least during waking hours.

She hired a local couple to act as caretakers in her absence and turned her attention back to her tennis, much to Hal's relief. He was eager to resume training, anxious for Melissa to thrive under his sole tutelage – some of Katy's disparaging remarks still rankled bitterly!

Nick was in London, thankfully free of Jessica and Juliet, although the latter phoned him constantly in the hope that he would pay for her to have a full-time coach. He was driving himself, and everyone else, crazy, waiting for Melissa and Ace to announce their engagement. He almost wished they would, hoping that would enable him to finally exorcise Melissa from his mind.

He was startled to learn that it was Katy, not Hal, who had split from Melissa and, telling himself he was doing Juliet a favour, tracked Katy down at her parents' house in New York and offered her a job. Katy, still smarting over what she believed had been a joint Farrell-Renwick conspiracy against her, flew to London and put Juliet through her paces.

'She'll never be as good as Melissa,' she said frankly. Nick shrugged carelessly.

'Will you take her on? Say, for a year?' he asked. Katy frowned slightly; she had her reputation as a coach to consider and she felt she would be lucky if Juliet scraped into the top one hundred. On the other hand, taking Juliet as a pupil would annoy Melissa intensely – only helping Lucia would anger her more. So she agreed, but shrewdly demanded a set salary, not a percentage of Juliet's earnings.

She guessed Nick's reason for hiring her had a lot to do with Melissa, but it was she who broached the subject, curious as to what had happened in London after she had walked out.

'Why didn't you and Melissa patch things up?' she asked. 'I was sure you would, especially after you supplied her with minders.'

'Yes, well I didn't know about her and Ace when I arranged that,' Nick said moodily.

'Melissa and Ace?' Katy repeated, surprised.

'She's agreed to marry him – surely you knew?' Nick asked incredulously.

'No,' Katy shook her head. 'But I never noticed anything going on between Jack and Lisa, either' she said bitterly. 'I must have been walking around with my eyes shut!'

'But you always watched Melissa like a hawk,' Nick said feelingly.

'True,' Katy acknowledged thoughtfully. 'I'd have sworn she got over all that nonsense years ago – she has no illusions left about Ace. Who told you they were getting married? Ace? He'd say anything just to wind you up,' she said. Nick hesitated.

'I heard it from Melissa,' he said guardedly.

'I still find it hard to believe. Maybe she just said it to, well, get back at you for something?' she hinted, remembering the bruises he had inflicted on her the year before.

'No!' Nick ran his hands impatiently through his

hair, but he couldn't bring himself to divulge the source of his information. 'I know for a fact that she slept with him and she said,' he swallowed painfully, 'she said she loved him and wanted to marry him.'

'Oh,' Katy grimaced; she felt really sorry for him, he looked so hurt and was trying desperately to hide it. 'Any idea when this was?' she asked.

'Not really. Maybe in Paris? It had to be fairly recent – Ace had short hair,' he added. Katy's eyebrows shot up: how the hell did he . . .? The only possible answer came to her and she winced. Ace was such a sod!

'Er, not Paris,' she said finally. 'Ace pulled out of the French Open.' She paused and thought back over the months. Melissa and Ace's paths had rarely crossed; she'd missed the mixed tournament at Key Biscayne through illness . . . 'Of course! I knew there was someone, I just didn't think she would be so stupid as to get involved with Ace. It was in Melbourne, in January,' she said positively.

'You're sure?' Nick smiled suddenly: January – it was now August! She changed her mind, he thought, she's realized what a bastard he is! 'Where is she now?' he asked eagerly.

'She's not competing this week,' Katy said promptly; she still knew Melissa's schedule by heart. 'She'll be in Montreal next week, though, then has another free week before the US Open.'

'I've never been to Canada,' Nick mused out loud, and Katy grinned. Now that she wasn't responsible for Melissa's career she didn't mind at all if Nick ruined her game.

'Good luck,' she said, and they parted amicably, Katy

to bully Juliet into some hard work and Nick to make his travel arrangements.

However, he was evidently not destined to visit Canada. The night before he was due to leave, Coop was rushed to hospital with acute appendicitis. The poor man had barely shaken off the effects of the anaesthetic before Nick was pacing his hospital room.

'Surely you can just supervise?' he demanded irritably, but resigned himself to remaining in London a while longer. He finally made it to New York for the start of the last and richest of the Grand Slams, the US Open at Flushing Meadow.

Juliet had competed in the qualifying rounds, but had failed at the last hurdle. However, Katy had decided to remain for a few days – watching real pros at work would be good for her, she informed Juliet tartly. Besides, Katy didn't want to miss the fireworks between Nick and Melissa!

Hal and Melissa arrived the weekend before the Championships began and, after checking in at the hotel, went straight to Flushing Meadow. It was there, while changing in the locker-room, Melissa discovered that Katy had resurfaced.

'I've just seen Katy Oliver,' Bev Hunter told her.

'Yeah?' Melissa feigned disinterest.

'She's coaching another Brit, Julie somebody . . . Standing?' Melissa froze.

'Juliet Stanton?' she asked carefully.

'Yeah, that's it. Do you know her?'

'Afraid so. She hates my guts,' Melissa said heavily. And, obviously so does Katy, she thought sadly. She was missing Katy more than she would admit, and not only for the amount of work she had done, which had been considerable. She simply missed having her around, even missed her criticism and acerbic tongue.

Dispirited, she wandered off to join Hal in the Players' lounge and imparted the news to him.

'Disloyal bitch!' he said heatedly.

'Juliet's not in my half of the draw, is she?' Melissa asked, in horror; as usual, she had not looked beyond her first round opponent.

'No, relax,' Hal said quickly. She breathed a sigh of relief, but knew that, sooner or later, she would have to take on Juliet.

'Hell!' Hal muttered and Melissa looked at him enquiringly, then followed his gaze. Katy and Juliet had just entered, and . . . Melissa's heart thumped painfully . . . they were accompanied by Nick. Of course, he must be paying Katy, she realized, with a pang. God, he must hate me so much, she thought wretchedly, staring resolutely at the floor as she sensed Nick's eyes on her. She wouldn't, daren't, look at him lest he see how hurt she was.

Nick had, of course, been prepared for seeing Melissa. At least, he had thought he was; he was stunned by the wave of longing which swept over him at the sight of her, setting his pulses racing. He carefully schooled his features; there were too many people around for him to approach her now. But the waiting was almost over, he consoled himself, watching with narrowed eyes as Hal put his arm familiarly around her waist and hugged her close to his side. He has to go, Nick decided firmly.

'What the hell is Lennox doing here?' Hal asked jealously.

'Who cares?' Melissa shrugged, and suddenly began delving in her bag for cash. 'Do you have any coins?'

'What?'

'Coins!' she repeated impatiently. 'And something to put them in.'

'What are you doing?' he asked, watching in bewilderment as she begged and borrowed small amounts of money from fellow players. Melissa didn't answer, but counted out her haul and tipped it into an empty glass.

She sauntered over to Katy, ignored Nick and Juliet, and put the glass in front of her ex-coach, ex-friend.

'Severance pay,' she said coldly, and immediately turned away.

'Melissa! Wait! How's Jack?' Katy asked. Melissa halted briefly and glanced back over her shoulder.

'In a wheelchair,' she said bleakly.

Katy frowned as she turned her attention to the glass, tipping the contents onto the table.

'It's just loose change, American, British, Canadian . . . what's she getting at?' Katy asked Nick. 'Is she saying I was only worth a few coins?'

'No,' Nick shook his head, counting out the money. 'Thirty pieces of silver,' he said quietly.

'What a cow!' Juliet exclaimed.

'Shut up!' Katy snapped, blinking back tears. 'Save your breath for practice,' she said, getting to her feet. 'Come on!'

'I thought I'd go sight-seeing this afternoon,' Juliet pouted.

'Do you want to be a tourist, or a tennis player?' Katy asked irritably, as she had once asked Melissa. Then, the answer had been a prompt and heartfelt 'tennis player'.

'This is my first trip to New York,' Juliet whined.
Katy sighed heavily.

'We'll see you later,' she said to Nick.

'Right.' He also stood up; there was no point in trying
to talk to Melissa here. 'Katy? Find out where Melissa's
staying, will you?' he asked quietly, and she nodded.

'No problem.'

'Thanks. I'll be at the hotel.'

The three walked out together, meeting Ace in the
doorway. The hostility between the two men was
immediate and palpable, and Nick had to struggle
against a strong desire to rip him apart.

'Seen any good movies recently?' Ace drawled, confident he had plenty of allies in the room. His gaze
flickered dismissively over Katy and settled briefly on
Juliet. Nick threw him a 'I'll deal with you later' scowl
and pushed past him.

'Come on, Juliet,' he ordered, through gritted teeth.

'You really are cradle-snatching this time, Your
Lordship,' Ace said mockingly.

'She's my niece, you filthy-minded cretin!' Nick
ground out. Oh? This could be interesting, Ace
thought; life on the tour had been so dull without Jack.

'Hi, honey, I'm Ace Delaney,' he smiled winsomely.

'I know,' Juliet squeaked, blushing furiously.

'Come ON, Juliet!' Nick snapped.

He was so furious, he walked for hours, trying to calm
down. He simply had to sort things out with Melissa
and he couldn't do that while he was eaten up with
jealousy and anger. Eventually, he returned to the hotel
and, along with his key, picked up a message from Katy
– the name of Melissa's hotel.

He showered and changed quickly, anxious to be on his way, and was annoyed when a stranger approached him in the lobby, wanting to speak with him. What the man had to say raised his temper once more and he was again fuming as he took a cab to see Melissa. She hadn't yet returned from Flushing Meadow and he had to wait, kicking his heels and trying to find the words to tell her what had happened.

'Melissa!' He moved quickly towards her, ignoring Hal. 'We have to talk, privately,' he said urgently. It sounded more like a command than a request and Melissa's chin jutted stubbornly. He'd stood her up in London, hired Katy to coach his bitch niece and now he expected her to talk to him!

'See if there are any messages, will you?' she requested sweetly of Hal, then gave Nick an icy glare that should have frozen him solid. 'What do you want?' she snapped.

'Not here,' Nick glanced around at the crowded lobby. 'It's important, Melissa.'

'Okay,' she shrugged, but pointedly waited for Hal before moving over to the elevator. With Hal glaring at Nick, and Nick totally ignoring Hal, they rode up to the tenth floor in silence.

'I said, privately,' Nick repeated, outside the door of her suite.

'I don't have any secrets from Hal,' Melissa said carelessly, walking into her sitting-room.

'Are you sure about that?' Nick asked, then glanced at Hal. 'I think your illusions are about to be shattered, Renwick.' He turned back to Melissa. 'A reporter, name of Flanagan, was waiting for me at my hotel earlier . . .'

'He's called here three times,' Hal interrupted; he'd been rifling through Melissa's messages.

'What does he want?' Melissa asked edgily. 'Why did he want to talk to you?' she asked Nick apprehensively.

'He asked me if there was any truth in a rumour that you aborted my child two years ago,' he said bluntly.

'Oh, hell!' Hal muttered. Melissa was dumbstruck; she had been anticipating only dredged-up gossip about their affair, certainly not this nightmare come back to haunt her.

'Sorry, Renwick,' Nick said insincerely. 'But I did warn you about shattered illusions. Welcome to the club.'

'It's not news to me,' Hal said stoutly. 'And I'm not the one you should apologize to. You got her into the mess and then treated her like a criminal when she dealt with the problem!' he said furiously.

'Apologize?' Nick gaped at him. 'She aborted my child and you think I should apologize?' His voice rose incredulously; he had come to New York with the sole intention of patching things up, but this had rekindled all the old emotions; the anger, the sense of rejection, the conviction that she could never have loved him.

'Stop it, you two, please,' Melissa begged. 'What did you say to him?' she asked Nick anxiously.

'I denied it,' Nick said. 'But I doubt that will be the end of the matter. Rumours like that don't just disappear.'

'There's never been a whisper of it, until now,' Hal glared accusingly at Nick, who arched one eyebrow in disdain. He didn't give a damn about Hal's suspicions.

'Katy,' Melissa said suddenly. 'It must have been Katy who tipped him off.'

'Yeah,' Hal agreed, and forbore to mention that Melissa had probably precipitated the action by her gift of thirty pieces of silver. This really was a betrayal! 'Can she prove it?' he asked. 'Does she have the medical bills?'

'I don't know. I was there under an assumed name,' Melissa said slowly. 'And Ace told her to pay cash.'

'Ace!' Both men stared at her, momentarily united in horror.

'I bet he's the culprit, not Katy,' Nick decided grimly. Hal nodded thoughtfully.

'Why would he blab?' Melissa objected, to Nick's fury. 'At least Katy had some provocation,' she conceded.

'Since when has Ace needed a logical reason to hurt someone?' Nick asked bitterly, deeply hurt that she had confided in Ace, but not bothered to tell him until it was too late. 'Why the hell did you involve him?' he demanded.

'I'm not sure.' Melissa put a hand to her temple and frowned. Hal recognized the signs of an impending migraine and went quickly to fetch her medication. 'I don't know, I can't remember!' she burst out.

'Here, take these,' Hal handed over two tablets and a glass of water. 'You have a match tomorrow,' he reminded her. Nick snorted his disgust. Matches! Was tennis the only thing that mattered to these people?

'Don't worry,' Hal continued speaking to Melissa. 'You can brazen it out. Even if Katy, or Ace, has the bills, your name's not on them. They can't prove it.'

'How can we be sure?' she asked fretfully. 'I can't live with this hanging over me like the Sword of Damocles!

Maybe I should act first, go public and give a Press interview?' she suggested.

'God, no!' Hal was horrified. 'There's a powerful pro-life lobby in the States,' he reminded her.

'There's also a powerful pro-choice lobby,' Melissa retorted.

'Your sponsors will go ballistic,' Hal warned next.

'Sod 'em,' Melissa said recklessly.

'Melissa, listen to me,' Hal said earnestly. 'They pay you millions of bucks because every little girl playing tennis wants to wear clothes like yours; use the same equipment you do. They want to grow up to be just like you. But they do NOT want to have an abortion!'

'What's the matter, Renwick? Worried about your percentage?' Nick enquired nastily. Hal ignored him; Melissa didn't even hear him, she was trying desperately to think.

'I don't see that I have any choice,' she said slowly. 'Nick's right – rumours like this don't just go away.

'Talk to Greg Reynolds – he'll know how to handle it,' Hal said next.

'No, this is private, not business,' Melissa said stubbornly. For the first time, she looked directly at Nick. 'What do you think I should do?' she asked quietly.

'When has my opinion ever mattered to you?' he countered bitterly. 'Do what you want to – you usually do.' With that, he spun on his heel and slammed out of the room.

He walked the ten blocks to his hotel, his thoughts buzzing around his brain like angry wasps. He had earlier left a message for Katy, telling her to wait for him and not to talk to the Press, and she was pacing the lobby when he arrived.

'What's going on?' she asked.

'Come over here.' Nick led her to a secluded table in the bar and sat down, watching closely for her reaction as he told her what had happened.

'Oh, God, poor Melissa,' Katy said softly, sounding genuinely sorry for her. 'This is bound to affect her tennis.'

'Oh, for heaven's sake!' Nick exploded. Tennis!

'It *is* The Open,' Katy said indignantly. 'She has a good chance to take the title – she'd have won Wimbledon if it hadn't been for Jack's accident. The mental stress wore her out . . .' she broke off, realizing Nick didn't want to hear a post-mortem on Melissa's defeat. 'Why did you lie to Flanagan?' she asked curiously.

'I resent the intrusion into my private life,' Nick said stiffly, refusing to admit, even to himself, that he would give his life to protect Melissa. 'Huh! Private life! That's a joke,' he said bleakly. 'I was the last to know. It was you and Ace she confided in.' He paused, struggling with himself, then the agonized words were torn from him. 'Was it my baby?' he asked painfully. 'Why did she tell Ace and not me? Was she sleeping with him even then?'

'No, she wasn't' Katy said quickly. Briefly she considered the consequences of telling him the truth – the worst he could do was sack her, and she'd already had enough of Juliet's whingeing and aversion to hard work. She took a deep breath. 'Melissa didn't tell Ace – I did. I thought he would know of a discreet clinic, which he did; it was all arranged before Melissa even knew she was pregnant.'

'How could she not know?' Nick frowned; he wanted to believe her, but it seemed incredible.

'She suspected she might be, but I lied to her and told her the test was negative,' Katy admitted.

'Why? What was the point?'

'Well, it was just before the tournament, and I didn't want her worrying about anything other than tennis,' Katy explained. Nick sighed; why had he bothered asking? He shot her a look of intense dislike and she squirmed in her seat.

'She didn't want to have a baby,' she said defensively. 'If she had been the slightest bit disappointed because the test was negative, I'd have acted differently. When she did know the truth, she wanted to talk to you, but Ace and I persuaded her not to. I knew that would have been the end of her career, and it would have been a terrible waste of talent.' She paused, but Nick remained silent, his features again impassive, so she plunged on. 'If she'd married you and had the baby, you'd probably be divorced by now.'

'No,' Nick refuted that firmly.

'She'd have felt trapped, and resentful,' Katy insisted. 'That's hardly a basis for a happy marriage.'

'Thank you, Dr Ruth,' Nick snapped. 'Didn't it occur to you that that was a decision for Melissa and me to work out, together?'

'No,' she admitted honestly. 'I blamed you for the mess she was in. Melissa didn't want to have a baby, and I knew I had to act fast, before the Press got wind of it. I waited until the end of the tournament, told her on the Sunday evening and she was already booked in at the clinic for Monday morning. She just wanted it to be over, but she didn't realize how she would feel afterwards. Neither did I,' she added softly. 'It was awful, the tears and self-recrimination, the nightmares and the migraines . . . God, those migraines,' she shuddered. 'I thought she'd die.'

'I saw her at Bellwood,' Nick said quietly, remembering her anguish. He looked at Katy and pictured her and Ace bombarding Melissa with reasons to get rid of the problem as quickly as possible. 'I thought her distress was caused by guilt.'

'It was, partly. But, mostly it was grief,' Katy said. Nick sighed heavily, and chalked up another black mark against Ace. That bastard has interfered in my life once too often, he decided grimly.

'How is Melissa going to handle this?' Katy asked him.

'I'm not sure. She and Renwick were still arguing when I left,' he said, getting to his feet. He paused. 'Thanks for telling me – I'm sorry you didn't do it two years ago,' he said bleakly, and headed for his room. What a mess!

Melissa awoke knowing she was going to tell the truth – keeping quiet about such a personal matter was one thing, lying about it was quite another.

She phoned Bellwood and warned Jack to be prepared for the Press descending on them like a swarm of locusts. He was sympathetic but added his voice to Hal's, advising her to sit tight and warning of the possible loss of sponsorship money.

'I've considered all that, but I've made up my mind,' she said firmly. Jack sighed but recognized the futility of further argument.

'Did you ever tell Dad?' he asked. There was a short, tense silence.

'Damn,' Melissa swore softly. 'No.'

'I'll tell him,' Jack offered.

'No, I'll do it,' Melissa decided. If she could tell her father, the rest of the world should be a breeze, she thought. She immediately re-dialled before she could lose her nerve and emerged, red-eyed, from her bedroom ten minutes later, when Hal knocked on her door.

'Hi,' she greeted him with a wan smile. 'Whoever said confession was good for the soul must have been a complete moron,' she declared.

'You haven't spoken to the Press, have you?' he asked, in alarm.

'Worse than that – I've just told my father,' she said hollowly.

'Oh,' Hal grimaced. 'Was he angry?'

'No. Sad, shocked, disappointed,' she said, blinking back tears. Then she drew a deep breath. 'Let's get to Flushing Meadow and do some work,' she said briskly.

'Fine, but we're going out through the back door,' Hal said. 'That reporter, Flanagan, has been hanging around the front lobby.'

'Oh, God,' Melissa muttered. She hated sneaking through the kitchens, subjected to the curious stares of the staff, but, for the next few hours, she had to put all this to the back of her mind and concentrate on the forthcoming match. If Nick has any sense he'll be on a plane to London by now, she thought, rather sadly. She knew he must be hating all this, and there was nothing for him here except a lot of hassle from the Press.

Her match was due to begin at eleven and, after a

short practice, she changed and limbered up in the locker-room. She guessed at once that Flanagan, or some other reporter, had already been questioning the players. They were mostly concerned with their own matches, but the sidelong glances and strained smiles told their own story. There wasn't usually this much tension in the senior locker-room until much later in the tournament, when they had to compete against each other for places in the final rounds.

She was a little nervous as she made her way onto court, but evidently any gossip hadn't yet filtered down to the spectators and she was greeted with the usual warm applause, despite her opponent being an American. The court seemed a familiar friend, a sanctuary, and she played extremely well, winning easily 6–1, 6–2. She hung around to scribble some autographs, enjoying the acclaim, but couldn't help wondering what the response of these people would be to the news that was about to break.

She showered and changed before facing the Press, even taking time to put on make-up to boost her morale.

'Make sure there's a car waiting,' she muttered to a scowling Hal, before marching into the Interview Room. A quick glance was enough for her to realize they had all heard the rumour; there were far more present than was usual for a routine first-round victory.

With her heart thumping, she took her seat behind the microphones and faced them coolly. The first few questions concerned tennis, but then there was a subtle change in the atmosphere and Melissa braced herself, then decided to jump before she was pushed.

'I have a short statement to make,' she began,

sounding much calmer than she felt. 'Some of you may have heard a rumour that I had an abortion two years ago.' She paused and took a deep breath. They waited, motionless, for her to continue. Hal closed his eyes in despair. 'I refuse to answer questions concerning such a private matter, but I am confirming that the rumour is correct.' She ignored the sudden buzz of conversation and cleared her throat, instantly quietening them. 'I would just like to add that I was nineteen at the time, unmarried, and, as an athlete, felt I had no alternative but to terminate an unplanned pregnancy. That is all I'm prepared to say on the subject, now and in the future.' She stood up and made her way to the door, her head held high.

'Get me out of here,' she said desperately to Hal. She began shaking uncontrollably and needed his supporting arm. The walk to the car-park seemed endless, but finally she was able to collapse into the limo, hiding behind its darkened windows.

'I admire your guts, if not your business sense,' Hal remarked drily.

'I didn't have any choice; I couldn't lie about it,' Melissa said simply, and they rode in silence to the hotel, which was mercifully free of reporters, but not for long, Melissa guessed correctly.

She headed straight to her suite while Hal made security arrangements and borrowed hotel staff to deal with the expected influx of calls, all of which were diverted to his own room, leaving Melissa undisturbed.

Alone, she changed into a leotard and put on some music to soothe her while she went through her routine of yoga-style stretching and relaxation exercises. She felt strangely detached from what was happening around her; she had done her part and had no control over what consequences there might be. No doubt this period of peace in the privacy of her suite was merely the lull before the storm, but, right now, she felt untouched by the tempest surrounding her. Even when she wandered over to the window and saw the knot of Press, including a camera crew, gathered below, she felt unthreatened by their presence.

Hal and his temporary secretaries fielded calls from the media, players, sponsors and members of the public for hours. Eventually, tired and hungry, he'd had enough and went to check on Melissa.

'Hi,' she greeted him calmly, uncoiling her body and getting slowly to her feet in order to switch off the stereo. Despite his exhaustion and worry, Hal reacted physically to the sight of her perfectly toned body in the clinging leotard. But he was resigned to the fact that she regarded him as a friend, almost a second brother, and tore his gaze away. Coaching her, being constantly with her, was both a pleasure and a torment. Today, it was a nightmare!

'So? What's the verdict?' Melissa asked lightly.

'Mm?' Hastily he gathered his thoughts together. 'So far, so good,' he said cautiously. 'Greg was furious, but he's calmed down a bit now – it seems as if most of your sponsors will stand by you, unless public opinion forces them to change their stance. Most of the calls have been supportive,' he decided there was no point in telling her about the others. Probably from cranks, anyway, but, just to be certain, there would be an armed guard constantly at her side until some of the furore had died down. 'Katy rang; she seemed genuinely concerned and sent you a message: don't let the bastards get you down,' he repeated and Melissa smiled slightly.

'A lot of players have called . . . here, I made a list,' he handed it over and Melissa put it aside to peruse later. 'You've been invited to give interviews, appear on chat-shows . . . don't worry, I turned them all down,' he said quickly, noting her reaction.

'Thanks. You look tired,' Melissa realized suddenly. 'I'm sorry, you didn't count on all this when you agreed to coach me, did you?'

'I'm not complaining,' Hal smiled warmly. 'But I am tired. And hungry. Have you eaten yet?'

'No, I . . .' she stopped speaking and frowned slightly. 'What's that commotion outside?' she asked, more puzzled than anxious. They both listened intently as what sounded like a herd of elephants came crashing along the corridor, coming ever nearer.

'It could be trouble,' Hal said quickly, reaching for the phone to summon assistance. 'There's an armed guard at the door, but you'd better go and lock yourself in the bedroom. Go!' he insisted, thinking that his decision not to tell her about the death threat phoned into a radio station hadn't been one of his brightest ideas.

'Melissa!' he yelled, as she headed in the wrong direction. He dropped the phone and ran after her, but she shook off his arm. Muffled curses and groans of pain were now clearly audible and, as Melissa recognized one of the voices, curiosity overcame her and she flung open the door.

CHAPTER 15

Melissa had been right about one thing – Nick detested the attention from the Press, especially after he was offered money in return for his story about his affair with the English Rose. But he hadn't returned to England and he was fortunate in that, once away from his hotel he became just another, anonymous tourist.

He was in a crowded coffee-shop when the news of Melissa's 'confession' broke on TV. Although he had thought of nothing else all day, it was still a shock, and he sat in dazed silence as the vociferous and outspoken New Yorkers discussed the rights and wrongs of one of the most painful episodes in his life.

'Good for her!' declared the waitress. 'If I had to make a choice between earning millions and having a kid, I know what I'd do!' There were nods and murmurs of agreement, especially from the women.

'Yeah, it's her body. She can do what she likes,' said another.

'I know what I'd like to do to her body!' a man leered and was promptly shouted down. Nick made an angry move towards him, then sat down again. Not a clever idea, Lennox, he told himself.

'It's not fair – the male tennis players can have a family and a career, the women can't,' someone else put in.

'Abortion's always wrong,' protested a lone, male voice.

'Trust a man to say that,' the waitress scoffed. 'It's easy to moralize when you know you can never get pregnant!'

'She should have been more careful,' the man persisted.

'What about the guy who knocked her up? It takes two . . .'

Nick stood up and beckoned for his bill, fishing in his pocket for change. As he waited, he glanced up at the TV screen and saw, with horror, that the station was running a phone-in poll on the subject. 'Do you think Melissa Farrell was right to have an abortion?' Two phone numbers flashed up, one for 'yes', the other for 'no'. This is sick, Nick thought, and hastily left.

He guessed Melissa would be holed-up in her suite, and strolled casually past the hotel. The vultures had gathered, he noticed irritably, but were being kept on the pavement by security staff. He scanned the group of reporters for a glimpse of any who had already approached him, but, when he saw no one who might recognize him, he retraced his steps and walked inside the hotel, nodding coolly to the porter.

As he made his way to the elevator, there was a sudden increase in the noise from outside and he glanced over his shoulder to see what had happened. Fury erupted in him when he spotted Ace pushing his way through the throng.

317

Nick stepped inside the elevator and was whisked up to the tenth floor. He noted the presence of the guard outside Melissa's door, then ignored him, flattening himself against the wall and waiting for Ace to emerge from the lift, which he did, only moments later.

'Delaney!' The voice was soft with deadly menace, and Ace whirled round to confront the danger, instantly adopting the half-crouch of the street-fighter. Quick as he was, he was too late to avoid Nick's fist in his face, and his head snapped back under the force of the blow.

'That's for arranging the abortion!' Nick snarled, before doubling him up with a punch in the guts. 'And that's for the video!' Ace went down on one knee, but came up fighting, the heavy gold rings on his fingers as effective as knuckle-dusters.

'That's for getting her pregnant, you stupid asshole!' he hissed, landing two, fast punches before Nick retaliated with a right hook that sent Ace crashing back onto a table, which splintered beneath his weight.

Ace picked up one of the broken-off table legs and advanced, putting all his strength into the blow. Nick deflected one aimed at his head, then grunted in pain as Ace, with the power of one who regularly swung a tennis racket at balls travelling at over 120 mph, used Nick's ribs for practice.

Nick staggered back, but succeeded in grabbing Ace's weapon and wrenching it from his grasp. He tossed it aside and Ace's sneer told him what he thought of that gesture towards fair play.

'I forgot you're a kid from the slums,' Nick said, feinting with his right fist before landing a vicious punch with his left. Ace reeled back and tripped over a Room Service tray which a guest had left outside the door to be collected. He snatched up a steak knife, small but sharp, and waved it menacingly in front of Nick's face.

'Where are your manners, Delaney? Haven't you learned how to use a fork?' Nick taunted, and regretted it a moment later when he had to dodge a jab at his eyes from a hastily snatched-up fork. God, his reflexes are quick, Nick thought, gripping Ace's wrist as he lunged, and using his momentum to flick him over onto his back.

Ace landed heavily but quickly rolled away and, cat-like, and was back on his feet in an instant, still holding onto his weapons, like a hungry cannibal too impatient to wait for his dinner to be cooked.

Nick rushed him and speedily disarmed him, then they both went down, watched with amused interest by the man guarding Melissa's door. They were both fit and strong, almost evenly matched in height and weight, and both landed some telling punches. But Ace had no scruples about fighting dirty and, after a well-aimed kick to his groin, Nick abandoned any notion of fair play; it was simply too much of a handicap!

Furious, and in intense pain, he grabbed Ace from behind and smashed his face against the wall, shattering a picture that hung there, then unerringly stabbed at Ace's kidneys.

'Bastard!' Ace spat a tooth and blood, driving his elbow backwards into Nick's already-damaged ribs. The pain caused Nick to momentarily release his hold and Ace snatched up a coffee-pot, dashing its contents into Nick's face. Fortunately the coffee was cold, but, as

319

he blinked the liquid from his eyes, Ace brought the heavy silver pot down heavily onto the back of his head.

Nick fell to the floor but his fist in Ace's shirt brought his adversary down, too, and they again grappled for supremacy, unaware of doors opening and guests peering out apprehensively to see what was going on.

They had also been steadily progressing along the corridor, moving nearer to Melissa's suite, and the guard fingered his pistol, watching more warily now. But he didn't interfere; he was enjoying it too much, although he occasionally winced in sympathy with first one, then the other.

Weaving drunkenly, they squared up to each other yet again, both winded and in considerable pain. Ace knew he had to finish it, fast, and charged at Nick, who side-stepped smartly and kicked Ace's knee-cap, bringing him crashing down. He looked likely to stay down, this time, and Nick staggered back, holding onto the wall for support, trying to regain some of his strength while he waited to see if Ace would try to continue, and hoping fervently that he would not.

At that moment, the door opposite was flung open and Melissa stood, hands on hips, glaring at the two protagonists and surveying the wreckage; the overturned tables, the smashed vases and crockery, the pictures knocked off the walls. An angel, Nick thought light-headedly, squinting at her leotard-clad body. An avenging angel, he amended, seconds later.

'What the hell's going on?' she snarled. Nick's right eye was rapidly closing up altogether but, as if to compensate, he had double-vision in the other. Two Melissas!

'I came to help,' he said, the words coming out slurred, as if he were drunk.

'Help? Help?' Melissa screeched, at a volume a regimental sergeant-major would be proud of, Nick thought, wincing. 'You call this helping?' she enquired sarcastically, gesturing to the trail of destruction. The corridor looked as if a hurricane had hit it. 'Aren't I getting enough publicity, right now? There's a camera crew downstairs – why didn't you bring them up with you?' There's no answer to that, Nick thought, beginning to slide down the wall.

'Why didn't you stop them?' Melissa demanded of the guard. He shrugged.

'I'm here to stop people attacking you, not each other,' he said calmly, so she turned her attention to a guest who had opened the door of the adjoining suite and peeked out.

'What are you looking at?' Melissa glared at the woman, who promptly disappeared.

Ace, feeling as if his right leg might have to be amputated, tried a winsome, if rather lop-sided smile, pleased that Nick was on the receiving end of Melissa's fury.

'He jumped on me for no reason, honey,' he said. 'Jack asked me to come and give you moral support . . .'

'Moral?' Melissa glared at him. 'You don't know the meaning of the word,' she said scathingly. 'For God's sake, stand up, both of you,' she said irritably. They would both have preferred not to, but pride dictated that they did, and, trying not to groan with the pain of the effort, they tried unsteadily to get to their feet.

'Now, get out!' Melissa ordered. 'OUT!' she yelled,

when they both tried to argue. She turned to the guard. 'If you see either of them here again, you have my permission to shoot them!' With that, she turned on her heel and stormed back into her suite. Hal, who'd been trying not to laugh, now openly smirked, but his smile faded when he realized Melissa had locked him out.

At this point, the hotel manager, alerted by anxious guests, arrived, flanked by security staff. Hal quickly hauled both Nick and Ace upright, ignoring their moans as he steered them away from Melissa's door.

'Keep Melissa out of it!' he hissed. 'Apologize, pay for the damage, but keep quiet! And stop dripping blood all over the carpet,' he added callously.

The three of them managed to defuse the situation, mollifying the manager with wads of cash. He didn't relish any more publicity, either, and was more than happy for them to sneak out of the staff entrance to avoid being spotted by the Press lurking outside.

'Stay here, out of sight, while I fetch a cab,' Hal said, propping them up against a wall. Ace promptly slithered down and sat on a garbage can. Unthinkingly, he kicked out at a scavenging cat and let out a howl of agony, clutching at his kneecap.

'Two cabs,' Nick corrected.

'Hell,' Hal muttered, walking away and shaking his head. He wouldn't have been surprised, or too displeased, to find two corpses upon his return, but they were both hurting too much to resume hostilities, and he got them safely into separate cabs. Then he returned indoors and tried to gain entrance to Melissa's suite.

''Lissa, it's me. They've both gone,' he said, rapping loudly on the door.

'Go away!'

'There's no justice,' Hal said disgustedly to the guard. 'What have I done wrong?'

The noise from a pneumatic road drill boring into his skull finally roused Nick and he opened his eyes. Well, he opened one, the other wisely refused to face the day. He was still fully clothed, sprawled across his bed where he had fallen the night before, and it was the ringing of the phone which had awoken him.

He reached for it, forgetting his injured ribs, and groaned, easing himself more carefully over to the infernal machine, more from a need to silence it than from any desire to speak to whoever had been so inconsiderate as to call.

'Mm?' he managed.

'Nick? It's Katy. Have you seen the news?' she enquired brightly.

'I haven't even seen daylight yet,' he grunted morosely.

'Oh, sorry. Were you asleep? You'll never guess – Ace got mugged in Central Park last night, and he's had to pull out of the tournament,' she said, trying not to sound gleeful. 'Juliet and I are leaving today – it's impossible to get any work done with the Press pestering me about Melissa. If I say 'no comment' one more time, I'll turn into a parrot!'

'Mm. Er, Katy . . . do you have any painkillers?'

'Yes. Do you want me to bring some over?'

'Please. And Katy, don't say anything to Juliet.'

'Oh. Okay,' she agreed, after a pause. 'I'll be there in a couple of minutes.'

Nick eased himself carefully off the bed and, still doing a passable imitation of John Wayne, staggered over to unlock the door, then propelled himself into the bathroom, and splashed cold water over his head. He stared at his reflection in the mirror; the right side of his face was swollen and discoloured, he looked much the same as Melissa had once . . . poetic justice, he decided, lurching back into the bedroom and collapsing onto the bed.

'Come in,' he croaked, when Katy knocked.

'These should do . . . Holy Cow!' she exclaimed, in awe, catching sight of his face. Nick said nothing, but held out his hand for the bottle of painkillers.

'Ace,' Katy realized immediately, and had to bite her lip to stop herself laughing. 'Does he look as bad as you?'

'I hope he feels a lot worse,' Nick growled.

'Why is he blaming a mugger? It'd be more like Ace to sue you for damages and loss of earnings,' Katy said.

'I suppose he wants to keep Melissa's name out of it,' Nick said, rather shame-faced.

'Melissa?'

'We had a fight at her hotel,' Nick admitted.

'Oh, that was sensible!' Katy said sarcastically.

'I know, I know,' Nick sighed, clutching his head and trying to decide if that needed his support more than his ribs.

'You ought to see a doctor,' Katy frowned; beneath the cuts and bruises, he was ashen.

'I will, but I want to talk to Melissa first,' Nick said, although God knew what he could say. Ace had had it coming, but Nick had to admit his timing had been lousy.

'She's still not taking calls – I tried earlier. Do you want me to see if I can reach Hal?'

'Please,' Nick nodded, then wished he hadn't; his head felt likely to fall off.

After Katy left, he slowly stripped off his clothes and stood under a steaming hot shower. That, plus the painkillers, helped his general aches and pains, but, as he gingerly fingered his ribs, a wave of nausea engulfed him and he realized he definitely did need medical attention – Ace's swipe with the table leg had fractured two of his ribs.

Melissa had cried herself to sleep, which had released some of her pent-up tension and she greeted Hal calmly when he joined her as she was eating breakfast. He was carrying a stack of the morning's papers and she eyed them warily.

'Good news or bad?' she asked.

'They're mostly sitting on the fence, waiting to see what the public opinion is,' he told her, sitting down and pouring coffee. He had already eaten, but enjoyed the intimacy of sharing her breakfast. 'Some of the radio and TV stations are conducting phone-in polls on whether you were right to do what you did. So far, you're getting around eighty percent support.'

'Good,' she said, rather absently. She knew it was important, from a sponsorship point of view, but she'd had to live with her own, and Nick's, opinion for two years and what Joe Public thought didn't much concern her.

'Ace has a busted knee, amongst other things. He's had to pull out of the Open,' Hal told her next.

'Oh, no!' Melissa was distressed to hear that. 'Damn Nick!' she said furiously.

'Mm. Katy phoned earlier – he'd like to have a word with you.'

'He won't like the words I have in mind,' Melissa said ominously. 'Do you have the number?'

'Yes.' Hal passed it over, and tried not to feel hurt when she shut herself in the bedroom to make the call.

Nick's pleasure at hearing her voice was short-lived.

'You could have ended Ace's career, you big bully!' she stormed. 'And for what reason? Because he had a brief affair with me! It's none of your business – I'll sleep with every player in the men's locker-room if I want to!' she yelled, intensifying the pain in his head – and his heart.

'No,' was all he could say to that.

'You said you wanted to help – did you mean it?' she asked, rather more quietly.

'Yes. What can I do?' he asked, eager to atone.

'Return to England,' she said, and his wince of pain had nothing to do with his physical injuries. 'No-one will believe Ace was mugged by a stranger if they see you,' she pointed out.

'I'm unrecognizable,' he said heavily. 'I'd prefer to stay. The Press keep asking me for an interview. I can help by saying I supported your decision.'

'But you didn't, did you?' Melissa said flatly. 'You didn't even try to understand.'

'You didn't give me the chance to,' Nick shot back, then sighed. 'Sorry.'

'Even if you did perjure yourself, it wouldn't mollify the pro-lifers,' Melissa said. 'Please, Nick, just leave. I know you didn't leak the story, but your presence here was obviously the catalyst.'

'That's not fair,' he protested, hurt. 'And, as for who leaked the story, who else could it be but your precious Ace?' he asked bitterly. 'He saw me at Flushing Meadow on Sunday, and he wanted to drive a wedge between us.'

'It wasn't Ace,' Melissa refuted, so confidently that he became infuriated. Why the hell was he pleading to be allowed to remain in New York?

'I'll catch the next flight home!' he snapped, and slammed down the phone. It was much later, after hospital treatment, and when he was halfway across the Atlantic, that he realized the import of the first words of Melissa's verbal assault on his eardrums. 'Because he had a brief affair with me . . .' Had? Past tense? Brief? And Ace had said he'd gone to see her in response to a request from Jack . . . hardly the action of a man romantically involved with her. A broad smile curved his mouth and he leaned back, relaxed, and finally drifted off to sleep.

After speaking to Nick, Melissa paced her suite restlessly, unable to settle to anything. Briefly, she watched a group of demonstrators which had gathered outside, some bearing placards, but they were quickly moved on by the police.

Her fury with Nick gradually abated, leaving in its wake a depression and sense of loss. It had been a gallant gesture, his offer to publicly support her action, and she hadn't even asked about his injuries, she realized guiltily. She decided to phone him again, but he had already checked out of his hotel.

She watched TV for a while and made some calls – to the 'yes' number of the phone-in poll being conducted. But that soon palled, and she rang Hal's room.

'I want to go and practise,' she said. 'I'll go crazy if I stay in here all day. And I'm not sneaking out through the kitchens, either – I've done nothing illegal.'

'Okay,' Hal agreed. 'I'll arrange a car and an armed escort . . .'

'Oh, God,' Melissa sighed, and hung up. She changed into her sportswear and, while waiting for Hal, decided to call Ace. It had been sweet of him to blame Nick's attack on an unknown assailant, she thought, and, as a fellow pro, she was horrified that he was unable to compete in the biggest tournament of the year.

'Hi, honey,' he said, quite cheerfully. 'Sorry about last night – have you been chucked out of your hotel?'

'Not yet – Hal's been handing out $1,000 bills like confetti,' she said gloomily, and he laughed.

'Any idea which sod dropped you in this mess?' he asked.

'No. You seem to be at the top of everyone's list of suspects,' she told him.

'Yeah?' He sounded interested rather than annoyed. 'Do you think I did it?'

'No,' she said promptly. 'There would be nothing in it for you and you wouldn't risk losing Jack's friendship again for no good reason,' she added shrewdly, and he didn't bother to deny it. 'How bad are your injuries?'

'My knee is as big as a football and I feel as if I need a kidney transplant, but it could be worse,' he said philosophically. 'I've decided to go to Bellwood while

328

I'm out of action and borrow Jack's physiotherapist. I'm thinking of turning the place into a convalescent home!'

'Give my love to Jack, and to Mum and Dad,' Melissa said, rather wistfully.

'Sure. Do you need anything? Drugs, booze, sex?' he offered, and she smiled.

'I thought you were out of action? You could create an even bigger scandal to take the heat off me – it's a pity you're out of the tournament; you could have hit an umpire, or something,' she said lightly.

'I don't need to be in the tournament to hit an umpire! There are one or two . . .'

'I was joking!' Melissa said quickly. 'I'm fine, really. I'm going out to Flushing Meadow soon . . . oh, here's Hal, now. Gotta go. 'Bye.'

''Bye, honey. Good luck.'

'Are you sure you want to do this?' Hal asked worriedly. 'There's quite a crowd gathered outside.

'I know, I've seen them,' Melissa said airily, picking up her racket case, then a look of horror crossed her face.

'What's up?' Hal frowned.

'Ace and Nick – they're both returning to England – what if they're on the same flight?'

'With any luck, they'll start fighting again and the captain will chuck them both out at thirty thousand feet, without a parachute,' Hal said callously. 'Come on, the car's waiting.'

Two armed guards fell into step behind them and they made their way downstairs. Melissa faltered slightly as she approached the glass-fronted doors;

the crowd seemed more menacing now she had left her tenth-floor sanctuary.

Some of the demonstrators were waving banners; one bore a crude painting of a foetus, another denounced her as a baby killer. Melissa drew in her breath sharply, losing her courage, but, just as she contemplated turning back, she was spotted and a chorus of jeers and cat-calls assailed her.

'You're not going out there!' Hal declared.

'I am,' Melissa said stubbornly, but her legs were trembling as she ventured outside. Ugly taunts greeted her appearance and she held her head high, ignoring the questions fired at her by the Press, but she was unable to hide from the barrage of camera lenses.

'Hell!' Hal swore. 'The car! The cops must have told the driver to move on,' he groaned, scanning the street anxiously for a glimpse of the limo, or even a taxi.

The two guards were watching the crowd for potential troublemakers, and, suddenly, all hell broke loose.

'Get that guy in the red sweatshirt – he's got a gun!' As he yelled the warning, the guard dived at Melissa, knocking her to the ground, shielding her with his body while he reached for his own weapon.

She fell heavily, her arm trapped agonizingly between the unyielding pavement and the hard edges of her racket case. Instinctively, she moved to try and ease the pressure on her wrist but the guard, misinterpreting her attempt to rise, pushed down firmly, making matters worse. Melissa bit her lip against the pain, refusing to cry out in front of such a hostile crowd.

'Stay down!' he ordered, watching as a police officer wrestled the man to the ground, cuffing his hands behind his back. 'Okay, you can get up now.'

'I can't,' Melissa muttered, then, 'Don't touch me! You've broken my arm!' she sobbed, struggling to get to her feet and swaying, her face ashen. 'At least it's the left one,' she said, before passing out and crumpling into Hal's arms.

She was oblivious of the near-riot which followed. While she was whisked to hospital, the pro-lifers exchanged insults and blows with the pro-choice lobby. When the police finally had the situation under control, fourteen more people needed medical attention and more than twenty had been arrested. The gun that had sparked off the incident proved to be a fake.

Nick's plane landed at Heathrow just as dawn was breaking. Exhausted, his body stiff and aching, he collected his car and drove back to central London. Fortunately, the traffic was light and he arrived without mishap, slowly climbed the stairs to the flat and, pausing only to pull off his clothes, fell into bed.

It was dark when he awoke and he lay still for a moment, bracing himself before making the effort to move. But the long sleep had worked wonders; his strapped ribs still ached, but his headache had subsided to a bearable level, and he was able to move around much more easily.

Hunger forced him into the kitchen and he prepared a snack, which he took into the sitting-room. He switched on the TV, tuning to a sports channel, wondering how Melissa had fared in her second-round match. A Men's Singles was in progress and he watched absently, but began to pay close attention as the commentator brought viewers up to date on the day's results during a changeover.

'. . . Lucia Conti is also through, in straight sets. We were all hoping for a repeat of her Wimbledon quarter final against Melissa Farrell, but of course that won't happen, not after yesterday's unfortunate incident . . .'

'Unfortunate incident?' Nick repeated: what the hell had happened? Fear dulled his brain and his hand shook as he reached for the phone, and he had to think hard to recall the number. I shouldn't have left her, he thought, over and over, as he waited for someone at Bellwood to answer the phone.

It was an age before he realized from the tone that they had unplugged the phone, and he quickly re-dialled. Coop would know . . . everyone would know, except me, he thought wretchedly. While he had been asleep, an 'unfortunate incident' had befallen Melissa.

'Coop! Thank God – what's happened to Melissa?' he demanded.

'Weren't you there?' Coop yawned, having been roused from sleep.

'No, dammit! I'm in London!' Nick exploded. 'What's happened to her?'

'She's okay,' Coop reassured him quickly. 'There was a demo outside her hotel yesterday and she was knocked to the ground, but she's not badly hurt. She has a hairline fracture to her arm and sprained wrist ligaments.'

'Oh,' Nick expelled a sigh of relief. 'Which arm?' he asked, knowing how crucial that could be to her career.

'Left,' Coop said.

'That's not too bad, then,' Nick decided. 'But I'm going back to New York . . .'

'Don't do that,' Coop interrupted. 'She's coming to England.'

'Are you sure?'

'Positive. Her coach – Renwick? – was interviewed on TV this morning. He'd already booked her flight.'

'So she might be at Bellwood right now?' Nick smiled happily.

'Yes,' Coop hesitated. 'But so is Ace Delaney,' he added reluctantly.

'Oh, hell!' Nick groaned. 'And I put him there!'

'I wondered if you had,' Coop said. 'A mugging seemed to be too much of a coincidence, even in New York! At least the Press aren't mentioning you, so it won't damage our business interests. I knew you'd have to fight it out one day – who won?' he asked interestedly.

'I think it's what's called a Mexican stand-off, or, to be accurate, a Mexican lie-down,' Nick said drily. 'We were both knackered. God, he fights dirty,' he added feelingly. 'Even if Melissa had been interested in a reconciliation, I'd have been in no condition to accommodate her!'

'Ouch!' Coop tried not to laugh, wishing he'd been there to witness it. 'You won't be coming into the office tomorrow, then?'

'Not unless you really need me. The way I look now, I'd frighten the clients.'

'That bad, huh? Don't bother then.' Coop paused, wanting to ask Nick not to go to Bellwood, but, realizing the futility ot it, he merely said goodnight.

Nick, wide awake despite the lateness of the hour, returned to his snack in front of the TV, half-heartedly watching a late-night movie. He had more sense than to say as much to Melissa but, on balance, he felt the 'unfortunate incident' had been a blessing. It would keep her out of the public domain for some time, and surely the present fuss would have died down, new scandals taking precedence, long before she was fit enough to return to the circuit? She was coming home, was maybe already here! He dismissed negative thoughts about Ace – after all, Rose and Jack were also at Bellwood, he consoled himself.

Melissa, lying in her hospital bed, had been planning her immediate future. At first, shaken and upset by what had happened, she had wanted desperately to go home, to her mother, and had asked Hal to book her a flight. But now, having had time to think, she had changed her mind.

'The British Press will be worse than the reporters here,' she said to Hal. 'Get onto a theatrical agency and hire someone to travel to England in my place. You can escort her to the airport and hopefully everyone will believe I've left the States. Once she arrives in England, she can simply disappear.'

'Where will you be?' he asked.

'California. Hardly anyone knows about Rose Arbor. I'll travel under an assumed name, of course, and hope no one recognizes me.'

'I'll come with you,' he offered.

'No, that would increase the chance of being spotted. Stay here for the rest of the Open, then you can tell the Press you'll be staying with your parents in San Francisco until I'm ready to resume training.'

'They won't be fooled for long,' he said doubtfully. 'They'll quickly realize you never arrived in England.'

'Mm, I've considered that. Book me in at various hotels around the Caribbean – that should keep them off the scent for a while.'

'Okay, I'll arrange it,' he agreed.

Melissa's plan worked beautifully. An aspiring actress of Melissa's height and build agreed to impersonate her, donning a wig, dark glasses and a sling for her left arm. Shielded by security guards and escorted by Hal, she dived from the hospital entrance into the waiting limo which drove them to JFK, closely shadowed by the Press.

Meanwhile, a helicopter landed on the roof of the hospital to whisk Melissa to an airport outside the city. From there, she travelled by private jet to the West coast, transferring to a smaller plane at LA for the last leg of her journey. She arrived exhausted, but with no reporters in tow, at a small airstrip only a few miles from Rose Arbor, where she holed up as furtively as if she had just robbed Fort Knox.

When the Open finished, media and public interest in tennis players, including Melissa, waned, although some members of the British Press corps chased an invisible Melissa around the Caribbean, much to her amusement. She felt she was doing them a favour – they were travelling on expense accounts, after all!

Hal arrived openly in San Francisco and remained in the city for a few days before driving out to Rose Arbor, making sure he wasn't followed.

Melissa had been keeping as fit as possible and began practising with Hal as much as she was able, but, each

335

week, her ranking slipped a little lower as she failed to defend the computer points she had earned the year before.

Once the plaster cast had been removed, she had daily physiotherapy to rebuild the strength in her left arm and wrist, but progress was frustratingly slow. Hal remained cheerful and optimistic about a full recovery, but confided his worries to Jack, himself still on the slow, painful road to fitness, as indeed was Ace, who had required surgery to repair the damage Nick had inflicted on his knee.

'She has around ninety percent power back in her left arm, but she's afraid to use it,' Hal told Jack. 'That double-handed backhand has lost its sting; it's a defensive shot, now, not an aggressive one.'

'She has too much time to worry about it in practice,' Jack said. 'She's too competitive not to use it fully in a match situation. Get it strapped heavily and enter her in a tournament as soon as possible,' he advised. 'She's already dropped out of the top twenty – you have to get her back soon or she'll face next year's Grand Slams as an unseeded player.'

'I know. And a first-round loss to a top player would send her self-confidence plummeting even lower,' Hal sighed.

'Is her problem just physical? Or is she afraid of appearing in public?' Jack asked next.

'She says not, but I think she is apprehensive,' Hal said. 'Most people seem to support her, or at least, think it was her decision to make, but there's always a chance of a group of anti-abortionists staging a protest during a match.'

'I know, but she has to face it, sooner or later. Either that or give up her career,' Jack said bluntly. 'When you think she's ready, enter her in a tournament. Incidentally, Nick Lennox was here demanding to know where she is.'

'You didn't tell him?' Hal asked, alarmed.

'Of course not. I said she was holidaying in the Caribbean! I don't think he believed me, but apparently he draws the line at beating information out of a cripple,' he added bitterly. 'Sorry,' he said quickly, hating his moments of self-pity, which were fortunately becoming rarer. 'No, I didn't tell him – he'll just have to wait and read about it in the Press.'

Nick didn't have long to wait. Just two weeks later, the director of a tournament in Texas announced that Melissa had been granted a last-minute wild card entry into the event which was to take place the following week.

CHAPTER 16

Melissa paced her hotel room nervously, beset by doubts, not at all sure she was ready to face the world. She had been out on the practice court earlier, keenly watched by the Press, who had turned out in far greater numbers than was customary for such a small tournament.

None of the top players were competing, so, although ranked a lowly twenty-seven, she was seeded four, and due to play a qualifier in the opening round. What if her courage deserted her and she lost to a complete unknown? She shuddered at the prospect, then whirled around to greet Hal as he entered the room, noting immediately the rather guarded expression on his face.

'What is it?' she asked fearfully.

'Your first opponent – it's Juliet Stanton,' he told her.

'Oh, God,' Melissa sat down abruptly.

'You'll beat her easily; I've just been watching her play and she has nothing that can hurt you,' he said soothingly.

'She has; she's got Katy,' Melissa said flatly. And Nick's support, she added silently. 'No one knows better than Katy how to win against me.'

338

'Knowing the theory is one thing, actually doing it on court is quite another. I'm telling you, she hasn't got what it takes to beat you,' he said firmly. 'I managed to get a tape of one of her recent matches – come and watch it and you'll see I'm right,' he coaxed.

'Okay.' Melissa gradually relaxed as they watched and discussed tactics, quickly falling back into the old, familiar routine. Hal was pleased that she had recovered her equilibrium so easily, but wondered how she would react to the item of news he had yet to impart – that Nick had arrived to watch his niece play.

He eventually told her over dinner. Melissa paused, then shrugged carelessly and continued eating, but the food had lost its flavour and, inside, she was seething with hurt resentment. He hardly ever bothered to watch my matches, she thought angrily, yet he's flown all this way to watch Juliet attempt to achieve her ambition of beating me!

'I'm going to win two golden sets,' she announced suddenly, a 'golden' set being one in which a player conceded not a single point.

'Steady on, don't put that much pressure on yourself,' Hal protested.

'You worry too much,' she told him blithely.

Melissa avoided eye-contact with Katy and Juliet in the locker-room, but sensed Katy's sidelong glances. She had practised with Hal earlier and was keyed-up, eager to begin. Luckily, her match was the first on Centre Court, filled to its 2,000 capacity, not a large crowd by Melissa's standards, but hopefully a daunting prospect for Juliet.

Thus far, Press, players and the general public had

reacted favourably to her return, and there was only a slight fluttering of butterflies in her tummy as she walked onto court, with Juliet a few paces behind her. The applause was warm and welcoming and Melissa smiled, glancing around at the massed stands. It felt good to be back.

Juliet won the toss – that's all you are going to win, Melissa thought determinedly – and decided to serve first. Melissa chose the end nearest the Players' Box and smiled brightly at Hal as she walked out to begin the warm-up.

She saw that Katy had joined Nick, who was sitting with his arms folded across his broad chest, his face inscrutable behind dark glasses. It was unnerving, not knowing if he were watching her, or not, and Melissa averted her gaze.

As she turned away, a movement in the crowd caught her eye and she stared disbelievingly as Lisa, and far more importantly, Jack, made their way to the front of the stands. Jack was relying heavily on crutches, but was moving much more easily than when Melissa had seen him last.

She stood stock-still, and sections of the crowd followed her gaze, breaking into spontaneous applause, some even standing to welcome him back. Jack waved an acknowledgement before grinning broadly at Melissa as he took his seat, stretching his injured leg out before him.

Melissa wanted to rush over to him but contented herself with blowing him a kiss. Nick, sitting only a few yards away, felt an insane urge to stretch out his hand and capture the kiss for himself.

'She'll be unbeatable now,' he murmured to Katy.

'I'm not so sure. It's great for her morale, but bad for her concentration,' Katy replied, rather absently. She had been watching Jack covertly, feeling pity for his continued disability, but she was surprised and relieved to discover she was no longer in love with him. Without her being aware of it, the months apart from both Jack and Melissa had cured her of her unrequited love.

The five-minute warm-up was over too quickly for Melissa; she was distracted both by Jack's arrival and Nick's presence. She took some deep, steadying breaths as the crowd quieted, waiting for Juliet to begin serving. Juliet greatly resembled Jessica, but was a far better player; faster, fitter, and she hit the ball harder and more accurately than her sister ever had.

It was always difficult playing someone for the first time and Melissa deliberately prolonged the early rallies, playing safe, steady strokes to both test Juliet's strengths and weaknesses and also to reacclimatize herself to the surroundings and pressures of competition.

The first game went, three times, to deuce, then Melissa made an error on a volley to give Juliet the advantage. Grimacing, Melissa returned to the baseline and proceeded to reel off three brilliant returns of serve to take the game, walking back to her chair with a brief nod of satisfaction.

'Damn, she's settled down faster than I thought she would,' Katy muttered, but she didn't sound too displeased, Nick noted, and he smiled slightly.

Melissa was confident about her own serve, and now felt she had all the information she needed to counter anything Juliet might try. She won four straight points on serve and, at 2–0, went onto the attack.

Juliet, despite eventually losing the first game, had been lulled into thinking Melissa had difficulty in reading her serve, a notion of which she was quickly disabused as she found herself trailing 3–0. Within minutes, the score was 5–0 and Melissa served out the set, 6–0, not the 'golden' set she had vowed to win, but near enough.

Juliet's confidence was in tatters, and she was further demoralized when she again lost her serve. Nick, watching closely, had a sense of déjà vu – although the standard of play was far greater, the scene was reminiscent of the day he'd watched Melissa beat Jessica. On that occasion he had felt her contest with Jess was as unmatched as a race between a thoroughbred and a carthorse. He had much the same feeling today.

Melissa broke again to lead 3–0, and was thoroughly enjoying herself. It was wonderful to be back in front of a supportive crowd, listening to the appreciative oohs and aahs, the warm applause. She began to play as if she were taking part in an exhibition match, purely to entertain.

Katy realized, even quicker than Hal, what she was doing and unthinkingly caught her eye and gestured to her, using one of their old signals that basically meant; stop mucking about and get on with it! Melissa stared at Katy for a moment, then grinned broadly, and Katy dropped her head in her hands.

'Oh, God, I'm sorry, I've just been coaching Melissa,' she groaned, but Nick laughed.

'I don't think she needs it,' he said easily, wondering

if anyone amongst the crowd wanted Juliet to win. He certainly didn't, despite the vast sums of money she was costing him.

Juliet, losing badly from the back of the court, rushed forward in an attempt to wrest the net position, from where Melissa was winning so many points. Melissa's answer was to hoist up a perfect top-spin lob which landed an inch inside the baseline. Juliet scurried back, red-faced and panting with exertion, but failed to reach the ball.

After another volleying duel at the net, which Juliet lost, she threw away her racket in disgust. It hit the top of the net and bounced over, landing near Melissa's foot. It had been accidental, but earned her the disapproval of the crowd and a stern look of warning from the umpire. Had Melissa not felt herself to be 'on probation' with the public, she'd have thrown the racket back. Instead, she picked it up and silently handed it over, with a slight smile and a virtuous expression on her face.

'Look at her – butter wouldn't melt in her mouth,' Jack said, laughing. Hal nodded, but he wished she would wrap the match up quickly.

A twinge of pain in her left wrist gave Melissa the impetus to do what he wanted, and she ended with four terrific serves for a 6–0, 6–0 whitewash.

Juliet avoided looking at her as they exchanged the briefest of handshakes, then pushed past her to speak to Nick and Katy.

'I suppose you're going to moan on about what I did wrong,' Juliet said sulkily to Katy.

'She could spend the rest of her life having that

343

conversation,' Melissa remarked, to no one in particular. Nick's lips twitched with amusement, but he said nothing and watched her rush over to greet her brother.

Once again, fate had intervened to delay the showdown he was determined to have with Melissa. First, he'd felt compelled to wait until the contest with Juliet had been settled, and now Jack's unexpected arrival had caused another postponement.

'Jack!' Melissa hugged him tightly. 'Thank you for coming; I'm so glad you're here! But you shouldn't have travelled all this way,' she added.

'I'm fine,' he assured her. 'The plane was half empty and I was able to stretch out and sleep for most of the journey.'

'Well played,' Lisa put in, and Melissa hugged her, too, then turned to Hal and kissed his cheek.

'I guess this was your idea?'

'Yep. Their flight was delayed, though. I was afraid they weren't going to make it.'

'Well done, Melissa,' Katy stopped by to say. 'Hello, Jack,' she added shyly.

'Katy,' he acknowledged her briefly and unsmilingly; he still felt she was the person most likely to have leaked the story about Melissa's abortion. She hesitated, then continued on her way. Melissa turned to watch her go, her gaze lingering on Nick as he shouldered his way through the crowd. She sighed, then turned back to her brother and began bombarding him with questions about what was happening at home.

Later that evening when Jack, exhausted from the journey, had gone to bed, and Hal and Lisa were

344

catching up on family gossip, Melissa wandered outside the hotel for a breath of fresh air before retiring to her room.

'Should you be out here without a bodyguard?' Nick's deep voice startled her and she put a hand to her mouth to stifle a cry as he stepped out of the shadows. She vividly recalled his anger when she had thrashed Jessica at Eastbourne, and was damned if she was going to listen to more of the same for putting Juliet in her place!

'Obviously not,' she bit out. 'If I'd known there was an undesirable character lurking about, I'd have stayed indoors!'

'Why are you angry?' Nick sounded genuinely puzzled. 'You're not still upset because I fought with Ace?' he asked, his heart sinking.

'Partly – he's still not fit enough to compete. But, no, it's . . . oh! When I have a couple of hours to spare, I'll write you a list!' she said, furious that he needed to ask.

'No. Tell me now,' Nick said, moving closer. Too close for comfort and Melissa turned her back on him. He stepped even nearer and reached out to touch her shoulders, but the rigidity in them stopped him. 'Tell me,' he insisted.

'Okay, I will. Glengarry, for starters!' she snapped.

'Glengarry?' Nick's brows rose in astonishment. 'What about it?'

'You always said it was your duty to live there, and you expected me to give up my career and act as an unpaid social worker to the villagers! But now you've set up business with Coop and live in London,' she said; it still hurt that he had been so close during those first, dreadful days after Jack's accident, yet had let her believe he was in Scotland.

'The estate IS still in the family – Sheena married a distant cousin of mine,' Nick explained briefly. 'I was glad to hand over the reins, not least because I knew you would never want to live there,' he added calmly, and Melissa spun round to meet his clear gaze. 'Next grievance?' he prompted. Melissa bit her lip and looked down at the ground.

'You hired Katy to help Juliet. You take more interest in her career than you ever did in mine,' she mumbled, beginning to feel rather childish.

'I became involved in the sport because you love it so much, and I hired Katy because she's a good coach, and because she's close to you, certainly not to hurt you. And I didn't come here, or go to New York, to support Juliet. It was to see you; to try to put things right between us,' he added softly.

'It was?' Melissa whispered.

'Yes. What's the next item on your list?' he enquired, and she swallowed, trying to gather her scattered wits. She was trembling so much she could barely stand, let alone think.

'London,' she gasped. 'You sent your employees to help me, but didn't come yourself. I . . .' she just stopped herself from saying, 'I needed you'. Instead she continued her attack. 'You stood me up. I was on my way to the Red Lion when Coop told me you wouldn't be there!' She glared at him accusingly.

'I couldn't. I wanted to, desperately, but I couldn't trust myself near you – I'd just learned you'd agreed to marry Ace,' Nick said hoarsely. Melissa's head jerked up.

346

'That's not true! If he told you that, he was lying, and you certainly wouldn't have believed him,' she said scornfully.

'No, but I believed you,' Nick said flatly, his voice hardening as he re-lived seeing the film of her with Ace.

'I don't understand,' Melissa shook her head in bewilderment. 'I never said I would marry him. Well, not since I was seventeen,' she amended. Nick sighed heavily, then reached out and gripped her shoulders.

'I saw you. I heard you,' he ground out. 'Ace made a video of the two of you in bed and kindly sent me a copy! You said you loved him and you'd marry him!' Melissa stared at him and he saw the look of confusion gradually give way to one of horror.

'He . . .?' She couldn't speak and turned in an attempt to run away from the shame of it all, but Nick held on tightly, so she hung her head instead to avoid having to look at him. 'I do remember saying that, but I didn't mean it; it was . . . just a game,' she mumbled. 'And it didn't count – I had my fingers crossed when I said it.'

Nick stared at her downcast head for a moment, then, feeling a heavy burden lift from his heart, he threw back his head and laughed. A game!

'Oh, don't laugh; this is awful,' Melissa said wretchedly, close to tears and vowing to kill Ace at the earliest opportunity.

'It's not awful, it's wonderful,' Nick contradicted. 'Don't you understand? When I saw that tape, I thought I'd lost you. Until that moment, I had always considered you were my girl, despite all that had gone

347

wrong between us . . . which brings us to the next grievance on your list.' He reached out and touched her right cheek, as gently as if it were still bruised and swollen. Melissa automatically pushed her face against his palm, like a kitten seeking affection.

'It does?' she queried breathlessly. His girl?

'I hurt you. I almost raped you,' Nick said painfully.

'Oh, that,' Melissa said dismissively. 'I'm not angry about that. I never was, not really. Upset, yes, but not angry.'

Nick regarded her quizzically: she was annoyed because he had left Glengarry, and was helping Juliet, yet bore no grudge over his unforgivable attack on her?

He glanced around at their surroundings; a hotel carpark wasn't the venue he'd had in mind, but he couldn't bear to wait any longer. He reached into his pocket and held out his hand towards her, palm upwards. On it, the sapphire and diamond ring gleamed brightly and Melissa stared at it, mesmerized.

'Will you take it back? Take me back?' Nick asked huskily. 'I love you, Melissa. Will . . . will you marry me?' Melissa swallowed, her heart thumping painfully against her ribs. She was trembling like a leaf, or was that Nick?

'Marry?' She shook her head, in confusion, not refusal, but Nick misunderstood the gesture and strove to keep the desperation from his voice.

'Do you need time to think it over? That's okay, I . . .'

'No,' Melissa interrupted. 'I mean, yes, I'll marry you, if . . .' Her words were stopped by his kiss as he swooped her up into his arms. All the old magic was there, sparking desire and she melted against him, winding her arms tightly around his neck. Dizzy with happiness, she clung to him, oblivious to their surroundings, hardly daring to believe in the miracle that was happening, but there was no doubting his passion and the wonderful strength of his embrace. At last, she was back where she belonged! Almost overcome with emotion, she squeezed her eyes shut to stem the tears. No more tears, she told herself joyously, no more tears.

'Excuse me, can I have your autograph?'

'Only in America,' Nick muttered, as he reluctantly set her back on her feet. For a moment Melissa stared blankly at the woman who had approached them, proffering a copy of that day's programme and a pen.

'Oh, yes, of course,' she said, shooting Nick an apologetic glance as she complied with the request.

'My husband and I watched you play today, and we'll be at your match tomorrow. I sure hope you win the tournament.'

'Thank you,' Melissa smiled at her. 'Sorry about that,' she eyed Nick rather anxiously.

'I don't mind, just so long as they don't start calling me Mr Farrell,' he said drily. 'I'll have to get used to sharing you with the world, won't I?' he asked cheerfully. Melissa stared at him as she realized the import of his words.

'Share me? You don't mind if I continue playing for a while?' she asked, in amazement.

'You'd be prepared to give it up?' he countered, equally astonished.

'If I have to make a choice, I'd give it up,' she said promptly.

'I won't ask you to do that. I figure we'll be married for the next fifty years, so if you want to compete for five, or even ten, of those years, it's okay by me,' he assured her.

'Oh, it won't be that long,' Melissa said quickly, feeling exhausted at the prospect. 'Will you travel with me?' she asked, hardly daring to believe.

'Of course. Coop can easily replace me – there are plenty of ex-Army officers around looking for work. I'm not letting you go, not again,' he said firmly. He hesitated, then decided to continue. 'If I had been with you when you first suspected you were pregnant, you'd have turned to me, not Katy, and we'd have worked it out, together. I was a stubborn fool, twiddling my thumbs in Glengarry and hoping you'd miss me enough to give up your career. You were alone, young, in a panic and under a lot of pressure . . .'

'Oh, please, don't make excuses for what I did,' Melissa begged.

'I'm not, I'm trying to tell you I understand how it happened, and that it's in the past. I have to take my share of the blame, too. I wasn't concerned about contraception; in fact, I think I subconsciously hoped you would conceive, which was unforgivably selfish when I knew how much you valued your career. We can't alter what we did, but we can put it behind us and start again. And, this time, I'll help your career, not hinder it. Just to prove that, I'm now going to escort you to your room – and then leave,' he said; the autograph-hunter had reminded him she had a match the following day.

'Goodness,' Melissa said, in awe.

'Precisely,' Nick sighed, then he grinned. 'My girl?'

'Your girl,' Melissa confirmed happily. They made their way slowly indoors, hands entwined. Melissa unlocked her door, then turned back to him, aching to be held.

'Don't look at me like that,' Nick groaned, determined to keep to his good intentions. He gathered her in his arms and kissed her with a thoroughness that left them both breathless and wanting more, much more. Reluctantly, Nick moved away, but first slipped the ring on to her left hand, kissing her finger, then, very gently, her injured wrist.

'I wish I'd stayed in New York, to protect you. No-one will hurt you again,' he promised. 'Dream of me,' he said huskily, dropping one more kiss on her mouth before summoning up all of his resolve and walking away.

Melissa watched until he was out of sight, then entered her room and threw herself down on the bed. He loves me! He still loves me, she thought, over and over, until she began to believe it. The ring was tangible proof and she touched it to her lips, then laughed out loud with joy. But she wished he hadn't left . . . I hope he's not going to take my career TOO seriously, she thought, grinning happily as she prepared for bed. Despite his final words, she slept deeply and dreamlessly, truly at peace for the first time in years.

Nick didn't return to his hotel, but roamed the streets with a foolish grin on his face and Melissa's scent in his nostrils. Eventually, he wandered into an all-night bar and ordered a round of drinks for everyone, a gesture which won him a dozen new-found and already-drunk friends.

'I'm getting married,' he told them.

'Yeah? Get a pre-nuptial agreement signed,' advised the sour-faced barman. Nick laughed.

'This is going to last forever,' he said confidently.

'Sure.' The barman shrugged: he'd heard that before.

Slightly drunk and still euphoric, Nick returned to his hotel at eight o'clock, meeting Katy and Juliet in the lobby. Katy noticed he was wearing the clothes he'd worn for dinner the evening before, that he needed a shave and, above all, that he had a broad smile on his face and the light of happiness in his eyes.

'You've made it up with Melissa,' she guessed. Nick's smile grew even wider.

'Clever girl,' he approved.

'You can't have,' Juliet said crossly. 'You hate her!'

'You are *not* a clever girl,' Nick eyed his niece with disfavour.

'But . . . you did. We came to stay at Glengarry for Christmas, months after the abortion. You hardly spoke to any of us! Sheena said . . .' she stopped, belatedly aware of the hole she was digging for herself.

'Sheena has a big mouth,' Nick said coldly.

'She's not the only one,' Katy put in thoughtfully. 'Little Miss Innocent here was so shocked and surprised to learn about the abortion when the story broke in New York, yet apparently she already knew about it. Why the play-acting, Juliet?' she asked sharply. Nick was stone-cold sober now and stared at his niece. She couldn't meet his gaze; her crimson cheeks a picture of guilt.

'You told the Press?' he asked incredulously.

'I didn't mean to,' she mumbled. 'That reporter,

352

Flanagan, thought he recognized you as being Melissa's ex-boyfriend and he kept on asking questions . . .'

'I suppose he used thumbscrews?' Katy said scornfully. 'You vindictive bitch! Don't you know how rough that was for Melissa?' She turned to Nick. 'I know I agreed to coach her for a year, but I want out. You're wasting your money, anyway,' she added.

'Not for much longer,' Nick said coldly, glaring at Juliet. 'I'll settle this hotel bill and buy you a plane ticket – it's your decision whether you go on to your next tournament or return to your parents,' he told her.

'You can't do that!' Juliet wailed, but she was talking to herself. Katy had stalked off in disgust and Nick had disappeared into the elevator.

As soon as he reached his room, he put through a call to Melissa, unhappily aware that the blame for the leaking of the story, and the ensuing misfortunes, lay indirectly at his door. He caught her just as she was about to go and practise and quickly explained what he had learned.

'I'm really sorry, sweetheart, I should never have told Sheena,' he apologized.

'It doesn't matter,' Melissa assured him. 'Actually, I'm glad to know it was someone I dislike – I hated to think Katy might have done it. Besides, I gained my revenge yesterday – do you think she enjoyed the tennis lesson I gave her?' she asked, and Nick smiled.

'No, but it's certainly one she'll remember . . .' he paused, frowning a little as he heard Hal's voice in the background, urging Melissa to hurry. He reminded himself of his resolve not to undermine her career – Renwick was just her coach, nothing more. 'You go and practise; I'll see you later,' he said casually. 'I haven't been to bed yet, so I'm going to crash out for a couple of hours.'

'Where have you been all night?' Melissa asked suspiciously.

'On cloud nine,' he told her.

'Me too,' her voice softened. 'I'll see you soon?'

'Count on it.'

'Okay. 'Bye.' They each waited for the other to hang up, then both laughed and broke the connection.

Nick stripped off and took a quick shower before climbing into bed, almost instantly falling asleep. He began having the most wonderful dream; at last, the girl he loved was once again lying naked beside him. It was so real, he pulled her warm body into his arms; no one else had skin so soft, or hair so fine and fragrant.

'I bribed the maid to let me in,' Melissa whispered, and he came fully awake.

'You're making it very difficult for me to put your career first,' Nick warned, running his hands hungrily over her curves and drawing her close.

'I've got a walkover into the next round – Ludmilla pulled a back muscle yesterday and has decided not to play,' Melissa explained, rather breathlessly.

'Poor Ludmilla,' Nick said insincerely, making her smile.

He turned swiftly and held her captive beneath him, ravishing her mouth with his tongue while his hands eagerly rediscovered every inch of her luscious body. When he slipped his fingers between her thighs he found she was hot and wet, as ready for consummation as he.

354

'Damn. Condoms,' he muttered: only Melissa could make him forget – he always wanted her so badly, and his past carelessness had cost them dearly.

'I brought some,' she said, and quickly and expertly unwrapped one and rolled it onto his erection, caressing him to even greater hardness as she did so. Who taught her that? he wondered jealously. Ace? Hal? Or one of the dozens of other men her name had been linked with in the Press? An image of her on the bed, pleading with Ace to be made love to, flashed into his mind, but he pushed it aside. There had been others for him, too; they didn't matter.

Wordlessly, he parted her thighs and thrust into her. Melissa welcomed him with a glad cry and wrapped her arms and legs around him, pulling him deeper and deeper into the softness of her body.

'God, Melissa, it's been so long, I've missed you so much. I'm only half alive without you,' he groaned. Already he was near to climaxing and didn't try to hold back. This was an act of repossession, reclaiming her as his. He had been her first lover and he would be her last.

He eased his weight from her and leaned on one elbow, gazing into the beautiful navy-blue eyes, even darker now in passion and soft with love.

'I never stopped loving you,' she gave voice to the emotion he had seen in her eyes, and he bent to kiss her.

'The others?' He felt compelled to ask. 'I don't want a list of names, or any explanations, but . . . did you love any of them?'

'No, I didn't, and there weren't as many as the Press would have you believe. Ace . . . that was lust, and curiosity, I suppose. Hal . . . he was so sweet to me at a time when I was feeling bad about myself. But that was over, long before he became my coach. That's the lot,' she smiled slightly. 'The gossip columnists would be most disappointed to know that!'

'Well, I'm not,' Nick said fervently.

'I don't think I want to know about . . . your girlfriends,' Melissa said, rather painfully. 'Unless . . . am I likely to meet any of them?'

'No,' Nick said, correctly guessing she was thinking of Sheena. 'I've only ever loved you,' he assured her. He bent and kissed her eyes, her mouth, then trailed hot kisses down the column of her throat, unerringly finding the ultra-sensitive spot above her collar-bone.

Melissa arched her head back and began to squirm with delight as his mouth closed over one nipple and teased it into a hard peak before he leisurely transferred his attention to the other breast. His palm rotated gently over her ribcage and then her tummy, moving tantalizingly slowly downwards until she could bear to wait no longer.

This time his lovemaking was slower and more controlled. He whispered endearments against her mouth and watched the play of emotions on her face, listened to her ragged breathing as he took her inexorably to the brink of orgasm.

He felt her nails dig into his back as she came nearer and nearer, heard the soft moans emitted from deep in her throat. Her head moved restlessly on the pillow, then she arched upwards as spasm after spasm racked her body.

Her release triggered his, the intensity of which surprised him so soon after the first. Spent, he turned on his side and cradled her in his arms, smoothing her tangled hair back from her face. She fitted snugly into his body, as if they had never been apart, burying her head contentedly in his shoulder and wrapping her arms around him.

'Don't ever leave me again,' he said fiercely.

'No, I promise. And I'll never again give you cause to leave me,' she said, shivering in remembered horror of that day at Bellwood, when she'd had to tell him about the baby. 'I'm sorry, so sorry,' she whispered, and he knew instantly what she meant. 'If I could undo it, I would, but I can't. It's no excuse, but I had no idea how I'd feel afterwards. It sounds stupid, but I didn't even think of the baby until it didn't exist any more . . .' She took a deep, shuddering breath and Nick held her close, hearing the raw pain in her voice.

'Even if I have a dozen children in the future, I'll never have that one back,' she continued sadly. 'It was so strange – I don't know if it was my hormones or just my imagination, but it was as if I was still pregnant, right up to the time when I would have given birth . . .' she stopped and swallowed, then lifted her arms helplessly. 'I ached to hold my baby. My arms felt so empty . . .'

'Hold me,' Nick said gruffly, pulling her even closer and feeling her hot tears soaking his chest. 'Stop torturing yourself,' he urged, trying to soothe her with his hands, stroking and caressing her until her shivering ceased. He struggled to find some words of comfort, anything that might possibly help, and finally told her of Katy's duplicity.

'She didn't make me do it,' Melissa said dully. 'I

could have told her and Ace to go to hell, but I didn't. I just wanted everything to be back to normal.'

'I know,' Nick continued his rhythmic stroking of her back and shoulders, purposely lulling her to sleep. He meant to stay awake, but was so warm and comfortable that he finally succumbed to his tiredness.

When he awoke, it was to the sound of voices, and he looked up to see Melissa, wrapped only in a towel, tipping a Room Service waiter – who seemed to be in no hurry to leave, Nick noted jealously. He cleared his throat noisily and the waiter hastily departed.

'I ordered lunch. I'm starving,' Melissa announced. She seemed bright and happy again, Nick thought, watching her closely; the shadows had gone from her eyes, the tension from her voice.

They ate in bed, making wedding plans and talking about anything and everything. Melissa told him about her purchase of Rose Arbor, eager for him to see it.

'I love it there; I think you will, too,' she enthused. 'It's virgin territory,' she added, with an impish grin. 'Hal's been out there, but only to play tennis. Ace doesn't even know I've bought it.'

'In that case, I'm sure I'll love it,' Nick decided, reaching for her once more. With one hunger sated, another arose and they made love again; it was even better than before.

Much later, they were sharing a bath, splashing each other like children when the phone began to ring. They ignored it, but a few minutes later it began again.

'It's probably the guests in the room below, complaining about all the water raining down on them,'

Melissa grinned, as another tidal wave swept over the side of the tub.

The phone stilled, but was followed a short time later by a furious pounding on the door.

'Nick! Are you in there?' It was Katy, and Nick groaned.

'Now what?'

'Nick! Is Melissa in there with you?' Katy called urgently.

'No!' Melissa yelled back, and giggled.

'Get serious!' Katy hissed. 'Jack's about to call the cops! Hal and Lisa have been looking everywhere for you – they're beginning to think you've been kidnapped!'

'Oh, God!' Helpless with laughter, Melissa dived for the phone, and was quickly put through to Jack's room.

'Where the hell are you?' His voice was rough with fear. 'How dare you just go off without a word to anyone when there are nutters out there threatening to kill you!'

'Sorry,' Melissa said blithely. 'I'm fine, I've had a bodyguard with me all day,' she twinkled at Nick, who grinned back. 'I'm on my way to see you, now. 'Bye,' she said, and disconnected before he could interrogate her further.

When Melissa entered Jack's room, with Nick at her side, Hal was the first to react. He glanced quickly from her radiant face to the ring on her finger, then stood up, his face ashen.

'I'll help you prepare for your matches this week, and then leave,' he said stiffly, hurrying from the room. Lisa exchanged a glance with Jack, then she stood up, too.

'I'll go after him. Don't worry, Melissa; he'll have to

let go, now,' she said quickly, then ran after her brother, leaving Melissa to face hers.

Jack had recovered from the panic which had gripped him when they had realized, at lunch, that Melissa had been missing since early morning. His fear for her safety had been replaced by anger, which he directed at Nick.

'We thought you'd left town,' he growled.

'Really?' Nick arched an eyebrow. Melissa decided to intervene and moved swiftly to where Jack was sitting, dropping to her knees beside him.

'We're getting married. Next week,' she said, gazing up at him and silently pleading with him to be pleased for her. Jack gaped in astonishment.

'Next week?'

'Yes, secretly, before the Press get wind of it. We'll have a church blessing and a big 'do' in England later, when the fuss has died down.'

'You seem to have it all planned,' Jack sighed. 'I suppose I can't stop you.'

'Why would you want to?' Nick put in.

'You're too handy with your fists!' Jack glared at him. 'I haven't forgotten that you beat her up, even if she has. And you have a lousy effect on her career,' he added.

'He didn't beat me up,' Melissa denied quickly. 'It was an accident, wasn't it?' she appealed to Nick.

'Yes, but I was responsible for it,' he said, and she sighed. Why did he have to be so damned honest?

'We both did things we're not proud of, but that's all over,' she told Jack. 'And he's going to support my career.'

'How? He's already lost you your coach,' Jack reminded her tartly. Nick was rapidly losing patience and counted slowly to ten, then repeated the exercise. Jack was obviously in physical pain; he'd feared for Melissa's safety and was understandably worried about her future happiness, he reminded himself, over and over.

'Please, Jack!' Melissa sounded as exasperated as Nick felt, then unwittingly said the words that mollified her brother. 'We need your help.'

'You do?' Jack stretched his leg and grimaced; this was the first time he'd felt needed since the car smash.

'Yes. With Ace,' she said, with an apologetic glance at Nick. 'You know how he hates to lose – a tennis match, a game of poker, or a girl, even one he doesn't really want for himself,' she said, squirming a little.

'Sure. But what does . . .' he stopped as enlightenment dawned. 'You and Ace?' he asked incredulously. At her nod, he raked his fingers through his hair and sighed. 'God, you're your mother's daughter, aren't you? But, what's the problem?' he asked, glancing at Nick's stony visage. 'Nick obviously already knows – what can Ace do to harm you?'

'Well,' Melissa blushed. 'There's a possibility that Ace has some porno films – with me in the starring role,' she said bitterly.

'Oh hell, Melissa!' Jack exploded. 'How could you be so stupid?'

'I didn't know! He must have hidden the camera . . . Jack, he'll level with you. If I ask him, he'll just laugh it off. I'll never be sure if he has any more films or not.'

'Okay, I'll speak to him for you,' Jack agreed. 'In fact, I'll do it now,' he levered himself painfully to his feet and limped over to the phone. 'He'll be asleep – the best time to get at the truth,' he added, as he began dialling.

Melissa moved over to Nick and placed her hand on his arm; the muscles beneath her fingers were rigid with tension.

'I'm sorry,' she said, gazing up at him entreatingly. Nick glanced down at her and relaxed, covering her hand with his own.

'It's okay, I understand,' he sighed. 'Just don't go near that bastard ever again,' he said roughly.

'I won't,' she promised.

The telephone conversation was a brief one and Jack looked a little shamefaced as he replaced the receiver and turned to them. He had almost forgotten asking Ace to ensure Melissa didn't meet up with Nick at Wimbledon, but, hell, I never expected him to do anything like that, he excused himself.

'He says there was only one film and that he sent it to you,' he said, regarding Nick with some sympathy.

'I destroyed it,' Nick said shortly. 'Are you sure he was telling the truth?'

'Yes,' Jack said, with more confidence than he felt – who could ever be certain about Ace and his actions? 'Are you sure you know what you're taking on?' he countered, nodding towards Melissa.

'I'm sure,' Nick said firmly.

'Thanks for your help, Jack,' Melissa went and kissed his cheek. He hugged her, then, rather awkwardly, the two men shook hands.

'And to think I still have to face your father!' Nick said ruefully, as they made their way to Melissa's suite. 'When Jack said you were like your mother . . . did he mean what I think he meant?'

'Afraid so,' Melissa giggled at the expression on his face. She unlocked the door, then turned to him.

'I have a match tomorrow, so I ought to have an early night,' she said solemnly. Nick tried to mask his disappointment. 'But I have to eat . . . how about dinner in bed?' she grinned up at him.

'Sounds good to me,' Nick murmured, following her into the room and closing the door firmly behind them.

CHAPTER 17

Eighteen months later, Melissa was sitting, outwardly composed, in the small waiting-room behind Wimbledon's Centre Court. Inwardly, she was quaking, for this was her first appearance in a Grand Slam Singles final; the famous trophy she had dreamed about since childhood just one match away from being hers.

Her opponent, almost inevitably she felt, was Lucia. Melissa had competed against her more often than any other player – twenty-four times they had faced each other, with twelve victories each. Today would be unlucky thirteen for one of them.

Melissa clutched her bouquet of flowers and tried not to fidget. God, these last few minutes of waiting were the pits . . . The buzz of excitement from the crowd was clearly audible, yet, inside the room, the atmosphere was tense and still. To calm herself, Melissa stopped thinking about the match and cast her mind back in time, to the tournament in Texas that had re-launched her career; re-launched her life, in fact.

Amazingly, she had won the tournament, the only note of sadness being Hal's abrupt departure. He had stayed to watch her clinch the title and then, his bags already secretly packed, had slipped quietly away without saying 'goodbye'. She and Nick had seen him only once since, at Jack and Lisa's wedding, which had taken place six months after their own, but in rather more style.

Rose had been horrified by Melissa's decision to marry in secret, mollified only by the prospect of organizing a lavish party to celebrate later. The news of the hasty marriage had sent shock waves through the tennis world – the 'experts' had gloomily predicted that Melissa's comeback would be short-lived and unsuccessful; a pronouncement which had infuriated Nick more than Melissa.

But, for a while, it seemed as if they might be right. Melissa, not wanting a third party travelling with them, had decided not to hire another full-time coach, and struggled to regain her form. Part of the problem was that she was almost too happy in her personal life to worry overmuch about losing tennis matches she ought to be winning. A humiliating first-round loss in the French Open had concentrated her mind – she had to put one hundred percent effort into her game, or quit, she told Nick, half expecting him to urge her to retire.

'Why don't you hire Katy?' he had suggested, to her surprise. 'She won't try and interfere in our private life again, and I never doubted her commitment to your career – she always knew how to make you produce your best tennis.'

So, Katy had been re-instated, and, for the past year, they had worked hard for Melissa to reach her current world ranking of four. Lucia was number three, but they were so close in computer points that, if Melissa won today, she would take over that position. They had both played brilliantly thus far, knocking out the top two seeds in the semis, and both were incensed by Press reports suggesting they had peaked too soon and predicting that the final would be a lacklustre anti-climax.

After what seemed hours, but was in fact only minutes, Melissa and Lucia followed the tournament referee onto court, awkwardly clutching the unfamiliar bouquets. Melissa glanced up at the row of commentary boxes – Jack now worked as a presenter on satellite TV, but had been invited to join the commentary team for this one match. Jack, her inspiration: what would I be doing today if you had picked up a cricket bat instead of a tennis racket? she wondered.

Jack caught her eye and smiled broadly: he was so proud of her, and all she had accomplished. Even if his own career hadn't been cut short by the car smash, he would never have been as successful as his little sister; he thought ruefully, but without even a hint of bitterness.

He had fully recovered from his injuries but, at twenty-eight, had decided not to attempt the long haul back up the rankings. In addition to his TV work, he ran Bellwood, with Daniel's help. Ace was rarely in England these days, having quit the tour on his thirtieth birthday in favour of carving out a new career in Hollywood. Because of this, he had agreed to sell the estate back to the family which had owned it for over three hundred years.

Melissa and Lucia reached the service line, turned in unison and bobbed a curtsey to the occupants of the Royal Box before continuing on their way to the umpire's chair. Melissa selected a racket and glanced around at the crowd – playing on Centre Court was always an awesome experience but there was an extra sense of anticipation and excitement today.

Courtside, there were rows of photographers and the girls dutifully posed for pictures, then turned to face those on the opposite side. Melissa was jumping with nerves, now, wanting to get started, and she glanced over to the Players' Box for last-minute reassurance. Nick was leaning across Katy to talk to Daniel, but seemed to sense her need and turned at once, meeting her gaze and smiling.

The love and pride he felt was evident for all to see, and instantly she felt calmer. It never ceased to amaze her that this one man could excite her so effortlessly yet be such a steadying influence on her life. Katy grinned encouragingly and gave her a 'thumbs up'.

'She'll be okay once they start to play,' Katy said to Rose, who was commenting worriedly on Melissa's pallor.

'Yes, she's fine; she's looking forward to it,' Nick added his voice to Katy's. He watched his wife as she prepared to play the most important match of her career. He was no longer baffled by her motivation; first had come acceptance, quickly followed by admiration once he realized just how hard she continually worked to improve her game.

The eighteen months had flashed by, each one happier than the one before. The Glengarry estate was flourishing under Richard's care; Lennox and Coupland was making a healthy profit, so Nick felt no guilt at being out of the country for such long periods. He was able to help Melissa, too, taking care of her business interests, dealing with sponsors and the Press, and generally ensuring she had nothing to trouble her other than how to compete to her highest ability. Melissa was grateful for his participation in her career, and gladly gave him – and his tender love and care – full credit for the cessation of her migraine attacks.

'Miss Farrell won the toss and elected to serve,' the umpire informed the crowd, as the two girls walked onto court to begin the five-minute warm-up. It had been Nick's suggestion that Melissa continue to use her maiden name whilst playing, and, over the months, he had successfully impressed on Press and fans alike that, while Melissa Farrell was public property, Melissa Lennox most definitely was not.

Melissa began to close her mind to all outside distractions, concentrating only on the court, the ball and her opponent. She had practised earlier with Jack and Katy and they both watched her closely from their different vantage points, both pleased with her fluid movements around the court and the accurate placement of her shots. Melissa gradually relaxed and there was only a slight fluttering of nerves as she waited for the balls to be gathered up. Then 'Play,' intoned the umpire.

They knew each other's game so well, Conti and Farrell – Lucia so solidly accurate on her groundstrokes, able to blast passing shots down either wing against the net-rushing Melissa. Melissa was confident she could hold serve; she had lost just one service game throughout the tournament, and that when leading by a set and 5–1, hurrying to clinch the match before an imminent shower of rain postponed her victory.

She did hold serve, but so did Lucia. Lucia wasn't one of the fastest servers on the tour, but was difficult to attack, adept at disguising the direction of her serve and adding exaggerated spin on the ball so it kicked up viciously into her opponent's face. The score remained even; 4–4, then 5–5, and it became a battle of wits as well as a physical test of strength and talent. At 6–6, they began the lottery of the tie-break.

Melissa served the first point. It was a great serve, sending Lucia scrambling for her return. Melissa felt she was in control of the point, when, on the third stroke, she heard, with horror, the unmistakable sound of a string snapping. She hoped desperately that Lucia wasn't aware of her predicament and might make an error on her return, but, of course, Lucia had realized what had happened and knew she needed only to keep the ball in play to win the point.

Melissa risked a split-second glance down to check the damage; two strings had broken in the centre of the racket. Damn! It would be like playing lacrosse! Lucia hit her return carefully, deep to the baseline; Melissa did the best she could but her reply fell short of the net. '1–0, Conti.'

The crowd groaned; some knew what had happened, others obviously did not and were disappointed by Melissa's poor shot. She held the racket aloft as she walked to her chair to exchange it, ostensibly to show the umpire, but mostly to prove to the crowd that she had not lost her nerve at a crucial point.

The murmurs of dissatisfaction changed to ones of sympathy as she took her time over choosing another racket, needing a few moments to compose herself. It's only one point, she reminded herself, over and over. But that one, vital break was enough; Lucia held grimly on to her own service points and won the tie-break, 7–4.

'Game and first set, Conti.'

Lucia strutted jauntily over to her chair and sat down. Melissa followed more slowly, trying to hide her disappointment and annoyance. She purposely didn't look over at the Players' Box – Lucia's supporters would be wearing huge grins while her own would be trying to mask their dismay.

The mostly partisan crowd offered Melissa vociferous encouragement as she walked out to begin the second set. This time, Lucia served first and managed, despite Melissa's best efforts, to stay that one game ahead. As the score steadily mounted, Lucia began to play inspired tennis, as if already scenting victory.

She's never played this well against me, not even on clay! Melissa thought frantically as, yet again, she was pinned to the baseline by the depth and accuracy of Lucia's groundstrokes.

Leading 4–3, Lucia piled on more pressure, stepping in and attacking Melissa's serve, determined to keep her away from the net. At 30–40, Melissa knew she was in dire trouble, a break point down at this stage almost amounted to match point. If Lucia took this game, she would be serving for the Championship.

Melissa wiped her palms and breathed deeply for a few moments. As she was about to serve, Lucia held up her hand to stop her and then dropped to one knee to re-tie her shoelace – unnecessarily, Melissa was certain.

'Bitch,' she muttered, under her breath, but she was too accustomed to Lucia's behaviour to allow the interruption to break her concentration. Her response to Lucia's stalling tactic was to produce an ace.

'Deuce.' The crowd yelled encouragement; the noise was deafening as Melissa selected another ball. The ace had been the best possible answer to a break point and she felt a surge of confidence as she prepared for the next point. Lucia mis-read the direction of the serve and Melissa ran in to put away an easy volley.

'Advantage, Farrell.'

Another ace clinched the game to level at 4–4 and Melissa stepped back, relieved to have come safely through the test.

'Come on, Melissa! Break her NOW!' Katy's voice was clearly audible above the din, and Melissa felt momentary sympathy for the eardrums of those sitting close to her. She didn't need Katy's exhortation; she knew that Lucia would be momentarily vulnerable – having hoped to be serving for the match, she was instead back on level terms.

Lucia had successfully mixed her serves all after-noon; guessing the direction was just that – guesswork. When Melissa guessed correctly, she was able to attack, when she didn't, she could only play a defensive shot, giving Lucia the advantage in the rally. It was as much a game of chess as of tennis, now, trying to out-think as well as out-play each other.

At 30–30, Lucia faltered a little; her first serve was a fault, the second, rather tentative, and Melissa pounced, punching it deep into the corner and running to intercept Lucia's scrambled reply. Too high, it gave Melissa the perfect opportunity to volley it into the opposite corner, out of reach.

'30–40.'

Melissa paced restlessly, almost pawing at the ground in her eagerness, focusing on the ball with every fibre of her being. Determined to attack, she stepped forward as Lucia served. It was fast, over 100 mph, and kicked up after landing on the line. Melissa had to take it at shoulder height, twisting her body to gain a wide angle on her shot, drive-volleying the ball back before Lucia had even recovered her balance after serving.

'Game, Farrell. She leads by 5–4. Conti leads one set to love.'

The applause was thunderous as Melissa walked to her chair, followed by a rather despondent Lucia. Melissa sat down and gulped thirstily from her cup of water before towelling down. Eager to resume, she was back out on court before the umpire called 'time', bouncing a ball impatiently as she waited for Lucia.

The noise was almost tangible, pressing down on her, the expectations of the crowd both an inspiration and a burden, so great would be the disappointment if she failed to turn the match around. Several Union Jacks were being waved, as if the victory were already hers. A bit premature, guys, she thought, then pushed everything out of her mind except for the task in hand; it was imperative she keep her nerve and not allow Lucia even the slightest hope of breaking back.

She glanced across at Lucia, unsurprised and unfazed to see her again re-tying her shoelaces, then she looked briefly at Katy, who was scowling at Lucia's tactics.

'Someone ought to throttle her with those damn laces!' Katy had often declared and had, on one occasion, enquired sweetly if Lucia needed help with them as she and Melissa left the locker-room to begin a match. Melissa smiled slightly at the memory. Lucia, finally straightening up and preparing to play, caught the smile and was discomfited by it.

Melissa served well, fast and placing the ball deep, following up with crisp, decisive volleys. The cheers grew louder with every point and were deafening when she clinched the game, and the set.

'Game and second set, Farrell. 6–4. One set all. Final set, Conti to serve.'

Melissa stepped back and briefly allowed her relief and pleasure to show, as much for Lucia's benefit as anything. After hoping to win in two sets, Lucia now faced a third, which was, of course, what Melissa had been hoping for since the conclusion of the first.

Adrenalin flooded back and she felt full of renewed energy as she prepared to receive, determined to try and break Lucia immediately while she was feeling down after the loss of the second set.

'Now, Melissa!' Katy screamed, evidently with the same thought. Melissa needed no urging but, although she took the score twice to deuce, she was unable to break. She towelled down quickly and was again purposely the first back on court, both to indicate a lack of tiredness to Lucia, and also because she wanted to serve and level the score as soon as possible.

It was now she reaped the benefit from holding serve so easily throughout the tournament. Four excellent first serves gave her a love game and Lucia was again under pressure. This time, after two deuces, Melissa broke through to take the game – and the lead.

'2–1, Farrell, final set.'

The cheers and whistles were ringing in her ears as she returned to her chair. Lucia followed more slowly, her shoulders slumped as if already conceding defeat; her body language adding to Melissa's confidence. Katy could barely contain her excitement. Jack, in the commentary box, was trying to remain unbiased, but his delight was evident in his voice.

The noise now rivalled anything ever heard from the Stadium Court crowd at Flushing Meadow, the umpire's pleas for silence going unheeded. Melissa knew she couldn't afford to relax; Lucia, just one break down, could still claw her way back into the match.

After serving again to lead 3–1, Melissa felt more confident; Lucia seemed too downhearted to resume the fight. Melissa pressed too hard, trying to gain a second break, and made a couple of errors to allow Lucia to narrow the gap to 3–2.

Melissa sat down and held her towel to her face, trying to shut out the sight and sound of the crowd. That was a bad game, she chided herself. Calm down, take it steady, one point at a time, she told herself silently. She couldn't afford to let Lucia regain her confidence by giving her easy points.

Composed, she put the mistakes behind her and walked out to serve. She had to wait for Lucia, who was complaining to the umpire about some imagined grievance. Melissa ignored it for the attempt at distracting her she knew it to be. The umpire knew it, too, and told Lucia to resume play.

'Don't forget to tie your laces!' someone yelled. A ripple of laughter followed and Melissa bounced the ball on the strings of her racket as she waited for the commotion to die down, trying to ignore it, for it was as unsettling to her concentration as it was to Lucia's.

'Quiet, please! The players are ready,' the umpire called.

Lucia knew she had to break back to stay in contention, knew, too, that she would gain nothing by being tentative. The earlier, long rallies had sapped her energy and she attempted spectacular shots on her return of serve, two of which Melissa could only stare at in grudging admiration.

At 30–30. Melissa varied her serve, taking off pace and adding more spin, causing Lucia to mis-hit, sending one return long and hitting another too high, thereby presenting Melissa with an easy volley. 4–2. Melissa stepped back and heaved a huge sigh of relief as she briefly towelled down.

However, Lucia wasn't a quitter, and Melissa was well aware of that as she buckled down to the next game, one which was vital for Lucia to win. Three times the score levelled at deuce, but each time Lucia played brilliantly to get herself out of trouble. Then, tiring, and pressing too hard on a second serve, she double-faulted.

'Advantage, Farrell.'

The volume of noise increased even more, but Melissa barely heard it. She was watching Lucia, trying to out-guess her. She won't risk serving to my backhand again, she thought, then suddenly changed her mind. Yes, she will! Double bluff! She reacted instantly, moving forwards and sideways, perfectly positioned and throwing the whole of her body weight behind the shot.

The ball was a blur as it rocketed back, landing within

an inch of both the base and side line before slamming into the back wall of the court, causing the linesman to duck sharply. But Melissa wasn't concerned about his head, just his hands, which he held outstretched, palms down, indicating her shot was in. She began walking towards her chair. Only one more game and the title would be hers!

'Game, Farrell. She leads 5–2, final set.'

'No! That ball was out!' Lucia screamed, glaring at the umpire and then the linesman she thought to be at fault. 'You only want her to win because she's British!' she added bitterly, a remark which the German umpire considered to be both unfair and somewhat incomprehensible.

Melissa sat down and let her rant, closing her ears to the exchange. Sections of the crowd were performing a Mexican wave, rising in their seats, cheering and hoisting up Union Jacks as if she had already won, but the last game was always the hardest to win . . . Suddenly, the cold water she was drinking lay heavily on her stomach, her heart began to thud painfully against her ribs, and she was drenched in icy perspiration that had nothing to do with her physical exertions. It was caused by panic. She wiped her palms and then her racket handle repeatedly, but it remained slippery, and she couldn't seem to grip it properly.

She leaned down to pick up a new racket, then paused. It would be madness to switch rackets now . . . but what if another string broke? Torn by doubt, she again reached for a fresh racket; again she hesitated.

'Oh, my God, she's lost her nerve!' Katy gasped in horror.

'Of course she hasn't,' Nick refuted, but he could see how the colour had drained from her face, how wild-eyed she looked as she glanced, not to him or Katy, but to Jack for reassurance.

For Melissa, memories of her first match on Centre Court, with her brother, flooded back, and then she recalled their Mixed Doubles final here, when she'd had to serve for the title, hampered by a bruised face and even more bruised heart. She walked unsteadily out onto court and glanced beseechingly across at her supporters.

'Don't let her see you're worried,' Nick hissed at Katy, who nodded and forced a cheery smile. Rose did the same, unaware of her nails digging into Daniel's arm. He didn't notice, either.

'This is sending my blood pressure sky-high,' he muttered, hardly able to watch.

Nick willed Melissa to look at him and, finally, she did. He sat back, arms folded, seemingly completely relaxed and confident. Of course you're nervous, his smile seemed to say, but I know you can do it. Melissa's world steadied around her, her legs ceased trembling and she held his gaze for a moment before straightening her shoulders and turning towards the ball-boy, ready to play the most important game of her life. The umpire had been calling repeatedly for silence and, when the hubbub died down, there was an almost deathly hush around the vast arena.

Lucia, knowing she faced defeat, lost her pin-point accuracy, missing the lines by an inch as she fought a last-pitch battle.

'40–15.' Two match points. Again, they had to wait

for silence, although Melissa barely heard the uproar above the hammering of her heart. She tossed up the ball and swung the racket over, her body arching in a fluid movement that propelled her towards the net before the ball had even bounced. Lucia tried one, last passing shot that hit the top of the net before falling back.

'Yes!' Jack's exultant cry nearly deafened millions of listeners. Katy punched the air in delight, while Nick let out a breath he hadn't even been aware of holding.

'Oh, Daniel! She's done it!' Rose sobbed. He nodded, too full of emotion to trust himself to speak.

'Game, set, match, Farrell! By two sets to one, 6–7, 6–4, 6–2.'

In a daze of disbelief, Melissa walked automatically to the net and waited for Lucia. They shook hands in silence, then turned to thank the umpire. Melissa, trembling like a leaf, stumbled to her chair and sat down, covering her face with a towel as she tried to absorb the enormity of what she had accomplished. Wimbledon Champion!

She looked over to her family, her vision blurred by tears of joy, and saw her parents hugging each other, while Katy was jumping up and down in excitement. Nick had risen to his feet to join in the applause, a broad smile on his face.

Seemingly the calmest of them all, he was bursting with pride as he watched his wife. He, more than anyone, knew of the physical toll the five years as a pro had taken on her muscles and joints; how, the morning after a tough match, she could barely move until a hot shower and lengthy exercise routine had

eased the stiffness from her body. One thing's for sure –
she's not feeling any pain right now, he thought fondly,
as she beamed at him in delight.

Melissa briefly considered going over and clambering
up into the box, but dismissed the idea almost at once. It
was too undignified; it had already been done and, more
to the point, she was too knackered! Instead, she walked
slowly over to Lucia, who was slumped in her chair, her
face etched with lines of exhaustion and despair.

'It was a great match,' Melissa said tentatively,
hoping she wouldn't sound patronizing. 'No-one can
say women's tennis is boring after that,' she added.
Lucia shrugged slightly but neither looked at her, nor
gave a reply. Melissa sighed, but nothing could dim her
excitement or happiness.

The ball-girls and boys had lined up in two neat rows,
waiting for the Duke and Duchess of Kent to come
down from the Royal Box. The couple emerged and
paused as usual to speak to several of the youngsters
before moving to make the presentation. Melissa's gaze
was fixed on the golden trophy; she wouldn't fully
believe she had won until she held it aloft, as so many
of her heroines had before her. Her childhood dream
was about to become reality!

She tried to mask her impatience as the familiar ritual
got under way; this time, though, she was a participant,
not an envious onlooker. First, the umpire received his
award, then Lucia moved forward, either forgetting or
deliberately omitting to curtsey as she accepted con-
dolences and the runner-up plate. Melissa politely
joined in the applause for the girl who had so nearly
won, then it was her turn to approach.

The cheering grew to a crescendo as she was finally handed the huge circular trophy, engraved with the names of all previous champions. It was heavier than she had expected and her hands gripped the rim tightly. It was solid; real, not a dream. I've done it! I've really done it, she thought ecstatically.

Some of the spectators began calling out to her, cameras at the ready, waiting for her to show off her prize. As soon as the Press had taken their pictures, she began a lap of honour, walking slowly around the court, posing for photographs and wishing the moment would never end. She hugged the trophy to her and caused a ripple of amusement when she engaged in an only half-joking tug of war with the official who tried to wrest it from her, to take it back into safe-keeping.

'You won't forget to have my name engraved on it, will you?' she asked anxiously, as she reluctantly handed it over.

Lucia had left the court, as had the linesmen, but Melissa remained, chatting to the crowd, signing autographs and accepting gifts of flowers. She left only when the players for the Doubles match that was to follow came onto court, blushing hotly when Al Montoya grabbed her and kissed her soundly.

'That's from Ace,' he whispered, grinning. 'He said to remind you he prefers married women and to give him a ring when you get bored with monogamy!'

'Stop encouraging him!' Melissa chided, trying not to laugh; actually, Ace had behaved very well about her marriage – by his deplorable standards, anyhow. He had been unable to resist winding Nick up a little at Jack's wedding, but hadn't said or done anything too awful, merely taking great pleasure in the knowledge that both Melissa and Rose were on the edges of their seats while he made his speech as best man.

With one final wave to the crowd and a long, lingering backwards look at the scene of her victory, she left the court and forgot all about Ace as she greeted her family. Rose reached her first and hugged her tightly.

'Well done, darling! We're so proud of you!'

'Thanks, Mum. For everything,' Melissa choked, remembering how often her mother had given up her time to drive her to junior tournaments and cheer her on. 'You always supported me. You too, Daddy,' she added, reaching up to kiss her father.

'Me? I was the one who threatened to dig up our court at Bellwood if you didn't concentrate on your schoolwork,' he said ruefully. Melissa grinned.

'I always knew that was an idle threat,' she said, then turned to Nick, gazing into his eyes. He loved her, helped her in a hundred different ways, putting his own life 'on hold' while she pursued her dream. 'I couldn't have done it without you,' she whispered, tears of emotion welling once more as she moved into his embrace.

'I just carry your luggage,' he said lightly, to stem the tears and make her laugh. 'The Press want you – and Katy's waiting for you in the locker-room,' he told her. 'Go on,' he urged, sensing her hesitation in leaving so swiftly.

'We'll go and have some tea while we wait,' Rose said. 'And we're all having dinner together this evening – we didn't tell you before, but your father's already booked a table at San Lorenzo to celebrate.'

'Oh,' Melissa glanced quickly at Nick, then realized he already knew about the plan and didn't mind sharing her with her family. 'Thanks, Dad, that's a lovely idea,' she said, and kissed them all quickly again before rushing off to shower and change.

Katy was alone in the locker-room, holding a bottle of champagne aloft. Never a tactile person, she didn't attempt to hug Melissa, now, just grinned broadly and slapped her open palm in a 'high five'.

'I did it, Katy, I did it!' Melissa said excitedly, as if Katy hadn't avidly watched every single point. 'A million childhood fantasies have just come true.'

'Yeah,' Katy nodded, popping the champagne cork and shaking the bottle as if she were a racing driver on the winner's rostrum, spraying most of the contents over herself and Melissa. 'Lucia's already gone off in a huff – she refused to talk to the Press. She'll be fined for that and they'll give her a bad write-up for being a sore loser.'

'She looked absolutely gutted at the end,' Melissa said; she loved the whole world at that moment and could imagine how Lucia must be suffering. 'I feel sorry for her – that was her third Grand Slam Singles final and she's lost them all.'

'She should be used to it by now, then,' Katy said callously.

'You are awful,' Melissa scolded, suppressing a grin. She barely sipped at her champagne, already high on excitement, and put the glass aside to begin stripping off. 'I'm Wimbledon Champion,' she said dreamily. 'I really am, aren't I? For a whole year, I'm Wimbledon Champion . . .'

'Just the one?' Katy enquired tartly. 'What's wrong with coming back and successfully defending your title next year?'

'Slave driver,' Melissa groaned, as she stepped under a hot shower.

They continued discussing the match, point by point, while Melissa prepared to meet the Press. A cheer went up from the British contingent when she walked into the Interview Room and she grinned broadly as she sat down behind the bank of microphones. The win began to seem more real as they fired questions at her about the match, and then about Lucia's conduct, but Melissa adroitly side-stepped the latter.

'What are your immediate plans?'

'A holiday,' she said promptly. On Monday, she and Nick were flying to California, to spend three weeks alone at Rose Arbor. 'And don't ask me "where?", because I won't tell you,' she added.

'Why? Is it a second honeymoon?'

'No, the first one hasn't ended yet,' she replied, then blushed when they laughed.

A little later, she did a televised interview for the BBC, then, most bizarrely, one with Jack. She couldn't take it seriously at all and laughter was never far away as she struggled to answer his questions in a professional manner. But, when he asked her about Lucia's behaviour, she replied as candidly as if they were alone. Too candidly, and Jack began to look alarmed.

'Oh, sorry – can you edit that bit out?' Melissa asked blithely.

'No – we're transmitting live!' Jack reminded her, his expression now one of absolute horror. That did it for

Melissa; she could no longer hold back the giggles and, after a few seconds spent glaring at her, Jack grinned reluctantly and turned to face the camera.

'See what I've had to put up with all these years?' he sighed. The technicians hurriedly switched to a recording of the final game of the match and Melissa was back in control when the interview resumed.

Her eventual departure from the All England Club was a lengthy process, for hundreds of people had gathered outside to wait for her, to offer congratulations and flowers, and to request autographs.

'I feel like royalty!' she whispered to Nick, who was waiting patiently and even joined in chatting to the crowd.

'Will she be back next year?' someone asked him. He hesitated momentarily, then nodded.

'I expect so,' he said casually.

Melissa had been asked the same question, seemingly a thousand times, and had replied affirmatively without even thinking. But later, relaxing in a hot bath before dinner, she began to wonder if she would. Whatever else I achieve in tennis, I'll never feel as good as I do right now, she thought. She had fulfilled her childhood ambition – how many people could claim that much? Was it time to quit?

She leaned forward and ran more hot water into the tub, then lay back again, listening to Nick's deep voice as he fielded phone calls from friends and family. It was five years since she had told Nick she needed to know how good she could be – well, for her, for any British player, Wimbledon Champion was as good as it got.

There were still goals to aim for, of course – the US

384

Open, the number one ranking, defending her Wimbledon title, and she was still only twenty-three . . . was she ready to turn her back on the fame, the money? Not to mention the hard work, the physical and mental strain, the constant travel . . . she grimaced. How will I feel if I'm just a spectator at Wimbledon next year? she asked herself. How will I feel watching someone else hold the trophy?

Nick finally tired of answering the phone and unplugged it before dressing for dinner. He glanced at his watch and frowned slightly; they would be late. Melissa looked up and smiled as he entered the bathroom, but decided to say nothing of what was on her mind; not until she was sure.

He had never complained about their nomadic existence, but she knew he would be delighted if she decided to retire from competition. Richard and Sheena now had an adorable baby son, and Nick's tenderness with the child brought a lump to Melissa's throat, and twisted the knife of guilt in her heart. But she had to be certain she would have no regrets – not for her the option of picking up her career again once the kids were in school!

'Come on, Champ, out of that bath,' Nick instructed, wrapping her in a towel and lifting her to the floor. Melissa wound her arms around his neck and pressed against him.

'I love you,' she said softly, her dark eyes glittering with desire. 'Would it be awfully rude of us to keep the others waiting?' she murmured.

'Awfully,' Nick agreed solemnly, already hardening at the feel of her pliant body against his. 'But I guess the

Wimbledon Champion can do what she wants.'

'Oh, good,' Melissa whispered, her questing hands and tongue leaving him in no doubt as to what she wanted. He carried her through to the bedroom, quickly tearing off his clothes and joining her on the bed, covering her body with his.

As always, desire sparked and ignited immediately; marriage hadn't dimmed their passion, only enhanced it. They were so attuned to each other's needs, knowing just how to arouse and excite to a fever pitch. This time, neither needed nor wanted foreplay, and their love-making was fast, intense and deeply satisfying.

Drained, Nick rested his head briefly on her shoulder, then raised himself and lovingly kissed each of her breasts before rolling away from her and reaching for his clothes. Melissa felt too sated to move, until she caught sight of the time, then she clambered off the bed and slipped into a clinging midnight-blue silk dress before applying just a touch of make-up.

'The car's here – again,' Nick called from the drawing-room, as she was searching for her shoes. 'The poor guy must have driven around the block a hundred times! Are you ready, sweetheart?'

Melissa grabbed a matching purse from the dressing table then paused and picked up her pack of contraceptive pills. She looked at them thoughtfully for a moment, then tossed them into the waste paper basket, a slow smile curving her lips.

'Yes, I'm ready,' she said softly.

 **THE EXCITING NEW NAME
IN WOMEN'S FICTION!**

PLEASE HELP ME TO HELP YOU!

Dear *Scarlet* Reader,

As Editor of *Scarlet* Books I want to make sure that the books I offer you every month are up to the high standards *Scarlet* readers expect. And to do that I need to know a little more about you and your reading likes and dislikes. So please spare a few minutes to fill in the short questionnaire on the following pages and send it to me.

Looking forward to hearing from you,

Sally Cooper

Editor-in-Chief, *Scarlet*

QUESTIONNAIRE

Please tick the appropriate boxes to indicate your answers

1 Where did you get this Scarlet title?

Bought in supermarket ☐

Bought at my local bookstore ☐ Bought at chain bookstore ☐

Bought at book exchange or used bookstore ☐

Borrowed from a friend ☐

Other (please indicate) _____

2 Did you enjoy reading it?

A lot ☐ A little ☐ Not at all ☐

3 What did you particularly like about this book?

Believable characters ☐ Easy to read ☐

Good value for money ☐ Enjoyable locations ☐

Interesting story ☐ Modern setting ☐

Other _____

4 What did you particularly dislike about this book?

_____

5 Would you buy another Scarlet book?

Yes ☐ No ☐

6 What other kinds of book do you enjoy reading?

Horror ☐ Puzzle books ☐ Historical fiction ☐

General fiction ☐ Crime/Detective ☐ Cookery ☐

Other (please indicate) _____

7 Which magazines do you enjoy reading?

1. _____

2. _____

3. _____

And now a little about you –

8 How old are you?

Under 25 ☐ 25–34 ☐ 35–44 ☐

45–54 ☐ 55–64 ☐ over 65 ☐

cont.

9 What is your marital status?

Single ☐   Married/living with partner ☐

Widowed ☐   Separated/divorced ☐

10 What is your current occupation?

Employed full-time ☐   Employed part-time ☐

Student ☐   Housewife full-time ☐

Unemployed ☐   Retired ☐

11 Do you have children? If so, how many and how old are they?

_____

_____

12 What is your annual household income?

under $15,000	☐	or	£10,000	☐
$15–25,000	☐	or	£10–20,000	☐
$25–35,000	☐	or	£20–30,000	☐
$35–50,000	☐	or	£30–40,000	☐
over $50,000	☐	or	£40,000	☐

Miss/Mrs/Ms _____

Address _____

_____

_____

Thank you for completing this questionnaire. Now tear it out – put it in an envelope and send it, before 31 December 1997, to:

Sally Cooper, Editor-in-Chief

USA/Can. address	*UK address/No stamp required*
SCARLET c/o London Bridge	SCARLET
85 River Rock Drive	FREEPOST LON 3335
Suite 202	LONDON W8 4BR
Buffalo	*Please use block capitals for*
NY 14207	*address*
USA	

Scarlet titles coming next month:

SWEET SEDUCTION Stella Whitelaw
Giles Earl believes that Kira Reed is an important executive. She isn't! She's been involved in a serious road traffic accident and is in Barbados to recover. While she's there she decides to seek out the grandfather who's never shown the slightest interest in her. Trouble is – he's Giles's sworn enemy!

HIS FATHER'S WIFE Kay Gregory
Phaedra Pendelly has always loved Iain. But Iain hasn't been home for years. Last time he quarrelled with his father, Iain married unwisely. Now he's back to discover not only has Phaedra turned into a beauty . . . she's also his father's wife.

BETRAYED Angela Drake
Business woman Jocasta Shand is travelling with her rebellious niece. Sightseeing, Jocasta meets famous soap star Maxwell Swift – just the man to help her get even with Alexander Rivers. But Maxwell already has a connection with Alexander . . . and now Jocasta is in love with Maxwell.

OUT OF CONTROL Judy Jackson
Zara Lindsey stands to inherit a million dollars for the charity of her choice, _if_ she is prepared to work with Randall Tremayne for three months. Zara can't turn down the chance to help others, but she thinks Randall's a control freak, just like the grandfather who drove her away from home ten years ago. So _how_ can she have fallen in love with Randall?